THE CUP

RUNNING ON EMPTY

A Novel by Godders.

1 3 1673946 6

Copyright © 2021 by Godders
All rights reserved.
ISBN:

Table of Contents

Preface iv
Chapter One   In the Beginning 1
Chapter Two   Excitement 9
Chapter Three   Steiner 16
Chapter Four   Do or Die 31
Chapter Five   Preparations 47
Chapter Six   Learning the Ropes 56
Chapter Seven   Getting Serious 86
Chapter Eight   Exercise 110
Chapter Nine   Raising the Stakes 128
Chapter Ten   On a Mission 156
Chapter Eleven   Aftermath 182
Chapter Twelve   Conspiracy 215
Chapter Thirteen   Another Chance 270
Chapter Fourteen   A New Plan 312
Chapter Fifteen   Running on Empty 336
Epilogue 371

Preface

It is the 1950's and Britain is slowly beginning to rebuild itself after the devastation of the Second World War, rationing has ended but poverty is never far from everyday life. Post War children are seen as the LUCKY generation, with families now usually consisting of a Mother and Father, and with Father working, education and hard work are the Governments key manifesto pledges.

The war may be over, but memories can be a long time in fading, and across Europe the vanquished countries seem to be prospering much quicker than the seeming victors, and in the newly created state of Israel, partitioned from Palestine at gunpoint even the Jews were making plans for the future.

Into this cornucopia of worldwide discord a young boy is born, normal it seems in every way, a child of loving parents, one of four children in a caring hard working everyday family, Mother and Father practicing Christians and children Sunday Schooled as a matter of course rather than choice, how could he have ever known that his life or at least a major part of it was already planned for him.

He was drawn into a web of intrigue that even the great writers of fiction might struggle to make believable, breathless through each step of the way until at last he was done, and just Running on Empty.

Chapter One

In the Beginning

As the summer sun slowly dropped over the distant horizon, Ronnie leaned back into the wicker garden chair and closed his eyes. Three score years and ten or so the good book said, and maybe just maybe it was at least sometimes right. Well probably in his case anyway.

His still razor-sharp brain gently allowed his mind to drift backwards over the half century and more that had finally bought him to this place. "Bloody hell" he mused, you simply could not make it up, not in your wildest fantasy, what a life, fun, excitement, high drama, and yet.... such unlikely beginnings.

"Ting-Ting" the well-worn brass hand bell vigorously shaken by the deputy headmistress of the small village primary school signaled the end of another day, and as teachers began to tidy classrooms, the hundred or so pupils collected coats and satchels from the cloakroom pegs and spilled out into the asphalt playground and onto the village street. A few maternal looking mothers were clucking around some of the younger children, but this was 1960 and most of the children walked home alone or perhaps part of the way with friends.

Ronnie heaved his satchel over his shoulder and started up the pathway outside the school, it was hot, so his grey school jumper had been taken off in the cloakroom and now hung precariously over the well worn leather satchel and he was now only wearing his short sleeve white shirt and green school tie with grey flannel shorts, grey knee length socks and buckle across brown leather sandals.

He was a stocky child, blue-eyed with short brown hair cut flat with a straight frontal fringe, and he was in every way or so he thought, average and normal. There were most probably hundreds, perhaps thousands of boys like him all over England. Post war children whom, according to the newspaper stories he had tried to read and understand "had never had it so good".

Ronnie was not sure of what he had, that was "so good" but guessed that if it was reported in the newspapers then it must be true.

He shifted his satchel to the other shoulder as he walked around the corner away from the school, stopping opposite Ayres the village shop. He looked both ways to check for traffic, in truth this was not actually necessary as the villagers had few cars and the cars that passed through tended to be few and far between, and he had even started taking down the registration numbers for something to do.

He checked the road again as all the children had been drilled to do, and started to cross the road towards the shop, wishing he had some money to buy an iced lolly, but there was no money for such things now.

Stopping suddenly, he stepped back onto the path, about fifty yards up the road parked neatly to the curbside was a big blue car. Ronnie did not recognise the car, he was sure that he had not seen it before, but he knew it had to be a Humber as the top policeman in the area was driven around in a big black Humber.

His eyes focused on the registration plate REG 1 he read, making a mental note to add this to his list, he looked back at the shop and started his curb drill again, "look left-look right-look left again" and if the road is clear cross quickly, walk do not run but do not dawdle.

Hello young man its Ronnie isn't it, Yes, but how do you know my name, who are you, we are not supposed to talk to strangers said Ronnie.

The man rested his arm and hat on his right waistline and laughed, so I look like a stranger then do I young Godliman, My name is Ronnie Lamb stammered the boy, you must have made a mistake sir, now I must be going home, or I will be late, and I will be missed.

The man laughed again so Ronnie will be missed will he, Who will miss you Ronnie, do you not sometimes stop on the way home to play with young Julie at the garage, you really like her don't you and her mother sometimes gives you tea and cakes, so you will not be missed. Ronnie had absolutely no idea who this man was or how he knew his name and that he liked Julie, he was about to ask just that when the man spoke again.

Do you like chocolate. Ronnie did indeed like chocolate, after all how many children didn't, but for most it was at best an occasional treat, perhaps a visiting Aunt or Uncle might bring some for the children to share, but generally chocolate was not on anyone's daily expectations list.

The man had walked back to the big car and opened the boot lid upwards, he waited patiently as Ronnie slowly walked towards the car then stopped slightly aside so that the boy could see into his car boot. Ronnie's eyes opened wide, there were boxes of sweets of all types, Smarties, Fiveboys, Tiffin, so much more than Ayres shop had, a cornucopia of sweet treasure such as Ronnie had ever seen, or he reasoned was ever likely to see again.

Go on help yourself said the man, taking a bar of Cadbury Milk and handing it to the boy, it's okay, really it is, eat it and enjoy and you must take some home with you. The man collected up a big handful of a mix of sweets and slipped them into Ronnie's satchel, savoring the very welcome chocolate Ronnie asked, please sir who are you, how do you know me and what do you want.

My name is Regenstein, and I need to talk to you about your future young man.

Ronnie had never heard such a silly name, it must be foreign he reckoned but the man spoke perfectly good English, what do you want he said.

Well young Godliman you are going to be a useful fellow over the years, and as for me, just regard me as Uncle Reg for now and keep this between just the two of us okay. Ronnie was confused, there was that name again, Godliman, it meant nothing to him at all and he had so many questions but the man had already closed the car boot, replaced his hat and was holding out a large right hand to shake his.

Instinctively Ronnie held out his right hand and the man suddenly grasped it with both of his big hands, pressing something into Ronnie's palm he shook the joined hands up and down. Goodbye for now young man, we will meet again soon. The man pulled away and jumped into the car's driver seat, calling out as he pulled the door closed, don't spend it all at once now.

As the car roared into life and pulled away up the road, Ronnie opened his tightly closed hand and looked down. A shiny round silver coin nestled there, but it was not a sixpence or even a florin, but a whole half crown, two shillings and sixpence. Ronnie was rich.

He walked home deep in thought, what did all this mean, who was this person Godliman, why was this man interested in him and why give him so much money.

Ronnie did not get pocket-money like some of his school friends, his family were quite poor and while he considered himself loved and cared for, he knew that compared to some of his friends with wealthier parents his family were poor like most of the villagers, although better of than some as his mother was a skilled seamstress making all of their clothes and sometimes curtains and furnishings for well off townspeople, she did a lot of baking, she made jams, bottled beetroot, made elderflower and elderberry wine and looked after the vegetable garden and all the chickens. When able she provide food and sewing for the poorer villagers and she was highly regarded by everyone who knew her.

They lived on the farm at the Grove which had recently been taken over by a big farming group called Farmers Weekly and the family had needed to move out of the farm cottage and now lived across the road from the farmyard in a Pendley Estate semi-detached three bedroom house with a very long back garden, the far end of which Ronnie's father and mother had turned into vegetables and fruit.

Ronnie's father had lost his job on the farm where he had looked after the dairy herd and milked the cows twice every day, storing the milk in huge silver steel tanks, and then in the early morning filling up the steel milk churns ready for the big lorry to come and collect to take to the dairy, leaving empty churns behind. Apparently, his mother and father had met during the war when Ron senior his father had been smoking outside the dairy one day.

During the war Ron had been the churn lorry driver, collecting milk from the local farms and taking the full milk churns to the dairy in Apsley, which was opposite the munitions factory where the woman had to go outside to smoke cigarettes and where Ron had seen and chatted to Winifred a married lady who made shell casings on a machine for the war effort.

Her husband was away fighting, and they started to chat together regularly, the young couple fell in love and after her divorce they married and Winifred had her first child, a girl who they named Christine her first of what were to be four, two girls and two boys, the young couple worked and lived on farms until ending up at The Grove in 1950.

, Ron was herdsman and Win, as she liked to be called gave birth to the three other children. The family had enjoyed good times on the farm sharing in harvests and having free eggs and milk which Ronnie often collected in a white enamel jug straight from the milk tank, it was warm and wonderful. Now though with the farm house and job all gone, Ron had a job looking after some automated machines in a factory about ten miles away, and so the family had a small grey Austin A30 two door car which Ron used to travel to and from work and very occasionally take the family for rides with Ronnie's younger brother sitting on big sisters lap.

Ronnie knew money was not in plentiful supply and his mother repaired all the clothes and when she could, sold all her jams and homemade wines, so being giving a whole two shillings and sixpence really did make Ronnie feel rich.

Arriving home, he put the secret chocolate into a cardboard box that he kept under his bed, which had his list of car registrations, a school sports day ribbon, a slightly torn black and white photograph of Patch the family's much loved dog who had died last year and two cigarettes which he had taken from his sisters packet some time ago but had never had the courage to smoke. He neatly added REG 1 to his list of car numbers and hurried downstair to tea.

The next few months passed normally and in truth Ronnie had almost forgotten the mystery man, when one afternoon just as before there was his car parked at the roadside, and this time the boot was already opened and several children were helping themselves to sweets.

Ronnie felt so bitterly disappointed, after all that first time had made him feel so special, but now it seemed Reg was happy to share his sweets with all the children. Seeing Ronnie, Reg called out. Ah there you are young man, I thought that you were not coming, now take some chocolate I believe it is Cadburys that you like best if I remember correctly and he handed Ronnie a bar. When all the children had been given sweet's he said goodbye and drove away.

Over the next year Reg frequently waited in the same place handing out sweets to the children, some of the parents talked to him and even took sweets for themselves or perhaps other children.

Ronnie overheard some of the mothers talking about Reg saying, oh he's okay you know, he is one of those Yiddish refugees, lost everything in Poland and now he just likes to see children happy. Ronnie knew that Poland had been an occupied country during the war and also knew that the word Yiddish had something to do with being a Jew, because his older sister had used it once and their mother had become very cross, saying that it was not a nice word and that she must not say it again, so Ronnie guessed it meant Polish refugee.

In early 1962 Ronnie's mother started to have spells in bed with headaches and sickness, often she would need to lie in darkness for a week, sometimes more until these troubles eased. During which time his older sister cooked, washed, ironed and generally looked after the family including his father, although she was only just sixteen and sitting her end of school, college exams as she wanted to go to Art college and learn to be an artist. She had a friend called Julia who was already at the college and one day, when Ronnie got home from school she was there, she was black, totally black with white eyes and pink lips.

Ronnie stared and stared he had never seen anyone who was not white before. Julia had just laughed, cat got your tongue boy, has it. Ronnie wanted to touch her to see if she was real or did the blackness rub off, but all he could say was hello, she was just like his sisters big black doll. Julia came to the house several times that year, and he began to like her quite a lot, then suddenly in May Ronnie's world fell apart.

It was a Saturday and his younger sister had agreed to take him to the dentist as mother was ill in bed and father wanted to stay with her. As the two children turned into the street on their way home, they saw an ambulance leaving the house, running down the road and into the kitchen they found Aunty Pamela a neighbor hugging their brother and sister saying that everything would be alright and that father and mother had just gone to the hospital for some checks and that it would all be fine, Mother would be home soon.

But everything wasn't fine and Ronnie never saw his mother again, it was May 1962 and he was just Ten years old.

Chapter Two

Excitement

By summer 1962, Ron senior had resorted to liquid solace, and any time that he had previously set aside for the four children evaporated as he retreated into his own depressive world, leaving big sister now seventeen to be full time mother. Seeing this becoming a lifetime of drudgery she opted for marriage to a wholly unsuitable man, a speedy wedding and the taken-over tenancy of the family rented home.

Ron senior, apparently shocked out of his downward spiral, stopped the drinking and agreed to marry a divorced mother of two girls he knew slightly from the local church.

But true to form in young Ronnie's life things were never going to be a heady mixture of love, joy and peace, with his new stepmother announcing at her wedding to Ron senior, that whilst she intended to have the two boys live with them, her cottage was too small for the younger of the sisters who would just have to remain living with her now newlywed older sister, some honeymoon period there.

However. Ronnie soon discovered that stepmother was in fact correct because whilst the family home was far from spacious and luxurious, the cottage was tiny, four rooms only, a kitchen and a front room downstairs, two tiny bedrooms upstairs and a bathroom outside along a concrete alleyway.

Stepmothers oldest girl like Ronnie's sister had been summarily shipped off to live with an Aunt, Ronnie never actually met her in fact, and with her absence it left stepmother and stepsister to share one bedroom, Ronnie and brother the second bedroom, with father sleeping every night on the hard rickety old couch in the front room.

Ronnie always remembered the wall plaque "Home sweet home" but surprisingly, despite the cramped conditions the family lived okay, stepmother had several serious talks with Ronnie regarding stepsister, but although from talking amongst boys Ronnie knew about sex and babies, he certainly knew nothing about what to do.

These chats with stepmother became somewhat amusing as the truth was that stepsister was in fact, looking back, a precocious young madam far and away more sexually adventurous than young Ronnie and things might have been different with them living in such close proximity had not another twist started Ronnie along a pathway he could never have imagined.

July 1963 school holidays and with such limited space at home, Ronnie spent as much time as he could outdoors, cycling for miles, stopping to eat sandwiches thoughtfully prepared by stepmother. It was on one such cycle ride with Ronnie sat alongside the railway line that he saw a car he knew, a big blue Humber, number REG 1. The car pulled up and Reg and another tall thin man in a white zip up jacket got out and walked across to where Ronnie was sitting.

Hello young man said Reg, it is nice to see you again, isn't it Charlie. The tall thin man smiled at Ronnie and simply said hello, but in a funny sounding way which he had never heard before.

Now then young Godliman, I believe that you know this area quite well, where are we and what is this place called.

This is the LNER railway from London Euston station up to Scotland sir, and we are at Sears crossing signal box.

Well now said Reg, turning to Charlie, I told you he was a bright young thing didn't I. Tell me young Ronnie, said Reg turning back to face the seated boy, do you know of any old houses or barns that might be for sale around here, because me and Charlie are looking to buy something private like and hidden away.

Ronnie smiled, as it happened he did know of somewhere just like that, so he tentatively said, well there is an old airfield at Wing , its off the Cublington road but its deserted and falling down now.

Let's take a look, shall we said Charlie. So, they hid Ronnie's bicycle behind the hedge, and they got into the car. The seats were red leather and the car smelled of cigarettes.

Ronnie gave directions and explained that he had found the old airfield on one of his bicycle rides and that he hoped it would be what they were looking for.

When they pulled up on the old cracked concrete runway, all three climbed from the car, Reg took a bar of Cadburys chocolate from his pocket and handed it to Ronnie, wait here young man he said, Charlie and I will have a look around.

Ronnie sat and ate the chocolate, and it was about half an hour later that the two men came back to the car. Jump in young man said Reg, it`s time we got you back to your bicycle. As they drove, the two men talked about Landrovers and a Lorry and supplies.

When they got back to Sears signal box, Charlie lifted the bicycle out for Ronnie and then climbed into the car, Reg took out a fat brown leather wallet, opened it and taking out ten shillings handed it to Ronnie. Well done young Godliman, we will see you soon, and with that they drove off.

For the next three weeks Ronnie regularly cycled back to Sears signal box and out to the airfield but saw nothing or no one, he was quite disappointed. Then on Wednesday 7th August as he cycled along, two old army Landrovers and a lorry passed him but when he got to the airfield it all seemed quiet and deserted as usual, suddenly a voice shouted out, hey you clear off this is private property.

Ronnie saw a short stocky man in dark green wearing a beret coming towards him, he was about to jump on his bicycle and ride away as fast as he could when he heard that funny voice say, it is alright Buster, that's Godliman he found us this place he is okay.

Charlie waved across to Ronnie and beckoned him over, taking the bicycle and leaning it against one of the old derelict hanger doors, he said come along young fella, perhaps you would like to meet the boys.

Inside the gloomy hanger were the two Landrovers and the lorry and lots of men all in green boiler suit like clothes, several wore blue berets similar to the one which the man called Buster was wearing.

Seeing Ronnie with Charlie and Buster, the noisy chattering suddenly stopped, and Ronnie felt that everyone was looking directly at him. What do we have here, said a spotty faced man, who had a broad accent, Ronnie had a teacher who was proud of being what they called a cockney so he instantly knew the man was from London.

Charlie spoke up, this my friends is young Godliman, Ronnie Godliman, he helped us find this place for our filming. Ronnie you say, well that is ok then as my name is Ronnie too, have some lemonade and I will show you around.

Ronnie was shown the vehicles and given lemonade which he drank from a white enamel mug. We are making a war film, said cockney Ronnie, and it is about some German soldiers attacking the airfield which we will all defend, it should be good fun.

What about your guns and things asked Ronnie. Some of the men laughed, it is just a film sonny, make believe, never believe what you see at the movies, only the close-up shots are ever real and then not always.

Charlie suddenly appeared and held out a greasy black gun. You can hold it if you like he said handing it to Ronnie, go on it won't bite that's for sure.

Ronnie held the gun, it was very heavy, he desperately wanted to point it and pull the trigger and say bang like cowboys did to the Indians, but instead he handed it back and politely said thank you.

You should not be teasing the boy like that Paddy said Buster we don't want to be giving him ideas. Charlie laughed, don't you know it already to be sure, Mr Big has already planned this young fella's path, he's one of us, he just doesn't know it yet.

Cockney Ronnie called from the hanger doorway, time you were going little man, here's your bike. Ronnie had never heard a bicycle called a bike, and he guessed that was how cockneys talked.

As he climbed onto his bicycle, he asked Charlie, when are you filming. The day after tomorrow if the weather stays right said Buster, why don't you come back and watch, we would like that wouldn't we boys. The group of men nodded.

The following morning it was Thursday, Ronnie cycled to Sears signal box, but as he approached, he could see lots of police cars and vans. A large constable in his black and white uniform and big hat stood in the roadway with his right hand held up. Stop there boy he said, you cannot come this way, you need to go back. What is going on asked Ronnie. It is nothing to concern you young Lamb.

Ronnie looked at the big policeman's face and recognised him as the local beat constable, Sergeant Shaw, who knew his parents and lived in the same village. Ronnie turned his bicycle around and pedalled away.

Despite the Policeman making him turn back he desperately wanted to go to the old airfield to see the filming, so he took a shortcut through Mentmore Park and soon found himself cycling across the old worn concrete.

The hanger was empty, just some used food wrappings and fresh oil on the floor from the vehicles, but that apart the place was deserted, he could only assume that the filming had been postponed, anyway he would keep popping by to see when they were back.

By Saturday everyone was talking about what had happened, the great rail train robbery was what they called it, how a gang of men had held up the Scotland to London night mail train and robbed it of over two million pounds. It soon became clear that the men had been driving a lorry and Landrovers and they had coshed the train driver without need.

Not seemingly being one of the brightest of boys, it had taken Ronnie this long to understand, but it was all so clear now, there was no film, they had been the robbers, he must tell the police all that he knew he thought excitedly, but then stopped, suddenly remembering the money he had been given and what had been said to him, "he is one of us now" Oh lord, said Ronnie, to no one in particular, I am a train robber.

The saga of the robbery was headline news for simply ages, and although the police had found the robbers hideout, which was an old disused farm the other side of Aylesbury the gang were long gone with the money.

Over the next few years there were small developments, and some arrests were made, stories of gang members going abroad circulated around and the police even reported that the whole thing had been masterminded by a wealthy Mr Big, and it seemed that some of those who had been arrested so far, apparently knew of this mysterious Mr Big, but could not name or identify him.

Ronnie was back at school keeping quiet and trying to stay out of trouble, and as the next four and a half years evaporated, with his life, seemingly no different from any other boy at the time, it appeared his fantastic experiences had come to an end, but as had happened before it all changed quite suddenly.

Chapter Three
Steiner

June 1969 and Ronnie having left school in the previous month with eight O level and two A level passes all in academic subjects was considering his future and a possible University place.

It was Saturday 12th, and Ronnie had gone to the summer fayre with his girlfriend Amanda, and whilst wandering through the stalls past the steam rollers and traction engines they came to an army display area, with a Landrover, small tent and uniformed soldiers offering advice. Let us have a look said Amanda.

O dear I do not think so said Ronnie, he had never really been interested in anything military and his family had lost so much during the war. Come on, Amanda pulled Ronnie over to the display.

Almost immediately a smartly turned-out soldier in brownish khaki uniform with three white Vees on his arm stepped up to them. Good afternoon young man, I am Sergeant Groves, Royal Corps of Signals, are you interested in joining.

Well no, not really, I am more interested in going to University to gain a degree in engineering because I want to be a good engineer not a soldier with his gun, anyone can use a gun, not everyone can be a good engineer, but I know I can.

So then, you think soldiering is all about guns do you, let me show you something, Sergeant Groves led them into the tent and sat them down, switching on a projector they watched a short film of soldiers doing electronics, vehicle maintenance, telephony, and many other engineering trades.

Well then young man, a career in The Army can include engineering so tell me what you want to do with your life, Sergeant Groves looked directly into Ronnie's eyes, skilled engineering needs to be learned, it takes time, patience and commitment, do you have those attributes.

Ronnie suddenly found some confidence, of course I do he retorted, I am going to University to get an engineering degree and then a well-paid job.

Hmmm... said Groves, University will not do young man, it just will not do, wait here one moment, and he marched smartly out of the tent.

The two of them sat in silence looking around, suddenly Groves and another man filled the tent opening. This is the young man I have just been telling you about, said Sergeant Groves, 17 years old and thinks that he is going to University, he wants to be an engineer.

Ronnie studied the new man, he was about thirty, not particularly tall with a lean figure and most strikingly pale blue almost grey eyes, which seemed to sparkle. Shalom Ronnie, said the man holding out his right hand, which Ronnie took and shook firmly.

Tell me your name young man said the newcomer. It is Ronnie Lamb, why do you ask. So, Ronnie then replied the man, I wonder, do you have any other names. No of course not replied Ronnie, how could I have.

So, no one calls you anything else then. The man's voice was quite soft, but urgent and insistent. No, they do not said Ronnie, except. Yes, said the man even more urgently, except what.

Well, there is this man that I know, well I mean I do not know him at all really, but we have met a few times, Ronnie thought about mentioning the great train robbery but said nothing, after all no one except him knew of the airfield meetings or even the sweets. He called me Godliman, which I thought was him just being nice to me.

He called you Godliman did he, the man turned to sergeant Groves, I really think that we have taken up enough of these young people's afternoon already sergeant, take the young man's address and let them get on with their day out. Sergeant Groves wrote Ronnie's address down onto a piece of lilac paper and passed it to the man.

Enjoy your summer fayre said the man and both he and the sergeant walked away from the tent and started chatting to some boys playing on the Landrover.

How strange was that said Amanda then laughed, come on Ronnie, Chairplanes are the next stop, and putting aside the strange encounter with the two soldiers they had a fun afternoon.

On Tuesday, a cream-colored envelope arrived at Ronnie's house, Master Ronnie Lamb it read. Ronnie had never ever had a letter before, and he felt suddenly important.

Who is it from, said his stepmother with interest, I have absolutely no idea, Ronnie said, carefully prizing open the envelope and taking out a folded sheet of cream-colored notepaper.

The letter had Ronnie's name and address at the top and was dated 14th June 1969, yesterday thought Ronnie absently. Well, said stepmother who is it from then, and what does it say, It looks quite official, what have you been up to.

Ronnie's eyes scanned the brief letter before reading:

Dear Ronnie,
Steiner and Company would like to offer you a summer job to keep you occupied before any university term begins in mid-September. Please attend at our warehouse, (see address above) on Monday 21ˢᵗ June to commence work from 0830am
Signed-
David Steiner

It is a job offer, said Ronnie and I do not even know who they are, what they do or how they know anything about me.

Well, said stepmother, probably the school put out a list of leavers and they have taken your details from it, but the letter is strange, it assumes you will take the position without question, quite rude really.

Yes, I suppose it is said Ronnie, what do you think I should do about it. I think that you should at least go along and see what is on offer, after all you have nothing else to do and who knows you might enjoy whatever it is that they get you working at, and there will be pay.

Early the following Monday, Ronnie washed, dressed, and cycled to the Steiner warehouse in Aylesbury, giving his name and showing the letter to the young girl behind the reception desk he was asked to wait.

Sitting on a leather chair in the reception area, Ronnie picked up a pamphlet extolling the values of trading with Steiner and Co, apparently the best hardware wholesalers in the United Kingdom.

He had only just finished examining it when a vaguely familiar soft voice said, Hello Ronnie, glad you made it and on time, that`s good, shall we take the tour. Ronnie recognised the man, as the one from the Summer Fayre.

Come with me please, the man gestured for Ronnie to follow and led the way out of reception and into the warehouse.

They walked past rows of high shelves stacked with everything from dustbins to air fresheners or so it seemed, eventually coming to a small area of offices. The man opened a door and ushered Ronnie into a spacious office with a large red mahogany desk, large swivel chair with brass studs pinning down the dark green leather upholstery, a couple of similarly upholstered tub shaped chairs, a filing cabinet and to Ronnie's great fascination a large white flag on the wall with a blue star shape on it.

Settling into the big swivel chair the man told Ronnie to sit, which he did. What I am going to tell you must remain a total secret between us Ronnie, do you agree to that.

Ronnie was confused, secret, surely hardware sales did not warrant secrecy. Well, are you willing to keep the secret Ronnie. Yes of course I am, he replied, hopefully displaying a little more confidence than what he was currently feeling.

The man pushed a button and spoke into a desktop microphone, Hannah tea with milk for two please and some biscuits. The best thing for me to do is to tell you a story, is that alright with you, Ronnie nodded but said nothing.

From 1938 even before the war, the Germans specifically the Nazi`s, were gearing up for global domination and as part of their overall plan they set out to eliminate the Jews. On the 9th and into the 10th of November in 1938 on the direct orders of the Further, Herr Hitler, they commenced a campaign of oppression and tyranny against all Jews and minority groups across Germany. People were forced out of their homes at gunpoint, shops were looted, houses and businesses set on fire, personal belongings were looted, jewellery and art stolen.

In Berlin within one of the houses attacked, lived an old man called Franz Steiner, who had a prized possession that he kept in a purple velvet drawstring bag. When the Nazis came that night, smashing everything, with glass being scattered everywhere, the old man ran across the street, hammered on the door of a neighbour and begged them to take the purple bag and to keep it safe.

As the old man ran back towards his own home, he was shot dead, right there in the street. The Jews called that night Kristallnacht or night of the broken glass.

Once war was official from September 1939, the plan to eradicate Jews from the new Third Reich had become well established, and as country after country became occupied more Jewish people came under pressure to either flee or hide, with the occupying Nazi troops starting to round them up in large numbers.

When captured they were separated as male and female then herded like animals to the train yards and forced aboard cattle trucks. They were locked inside these cattle trucks with no food, no water, and no toilet facilities, they struggled to survive for days until they reached their destination, often a prison camp, and there were many.

One such place was called Auschwitz, where stumbling from the cattle trucks in excrement and filth, hungry and thirsty they were force marched at gun point into a barbed wired compound and everyone was forced to strip naked and hosed down with freezing cold water.

Personal jewellery, rings bracelets necklaces watches and even shoes were all confiscated, then the people were lined up and examined one by one, checking their hair eyes and teeth. Two groups were formed, one group were given simple smock tunics to wear with nothing else, the second group were marched to a big brick building with a large sign saying showers, they were never seen again.

The other "lucky group", were kept housed in wooden sheds in filthy conditions, poorly fed, and selectively sent to the showers, often on a whim of a guard. Hundreds of thousands of people, Jews, homosexuals, gypsies were sent to those showers Ronnie, hundreds of thousands.

Well yes, I know that sir, but what has any of this got to do with me. The door opened, and the young receptionist entered with a tray holding a teapot, water jug, milk sugar and biscuits plus two china teacups and saucers.

As Hannah closed the door, the man stirred the teapot and three quarters filled each of the cups. Always tea first Ronnie remember that, always tea first. after pouring the tea, he pushed a cup towards Ronnie, help yourself to milk and biscuits, he said taking two digestives and biting into one.

Now then where was I, oh yes when that camp was liberated only a few hundred survivors were left, starving and skeletal, witness to one of man's greatest human atrocities. I do know about this, said Ronnie even though his knowledge was fairly limited to the school`s modern history curriculum, but what has this got to do with me.

By April 1943 the Nazis had created a Jewish quarter or Ghetto in Warsaw, where living conditions were inhuman, some of the people started to complain and refuse to obey orders, so on the direct order from Hitler, as they had been on Kristallnacht they were all herded out of their homes again.

You remember those neighbours who took the purple velvet bag in Berlin, they had moved for safety to Warsaw, but even here they were persecuted. As they were forced from their home, they managed to take the little purple bag with them, but a Nazi officer saw the man clutching the bag and demanded it from him.

The Man clutched it even tighter and refused, so the officer simply took out his revolver and shot the man between the eyes and took the bag. Opening it he took out a small hand carved wooden cup, snorting loudly the officer put the cup back into the bag and put it into his pocket saying stupid Jew, dying for a wooden cup.

Sorry but I still do not understand what any of this has to do with me, said Ronnie. The old man on Kristallnacht was my great Grandfather, and the neighbours who he entrusted with the bag were called Jesse and Daisy Godliman. But I still do not understand what any of this has to do with me, said Ronnie. Jesse and Daisy Godliman were your Mothers parents Ronnie, your grandmother and grandfather.

What, said Ronnie, that is just not true, my name is Lamb not Godliman. Yes, of course it is now, said David as your Mother married Sidney Lamb, but your mother's maiden name was Godliman and Jesse and Daisy were her mother and father.

If any of this is true then tell me what happened to my Mother, why was she not in that Ghetto, and what happened to this Daisy who you say was my Grandmother, said Ronnie, was she taken to a camp like Auschwitz.

Your Mother was Just seventeen, your age when war broke out, and for her safety she was sent to England to stay with an aunt in Willesden North London. Our Great Aunt Vi, mumbled Ronnie.

No one is sure what happened to Daisy, there are no records, and anyway, this is not about my great grandfather or any of your relatives, this is about the wooden cup.

Now I do not understand at all stammered Ronnie, you tell me horror stories of persecution, cruelty robbery and death, then you tell me that the whole thing is about a simple hand carved wooden cup, that is madness, it cannot be worth anything, certainly not dying for.

My dear young friend, that is exactly what the cup was made for, and it is imperative that we find it and get it back, it must go home to Jerusalem soon.

Jerusalem, stammered Ronnie, for pity's sake it is just a wooden cup, what worth can it possibly have.

That wooden cup holds life and death in its power, it was carved by Jesus himself, and he used it to deliver and confirm the last covenant. You mean the last supper, gasped Ronnie. Exactly that Ronnie exactly that.

All of this is just unbelievable said Ronnie, you cannot seriously expect me to simply take your word, I mean everyone knows that the cup from the last supper is supposedly made of pure gold, but no one knows where it is or even if it still exists.

After the death of Jesus, and the tomb being found empty, everyone who was, or had been one of his followers was scared, rumours abounded of his resurrection, of sightings and miracles, the occupying romans were going from house to house seeking out his people to torture them for information on the missing body, and then killing them.

A group of his closest followers including Mary from Bethany took a boat to Crete then later onto France, taking with them the linen grave cloth which had covered his body and the marble flask containing the remainder of the perfume which the stargazers had given at his birth, however the cup which Jesus used to establish the last covenant was entrusted to Joseph a merchant whose tomb Jesus had been placed into.

But, interrupted Ronnie, even if that were true it was two thousand years ago, surely the cloth and the cup wherever they might have been taken would have rotted away by now, there would be nothing remaining.

You would think so, but to the contrary, both are in exactly the condition as they were then.

How can you possibly know that, what evidence is there to support such a claim.

We can start with a linen cloth in a museum in Italy, behind glass and very secure under lock and key. You are now talking about the shroud of Turin whispered Ronnie, then louder, you believe that it is real.

For certain it is real, the only good news is that the so-called experts, cannot agree on its authenticity, so the arguments rage on whilst the cloth is safely locked away. But what does it matter sighed Ronnie, I mean after two thousand years, except for historian interest, it must be pretty meaningless by now.

You just do not see yet Ronnie, that cloth was used to wrap up Gods dead body in its human form, it has body fluids, his human body bloodstains, his human DNA locked into the fabric forever. Oh, I see, said Ronnie, not quite sure of what he was supposed to be seeing.

If that cloth were to fall into the wrong hands then who knows what might happen said David. But surely it is harmless said Ronnie, after all the experts have all touched it and come to no harm, what can it do.

To be truthful we do not yet know, but whatever its power if any, it needs to be held in the right hands. Okay then so what about the wooden cup that you mentioned, where is it now, do you know.

Not exactly, or at least not yet, but we will and hopefully soon. Ronnie noted that "we" had been used again but said nothing.

We will find the cup, get it back and take it to Jerusalem where it will be housed safely in the temple. Okay, so assuming that all or any part of this crazy story is in fact real, how will you find the cup and how will you get it back. We will not be getting it back Ronnie, that is now your job.

Laughing loudly but somewhat nervously Ronnie said that is crazy, I mean we have only just met, I do not even know your name. You tell me fantastic stories about the war, the Jews and relics from two thousand years ago and that you expect me to somehow find the cup that you talk about and get it back.

I received a letter in the post offering me employment here, so as instructed I am here to work in the warehouse before I go to university, I think that someone has made a mistake and that I am not the person that you think me to be.

Oh dear, what must you be thinking Ronnie, come with me please and let me show you round and introduce you, I am David, David Steiner, and what we have just talked about, well, it can wait but we will talk again.

The Steiner warehouse seemed vast to Ronnie and as David led him round aisle after aisle of tall shelving each filled with all manner of items, they stopped every so often to greet people and Ronnie was introduced as the new banksman.

The aisles were on both sides and down the middle corridor an overhead chain drive pulled along wheeled trolleys, each capable of carrying up to nine galvanized steel dustbins, Ronnie knew this because several trolleys had exactly that, three bright shiny household dustbins and lids, laid side by side on each of the trolley shelves.

David showed Ronnie the employee toilets, the canteen and what would be his locker by the clock card. Eight thirty until five pm Monday to Friday only said David, any Saturday work will be optional and paid at overtime rate. You will clock in and out each day and take half an hour midday or when you can fit a break in, to eat lunch.

They continued the tour with David explaining that the warehouse supplied hardware shops in London and the home counties. We have twelve lorry drivers said David, each with his own shops to supply, they generally have eighty to hundred shops each and usually make five drops each day calling at each shop roughly once a month. The shops send an order for what they want here to the warehouse, where we process it for costing, update the shops accounts then issue the picking order to the warehouse. The picking team fill the order as the shops trolley is pulled around the warehouse until it finally ends up here.

They were walking up a short slope, rounding the corner Ronnie saw a row of twelve doors along one side and twelve double sided shelving bays opposite each. This is the loading bank Ronnie, as you see we unhook the full trolleys and place the items from the order onto the storage shelves opposite the right door for that customer.

Each afternoon as the drivers return here from that day's deliveries, they back the lorry to their door, open it and load tomorrows delivery from their storage bay. Your job will be helping our current banksman Reuben to offload the trolleys and help the drivers load their lorries.

Just then a lean wiry man of about mid-twenties came out of a storage bay, he had extremely long hair tied behind his head with a black and white cloth, he was unshaven and to Ronnie looked scruffy. Reuben, called out David, this is your new helper Ronnie, show him what to do please, I think you will both get along fine, and with that David walked off along the concrete bank and disappeared.

Reuben eyed Ronnie up and down then grinning widely said come on Ronnie I will show you what to do, he showed Ronnie how to unhook the full trolleys and hook them up again when emptied. He pointed out lists of names at the end of each bay and explained that every trolley would have a shop delivery note on it, which you check off as you unload the items into the correct bay for that shop. If anything on the order was missing from the trolley you went to the stock controller Vish and told him. Sometimes the order pickers had simply missed the item, but also sometimes there was no stock available, so we are to write n/s against the item.

Simple isn't it said Reuben, and not too hard, our quiet time is first thing every day and busiest is in the afternoon when we help load the lorries, as all the drivers want to be done first so that they can sort paperwork and get off home.

The following morning at eight fifteen Ronnie put his cycle in the rack, walked into the warehouse and over to the clock machine, he looked at the cards but could not see Lamb anywhere. Vish the stock controller came up, good morning Ronnie, everything all right. Yes I am fine, but cannot seem to find my card anywhere said Ronnie.

Vish reached up and took a card from a slot handing it to Ronnie he said here you go, he took his own card punched it into the clock and placed it back in the rack, see you later he called out as he walked away. Ronnie looked down at the card in his hand, Godliman R. was neatly hand-written in black ink.

A new job and now a new name Ronnie thought to himself as he punched his card into the machine, whatever next I wonder, a new life.

June and July evaporated in the process of daily work, which whilst never boring or even particularly arduous, was just the same routine each day. Ronnie got to know the drivers and where they went, such exotic places as Farnborough, Leatherhead, Dorking, Camberley, Wokingham, Croydon, Basildon, Ilford, Hertford, Ware, Potters Bar, Bushey, Amersham, Luton and Leighton Buzzard, and of course all London.

He also got to predict which shops sold the most dustbins, these being in the new towns of Harlow and Welwyn Garden City. The most air freshener consumption in Airwick jars was by far Battersea which surprised him until the driver explained about the coal fired power station smell`s.

Early in August, David had Ronnie called to his office. Hello Ronnie, how do you like working here. Oh, it`s okay thank you, secretly Ronnie loved the job, it was easy and well paid with almost no responsibility.

Well, you only have a few more weeks and then you are off to University. Ronnie was shocked, how could that be possible as he had not actually made any applications, thinking that he might spend a year working at Steiner before going to University.

What do you mean, I mean how is that possible, I mean who has arranged for this to happen. Slow down, said David, everything is fixed, you will join the 16th Regiment Royal Corps of Signals on September 14th who are based at Harrogate in North Yorkshire, you will be a communications technician, as far as anyone and everyone is concerned, but during the week you will be taken to Leeds university to study and of course when not at university you will be given training.

So, I will not be a soldier like the others said Ronnie. No, not like the others, you are being schooled for your future and trained for our needs, do you have any objections, after all an engineering degree from a University is what you wish for, I believe. Yes it is, Ronnie said thank you and that was that.

A rail pass and some documents arrived in the post, Ronnie left Steiner's, packed his few clothes, said goodbye to his father, stepmother, stepsister and his brother and set out from London Euston station on his next adventure.

His stepmother and stepsister actually kissed him goodbye, little did Ronnie know that he would never see them again.

Chapter Four
Do or Die

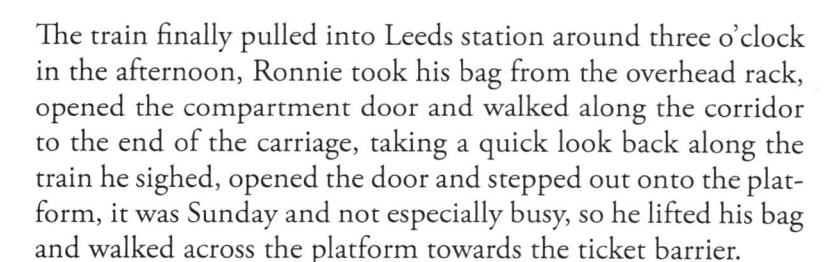

The train finally pulled into Leeds station around three o'clock in the afternoon, Ronnie took his bag from the overhead rack, opened the compartment door and walked along the corridor to the end of the carriage, taking a quick look back along the train he sighed, opened the door and stepped out onto the platform, it was Sunday and not especially busy, so he lifted his bag and walked across the platform towards the ticket barrier.

A uniformed platform attendant took a very brief almost cursory look at Ronnie's rail warrant and ushered him through the gate and into the main station concourse. Feeling thirsty, he walked across the hall area towards a sign reading station buffet, as he got near to the buffet, he noticed a Soldier holding a piece of card to his chest that read, LAMB, so realising this was his connection, he changed direction, walked over to the soldier and said I am Lamb.

Welcome to Yorkshire Corporal, the transport is outside, and taking Ronnie's bag he led the way outside to a parked, dark green Landrover, with Military insignia. Putting the bag into the back of the four doored vehicle and climbing into the driver's seat, the soldier said, hop in Corp, we haven't got all day.

Seeing Ronnie looking around the vehicle, the soldier said, nice isn't it, new Model, Long Wheelbase Defender 90, much better than the old ones that we had, it even has a synchro gearbox, so no more double de-clutching. Ronnie nodded as if in agreement although he had absolutely no idea what the soldier was talking about.

Is it far, he asked, I mean to the barracks in Harrogate. About half an hour or so replied the soldier, maybe a bit longer, it really depends on traffic around the City, but as it is a Sunday, we should be okay, just relax and enjoy the trip, we will be in plenty of time for scoff.

Once out of the City, Ronnie noted that the fields and hedgerows were not that much different from those at home, and sensing his gaze the driver asked, your first time in Yorkshire is it. Yes, it is replied Ronnie, and to be truthful I expected it to be more, bleak and wild, you know moorland.

The soldier laughed, it can be all that and more Corporal, just wait until you get up to the ranges in Outhwaite or Otterburn, you will get as much of wild and bleak that anyone could wish for. An exercise, even only a Minival, can be bloody hard going out there, but then that`s why they use those place`s I guess.

Some thirty-five minutes after leaving the station, they pulled into the entrance of the army camp past a large painted sign which carried the emblem of the Signals Corps and the wording, 16th Signals Regiment, Pennypot Camp. A neatly hedged short driveway led to a double barrier system for both in and out traffic with a centrally positioned gatehouse. Ronnie could see several figures inside the small building, but his primary focus was upon the uniformed soldier stood outside cradling a black machine gun in his arms.

The soldier on guard stepped into the roadway and looked at the pass proffered by the driver, was it a good trip Steve he asked. Yes, it was quiet, but that`s to be expected as it is Sunday, I will just drop of the Corporal and see you later for a jar if you like.

As they drove around the camp, Ronnie caught glimpses of parked military vehicles, brick and steel buildings, he saw what was labelled Medical Centre, a well-lit building with a sign saying NAAFI, a small general store and post office, what seemed to be a pub, and several lit buildings with activity inside them, one with a sign saying NCO Mess. That`s where you get your scoff Corporal, on a Sunday it`s from half past four until half past six, weekday times are on the notice board, right ho, here we are.

The driver had stopped outside a three floor, brick building, there is a staircase at each end of the block Corporal, your room is on this end staircase, middle floor, bunk four. Ronnie climbed from the vehicle, took his bag from the back and watched the driver move away.

Looking around there was no one to be seen, so taking his bag he entered the building and climbed to the first landing, there were two doors numbered three and four, and four had a key in the door lock and a note pinned to it, pulling the note down and unfolding it he read. Settle yourself in

Corporal Lamb, and get some food this evening, I will catch you tomorrow and get you started Harry.

Inside the sparsely furnished room were a small wardrobe, three door chest, low cabinet and a solitary chair next to the single bed. Laid on the mattress were two white linen sheets, and two dark brown woven blankets, a single pillow and one white linen pillowcase, all neatly folded and stacked at one end.

To the other end was a uniform, again neatly folded with a small scrap of paper bearing the name, Corporal Lamb which had been hand-written on it.

Opening the wardrobe, he found a khaki colour, uniform jacket with Signals Corps Badges on the epaulettes, and two white vee shaped stripes sewn onto the left arm. On separate hangers where a matching pair of thirty four inches waist, short legged trousers neatly pressed to give well defined creases, and two linen shirts both chocolate brown. A thin brown woollen tie, two pairs of size eight nylon socks,. a white plastic belt with gleaming brass buckle together with a small sewing kit placed onto the only shelf, completed the contents.

On the bed were two pairs of light green denim work trousers, three wool mix shirts, two green pullovers with vee necklines, three pairs of wool socks, a brightly coloured regimental belt made from woven elastic with a hook fastening, three pairs of linen pants in a cream colour, and one pair of rubber soled leather work boots in size eight, and a pair of black leather lace up shoes. He neatly put each of the items into the wardrobe and drawers, then unpacked his own bag hanging his shirts and trousers at one end and his uniform the other in the wardrobe, with his civilian socks and pants in a separate drawer in the small chest.

His little travel alarm clock went onto the small cabinet which he dragged next to the bed, along with the small bottle of aftershave which he had yet to use and the small travel bag which held a razor, some shaving soap, horsehair brush and a toothbrush and some paste.

A light knocking on the door attracted his attention, come in he called out, and the door opened to reveal a tall, thin scrawny youth of about twenty in khaki work clothes and open necked shirt carrying two folded white cotton towels. Hi corporal, I am technician second class Blythe, and your helper, the stupid store clerk forgot your towels, so I managed to find a couple for you, as I thought that you might want to shower before scoff.

Your mess is next to the main one so easy to find and on Sunday, grub starts from half past four and gets served until half past six. This floor houses Signals Techs, linemen and drivers, there are two sets of washrooms with bogs, showers and sinks, and a laundry room with three machines and a drying and ironing room. The NCO Bogs and Showers are marked on the doors, but the washing and ironing is first come first use.

I will make your bed and keep your room tidy, bring you tea and coffee and sometimes biscuits if we can nick them from the mess, we don't have a kitchen here in the block, but a cupboard has been turned into a small tuck store with a fridge and kettle which we all use, do you prefer tea or coffee.

Well, that depends on when it is and how I feel said Ronnie, right now I would love some tea, I was going to get one at the railway station, but the driver was already waiting and keen to get away. No problem corp, leave it to me.

Ronnie undressed and with just a towel wrapped around his waist padded along the vinyl floored corridor to the first washroom area, as explained two of the twelve toilet cubicles had signs reading NCO as had one of the eight shower stalls, the central area being filled with two rows of twelve sinks fitted back-to-back, with mirror walling between them. The washroom was deserted, so after using the toilet he enjoyed a leisurely shower, a new experience for him, dried his hair using a wall mounted drier and went back to his room feeling much more relaxed.

On the cabinet was a mug of steaming tea and two digestive biscuits, a tap at the door was followed by Blythe entering carrying a sugar bowl and spoon, sorry corp I forgot to ask if you take sugar in your drinks. Yes, please, two spoons. Blythe spooned in the sugar and stirred the mug, tea at six thirty tomorrow morning corp, and I will bring you some cocoa tonight around ten thirty if that's okay. That will be fine thank you Blythe replied Ronnie as the door closed behind the soldier.

Taking the uniform jacket from the wardrobe, he tried it for fit and found it was just perfect, the trousers also fitted, if a little long in the leg, however the work shirts were a little baggy, but he solved this by gathering the slack at the rear and tying the belt tighter.

Undressing he looked closer at the multi coloured regimental belt with the interlocking silver clasp, the colours were in three segments of blue, lighter then darker, below which was a green segment, Land Sea and Air he mused to himself the Corps Motto, communications by each of those elements being the mantra. The buckle clasp carried the Signals Emblem which everyone knew as the Jimmy, with the two-word legend, Certa-Cito, Swift and Sure he said out loud, finding his basic school Latin surprisingly useful. He was quite sure that the figure and Motto were from Greek Mythology and reasoned that the figure was a messenger from the God`s, which he considered appropriate as the Corps of Signals were indeed a communications regiment.

He checked the little clock and set the alarm for six thirty in the morning, it was after half past five, so finishing the tea and biscuits he dressed in a clean shirt, trousers, socks and his worn but comfortable shoes, pulled on his lightweight black zipper jacket and headed down the stairs, he passed several small groups of soldiers walking back towards the accommodation blocks, and a few nodded at him but most were talking amongst themselves.

The NCO mess was in fact an annexed area at one end of the main dining facility, each area containing wipe clean Formica topped tables and fold up style plastic chairs. Along one wall was a stainless-steel serving counter behind which white coated uniformed soldiers dished out food from the variety of dishes available, plates were stacked at one end of this servery and cutlery was in a sectioned tray unit at the other.

There were a few soldiers seated in the main area and four in the separated NCO section, walking the length of the food counter he noted that there were sausages, burgers, some sort of meat roast, pork he thought, carrots, mashed potatoes, peas, beans and chips, so taking a plate he took a couple of sausages, some chips and a few baked beans. At the end of the food counter he found some sort of what he guessed was a baked crumble desert with a bowl of yellow custard next to it, so he added this to his selection, walked through into the NCO area and sat down.

The food was quite good much to his surprise and liking, and the crumble was apple which he enjoyed immensely, on a table he saw a tea urn, coffee pot and cups set out, with a small milk jug and sugar basin and some biscuits on a plate, so with a mug of tea and some custard creams he sat back at the table considering the day.

No one had spoken to him or seemingly even acknowledged his presence, but he mused no one even knew who he was so why would they bother with him, and he had liked the food and had found himself quite hungry for it.

From the mess he took a walk around part of the camp being careful to note the names on some of the buildings for future reference and to make sure that he could find his way back to the accommodation block. He saw again the NAAFI building and popping his head inside saw it to be some sort of club with casual seating, a television, a small bar, a tea and coffee area which seemingly also sold burgers and chips, a table tennis table and a pool table, there were around forty or so soldiers in the club spread around in groups with by far the biggest being clustered around the television set watching high kicking dance girls perform on a revolving stage.

Past the NAAFI was a small shop which seemingly sold most things including cigarettes and newspapers as well as milk, tea, coffee and biscuits, he considered buying a newspaper, but decided not to as he had little knowledge or understanding of news or current affairs, and whilst he was interested in sport, he did not know enough about any individual one, to require news items.

Walking on further, he passed two churches one obviously the Anglican place of worship, the other similar but slightly smaller which he rightly guessed was Roman Catholic. The Medical Centre, a small Barbers shop, and on the end of the block a well-lit building with a sign saying Jimmy`s Bar.

Inside were half a dozen worn sofas, a dozen soft armchairs, a couple of round tables with upright chairs, and scattered around a few low tables most of which had been pulled in front of the sofas. There were around forty men inside sat in groups talking and drinking, a single table was occupied by four men playing cards, whilst over in the corner a pool table had a group of four men around it.

In one corner was a bar with a red leather front panel and hard wood countertop, a white coated bar steward stood behind polishing glasses with a grubby looking tea towel, he walked across to the bar and said, a pint of bitter please. Sam or John`s was the stewards reply. Pardon answered Ronnie looking puzzled. New here are you then, we have two bitters, Sam or John Smiths, both similar but a bit like the Scottish old firm rivalry, each thinks the other inferior, if you know what I mean. Ronnie didn`t but said nothing except John Smiths please.

He sat on a high stool at the bar sipping the cold beer which was quite hoppy in taste but still he decided much to his liking. New here are you then asked the steward who had gone back to polishing the glasses. Yes, I only arrived this afternoon, and I am checking out the camp to see what is here.

Where are you from asked the steward idly. From the Home Counties, north of London. Very funny, you sound just like guys from London, so I had guessed that you were from the south, I actually meant what regiment are you in, not everyone here is signal corps, and which base did you leave to come to this godforsaken hole.

Ronnie considered the question very reasonable, yet it was one which he simply could not answer. For the first time he considered his position, supposedly a corporal in the signals regiment, with all that entailed, service history, army number, military record, and yet earlier that afternoon he had been plain Ronnie Lamb, aged seventeen years and seven months, and most definitely a civilian.

He started to proffer what would undoubtably have been a very lame response, saying Signal Regiment, when loud voices from the pool table area took everyone's attention.

Two of the four pool players had squared up to each other brandishing cues as makeshift weapons. Hoi you lot, shouted the steward, you can cut that out or I will call the redcaps. He picked up a wooden baseball bat from a shelf under the counter and slipped out from behind the bar to walk across to the small group. Ronnie grateful for the interruption, finished his pint of beer and left the bar to walk back to the accommodation block. Hmm he mused to himself, someone needs to give me some information soon or I am going to have an awful lot of explaining to do.

Safely back in his room he took out the uniform jacket from the wardrobe, tried it on again and realised that there was a bulge in the inner pocket, pulling the offending item free he discovered it to be a folded blue beret with the signal corps badge on the front, and looking inside he read the stitched label, six and three eighths.

He pulled the beret onto his head and down to one side as he had seen other soldiers wearing theirs, at least it fits he said to himself, and I now know the size of my head.

THE CUP

The tapping on the door caught him by surprise, and he was still wearing the jacket and beret when it was pushed open and Blythe entered, putting the mug of coffee onto the cabinet along with three digestive biscuits he said, sorry no cocoa tonight corp, but it should be okay tomorrow. Coffee is just fine, thank you, replied Ronnie and the biscuits too, much appreciated. Blythe started to leave but stopped in the doorway.

Why did you need a whole new uniform corp, I mean what with you just transferring here from Catterick, I just expected you to have a full kit and more. I have been away on holiday, and it appears they somehow managed to lose all my belongings in transit said Ronnie, surprised at how easily he could seemingly lie convincingly.

Bloody logistics corps snorted Blythe, they couldn`t organise a piss up in a brewery, don`t worry corp I will take care of you and it will be my pleasure, have a good night tea at six thirty in the morning, and he was gone.

Ronnie sat on the bed munching the biscuits and sipping the sweet tea, so he considered he had been transferred from Catterick, he wondered idly where Catterick was.

The following morning, he had already completed his ablutions or as the army knew them the three s`s (Shxx Shave and Shampoo) by six thirty and returned to his room just as Blythe was coming out, tea and a couple of custard creams corp, have a good day.

Drinking and eating the biscuits as he dressed Ronnie was struck by the level of noise and looking out along the corridor saw soldiers in various stages of dress, bustling around in and out of the barrack rooms and washrooms how different from the previous evening.

He tucked his trouser bottoms into the top of his boots, pulled on the beret and sloped it down to the side of his head, checking his appearance in the mirror fixed to the inside of the wardrobe, he opened the door to step outside onto the staircase.

Several soldiers were already making their way down the stairs and none had a beret on their head, so turning back inside he pulled his off and threw it onto the bed.

The mess was busy, and several soldiers gave him a simple, morning corp, which he acknowledged with morning. He took two fried eggs, bacon, sausage and fried bread, and made his way through into the NCO area, there were no empty tables available, so he sat down opposite two lance corporals who both looked up and said good morning before continuing to eat their breakfast.

He had only just started to eat when everything went quiet and everyone stood up, a voice called out Corporal Lamb, and looking round he saw a smartly dressed middle aged soldier with brown leather gloves, red shoulder flashes, and with a highly polished stick under his arm standing in the exit doorway.

Is Corporal Lamb here the voice called out again. Suddenly realising, that he was the wanted soldier, he shouted out yes sir in response. My office nine fifteen sharp Lamb, the officer called back and turned on his heel and marched away.

As everyone sat down again and continued their breakfasts Ronnie was very aware that he was now the subject of quite a lot of attention, with soldiers obviously talking about him. One of the lance corporals sitting opposite said, bloody hell corp, your either extremely important, or in deep shit. Pardon me said Ronnie, what do you mean.

Well continued the soldier, I have been here for ten years now and in all that time I have never seen the old man go looking for anyone himself and he has never been in here, so what did you do, get his daughter up the duff.

I have not done anything that I am aware of, and who was that man anyway. The two lance corporals stopped eating and exchanged looks at each other.

What fucking planet are you from mate, that was the Brigadier himself, and if you want to accept a wee bit of friendly advise do not, and I mean do not be late to his office. They both cleared their plates to the trolley against the wall and left, Ronnie fetched a mug of tea and finished his food then also cleared his plate, mug and cutlery.

Back in his room he found Blythe wearing his new beret, smoothing the side down over his ear. Hi corp, just trying to work your cap, new ones are such a bastard to wear in. Thank you said Ronnie absently, it is good of you, do you know where the Brigadier`s Office is located.

Blimey, only here a day, and already for the high jump, you really are a rum egg, that`s for sure. His office is on the first floor of central admin, a red brick block on the far side of the square behind the flagpole.

At ten past nine he was standing in the outer, ante room, waiting nervously, a Lieutenant was seated at a large desk piled high with papers busily typing, he had informed the Brigadier of Ronnie`s presence and simply told him to wait before continuing to type. Just as the office clock hands showed nine fifteen a loud voice called come in Lamb, so he opened the inner office door and as smartly as he knew how, marched in and stood in front of the Brigadier`s desk. No need for ceremony here Lamb said the officer, sit down. He sat in a straight back chair only then realising that Sergeant Groves was also seated in the room.

I am sure that by now you must be wondering how it is that a civilian begins his service with her Majesty`s Royal Corps of Signals as a full Corporal, with no interviews, no testing no medical, and indeed no explanation, Ronnie opened his mouth to reply but the Brigadier held up his palm, the truth is Lamb that you are not actually in the army at all, well you are, and then you are not if you see what I mean.

It is all part of this intelligence charade, which we have agreed to play along with, at least for now, I personally hate anything to do with secrecy, that is how the enemy get inside the walls, but as it is for Queen and Country, we all need to do our bit.

Ronnie was not sure exactly what a charade was, he certainly did not understand how he could be in a soldier's uniform living on an army camp, but apparently not be a soldier, but he said nothing.

Good luck to you is all that I can say, and if possible, try to keep any trouble as far away from my camp as you can, and of course if all goes well, any mention of my cooperation would be most appreciated.

Of course, Brigadier said Groves, we are indebted to you and I will personally see that you get the mention that you deserve. Good show, the Brigadier rose to his feet, Ronnie and Groves did likewise. Take Lamb somewhere quiet Sergeant and get him up to speed on your plans, good luck to both of you.

In the Bar a different steward served them coffee as they sat at one of the tables with upright chairs, Right then, Sergeant Groves smiled, this explanation might take a while but I will try to keep it basic and simple.

David Steiner has I believe already outlined the events relating to the cup during the war, and the way that both his and your grandparents were involved, Ronnie simply nodded his agreement, good, and presumably he has also explained that we are determined to recover the cup and return it to Israel.

Something like that said Ronnie, but he seemed to have some notion that I was going to recover this missing cup, which is of course ludicrous, and as far as I can remember he did not actually know where the cup was.

Good, replied Groves, at least you have the basics of our plan, and like the Brigadier say`s it is wise to keep secrets safe, as who knows what the enemy will use them for.

Just let me try to get what you are telling me straight in my head said Ronnie, you believe for some strange reason that I can help you recover this cup, and that in order to do so, you have somehow managed to get me into the army presumably as some sort of cover for whatever it is that you expect me to do, even managing to convince the Brigadier that this is a National Intelligence Operation.

Very good Ronnie, and for what it is worth people much cleverer than me believe that you can identify the cup as authentic or otherwise, I only do what I am told, and in a way, it is a National Intelligence Operation, with real Intelligence Service backing and cooperation, just not actually for the greater good of this country.

So, who actually am I and who do I work for, surely I have a right to know at least that much.

That is quite a difficult question to answer replied Groves, in part of course British Intelligence, but then again, the project is Mossad controlled so they also have call on your services, but of course your pay will be from the British Army, direct into your account we already have the details from Steiner, so you can pick whichever employer suits you.

This is all totally unbelievable, I keep thinking that I have slept for too long and will wake soon to find that it is a silly dream. It is not a dream nor is it silly, a great deal of planning, preparation and politics has already gone into getting us this far, not to mention creating sufficient funding for the entire project which by itself was no easy thing, you are just another cog in the machine, an important cog but nonetheless still a cog.

Now for your basic details which you must memorise, Groves passed him a slip of paper, you are Army Number 24105567 Corporal Lamb R, 16th Regiment Royal Corps of Signals based at Catterick which if you did not know is about forty-five miles away in North Yorkshire. On a day to day basis you will live here working in a small hut workshop, supposedly on a secret mission to improve field radio communications, specifically within urban areas, and you will be liaising closely with the technical experts in radio comms at Leeds University where you will work three or sometimes four days each week.

The reality is however that you will be receiving training from myself and an intelligence officer colleague during your time here on camp, and you will complete a full engineering degree course at Leeds Carnegie University as you wished.

Why are you doing this for me, I could have applied for a University course myself, I did have the necessary grades. Yes, I know, those could not be faked, and in any case you will need the academic ability which you possess to gain your degree, we certainly will not be guaranteeing that for you, it will only be achieved by your own hard work and merit.

As for why we have set this up, it really is quite simple, we have bought you here because we might need you at any time night or day, perhaps at short notice, and we currently believe that the cup is located somewhere in Northern Ireland, so as a soldier you might have better access and freedom there.

In order to recover the cup, a degree of stealth subterfuge and secrecy will be required, getting it back might not be straightforward, a certain amount of risk and danger will doubtless be present so total discretion will be essential.

You expect me to go to Northern Ireland, find this cup and steal it, said Ronnie, and how might I ask am I expected to achieve that.

Not steal, recover, we are more than prepared to pay for it, and as it does not technically belong to anyone, it would not be legally possible for it to be stolen. Your main focus for now must be getting settled into a daily routine, letting everyone and anyone see you out and about acting naturally you will get few, if any questions asked of you as it is not that unusual for semi-secret operations to be carried out, it is what the army call Mushroom Management.

Mushroom Management replied Ronnie, that you will need to explain. Mushrooms are always kept in the dark and fed lots of shit laughed Groves, but it does make them grow quite quickly.

For our part we will give you all the training that you need, both in how to be a convincing soldier as well as specific tactics and abilities for the more physical aspects which might arise, and of course teach you to kill.

Why would I wish to kill anyone said Ronnie horrified, I have never even held a gun certainly never fired one, he suddenly remembered the airfield hanger and the black revolver he had been allowed to hold in his hand, but he said nothing.

Maybe not now, said Groves but trust me once this operation gets started properly there will be others who might wish you harm, and knowing how to protect yourself might save your life one day.

It is lunch time said Groves, enough for now, get your food and meet me back here outside at two pm, I will show you where we are going to wor

Chapter Five

Preparations

At two pm he met with Sergeant Groves as planned and they walked down past the medical centre to a wooden building which had a small sign reading Comms Hut underneath which was a white plastic notice with bold red lettering saying "No Unauthorised Access".

Twisting the round knob and pushing the door open, they entered what was a neatly laid out workshop with benches shelves and cabinets dotted around. At the far end, a partition separated a single office from the main area, and to one side a short worktop section with a sink. A shortish quite stocky soldier with two white stripes on his sleeve was making drinks at this little kitchenette, and looking up he called out, tea or coffee Ronnie.

Tea would be fine thank you, they walked down the hut and into the little office which had a desk with chairs a small filing cabinet a telephone and two soft seated upright chairs all set out on a threadbare square of carpet, whilst seemingly clean it looked very tatty. Hardly the Ritz I grant you said Sergeant Groves, but it is ours and has everything that we need, and in here we are away from any questions or enquiring ears.

The other soldier came into the office carrying three mugs in one hand and a plate of assorted biscuits in the other, putting the mugs and biscuits down onto the filing cabinet he passed one to Sergeant Groves and a second to Ronnie, picking up his own mug and placing the biscuits onto the desk he sat on one of the chairs.

Sit down Ronnie said Groves taking his seat behind the worn desk, this is Corporal John Stott also army intelligence corps, whose members are generally referred to as squeaky beaky`s in reference to their secretive snooping nature, whereas signallers, that`s you, are known as scaley backs, on account of the scarred backs suffered from leaking radio batteries in backpacks during the last war.

Sipping his tea Sergeant Groves began to talk. In here, we are just three like-minded people sharing the same end goal of recovering the cup with the least difficulty.

Each of us has his own personal jobs and things to do, and we will respect each other`s privacy in all things, not everything can or even needs to be shared.

It is possible that soldiers from the main unit stationed here might come into the hut from time to time, perhaps for advice, to borrow something or beg a repair job from us, but normally, we will be left alone. That said, there is no excuse for making anyone even slightly suspicious, so we all maintain standard military practices and procedures, when we are away from the hut or whenever anyone else is present here.

In here we will call each other by first name as friends should, I am Sergeant Harry Groves, British Intelligence but attached to the Royal Corps of Signals, this is Corporal John Stott of the British Army Royal Intelligence Corps, and for the purposes of our mission you are Corporal Ronnie Lamb of the 16th Regiment Royal Corps of Signals.

We all know that the aim of this little subterfuge is to recover the cup, and it is our job gentlemen to achieve that end with a minimum of disruption or danger, however we also know and must keep in mind, that we are not alone in seeking the cup, and therefore we need to consider our actions and what we say, and where we say it, as anyone watching could be an enemy.

Ronnie had not known this or if he were honest even considered it, but it was reasonable to assume that if they saw the cup`s possession as important then other`s might have similar thoughts.

He was struck by the constant use of we when Groves spoke about the mission, and slightly amused by the suggestion that it was all something of a boy`s comic wheeze, with expressions like little subterfuge, when the apparent reality of real intelligence personnel, and secret plotting inside a very real army camp suggested anything but.

Looking directly at Ronnie Harry said, we do appreciate that this situation might be somewhat overwhelming for you, and I am sure that you have loads of questions which you want us to answer, but for now at least you will simply have to trust both of us and follow our instructions is that okay.

Yes, said Ronnie, it seems that I have little choice in the matter. That is not quite true smiled Harry, you are neither prisoner or pressganged, you desire a University Course in engineering which we will provide courtesy of the army, you will get board and lodging, a reasonably decent standard of living, and of course you will be paid as well.

For those provisions we will expect you to assist us with our plan to recover the cup. We understand that you are at this moment, totally untrained unprepared and in no position to offer us anything, however that is for us to correct and as already mentioned when you are not attending university, we will give you the training that is required to work with us and achieve our goal.

What happens once we get the cup said Ronnie. Then that will be a job well done and we can all go back to our own lives happy in the knowledge that we have achieved something good was Harry`s response. You mean that I will not be a soldier anymore continued Ronnie, what about university.

We hope and expect that your degree will have been gained before this is over, but in the unlikely event that we succeed quicker than is anticipated, I guarantee that you will get to complete the university course, although there can be no promises regarding how well you do, after all I believe that you once told me that you would undertake the course on your own merit.

That is fair enough smiled Ronnie, I will help in any way that I can, but still do not know how I might identify the cup when I see it. We do not know that either, John Stott spoke for the first time, it is generally thought that descendants of the Levite Tribe are the only ones to be gifted with such knowledge, but we do not know how it is manifest yet.

Harry held up his hand, let us not get too far ahead of ourselves just yet, this is day one and we probably have a long road ahead of us, so before we befuddle Ronnie`s head with too much detail and knowledge, he needs to get a handle on army routines and basic regulations, so that his cover at least appears genuine.

You are Corporal Lamb R. 16th Regiment Royal Corps of Signals, army number 24105567, based at Catterick Garrison but seconded to army intelligence to work on field radio communications here, where you are attempting to improve radio transmission and reception signals in urban areas.

You are liaising with specialists at Leeds University, where you spend a great deal of your time doing both laboratory based and field trials around the suburbs of the city.

If you are ever challenged as to your identity, your army number is genuine, and records will show the details I have just given you, however personal knowledge and details which you will need to make your cover real must be down to you, so I advise that you watch other soldiers carefully and develop their mannerisms and habits, always remembering that you are a full corporal.

As such, you have your own room, the army refer to it as a bunk, and presumably a goffer, some young soldier who is tasked with keeping you supplied with tea and biscuits as well as tidying your bunk, they sometimes do the washing and ironing now I believe as well.

Ronnie thought of Blythe but said nothing. Anyway, continued Harry, as a middle ranking NCO you will not actually be expected to do anything, the daily routines are managed by the lance corporals and troop management comes under the sergeants, so it is very unlikely that you will get called to do anything and if you are, then you must make the best of it.

Most of the soldiers here are signals engineers, training on telephone line installations, transmitters and setting up signalling stations, both base camp and field operations, so do not be surprised to see mechanical diggers and teams with tools putting up poles and overhead lines, and of course in typical army fashion there is a lot of bull and drill, with regular parades and marching around.

That said there will be times when some of them will ask you questions mainly out of friendliness or plain old curiosity, and it is imperative that you keep our reality a secret, try hard not to offer any detail that might be considered odd or suspicious, particularly about other camps or soldiers, as most of the guys here have served a few years already and will know people and places that you do not.

Your presence here nor the trips to Leeds need not arouse any undue interest or suspicion, as the drivers who take and fetch you will soon discover that your work at the university is boring, a constant round of working out mathematical equations, and testing designs and theories, in short very boring.

This will be shared on the camp gossip system and before you know it, everyone interested will know who you are and what you are here to do, and they will at that point lose all interest in you.

How often will I go to university, and you mentioned that along with everything else I will be paid said Ronnie. Tuesday, Wednesday and Thursday during term times, whilst on Mondays and Fridays and during holidays you will come here to receive training from us.

A driver will collect you at the gatehouse every morning at 8am and you will wear dress uniform for university with a tie, here you wear work clothes, remember to wear your beret outside buildings, and salute officers with a gentle raising of your right arm bringing your hand to the right temple until the tips of the fingers just touch, like this. Harry saluted then smiled, it will start to come naturally after a while I promise.

Do we have any idea of timescale for this operation asked Ronnie, John Stott chuckled, "we" already eh Ronnie, it did not take you long to get yourself settled in. No, we do not, said Harry, but your university course starts next Tuesday 22nd September, and it normally takes three years at least to obtain an engineering degree so summer 1972 should see you fully qualified.

And the cup, do we actually know where it is, and how it might be recovered, Ronnie was amazed at his own sudden confidence. We believe that after the war it passed between various Nazi families, although there are no records as such, the suggestion is that it is currently somewhere in Northern

Ireland with Neo Nazi sympathisers, and intelligence are doing what they can to check this for us.

As for how we regain the cup, that will need careful planning once we have real time confirmation of its whereabouts, it has been out of sight and Jewish hands since 1942, so a few more years waiting will not be a problem, and we must get the recovery right, there is unlikely to be a second chance.

Do the people who have it know exactly what it is, Ronnie was becoming drawn into what he had already made up his mind was someone's personal fantasy.

We think so replied John, although it is unlikely that they know of its potential power, hopefully it will remain that way at least until we can send you to get it back.

Look chaps it is past four, Ronnie needs to collect the remainder of his kit from the stores, you can show him where that is John please, we will continue our discussions tomorrow, we start here at nine am every day, and as already mentioned you will need to be at the gatehouse for eight on university days.

Oh and as for pay, yes you will be paid, directly into the account that Steiner used for your wages as we have those details, I believe that it will be around £180 pounds each month less tax and national insurance of course, and around fifty pounds will be stopped for messing, so at a rough guess you might have around £80 pounds pay to spend, with everything provided.

Ronnie blinked, eighty pounds a month, he would hardly need to spend anything except on his beer and treats, so he quickly calculated that he might save as much as six to eight hundred pounds in a year, and a new Mini was around six hundred, not that he was able to drive yet.

What will my training consist of he said hastily, trying to give the impression that the pay was not that interesting to him.

You will learn basic electrical skills, how to setup and monitor listening devices, the correct use of radio transmission and wiring of base systems, then work with security systems and how to bypass or break them, moving on to explosives and of course firearms training and obviously personal protection and defence.

I cannot yet drive nor do I have a learner license will that be a problem.

No, as we will teach you to drive all types of vehicles and how to be evasive if being pursued.

Be in no doubt that we are all committed to recovering the cup, at almost any cost, so it is in everyone's interest to ensure that you get all of the training and knowledge we can provide.

Both myself and John are fully aware of your current limitations which are only to be expected, so our full time task is two-fold, firstly to train and guide you to a level where we can safely send you out to get the cup, and secondly to keep abreast of intelligence relating to its whereabouts, and when the time is right devise and execute a sensible plan which will allow you to collect and authenticate it.

You mentioned firearms and explosives, do you really think that these might play some part in any operation. We just do not know is the simple answer, but we would be failing everyone, you especially if we did not give you at least basic understanding of explosives and arms, after all it might be that you need to kill someone.

Kill, gasped Ronnie seemingly lost for anything else to say. Certainly, replied Harry forcefully, we are trying to regain possession of a valuable item, and presumably others will also be considering such action.

It is not likely that the cup will be handed over to you willingly, and even if a deal is done for its purchase, any other interested parties could well be plotting to steal it from us, and I can assure you that others will not hesitate to kill you if the need arises, the stakes are quite simply too high.

Now it is getting late and the stores close at half past five, so pop along and collect the remainder of your kit and we will start things properly tomorrow morning.

John showed him where the stores building was and left him, saying see you tomorrow. Inside a young stores clerk in uniform asked what he wanted, and he explained who he was and that he had been told to collect his kit. The clerk disappeared for a few minutes then came back with a bundle of items which he set down onto the counter.

One peaked dress cap, one pair putties, one dress uniform trousers size 34 short, three pairs of dress socks, three dress shirts, one dress tie, three pairs pants, two bath and two hand towels, and one pair denim work trousers, sign here.

After putting the new items away, he washed quickly and went for dinner, surprisingly good he ate chicken escalope with baked beans and chips, followed by a doughy pudding with currants in it which he heard the others calling cookies willy, it was only much later that he discovered that it was really called spotted dick.

Later he considered events so far, everything seemed to be happening fast, just two days ago he had been at home with family, now he was part of a secret operation to recover this cup, possibly from Northern Ireland.

In truth he had a nice room, the food was okay, he liked both Harry and John and best of all with his pay saved, in three years he could have his engineering degree, and be able to buy a new mini, yet still only be twenty years old.

Chapter Six
Learning the Ropes

Ronnie spent the next few days working in the hut, he learned basic wiring techniques, how to wire up a simple lamp holder onto a plug and make it work.

They taught him how to tap into telephone circuits at the local junction box using a handset with leads which had crocodile clips on their ends, using a knife edge to shave the insulation back on the two voice receive wires and simply clip the handset wires onto the bare wiring, this allowed you to listen to any conversation on that line.

As a simple test they picked a random line in the camps married quarters junction box, setting up a small tent and work barriers and putting on yellow over-jackets to look like workmen.

The line they tapped into was in fact an officer`s home and they listened in while the wife made plans with her secret lover to meet her next week, as the husband would be away.

Ronnie was quite concerned about what they had done and said so quite indignantly.

Both Harry and John laughed, we appreciate your sensitivity but in real life there is no such thing as privacy said John, anyone can be listening in to you or watching you or even filming you at any moment, and you will probably never know anything about it.

And bear in mind we are British Intelligence, we need secretive information such as this to counteract enemy activities, just suppose that the lady's lover is in fact an enemy agent, working his masculine magic on a bored officer's wife, what information about the camp, the personnel, the strength and weaknesses might she inadvertently give away without even realising it.

You must understand Ronnie that whatever cunning plan the enemy instigates, our responses need to be equally cunning, just to maintain the status quo, and if we are ever to gain superiority then we need to be proactive rather than reactive.

For the first time Ronnie began to see that morality was perhaps a principle that carried too high a price tag, it was easy to judge everything by his own set of standards and understanding, and those which his parents and family had adhered to, but as each day passed and new situations arose, with both plausible and acceptable explanations being given for the actions that needed to be taken, he saw that morality would be only one of life's measuring rods

He began to realise that the adult world was far from what he had imagined, and that evil was not just a word from the Bible, or part of a throw-away line from some angry encounter, but a harsh truth, there were people out there determined to cause chaos, destruction and even death, sometimes for personal motives and other times to achieve an ideal, but for whatever the reason, someone always suffered.

By the end of the week, he had mastered listening in, opening locked doors and cabinets, and disabling basic security systems, and was feeling quite pleased with himself.

Harry reminded him that part of his workload would be to research the cup as much as was possible, and to get his head around the realities of both good and evil being existent in the world, for although the cup was a simple inanimate object, its significance could be considered supernatural, a good power, even perhaps magical, and with that in mind, others intent on obtaining the cup might consider involving good or evil forces.

Ronnie asked John if there were a library on the camp, and was told that there was not, but that in the NAAFI club there was a trolley which had a pile of books which people took, read and returned, so popping in on his way back to his room on the Friday he found two books by Dennis Wheatley which he took and determined to read.

Over that first full weekend he read both books carefully, and soon saw that Wheatley had written them from a fact and fiction perspective. There was obviously some depth of truth and fact in the so- called black arts, and satanism or devil worship, and the author had used facts embroidered with fiction to give the book appeal.

Realising that the resources of a library would be required he decided that a trip into the nearby town was the next step and he made plans for it to be the following weekend, as it should be sooner rather than later, he reasoned.

In the evenings he began to frequent the bar, the John Smiths ale was good, and he discovered that his ability at pool and darts gave him lots of opportunity to play against other soldiers.

There was a short period when he played pool for money, not large amounts but a couple of pounds sometimes, but this stopped after he began to win consistently, usually only losing when in overexuberance or plain showing off he potted the cue ball as well as the black.

He had recognised quite early that using basic triangulation, balls could be potted in holes not immediately in line with them by bouncing them off the side cushions, and for as long as you kept the power of the shot correct and got your angles right, then games could be won easily.

This strategy which whilst entertaining to watch was not a pleasant experience for the losing player, a fact quantified by a bar steward one evening when Ronnie was almost alone in the bar moaning that he had no opponents to play against. Perhaps you should try losing occasionally, was the response, no one likes a smart ass.

On the Tuesday he was outside the gatehouse for ten minutes to eight, and the Landrover arrived a few minutes later, the driver was amiable enough and as Harry had suggested he might. asked quite a lot of questions. Ronnie explained the basics of his work and the need to meet with specialists at Leeds University on a regular basis to work out equations and theories, to which the soldier simply said right.

At the University his course work was already programmed, and after giving his name at reception, a pass was issued, together with a pile of books and folders, and an academic timetable detailing locations and times of all the lessons and seminars that he would need to attend during that term.

The start of the course was mathematics and he found this both enjoyable and relatively easy as this had been a favourite subject at school and he had gained A Level grade exam pass in both theory and practical.

The driver was already waiting at four pm and they were back on camp around quarter to five, giving him time to use the washrooms before the majority, of soldiers came back to the barrack block around five.

Meals were more than adequate if slightly monotonous, it seemed that the army`s idea of staple diet consisted of sausages, burgers, chicken or fish fingers with chips and baked beans, and whilst the chicken often took different forms such as escalope, burger, or even occasionally Tika Masala Curry, nonetheless, some Lamb or Beef would have been very welcome, even the traditional Sunday roast was either chicken or pork, and he knew that without the exercise which the other soldiers received on a daily basis his weight would simply rocket upwards.

On Saturday after breakfast, he went to the hut and finished off the detonator timing device which he had been working on and was quite pleased with. Instead of the more usual method of using a clock mechanism to make a circuit to initiate a power source, he had used some sodium inside the teapot on a standard Teas-Made unit, so that when the water boiled and poured into the pot, a chemical reaction fired the sodium, and with added plastic explosives this would create a significant weapon, he was looking forward to trying it next week.

After lunch he dressed in his civilian clothes, walked out of the camp gates and waited at a bus stop a short distance down the road, several other soldiers some in uniform joined the queue, and it was not long before a single deck bus arrived.

The trip into the town centre took fifteen minutes and stopped firstly at Queen Ethelberga's Ladies College, where four young ladies boarded to wolf whistles and catcalls from the soldiers, then at the exhibition hall before parking up on a stand at the central bus station, he noted the bus number to ensure the return journey would be okay and asked a passer-by for directions to the Library.

Harrogate was seemingly a busy market town and he enjoyed looking in the shops and at the food and produce stalls in the open-air market. The Library was not busy, and he asked for assistance to find books on black magic and satanism explaining that it was research for his university course.

Sitting at a table, he read about various types of so-named black arts, and both medieval and current witchcraft practices, including detail on a coven still practicing at a place called Pendle in Lancashire.

He found some books on white magic and its many practitioners some real but many just using the cover of magic for their own perverse needs, for which it seemed a naked virgin was always an essential part. However, he did find detail of an Oxford scholar who had apparently tried to summon the devil himself, but only the name rather than facts.

Asking the librarian again he was given a book called a treatise on white magic, and one section contained full details of Alister Crowley, an Oxford University undergraduate who broke away from the cult group he had joined complaining that they were not serious about seeking the devil's blessings.

Apparently alone, he locked himself into his rooms and allegedly tried using ancient potions and incantations to summon the devil himself rather than some mere demonic assistant. He was found the next day, naked and sitting inside a large Pentogram that he had carefully painted onto the floorboards. Foaming at the mouth and babbling about the goat of Mendes, he never spoke properly again and was confined into an asylum until he died.

Taking a Bible Ronnie searched under demons in the concordance section and found a passage in the New Testament where Jesus was alleged to have cast Demonic Spirits from someone, which issued forth from the mouth and entered a herd of Pigs which then hurled themselves from a cliff in frenzy.

So then, he reasoned, if the fiction and elaboration were chipped away, there was quite strong suggestion, if not evidence that both Good and Evil were plausible concepts.

As the Library closed at two thirty on Saturdays his research was limited and he found himself walking somewhat aimlessly through the town, only to realise that a small number of people wearing yellow and black scarves were making their way in the same direction, so guessing the reason to be football he followed.

The town football ground was a very low-key affair with a single, part covered stand at one end of the pitch, and white painted steel rails on concrete posts around the actual playing surface. At the opposite end of the pitch to the stand was a small clubhouse bar with changing rooms to one end, and in the corner by the entrance gate stood a smallish wood hut with a hatch opening and internal counter the notice above which, said Tea Hut.

The game was amateur level, and one of the few supporters told him that this was Yorkshire League Division One and that Harrogate were currently favourite to gain promotion into the Northern Premier League, with the man repeating, I mean the actual Northern Premier League, as if it were somehow a hallowed sanctuary.

Ronnie was very tempted to say, what goes up must come down, but seeing the man's look of awe at the words he had spoken thought better of it and simply said that is good.

At half time with the score level at one goal each, he wandered over to the tea hut and was pleasantly surprised to see a long-haired blonde girl of about his own age, on her own serving the teas and coffees.

Ordering a tea he was asked are you with the visitors, to which he truthfully replied no I am from the army camp at Pennypot. Oh, a squaddie, she almost spat the word, we don't get many in here, in fact I do believe that you are the first.

As it happens, I am only working at the camp, I am not what you call a squaddie retorted Ronnie comfortable that he was in fact telling the truth, after all even the Brigadier did not consider him to be a soldier.

Oh, sorry, that's all right then, its just that, well you know, they do have an awful reputation, especially where girls are concerned, only after one thing.

Ronnie wondered what the one thing might be but felt now was not the right time to ask, instead he said, are you always alone, is it not busy sometimes.

She laughed, busy, I doubt that I do more than forty or fifty drinks all match even on cold days, and a few pies or sausage rolls which I put in the little oven before the match. On rare occasions if we are playing a big team who bring a few supporters my mum has helped but usually just me.

He put his empty mug onto the counter and said thank you, to which she replied, you can come in if you like while I wash up, we can talk, if you want to that is.

The hut was a simple affair, a small counter and extended worktop on the inside, with double shutters which opened outward to create a servery, a small refrigerator, a small electric oven at one end of the worktop, a sink unit with and over-sink electric water heater, two wall cupboards housing glasses and mugs with a few plates, cups and saucers, and an under the worktop cupboard with drawer above housing tins of biscuits, tea, coffee and sugar. In the refrigerator, squash, milk and half a dozen cans of cola completed the itinerary, with a mop and bucket plus broom and dustpan making up the cleaning equipment.

As she washed the dirty mugs and plates the girl told him that her name was Sheila, she was seventeen and had left sixth form with a Math's GCE to work for the Milk Marketing Board.

Her father was the club groundsman, youth team manager, all teams coach and general handyman and that she ran the tea hut for something to do rather than any support for the town team. She collected fresh milk and biscuits before the home games to sell and over the entire course of a season often made around one hundred and fifty pounds for the club funds, and rinsing away the soapsuds she realised that he had dried the mugs and said thank you.

After sweeping and wiping the floor with the dampened mop they locked the hut door and she put the key into her small shoulder bag, right that`s me done, will I see you in a fortnight for the next home game.

Yes, well maybe, he answered. Good she smiled, then turned and walked away up the road without looking back. Ronnie watched and found her shapely legs, clumpy heels, and blonde hair cascading down her back over the green leather coat strangely exhilarating, after about a hundred yards she stopped, turned and looked back at him, then waved. He waved back and watched her walk away, perhaps he might just come back in two weeks, he thought.

Back at camp he asked Blythe if he had a Bible, to which the response was, only the King`s same as you corp, so he made the decision to go to church the following morning and find one for himself.

There were apparently three rather than two churches at the camp, with these being the Anglican and Roman Catholic facilities which he knew of and it seemed a smaller less formal protestant gathering which apparently took place in the sports hall.

The service was in fact held in a meeting room inside the sports complex and consisted of four people plus him, these all being from the town, a pastor and his wife their son and his girlfriend all of whom apparently came to the camp every Sunday to hold informal services and give teaching on the Bible.

Ronnie was welcomed and given a hymnbook and a Bible which said NIV on its cover, they sang a few hymns and read some scriptures, after which the pastor talked about Jesus being the way the truth and the life, recounting Jesus own words that, "No One Comes to The Father But By Me".

As an aspiring engineer, he saw the comparison of bridge building, reasoning that what Jesus had meant was that he alone had the Fathers Ear, and that anyone who wished to get close to the Father needed to undertake that through him.

After the service they shared coffee from a flask the family had bought with them, the pastor asked if he were new to which he replied yes, and he was told to feel free to attend or otherwise any Sunday.

He asked the pastor what he knew about the cup, which at first seemingly had the man confused, until Ronnie mentioned the Last Supper.

Oh that, laughed the pastor, what some call the holy grail, of course legends abound with regards to its whereabouts and its authenticity, but then where would we be without legends and myths.

But, pressed Ronnie, could it possibly have some magical powers.

Oh dear, said the pastor smiling, someone has been filling your head with mumbo jumbo that`s for sure, the cup used by Jesus at the last supper was almost certainly an everyday hand carved wooden vessel of no significance other than Jesus using it to offer wine to the disciples.

I am sorry to disappoint you young man, but any supernatural power at the time was from the man holding the cup, that being Jesus, the object itself held no power and after two thousand years would by now be rotted away.

Holding out the Bible Ronnie asked if he might borrow it and was pleased to be told that he might keep it as it could be useful to him one day.

After lunch, he sat in his room with the Bible and only after some searching found the part which told the story of the last supper, he read it several times only to end up quite disappointed as it contained almost no mention of the cup, and all that he could find was, "that after supper Jesus had taken the Cup and blessed it" which he considered a strange thing to do even for a God, after all it was Jesus who held the cup, so was he blessing the cup, its contents or perhaps both.

The next morning whilst chatting over coffee he mentioned to Harry and John that he had attended the little church and that he had been given a Bible.

Shit exploded Harry, the Bible, I forgot the Bible, at which he rushed from the hut, leaving John and Ronnie simply staring at each other.

About an hour later Harry returned carrying a small black, leather covered new testament with a silver cross on the cover. Asking Ronnie to stand he passed the little book to him and told him to hold it in his left hand.

Repeat after me he said, I, 24105567 Ronnie Lamb, hereby pledge to uphold and defend her Majesty`s Realm, and to protect Queen and Country even unto laying down my life. Harry then held out a silver shilling coin saying repeat again.

I accept this payment as the Kings sealing of this pledge, Harry passed the coin to Ronnie saying congratulations you have received the Kings Shilling and made your pledge to defend Queen and Country, you are now one of her Majesty`s Soldiers.

Bollock`s snorted John, that was about as official as a drag queen dressed as HRH, he is not, and never will be a fully-fledged soldier, at least not under our watch, he already knows that our mission is both covert and technically unauthorised, I really think that it is now time to level with him so that we can discuss things openly without consideration of any consequences.

You are right as usual sighed Harry, we do need to set the record straight, but Ronnie does need the testament and shilling to add credibility to his cover, who knows if anyone might decide to go through his things, at least finding the shilling with the testament might add some reality to our smoke and mirrors facade, put the kettle on John and we can sit down and chat.

Sitting together in the small office with tea and biscuits Harry spoke. John is right to say that we need to give you as much detail and information as we can, however you must understand that information is sometimes a dangerous commodity, especially if you do not know what to do with it. What you do not know can rarely harm you, but of course the converse is also true.

Whilst it is certainly true that as Harry Groves, I am a serving member of Her Majesty`s armed forces namely the Royal Corps of Signals It is also true that I work both for and closely with British Military Intelligence, and as you have possibly also guessed am a serving member in the Israeli Intelligence Service generally known as Mossad.

So presumably your name is not Harry Groves either then sneered Ronnie. There is no reason to be upset or sarcastic sighed Harry, in our profession deceit becomes second nature, sometimes it is hard to remember who we really are or were, but If it makes you less bitter, then my real name is Isaac Steiner, and before you ask my father was Franz Steiner`s only son which of course makes David and I brothers, and we have a sister.

Why did your family have the cup in the first place asked Ronnie, we have already explained that, Grandfather Franz was safekeeping it, he passed it to your Grandfather paying for that with his life, only for it to be stolen by the Nazi`s, a few years later.

If all of that is true, how can you know that this cup is the original used by Jesus, retorted Ronnie, I mean who has authenticated it, it might just be another cup.

In all honesty we do not know if the cup we seek is the genuine article, how can we, excepting you apparently no one in the team has the ability to know for certain that the cup is real or otherwise, which is why, since you were quite young we have monitored your progress and molded the way that life has led you, knowing you to be a Levite and hopefully therefore having the ability to tell the cups truth.

And if I do not what happens then, I guess I would be seen as a disposable asset spluttered Ronnie. Not at all responded Harry, contrary to what you seem to be thinking about us, this is a mission to recover the cup of Christ, which was taken into safe keeping two thousand years ago, it is not some sort of holy warfare, where we eliminate everyone involved to retain secrecy.

As for the mission failing, if you are unable to provide authentication, then that might mean the cup is a fake, but it might also mean that our understanding of the Levite connection is incorrect and the cup is genuine, just that we would not know it to be so.

Where does John fit into all of this and are there others that I do not know about asked Ronnie.

John is my nephew, my sister`s boy, and as you have already been told a genuine member of British Army Intelligence, his role is to help me and more specifically to train you to a level where the issues that are likely to be faced do not come as a complete shock. As for others, both British and Israeli intelligence services have an insight into our mission, albeit with only tacit approval and limited assistance, what is generally known as "deniability" if the shit hits the fan.

Surely if the cup is genuine, that poses several questions mused Ronnie. Such as, replied John. Well, for a start why has it not degraded and rotted away if it is just wood. Let me ask you a question in response to that said John do you believe in God. Well yes, I mean I suppose so, after all there must be some sort of higher power to have created all the universe, it did not just appear from nowhere.

But at this precise moment you have no committed belief in the Bibles version of creation, or in the claim that Jesus was indeed the Human form of God himself John persisted.

Well to be honest, I think that It is as good a possibility as the so called, evolution theories, after all where did life, in their claims originate from, and as far as Aliens are concerned, creatures from out of this world are repackaged Angels. Whatever you wish to call this higher power, God or otherwise, the answer is yes, I believe in its existence.

Good, smiled John, then as such, an object created by this higher power might not have normal properties, at least not as we understand them. Perhaps one day, as the Bible predicts, every eye will see, and everyone accept that Jesus was exactly who he claimed to be. Maybe replied Ronnie, we shall have to wait and see, but the burning question for me is does this cup have any real power, and if it does what sort.

Most certainly the cup has power and authority said John, just as Jesus himself had, but possibly not the sort of mythical magic and sorcery that you imagine.

Explain please said Ronnie, If I am to be the retriever of this cup, it is only fair to know what if anything that it might do to me.

There are three ancient Christian relics generally accepted as holding of any significance for proof or disproof of Biblical truth, these being the Ark of the Covenant which the Israelites made from Gold on Gods orders to hold the Ten Commandments, these represented the second covenant God made with mankind, the Holy Shroud or burial cloth in which Jesus dead body was wrapped when he was placed into the tomb, and the Cup of the Covenant or Last Supper, which represents the third covenant which God made with man, theoretically any single one might be used to offer proof of Biblical teachings, however there is a consensus of opinion that believes if all three items could be somehow bought together, then it would usher in Gods new kingdom.

Ronnie desperately wanted to ask what Gods first covenant with mankind was, but as John had not mentioned it, assumed he was somehow expected to already know, instead he said would that not be a good thing, surely if everyone had no choice but to believe In God, the world would be a much better place.

Such an idealist laughed Harry, do you think, that non-Christian faiths would just stand idle while Christianity effectively took control of worldwide religious beliefs, even today different faiths wage war on Christianity because it stands so much against what they believe. Were any determined effort be made to show proof positive of Gods existence, a global holy war would be the result, and for that reason alone we must not let the cup fall into the hands of others whose motives for its possession might be much different from our own.

I understand I think, said Ronnie, you have said that it is believed the cup to be somewhere in Northern Ireland, what about the other two items.

The burial cloth or Shroud of Turin is allegedly held in a museum in Italy, John Smiled, although some evidence exists to suggest that this is in fact a copy, with the genuine article already stolen and in the possession of Neo Nazi`s seeking to create a fourth Reich.

As for the Ark, we are confident that it is both genuine and in safe keeping, somewhere in East Africa, at this precise moment you do not need to know the exact location.

Fair enough responded Ronnie but what reason might there be for the cup to be in Ireland, are there any ideas.

We cannot yet, be one hundred percent positive that the cup is there but if it is, then you can bet any money that the IRA have a vested interest in it said Harry. Which of course is where you come in quipped John, we will train you, equip you, and get you into the province safely and secretly, so that you can recover it and bring it home.

Bloody hell, I am to be James Bonds sidekick, laughed Ronnie.

Not quite, Harry was not smiling, this is not a game or some movie script, bullets kill trust me I know, you are now part of a very real mission with a justifiable cause to fulfil, and therefore taking any part of it less than totally seriously will have extreme consequences, of that you can be sure.

Sorry, I got a little excited and carried away I guess. No harm done in here, smiled John, but Harry is right in what he says about secrecy and caution, this might seem very surreal to you, perhaps even the stuff of fantasy, but it is quite real I can promise you, and it carries very real threats to all of us, which can only increase.

After the evening meal Ronnie lay on his bed reading his new testament, he read the story of the last supper repeatedly but try as hard as his brain would allow could not get beyond the basic wording and find any particular significance for the cup, save that it was used for the wine sharing when Jesus spoke to his closest followers.

Suddenly he stopped reading and stared at one line of words, "Until I drink it with you in my Fathers Kingdom", why did Jesus make such a statement seemingly matter of fact if it were not true he mused, why even say it at all, more importantly why repeat in in writing if it were not important, perhaps this Jesus was real after all.

Days evaporated into weeks with him studying hard at Carnegie, whilst acquiring many new skills with John particularly, but some had Harry`s input, including learning to drive and gaining his license.

Harry taught him basic self-defence skills, and he started a fitness regime by cross country running around a seven mile course that he had worked out would give both flat and road running as well as climbing and rough terrain stuff, the route taking him from the front gates of the camp, down past the Ladies College, into the field and up over Brimham Rocks, before cutting back out onto the road and back to camp, he tried to do this run at least once but often twice and occasionally three times every week.

To give some semblance of soldiering, John taught him basic drill moves and then how to take drill parades, what commands to give and at what point during marching to give them.

Once he was deemed able, he and John joined in with some actual parade ground drill practice, marching with other soldiers which strangely he enjoyed although seemingly most soldiers saw drill as a chore and a needless army practice which achieved little.

After a few sessions with the soldiers John surprised him by suddenly telling him that today he was taking the parade, and while he marched the men around the parade ground John and the drill Sergeant watched from the side, afterwards the Sergeant was kind enough to say that his drill had been good enough to pass Cadre.

Later he asked John what Cadre was, to be told that it was the name for the tests which Corporals were subjected to when trying for promotion to Sergeant, which is what John had told the drill Sergeant Ronnie was working on.

Every other Saturday he went to the Football Ground and spent the time in the tea hut with Sheila, serving the drinks and washing up. As Christmas got closer, she asked him what he was doing over the holiday period, to which he truthfully replied that he did not know. That is settled then, you are coming to ours for Christmas dinner, I will sort it with Mum.

It seemed that the camp almost emptied for the Christmas period, with just a few single soldiers like himself remaining and of course those in married quarters, the NAAFI and bar were still open, and food was served as normal but with Sunday hours opening, and of course Guard Duties at the gatehouse still had to be maintained.

Ronnie decided that he should buy gifts for Sheila and her parents, although he had not yet met them, he chose a large box of shortbread biscuits for her Mother and a bottle of Whiskey for her Father, for Shelia herself he bought a gold cross and chain in a small presentation box hoping that she would like it.

Christmas Eve was a Saturday and Town had a home game, it was bitterly cold with few supporters braving the weather, so Sheila was able to lock the tea hut by midway through the second half of the game.

Ronnie walked Sheila home to the end of her road, as he had already done a few times, and taking a chance when they stopped to say goodbye, he kissed her. She looked at him smiled then reached up put her arms around his neck and kissed him hard on the mouth, sliding her tongue inside his mouth which felt both strange and yet nice at the same time.

They stood apart and she smiled again, be here at my house, for twelve o`clock tomorrow as we go to the pub for Christmas drinks before dinner, remember its number Eight and don`t be late, she giggled at her little ditty.

As she walked away from him down the pathway he stood watching, she half turned as she walked and called out, and don`t forget to bring something.

How on earth could she know that he had bought presents thought Ronnie then sighed to himself, it was probably the expected thing for a Christmas Dinner guest, so he was thankful that he had purchased the gifts.

Christmas Day 1969, he had breakfast then a relaxed shave shower and toilet. He dressed in a light blue, button-down collar Ben Sherman shirt, plain dark blue tie and navy-blue suit with a faint check pattern, finishing the appearance with his well-polished black oxford brogues. Putting the gifts into a sturdy carrier bag he took the bus into town.

Outside the house, he adjusted his tie and was about to knock on the door when it opened as if by magic. Sheila stood in the doorway smiling, she was wearing a canary yellow mini dress, stockings and black shoes with a small heel and a strap around the ankle, with her long blonde hair falling either side of her neck, Ronnie thought that she looked gorgeous.

Well, are you going to just stand there or come in she said. He stepped into the small front lobby area and she kissed him using her tongue again, happy Christmas Ronnie, now come and meet my family.

Inside the deceptively spacious front room he was introduced to Sheila`s parents, Mavis and Wilfred and her brother Colin and his wife Maria, he had said hello to her father at the football club but now he felt nervous as if he were somehow a specimen bought home by Sheila for the family to assess.

Despite his nerves, he managed to say happy Christmas everyone, and opening his bag offered the gifts to Sheila`s parents, who both said thank you as they opened them. Oh, my word said Colin as Wilf pulled the paper from the present, it`s Macallan, you have good taste Ronnie, dad will be a friend for life. And me said Sheila coyly, do I get a Christmas Present, her eyes on the small gift held in Ronnie`s hand.

He offered the present to her saying happy Christmas, she quickly ripped the paper away and opened the box, thank you she cried holding out the necklace for everyone to see. Her mother fastened it around her neck and the gold cross nestled neatly in the valley between her breasts.

It looks lovely said Ronnie, unaware that he was staring at her chest area, then realising stammered, I mean the necklace it suits you. They all laughed, and then standing up Wilf declared come along, I do believe that it is time for a Christmas drink. Not too many dear said Mavis to Wilf, and don't be late, dinner will be at two o`clock, not later.

Ronnie, Wilf and Colin left the house and walked up the road, we leave the ladies to do the dinner Ronnie, it is our tradition, we go and have a drink before dinner to celebrate Christmas day, then enjoy a Mavis special Roast Turkey feast.

The nearby pub was called the Claro Arms and was busy with mainly men chatting and drinking, drinks are on me said Colin, what will you have Ronnie.

Two pints of Tetley`s bitter later he had discovered that both Wilf and Colin worked at the ICI factory in the town, Wilf as a storeman, Colin in the design office, with both involved at the town football club. Wilf as Ronnie knew managed the grounds and youth team, with Colin in the reserve team.

After drinking up, they made their way back to the house, Ronnie had found both men agreeable, with Wilf suggesting that he might like to train with the youth team to see if he was good enough to play.

Christmas dinner was a traditional Yorkshire affair he was told, large open Yorkshire puddings filled with onions and gravy, followed by a full turkey roast, with cuts of beef, roasted potatoes, swede, brussel sprouts, cauliflower in a cheese sauce, roasted parsnips and little sausages wrapped in bacon which they called pigs in blankets.

For desert traditional plum duff Christmas pudding with whiskey poured over it and set alight, served with thick cream, and afterwards mince pies in the front room with tea.

The three women cleared dinner and did the washing up whilst the men each had a glass of the Mcallan whiskey Ronnie had given Wilf and sat chatting.

When the women had finished clearing, they joined the men in the front room with Christmas cake and more tea, Mavis embarrassed Sheila by telling Ronnie about previous totally unsuitable boyfriends, and made him blush a little when she said maybe she has found a decent lad at last.

Around six pm both parents and Colin and Maria put on their coats and gloves, said goodbye and left the house. Seeing the somewhat puzzled look on his face Sheila smiling said, another tradition, Mum and Dad go the pub with Colin and Maria for a couple of drinks then go to their house for supper, they will not be home until at least eleven o`clock.

Shelia made tea and cut some more cake and they cuddled together on the settee and as there was nothing to interest them on the small black and white television, Sheila put on the radio and they listened to some music.

You did bring something Sheila asked. Yes, I gave it to you earlier Ronnie replied. No silly, I mean something for protection, you know.

Ronnie did not know, and the look on his face obviously showed that fact. A Johnny Ronnie, Sheila giggled at her wording, then seeing Ronnie`s face, stopped.

Oh my, she gasped, I am your first girl. No of course not Ronnie spluttered, I have kissed quite a few, he felt terribly embarrassed. Kissed maybe, but you have never had sex have you she said.

No, he replied, not yet sorry. You don`t need to apologise she smiled, I will show you what to do, luckily I have a condom upstairs, wait here.

When she returned, he was stunned, wearing nothing but a blue suspender belt holding her stockings, and the strappy shoes she looked so at ease and confident, quite the opposite to how he was feeling.

Afterwards they dressed and cuddled on the settee, around ten thirty he decided to go as there was no late bus and it was quite a long walk, so they kissed goodnight and he said thank you for a super day.

Walking back to camp, it was if he had a spring in his step, Christmas 1969 he said to himself and I have had sex.

With both Harry and John away for the Christmas period he spent the next day`s playing with different types of detonator devices, and some plastic explosives. He created a normal looking lightbulb effect which was however most deadly, removing the bayonet cap carefully, he replaced the filament with a number four detonator wired across the lamp cap pins, and packed some PE all around inside the bulb.

Under a lampshade with only the top of the bulb displayed everything looked normal, but if the lamp was switched on, BOOM, the resultant explosion being enough to devastate a small area killing or badly maiming all present.

Feeling quite pleased with himself, he set up an outside test, borrowing, one of the life size dummy soldiers from the medical centre, which he presumed the medics used for training purposes.

He seated the dummy on a chair, with a small table next to it holding his special table lamp. Switching on the power from what he considered a safe distance he was shocked by the devastation, the dummy was literally blown to pieces, as was the lamp, and both the chair and table were damaged beyond any reasonable repair.

He disposed of the dummy, or rather its pieces into various wheelie bins around the camp, taking the remains of the chair and table to the wood workshop, throwing them towards the back of a pile of broken furniture.

After sweeping up the last of the evidence he returned to the hut only to be surprised at the pungent smell, marzipan he thought, so plastic explosives gave a smell which was not unlike marzipan, it was something new he had learned.

At the NAAFI shop he was pleased to buy a small Christmas cake, and taking it back to the hut, he scraped off the white icing exposing the marzipan layer spread under it and left the cake open on a bench.

As he locked up the hut, he considered everything. After just a few months he had learned such a great deal, he could drive, undertake basic electrical jobs, tap people's telephones, and create explosions.

Damn it all, he had made a bomb, crude maybe, but it was still a bomb. And of course, there was Sheila, a total new experience for him, as a younger person he had kissed and held hands with quite a few different girls, but Sheila was different, he thought about her a lot, and they had sex, that must mean something he reasoned.

On the Friday afternoon as he was walking back towards the accommodation block, he was stopped by Captain Baines, whom he knew to be the commanding officer in charge of the engineering training unit. Fearing some sort of trouble, he saluted the officer as smartly as he knew how.

Corporal Lamb I believe, the officer's tone was almost genial. Yes sir, replied Ronnie.

Look here Lamb, I fully understand that you are here on attachment and as such you are not part of our unit however, I also believe that you are expected to be on camp this weekend, is that true.

Yes sir, I have no plans to be anywhere else, he had considered seeing Sheila, but decided the officer did not need to know that, and as the town were playing away from home this weekend, he would only meet her in the evening anyway.

Good show, we need your help said Baines. Always happy to help where I can sir, what is it that you need asked Ronnie.

Every year the unit hold a New Year party, for the married couples and those singles who remain on camp over the season, nothing too grand you understand, a buffet supper, with dancing to our own little Jazz Band and of course a few fireworks to see in the new year.

Sounds fun sir, said Ronnie fully expecting an invitation was coming his way, it sounds too good to be missed.

Quite so Lamb, and there`s the nub of it, you see Sergeant Thorpe is our Jazz Band leader and also doubles as the MC, but he starts a week`s guard duty stint tomorrow morning, meaning of course that he is not able to be at the party.

I see sir, said Ronnie not seeing at all. That`s the spirit Lamb, I knew that you would be willing to take up the challenge, step into the breach as it were.

Catching the officers meaning at last Ronnie replied, and of course with all the other Sergeants needing to be at the party with their families, then any cover needs to be an outsider, a single man with no plans and willing to cover the Sergeants duty to allow him to also attend the party.

Exactly Corporal, or should I say acting Sergeant Lamb, good man, jolly good show. He Stepped back one pace and Ronnie saluted, turning on his heel captain Baines marched away calling over his shoulder, see Sergeant Thorpe at the gatehouse tomorrow morning around nine am, he will give you all the details.

Ronnie had never been inside the gatehouse, and found it to be totally unremarkable, a single storey brick-built structure, set in the middle of the entrance and exit traffic lanes in the sweeping gateway, with just one door, and windows on three sides.

A solitary soldier, gun cradled in his arms was standing directly outside the gatehouse on duty, whilst a second was standing at the far side of the entrance next to the barrier post, both access and exit barriers were lowered and everything was quiet.

Within the gatehouse the front area was open plan, with a desk in one corner housing a camera monitor, notepad and various pencils and pens, whilst sat in a hard backed chair in front of the monitor and writing in the book that was open on the desk was Sergeant Thorpe.

From his pocket Thorpe took an elasticated cloth which Ronnie saw had three white Vee Shaped Sergeant stripes embroidered onto it and slipping onto Ronnie's arm and up over the corporal's stripes Thorpe said, let me show you around Sergeant Lamb.

The camera monitor could be set up as four pictures or a single view, quite basic said Thorpe, Camp Armoury, Medical Centre, POL, and looking out from here at the entrance, the tape in the recorder is continuous loop lasting seventy-two hours and it simply overwrites every fourth day.

At the back of the room were three doors, the left opened into a row of four small cells each with a small toilet, barred door with lock and wooden bed complete with moulded wood pillow.

The middle door gave access into a square room with three sets of twin bunkbeds, a couple of upright chairs and a small table, four soldiers were lazing on the beds, and Thorpe introduced Ronnie as Sergeant Lamb, who would be duty Sergeant for the day, each of the soldiers said hi and went back to what they were doing.

The last door revealed a small kitchenette with a small countertop oven, small refrigerator, kettle, sink and cupboards, and at the rear a further door led into a toilet and shower room.

That's it said Thorpe, you have six soldiers for stag duty outside, each doing three-hour shifts, to ensure that they remain alert. They do three hours in pairs outside on stag, then have six hours rest, you will need to sort out a rota as today is handover and I have already taken over from the last team.

The guys here are all inexperienced but we are not expecting any trouble but I have not yet sorted out a duty rota. And my role, said Ronnie.

THE CUP

You monitor the cameras, you might be surprised what gets purloined even here on camp, so if you see anything suspicious send a couple of the guys to look around. You check the guys weapons, make sure that they are loaded correctly when outside on stag, but unloaded as soon as they finish their stint, ammo is kept locked in the desk drawer, the key is on a hook above.

You keep the stag duty going, and above all you make sure that no one unauthorised enters camp. And the guys here on duty are not allowed to leave for any reason unless an officer commands it.

You say that stuff gets stolen on camp said Ronnie. Oh yes, all the time, especially from the Medical Centre, Ronnie tensed up wondering if he had been seen taking the dummy, there is an endless supply of condoms, pills and other tablets which have a ready market, and fuel nicked from POL can also be worthwhile even if only for personal use.

Surely people get caught said Ronnie, and punished I mean. Sometimes said Thorpe, but usually it`s only a week`s LOP and to be honest what`s that compared to the benefits. Ronnie already knew that LOP meant loss of privileges, which for a basic soldier probably meant seven days confined to barracks and not allowed out of camp, which as Thorpe suggested might mean little hardship if profit were involved.

As he left Thorpe said thank you to Ronnie, adding I owe you one. What if anything does happen, called Ronnie as he disappeared. Nothing will mate, after all its New Year`s Eve and everyone will be too busy getting pissed to cause any trouble, and any drunkenness at the party will be sorted by the redcaps who operate from their own setup on camp.

It`s highly unlikely that you will have any issues, but worst case, push the big red button above the desk, it sets off camp wide alarms.

Bloody hell thought Ronnie, how sodding blaise could anyone get, a no combat totally inexperienced corporal, supervising a group of newbie soldiers, with only basic weapons training, in control of the entire camp.

The local WI could overrun the camp in ten minutes, God knows what any plausible militant group might achieve, and he realised suddenly, he did not even have a weapon.

Sitting at the desk he took a sheet of paper, pencil and ruler and created a simple rota chart, nine columns across and seven rows down. In the top row he detailed the columns Name, six until nine, nine until noon. noon until three, three until six, six until nine, nine until midnight, midnight until three, and three until six.

Going outside and with as much confidence as he could muster, he asked the names of the two soldiers on duty, 626 Watson and 647 Miller were the responses, and he said thank you, your stag duty finishes at noon, stay alert, it might be New Year`s Eve, but that is not an excuse for being sloppy okay. Both soldiers noticeably straightened and became more alert, he smiled, this sergeant thing was okay.

Back at the desk he filled in Watson and Millers names in the nine until noon column, then again under six until nine pm, and finally three until six tomorrow morning. Next, he went into the rest area and asked the names of the other four soldiers, noting these onto a pad, right Stevens and Appleby, you take over from Watson and Miller at Noon, be ready in the front for me to check your weapons at five to twelve, Collins and Hardy, your turn will be from three this afternoon, so ready at five to three okay.

Yes Sarn`t was the unison response, the duty rota is on the desk if any of you wishes to look at it, and just because it is New Years Eve, we still have a job to do so don't fuck around, got it.

THE CUP

Another yes Sarn`t greeted his final words and he turned to go out again, then stopping said, and Stevens, put the bloody kettle on, a camel could die of thirst in this place, they all laughed, and Stevens jumped down from his bunk and went into the kitchenette.

Ronnie filled out the remainder of the rota, and then checked through each of the four camera pictures eventually working out that you could get all four up at the same time as quarters of the whole screen, which he saw as the most sensible.

Checking his watch against the wall clock it read half past ten, and thanking Stevens for the tea and biscuits, he noted the compiling of the stag rota and the camera checks in the logbook on the desk against Saturday 31st December 1969.

Amazing he thought, just a few short months ago I was just another pimply teenage boy wondering what to do on New Year`s Eve, now here I am, a Sergeant in full command of an entire army camp and yet apparently, I am not even a bloody soldier, how crazy was that.

At five to twelve Stevens and Appleby came out from the bunk room carrying their rifles, which he checked ensured each had a round breached and the safety catch on. We do not need any show he said, just go out and take over, and like I said be alert, it is on days like this that the top brass can decide to check up on us.

The men went out and he saw them exchange words with each other before Miller and Watson made their way back into the gatehouse. He was not sure why he had said that about the top brass checking up, after all he had no experience whatsoever, but Miller spoke, we had not thought about anyone doing spot checks on us sergeant, we understand why we all need to be alert now, we will tell the others.

Just before One pm a Landrover arrived with seven covered dinner plates, all containing sausages chips and beans, plus some apple crumble in small bowls. The driver said that he would be back at six with dinner which was to be pie chips and peas, I will collect the plates and covers then he said.

Now understanding the need for the small oven to reheat food for the soldiers on stag, Ronnie placed two covered plates inside and turned it to low heat, reheated sausages he said to himself uggh.

Chapter Seven
Getting Serious

Excepting boredom, guard duty passed without incident, the highlight being when Miller had asked him why it was called stag, and before he could answer, Appleby who was apparently from somewhere in Scotland, explained for him saying, don`t you even know that fuckwit, it`s from when the head deer or Stag, watches over his herd whilst they relax. Oh, had been the response I didn`t know that. Ronnie had not known either so Appleby`s intervention had been most fortuitous.

Thorpe turned up around eleven am somewhat bleary eyed but nonetheless grateful to Ronnie for the stand in arrangements, and when asked if the party had been good, he affirmed that it was probably the best he had attended out of the five in total since he deployed there.

Ronnie started to remove the arm band to return it to Thorpe but was told to keep it on, as Captain Baines had told him that the acting Sergeant position was permanent, with full status being given upon completion of the cadre course.

A new year, 1970 had arrived and Ronnie really got stuck into both his academic and intelligence training, gaining his first exam results, an ONC in mechanical engineering in the spring from Carnegie.

He completed the Sergeants Cadre course with assistance from both John and Harry thus making his promotion to Sergeant permanent with a pay increase to match.

The shooting tests had been probably the most interesting of the various challenges, as despite his enthusiasm he found that shooting range accuracy was not his strongest ability, but perseverance and goading by John in particular, eventually pushed him over the line.

His promotion to sergeant and its reasons had interested Harry to such an extent that he had researched Captain Baines to see if there had been any ulterior motive involved, but everything pointed to Baines being a straight thinking, officer with no known political affiliations or interests.

Harry therefore somewhat begrudgingly accepted that the reason had been pure self interest in terms of the party, and that despite finally achieving cadre, Ronnie was nonetheless still a lucky guy.

Training on hand-held and open-air listening devices, was both good fun and extremely enlightening as he had never considered being able to hear quite clearly a conversation that was held up to a hundred yards away without being observed, this coupled with using night vision equipment gave a powerful ability to listen in on discussion and general conversation in total secrecy day or night and the most powerful units picked up conversation even through window glass, and by the autumn of 1970 he was becoming a proficient intelligence operative even though still young in years.

He saw Sheila regularly, and their relationship deepened, he met her closest friends, in particular Janet who she had known since primary school and Linda a work colleague who Sheila saw as the sister she never had. His friendship with her father Wilf also blossomed with Ronnie training with the town youth team, and then being signed by the town as a player available for any of the teams, whilst on camp his unusual working arrangements meant that he had little or no interaction with the other soldiers, nonetheless he did get to know a few, mainly from time in the bar.

THE CUP

The town youth team played matches on Sundays meaning that he could still be with Sheila in the tea hut on Saturdays, and for the last few months of the year, his life was a whirlwind of University, more training in the hut, Sunday Football and romantic liaison`s with Sheila, who somehow always managed to arrange for them to be alone in her house at least once each week.

In late November he was summoned to report to Captain Baines, although he was less concerned this time, however on entering the office and saluting, was slightly less self-assured when Baines said sit down Lamb we need to chat. I understand that you are playing football for Harrogate Town, is that true.

Yes sir, responded Ronnie, suddenly wondering where this was leading, as whilst anyone wishing to take up what the army knew as extraneous activities was required to seek the commanding officer`s approval first, he could not see how that edict applied to him, as he was technically not even a soldier.

I do not remember giving my permission for you to undertake that role Lamb, as you know all such out of camp activity requires my consent, however it appears that your ability on the football pitch might be something that we could use at this time, and from what I understand your reporting structure takes you out of our immediate control so we can ignore the lack of extra curricula protocol thus far.

However Irrespective of who you report to, you are nonetheless on my camp, in my accommodation, eating my food and therefore however technically, under my command.

Let me say now for the record, that I have no time for secret operations, especially when they are being undertaken from my camp, using my facilities, without any discussion or even simple basic acknowledgement of my role.

I understand from what I have already ordered researched, that no one based here has any real interaction with you or the two others, Stott and Groves who work in the hut with you, with both also living in quarters but again as attached NCO`s not being directly under my command, and it just will not do.

It seems that you, alternate your time between Leeds University and the hut, allegedly working on developing better communication systems, particularly within urban areas, and that as far as I know in the year that you have been here nothing practical has been achieved, seemingly a complete waste of time, money and my services.

Jumping in before the officer could continue his rant, Ronnie said, everything that you have said is correct sir, excepting the achievements aspect, our field radio comms have been notorious for being unreliable in poor weather especially strong winds, and also in built up or what you called urban areas.

So we are modifying standard equipment using stronger diodes and resistors, to try and bend the radio waves slightly to give better wave strength capability.

In the year up to now we have managed to maintain basic voice comms at over a hundred yards distance, which while nowhere near good enough is a distinct improvement on the basic system.

Bollocks Sergeant Lamb, complete bollocks, I have absolutely no idea what it is that you and your cohorts are cooking up in my hut on my camp, but radio comms is certainly not part of it, and to be truthful I am not sure that I wish to know, just get it done as soon as possible and then get the fuck off of my camp, as it has been made quite clear to me that someone way above my pay grade sanctions your continued presence here.

Anyway, consider your bollocking concluded, it is now time for you to repay some of the kindness that we have shown to you and your mates, we require you to do something for us.

Most certainly sir, Ronnie was relieved, he had been quite concerned that their activities were going to be stopped, which was now not so, and therefore he was much more relaxed as Baines began.

Look Lamb, our regimental football team, The Royal Engineers, have somehow managed to win their way through every round of competition into the final of the Army Cup, which as it happens will be against the cup holders, the Parachute Regiment, the match to be played at Aldershot Arena in just over two weeks.

That is a great achievement sir, well done, I hope that the guys win. We must win Lamb, it needs to be my legacy, the first and possibly only officer to lead the Engineers to win the Army Cup, and we have a slight problem in that our best forward has broken his foot during an assault course incident and is obviously ruled out of playing.

So how can I help asked Ronnie. We understand that you are a decent forward player, so you will take his place in the team and help us win that cup said Captain Baines.

But I am not an Engineer sir, I am enlisted in the Royal Corps of Signals, how can I play, surely any such thing would be cheating.

Listen Lamb, suggestions of covert or secret actions when coming from the likes of you seem somewhat shallow, and if I say that you are an Engineer then you are an Engineer understand. If you like and if it fits with your secrecy requirements, you might always say that you are an Engineer on secondment to the Signals.

Oh great, sighed Ronnie to himself, now I am a member of the Signals pretending to be an Engineer on secondment to the Signals, when in actual fact I am a civilian, one day I might work out who the hell I really am, but to the captain he said, you said two weeks sir, that is not much time to get working with the lads, and for them to accept me into the team, he thought back to when he had first been selected for the youth team, and the snide comments about being the managers pet as he was screwing the daughter.

Not an issue Lamb, the team need you, but of course it is up to you to show them what can be done, the problem is of course beating the Parachute Regiment who have a strong team, fighting fit so to speak, and not likely to relinquish the cup without putting up a good show.

I am sure that we can raise our game to meet the challenge sir purred Ronnie.

Right then, that is agreed stated Baines, I will tell the team captain. Sergeant William Loman, to expect you at training this afternoon on the pitch at two pm after lunch.

Sharing the news about the football, both Harry and John agreed that while unexpected, it would not necessarily hinder their progress and in fact might work in their favour, although trying as hard as he was able and examining every angle, Ronnie simply could not see how playing a football match whatever the outcome, might benefit their plans to recover the cup.

Two weeks of daily team training, practice matches, and motivating talks were more than enough to convince him that while the Engineers did not lack enthusiasm, sadly that by itself was a poor substitute for actual ability, and in truth most of the players might not even get picked for their local Sunday League Pub Team.

THE CUP

The real problem was that given the lack of ability and the teams intense dislike of his inclusion, as they saw him an upstart outsider, Ronnie found it challenging and on several occasions during so called friendly practice was hacked to the ground forcefully. After one particularly savage tackle from the giant of a centre-half, Loman, who was also the team captain, he sat upright and called out to the others, okay that`s it, I am done with you lot.

I have had it with being kicked all over the field by you fuckers, I did not ask to join your team, and if you do not want me that is okay by me, but in truth you need to be thinking about somehow fixing the game in your favour, because trust me you sure as hell are not going to win fair and square.

Well now, the young scaley back has certainly got balls after all laughed Loman reaching down and pulling Ronnie to his feet, okay smart guy, you are the supposed expert, can we beat the Para`s, do we have any chance.

Ronnie scanned his eyes around the bedraggled bunch, willing but hopelessly untalented, and then he looked across at the touchline to where the PTI`s, all corporals, who were managing and training the team stood watching.

Look Loman, your Physical Training Instructors have managed to get you all reasonably fit for a team game, although short sprinting needs to be improved, but football or more precisely winning at football requires ability, not just a bit of luck although that helps, and from what I have heard the Parachute Regiment boys are not likely to roll over for you, I believe that they play quite rough.

Well so what, we can play just as rough when it matters, the newcomer was one of the PTI`s who had walked onto the field to see what was happening.

I am sure that you can, replied Ronnie, I have first-hand experience remember, but kicking the other team off the pitch will not in itself win the match, and most likely earn red cards, which will make the job impossible.

Winning at football is about scoring more goals than the other team, and before you laugh and say obviously, some teams just do not consider how hard it is to score against a ruthless defence, the more a team tries to match their opponent`s level of skill and ability, the more opportunities the opponent`s will have to score goals, defenders dragged out of position by skilled attacking play cannot be there to defend goal-bound shots, you cannot be in two places at the same time.

That`s fair analysis said Willis, but what do you suggest we do then to improve our chances. We adopt the ancient Roman Army motto of "They Shall Not Pass" said Ronnie.

We train hard as a solid defensive unit, goalkeeper then two lines of five spread across the field, each man keeping to his own defined area and instructed to tackle hard anyone coming into his area with the ball, no one attempting heroics by running up the field with the ball, just solid defending.

I see the logic, but not how it helps us win, after all it`s a cup game, win or lose, the actual score is not important if you lose sighed Willis.

Even very skilled forwards find it hard to score goals against a well drilled and packed defence, if we do it right, we may stop them scoring altogether but at the least restrict how many they get replied Ronnie.

But then what asked Loman, like PTI Willis said a loss is still a loss even by one goal.

Hopefully, we can limit them to one goal, or even better no goals, then with ten or perhaps fifteen minutes of time left, we change tactics, we swamp their end with guys, leaving just a basic back line of four defenders whose role will be simply hoof the ball up into the opponents end if it comes near them or if unable to do that boot it out of play to allow regrouping.

In any game the underdog usually gets at least one chance of scoring a goal, we just need to make bloody sure we make the most of that chance, and if we do, who knows, we might just achieve the impossible.

What do you think Corporal Willis asked Loman. I think, said Willis smiling broadly, that it might just bloody well work, and in any case what have we to lose, we have no better plan, and by the time we change tactics on the field the Para`s will have assumed us to have no competitive spirit just being a kick and hope outfit, they might have to reorganise themselves if we were to suddenly attack their goal.

Resisting the urge to state that the Engineers were in fact not even at the kick and hope level of ability, Ronnie suggested that the basic team played some time as a two line, defence with himself and the substitute players making up an attacking force to try and score.

After forty-five minutes the defenders had retained a clean sheet, despite Ronnie hitting the crossbar with a more speculative rather than skilled attempt on goal, and at the whistle all the PTI`s whom Willis had explained the new team tactics to, were distinctly more enthusiastic.

Gathering around in a team huddle Willis said well done lads, we might just have something good here, let`s see what tomorrows session brings.

As they were breaking away, Ronnie said loudly, just one thing, I know that it is only football, but you never know who might be listening to what we say, so might I suggest that we do not make too much of an issue about our change of tactics, we do not want the Para`s to get any advance warning.

For the remaining period leading up to the match they trained well together and even though the attackers did manage to score goals, the principle of strong defence seemingly worked.

Ronnie got to know most of the players and grew quite close to William Loman a dour Scot from Motherwell who as the captain and natural leader the others all looked up to, he also had a very dry sarcastic sense of humour which Ronnie found likeable.

The team travelled down to Aldershot on the Thursday morning after breakfast, and on arrival were placed in rooms and shown how to get food.

In the afternoon, they did some light training, then on Friday they trained in both the morning and afternoon before being allowed to look around the Aldershot arena, and at the pitch where the match was to be played, a decent playing surface with concrete stands on all sides, changing facilities and a bar.

After the evening meal Sergeant Loman gathered all the team together and made a little speech thanking the PTI trainers and everyone for their hard work to get this far, he then produced a large bottle of Malt Whiskey called Glenmorangie which he opened then passed from person to person, with each taking a swig from the bottle neck, tomorrow we will give those Para Boys a bloody nose, he said, so tonight we get some good rest.

Laid upon his bed Ronnie considered his life, not yet nineteen years old he had been drawn into a secretive scheme to recover an ancient religious artifact, cleverly but illicitly registered as a soldier, was attending University, and had an attractive girlfriend to whom he had lost his virginity, now he was here at Aldershot, the home of the British Army, to play football in a

THE CUP

Regimental Cup Final, when technically, no in reality, he was a bloody civilian, whatever next he pondered as his eyes closed.

The following morning after breakfast he sought out Loman, pulling him to one side out of hearing of the others, look, we know that the Para`s tactics will be to kick us off the field right from the start, and if I get crocked then what use will I be to the team. Exactly what are you saying, replied the dour Scotsman.

You start the game without me, play fully defensive tactics as we have been practicing, kick the shit out of their forwards without getting yellow cards, and try to keep the goals that they score to a minimum, then in the later stages I can come on, fresh and ready, and just maybe we can get a result.

That`s quite good thinking for a Sassenach, Loman laughed, slapped Ronnie on the back and said, good on you, young scaley-back, come on let`s do this.

The arena was packed with red bereted soldiers lining three side of the pitch, with a much smaller green bereted contingent from the Engineers making up the fourth side, three Football Association Officials had been assigned to referee and run the lines, and at the start of the game the referee shook hands with the opposing captains saying, good luck to both of you, we want a nice clean game.

No bloody chance of that said PTI Willis cynically, and as expected the Para`s went straight onto the offensive, using their obvious physical superiority to force their way towards the Engineers goal. Wave after wave of strong attacks were launched, but to the Engineers credit at half time there was no score, and whilst players on both sides carried minor cuts and scrapes, it was the Engineers who were the most satisfied.

Loman asked Ronnie if he wanted to come on and play but was told that it might be better to keep going as it were for a while, to see how things progressed.

As the second half kicked off, Captain Baines appeared and berated PTI Willis saying, listen Willis, the whole point of having Lamb in the team was to give us a half chance of winning the bloody match, yet he is sitting on the sidelines, he is not going to score any goals warming his arse on your substitutes bench.

Quite so, replied Willis, but you will have to trust us, Lamb and Loman have a plan I do believe.

You believe do you, I thought that you were the bloody team manager, so damn well manage corporal, or I swear that you will be doing Stag indefinitely.

As Baines marched away Willis turned to Ronnie and said I do hope that you two know what you are doing, because if we fuck this up we will all be for the bloody high jump.

The second half of the game was every bit as physical as the first had been, with both teams needing to replace players who had received injuries, and with just over ten minutes to go it became obvious that the Para`s fitness was beginning to wear the Engineers down, with two goal bound scoring attempts both amazingly saved by the Engineers goalkeeper.

Ronnie told Willis that it was time for him to go on and the substitution was made.

The Engineers managed to gain a throw in just inside the Para`s half and during the short stop of play Ronnie swapped with one of the defenders, the ball was thrown into play and Loman collected it then chipped it forward into Ronnie`s path, his first touch of the ball sent it curling towards the top left hand corner of the Para goal, only for their goalkeeper to tip it around the post for a corner.

From the resulting corner kick, the Engineers first of the game, Ronnie managed to jump high enough to get his head to the ball only to be flattened by the goalkeeper who punched the ball away. Laying on his back he looked up into the Para goalie's eyes, as the man snarled, no fucking way spanner-head, this game is ours.

Ronnie managed to get several more touches of the ball, each time ending up flat in the mud, but with only one minute of the referee's extra time remaining a speculative shot from one of the Engineers was deflected for a corner kick.

Running over to Loman Ronnie said, listen William, you take the kick and try your best to put the ball straight into the goalkeeper's hands.

What said Loman, that's daft. Just trust me please, implored Ronnie, what have we got to lose. Ronnie ran back into the Para goal area and placed himself directly in front of the man-mountain goalie, who sneered into his ear, and you can fuck off little man, this will be my ball.

As asked Loman took the kick aiming it for the goalmouth, and as the ball flew towards the keeper's gloves, Ronnie reached behind his back and grabbed the goalie's testicles, squeezing as hard as he could.

Aggh you bastard, cried the man, instinctively putting both hands onto his groin area. The ball dropping from the sky, hit Ronnie on the shoulder and fell into the net, and despite the Para complaints, the referee had seen nothing wrong and the goal stood.

Immediately after receiving the cup and having the obligatory photographs taken, the team showered and were ushered directly onto the coach, as feelings were running high and lots of threats were being made against the Engineers by the disgruntled Para's.

On the coach the mood was jubilant, and Ronnie was the hero of the hour, who tried hard to play down his part saying that the team had all been great. Did you really squash his bollocks, asked Loman, to which Ronnie replied, I am sorry to say that I did captain, desperate measures and all that crap, please accept my apolgies if I let the team down.

Bloody marvelous that`s what it was, we really did it lads said Willis. Ronnie did it said Loman. Bollocks we all did it, if you lot had not kept those bastards at bay for so long, we would not have won replied Ronnie. Whatever you say, but the spannerheads have won the regimental cup, so from now on its William, and Lamon actually smiled.

From somewhere several crates of Tetley Beer were produced and the journey North seemed to pass quickly, with joking and singing helping to pass the time.

As the coach pulled into the camp entrance it became clear that word of the team`s success had preceded them, as an impromptu banner made from a large white sheet was draped across the front of the gatehouse declaring in big black letters "Engineers do it with tight nuts".

The coach went directly to the NAAFI where the place was buzzing, it seemed that everyone wanted to buy the team drinks, and there was chicken and chips served in little baskets, which whilst much needed, did little to soak up the alcohol and it was with a slightly teetering step that Ronnie eventually found his way back to his bunk, where collapsing onto his bed it took only moments before he fell asleep.

Despite a slight headache he was awake early and washed shaved and toileted when Blythe bought his morning tea, well done sergeant, everyone is so proud of you all, and even though it is Sunday, Captain Baines wishes to see you in his office at 10 am sharp.

Breakfast was a continuation of congratulations and being slapped on the back with praise, and he enjoyed bacon and eggs with toast and several mugs of tea, feeling much less heady when he went back to his bunk, putting on his work uniform he walked to the Captains Office, knocked the door and was called to enter.

Saluting smartly, he stood in front of the desk where Baines was sitting in civilian clothes. At ease Lamb, no need for all that it`s my day off, now then firstly well done lad the Regiment are proud of you and as a thank you the team will be honored at a special gala dinner and dance next Saturday evening in the officer`s mess, all the players and wives or girlfriends will be attending as guests of the Regiments Officers.

There will be some presentations and of course photographs, so full number one dress uniform is the order of the hour.

Will it not be considered strange that I wear Signals Regiment uniform sir. Certainly not, it will be explained that you are on secondment, so all will be fine. You mentioned girlfriend`s sir, my girl is local and lives in the town, will it be all right for me to invite her.

Most certainly Lamb, it will be good to meet her, explain that evening dresses are expected, either short or long, that will be for her to choose, and secondly, you will need these.

Opening a drawer in the desk he withdrew a small package which he handed to Ronnie, your sergeant stripes which will need to be sewn onto the dress jacket, there is a second set for everyday uniform, drop your clothes into the stores tomorrow and they will sew them for you.

Thank you, sir will there be anything else. No that is everything Lamb we will see you next Saturday dinner is at eight pm, but arrive any time from seven, and once again whatever our differences, well done.

After changing into his civilian clothes Ronnie took the bus into Harrogate and walked to Shelia`s home, she was delighted to see him and anxious to find out how the team had done, so when he said that they had won the cup she shouted with delight and insisted on telling her parents straightaway.

Ronnie explained about the Dinner Dance Invitation for the following Saturday and when asked about what she should wear, was able to say evening dress either short or long, to which Mavis commented, leave it to me.

What a bloody farce laughed Harry as the three of them sat drinking tea in the hut on Monday morning. You help the team win the Regimental Football Cup for the Engineers, have already been made up to Sergeant status when in fact you are not even in the army, have zero soldiering training, and cannot shoot for toffees, now you will be guest of honour at the Rupert's self-indulgent soiree next weekend.

Sorry, you will have to explain some of that to me said Ronnie, why guest of honour, I was only one player in the team, and what does Rupert mean.

You may have been one player, but you scored the winning goal, only goal, so all the officers will want Regimental photos of you and them holding the cup, and as for Rupert, that is army slang for an officer, especially one who is upper middle class and as such incompetent and scatter brained, like Rupert the Bear.

What about his permanent promotion to sergeant, will that create a problem, asked John.

I doubt it, replied Harry, no one will ask his age, or why one so young has such rank, it will be assumed that he just looks young, and in fact it works very well for us as it will be that much easier for him to gain access into Northern Ireland as a sergeant.

During the week Ronnie sought out Sergeant William Loman and asked him what the wives would be wearing on Saturday for the dinner dance. Evening Dress was the response, but some will be the more modern style and short whilst others more traditionally longer, however all of them know that the trick is to look smart, but not out dress the wives of the officers.

Ronnie wondered if he should relate the information to Sheila, but after consideration chose not to, worrying that she might think that he was trying to make her look dowdy.

Ronnie met Sheila from her Taxi at the main gate at seven thirty on the Saturday evening, and he was stunned as she climbed from the cab. She was dressed in a sparkling light blue mini-dress with matching blue ankle strap heeled shoes, a white fur cape around her shoulders and carrying a matching blue clutch style handbag.

Her blonde hair normally down around her shoulders had been piled up onto the top of her head in a knot which was pinned in place with sparkling diamanté brooch.

Wow, you look wonderful he gasped. Laughing she replied, well you brush up quite nicely too, admiring his smartly pressed dress uniform highly polished shoes white dress belt and blue forage cap with its Jimmy motif sparkling in the fading light.

They walked around the parade ground and down towards the officer's mess, seeing other couples also on their way to the dinner dance. Several of the men exchanged greetings with Ronnie and he felt quite proud to have Sheila on his arm as the others spoke their hello's.

The Team had been seated at a long High Table facing out towards the round tables seating the Officer's and as their wives or girlfriends.

The Ladies sat opposite their respective men and Ronnie found that he was seated next to William Loman and Corporal Willis, meaning that Sheila was seated between Loman and Willis's wives, who although attractive and smartly dressed were plain when compared to Sheila.

The dinner was quite formal and a sumptuous affair, and during the coffee and mints the RSM thanked the officers mess staff for putting on such a wonderful meal, and then reminded everyone that after dinner and photographs there was dancing until midnight.

Then he announced that the reason for the dinner was to honour the football team who had achieved something never done before, by winning the Regimental Football Cup.

He asked the team to stand and named them individually in army tradition using rank name and number, reaching Ronnie he said Sergeant Lamb 567, on secondment with the Royal Signals.

Ronnie half smiled, realising that anyone who was questioning why his uniform was different, now had their answer. As he concluded his team list the RSM called the dinner guests to stand and raise their glasses in a toast to the team, which was followed by a round of applause.

With the formal part of the evening now completed the requisite photographs were next on the agenda, first a team photograph with William and Ronnie holding the cup between them, then a series of photos with officers some with the players as a team, others with individual players.

Several officers wanted Ronnie and William with the cup in their pictures, and to round it off the players were invited to have a photograph with their wife, with or without the cup.

When it came to their turn Sheila picked the cup up to hold, but Ronnie said no, just the two of us please. She asked him why he did not want the cup in the photograph, to which he replied blandly, some cups are easier to get than others.

The following Friday the Harrogate Herald carried the photograph of Sheila and Ronnie on its back page with the headline. Town Star wins Regimental Cup, followed by a largely fabricated writeup claiming that not only was Ronnie engaged to Sheila the Harrogate Town Youth team managers daughter, but also that he was attached to a small elite task force unit based at Pennypot camp.

Asking John for his comments on the Friday morning, Ronnie was surprised to hear him offer congratulations on the engagement. I have not asked her said Ronnie the whole story is just bollocks.

Well, that is as maybe said John, but two things strike me. Firstly who told the paper that you are doing out of the ordinary work here, and secondly whether you have asked Sheila to marry you or otherwise is I suspect irrelevant now, as she and all her family will expect it to be confirmed or they will lose respect in their community, so I suggest that you take her shopping for a ring tomorrow.

Saturday was a town home game, and he was taken aback to see a white banner with black letters declaring congratulations Sheila and Ronnie, She, was red with embarrassment but also of the opinion that Ronnie had briefed the newspaper about the engagement rather than face her father to ask permission which was the accepted practice.

He tried to explain that he had said nothing, but heeding John`s words realised it would be pointless to try and get out of it, so instead he asked her what the family had said about it.

They were surprised just as I was, but at the same time they like you, and if it is what I want they are pleased for us.

And is it what you want asked Ronnie. Yes of course, I really do want to be Mrs Lamb. Well then after we finish today, there should be time to pop into town and look at a suitable ring. Sheila gasped out aloud, do you mean that. Yes of course I do smiled Ronnie, now I do believe that we have tea`s to serve.

Sheila chose a solitaire diamond in a nine-carat gold ring setting, and took Ronnie straight home to show her parents.

Ronnie apologized to Wilf for not asking him first, but Sheila`s father was not annoyed and simply said, times are changing lad, it`s hard to keep up anymore, I mean look at the length of Sheila`s skirt, catch a death of cold in that she will, but it is now the fashion, like I said times change, so be happy lad.

The four of them went to the local pub to celebrate, and everyone offered congratulations, Colin and Maria came later, as did Sheila`s best friend Janet and her Boyfriend Peter. Janet, admiring the ring nudged Peter and said loudly, isn`t it about time that you did the right thing.

Peter had just ordered himself and Ronnie bottles of Carlsberg Lager to celebrate, so holding up his bottle to show of the label replied, soldier boy here is special forces, I am more special brew.

It was late when after kissing Sheila goodnight, he climbed into the taxi for the ride back to camp, not yet nineteen, a make-believe soldier, part of a rag tag group chasing a mythical cup and now engaged to be married with Christmas only two weeks away, what could possibly happen next.

The answer to his self-imposed question came much sooner than he had expected when on the Tuesday a message was bought to the hut for him which stated simply. Sergeant Ronnie Lamb is to report at the main gatehouse on the first working Monday in the new Year with full kit, for a weeklong exercise at Otterburn.

What the hell said Ronnie showing the note to both Harry and John, did either of you have an input on this.

Certainly not they both asserted, possibly someone is trying to interfere with our plans said Harry, I will see if I can find out anything, although I doubt anything will be found.

Do I have to go asked Ronnie, I mean I hardly know enough to exercise with the others, I could end up being exposed as a fraud.

I am afraid so replied Harry, this is a formal note it appears that you have been placed upon a named list of soldiers being exercised, the question is why.

Well, someone wants me on the bloody exercise, and I think that if I am going to be constantly pushed around, then at the very least I deserve to know why said Ronnie, I think that it is high time for me to be told everything that you two know about this cup.

All right said Harry, sit down and I will share everything that I can, we will tell you the truth.

Truth, shouted Ronnie, you two would not know the truth if it bit your arse. Enough said Harry, our prime need is to keep you safe, and whatever grand ideal of yourself you currently hold, believe me you are not yet in any position to stand against any real opposition. Your training is going well but there is still a way to go.

John passed tea to each of them as Harry began. Irrespective, of what you personally believe, please hear me out before you jump in with questions okay.

Now then, Heaven or whatever you wish it to be called is the home of the angelic beings, headed up by God, some time ago, there was a falling out amongst these angels with a group led by an archangel called Bright Morning Star attempting to overthrow God, which failed resulting in banishment from God`s presence and blessings.

These rebel angels are still intent on winning their war against God and the faithful angels, and God in his unfathomable wisdom has decreed that until the final battle has been fought, the rebel angels can have unrestricted access to both heaven and earth including the authority over God's creation which also means us humans.

God will win that final battle of course, but in the meantime the fallen angels have full and easy access to us, trying to convince us individually to do bad things, which is exactly opposite to what God wishes us to do.

Their leader, Bright Morning Star is also known as Lucifer, The Devil, and Satan, to name just a few, and it was he, disguised as a serpent who tempted Eve, and Adam within the original Garden of Eden.

God had created Man and Woman in his own likeness to enable his fullest communication with them and to this extent, physically breathed life into them thereby making them totally different from any evolved being or thing.

However, it is part of Satan's plan to manipulate as many of those descendants from Adam and Eve as he can, so that the numerical balance of support for God in Heaven is diminished.

After the disgrace of Eden, which was in fact an extension of heaven here on earth, mankind was declared to be mortal, with an average lifespan of seventy years, and that women would bear children as offspring, borne out of labour pains, and who like their parents would have to work to survive.

After many years of watching as his created children, started to fail in their belief and support of their God, He himself made the decision to come to earth and experience first-hand what life was like as a believer in an unholy time, and to prove it was possible to live a blameless sin free existence.

THE CUP

That Human God form was who we know as Jesus, and as the historians confirm, both a real person and the subject of a Roman execution by crucifixion.

The Bible tells of a third day resurrection, and an eternal life after earthly death through a publicly proclaimed belief in God and an attempt to live as he desires us to. The cup, the shroud and the ark are all Biblical objects each with its own relevance at the time of its use, and for believers each has significance even today.

The Bible tells that anyone who touches the ark, other than priests designated by God, will die, so the assumption is that God does not wish the ark used for any ungodly activity, and several people who touched the ark were apparently suddenly struck down dead, so there is certainly some recorded evidence of the ark having power.

Whether the shroud and the cup also have some God given power is unknown, at least to us, however it is widely believed amongst theological experts and scholars, that individually each item has its own inherent capabilities.

Those capabilities, whatever they might be also suggest that with all three of the God given artifacts bought together, some sense of fulfilment will occur, so for us and hopefully you as well, finding the cup and restoring it to the safety of the Jews must be a priority.

Okay said Ronnie, thank you for that explanation, I am fully sold on the fact that the cup both exists and might have some power, although I have no understanding of how I might be able to give the item any authenticity, that is assuming that we can find it.

We will find it and you will recover it Ronnie said Harry, and I believe that when the time comes, God will show you how to prove if it is the genuine cup, so let us break for the holidays on a positive note, committed to moving our operation forward in the new year.

Christmas 1970 was for Ronnie, every bit as good as the previous year, and as tradition it was pub before Christmas dinner again. The dinner itself was delicious and around the table they began planning the wedding for two years or so later.

Ronnie worked in the hut during the holiday break as he had done previously although this new year, he was not called to undertake guard duty, so spent his first new year`s eve with Sheila, they had a few drinks with her friends and watched fireworks, all things considered a fitting end to what had been a turbulent year.

Chapter Eight
Exercise

Monday 4th January 1971, and a squeal of brakes announced the arrival of a Landrover at the main gatehouse,

Jumping out a young private picked up Ronnie`s kit bag and dropped it into the rear before climbing back into the driver seat saying, hop in sarnt, its time we were moving.

Pulling out of the gates, they took the road to Ripon, then passed through the town and out to the main A1 highway where they turned north towards Catterick. There had been no talking in the half hour or so since leaving camp so Ronnie casually asked, how long to the exercise area, to which the driver replied, about another hour sergeant, and before you start asking me questions like they said you would, I was told to collect a vehicle first thing this morning, collect you at the gate and take you to Otterburn training area for a Taceval exercise, sorry, but I don`t know nothing else.

Appalled at the young soldier`s poor grammar but recognising that he probably did not know anything useful Ronnie chose to remain silent, and some eighty minutes later the vehicle turned into an opening with a barrier across it guarded by two armed soldiers.

The driver stopped the Landrover, hopped out and taking Ronnie`s kitbag he dropped it onto the path saying, there you go sergeant have fun, and turning the Landrover around in the opening he started to pull away.

Thank you driver called Ronnie and added, please thank Captain Baines when you next see him, to which the young soldier replied Sorry sergeant, but I don't know a Captain Baines.

But you are Royal Engineers are you not queried Ronnie. Goodness me sergeant, not at all, I am squeaky beaky and proud of it. Like I said have fun, and firing the engine he was gone.

Picking up his bag Ronnie wondered what the hell the intelligence corps wanted with him, that seemingly neither Harry nor John knew about.

Giving his details at the barrier a field telephone call resulted in the arrival of a three-ton lorry with canvas sides its open rear showing soldiers in full kit and camouflage lining the side benches. Hop up sergeant Lamb, a grinning corporal said, we need to get rocking.

The truck slowly lumbered across the rough terrain, and Ronnie looked at the other occupants, he counted ten privates, one lance corporal, one full corporal, and a medic who was also carrying the groups radio set, so with him fourteen strong, a full troop.

The corporal who had spoken to him held out his hand, which Ronnie took and shook, welcome to C Troop sergeant, he swept his arm around the truck to indicate the others, Prince of Wales Fusiliers at your service.

Right, said Ronnie, Welsh Fusiliers, and the purpose of this little playtime is what exactly. Don't rightly know yet sergeant, we hoped that you might have that little bit of info, but not to worry we will be at the briefing soon.

But you know why I am here I presume. Again, not exactly sergeant, we know that this is a Taceval, which can mean any type of tactical evaluation of our troop capability, orienteering, general ability, progressiveness, spirit, flexibility, you know the sort of thing, the top brass just monitor how we cope when put to the test in so called field conditions.

Ronnie did not of course know anything about exercises but considered it wiser to say nothing, instead he asked, but why me, and not one of your own sergeants to lead the troop.

Here I go again said the corporal, sorry we have no idea, we thought that perhaps someone was trying to spice life up a little, you know to find out what might happen to a troop if the sergeant was lost in a battle, how they might react if placed under someone totally new. Ronnie wanted to add and green as grass, but just then the truck lurched to a stop.

A loud voice barked, all right you shower, out and line up sharpish, this is exercise, not a holiday. Dropping from the back of the lorry C Troop lined up in two rows of five soldiers with the lance corporal and the medic at each end of the front row and the full corporal stood to the side in front of the front row.

Ronnie went over and stood alongside the full corporal dropping his kitbag to the floor beside him.

They were in a clearing which was about fifty yards across, three sides were bordered by tree line seemingly stretching quite a distance, the fourth side was more open, being made up of chest high grasses, scrub, bushes and small trees. Inside the clearing were two field tents one seemingly a food station the other of unknown use, and off to a side were three tent latrines.

The loud voice barked again, and C Troop came to attention, Ronnie eyed the smartly dressed soldier issuing the orders, and recognising the crown insignia on the soldier's sleeve realised him to be a warrant officer, to his side a thinner slightly taller officer with three pips on his shoulder epaulets identified him as a captain.

Right then you lot barked the warrant officer, after briefing you can fall out and get some scoff from the field kitchen over there, he lifted his pace stick to waist level and swung it in the general direction of the tents, afterwards you will have some time to make any plans that you need.

It is now half past ten, kick off will be at fourteen hundred hours, Captain Adams will now brief you so listen up.

Good morning men, Ronnie was immediately struck by the difference in voice tone between the two men, Adams was soft and gentle, almost feminine, whereas the Warrant Officer had been hard and rough edged.

Adams continued, Sergeant Lamb, from the Royal Corps of Signals, will be leading C Troop Prince of Wales Fusiliers, on this tactical evaluation exercise, which has been designed to test team spirit, endurance, creativity, and of course C Troops ability.

This clearing is approximately one mile across, with a similar area to this, on the other side where your opponents are currently receiving the same briefing, in the middle of the clearing is a lake which is approximately two hundred yards across, with a small island in the center where a flagpole is mounted.

The objective of this exercise is straightforward, in that on the flagpole a Union Flag is currently flying, your objective is simply recover the flag.

Once the Flag has been captured you will bring it to me or the sergeant major by fourteen hundred hours tomorrow latest, or earlier if you are able, that is all.

To assist you in your task, each team will be provided with one Mortar Unit, two Bren LMG`s, a two-man ridged inflatable boat with paddles, thunder-flashes and smoke mortars. The rounds for all weapons will be compacted neoprene with marker dye.

Food and facilities, such as they are here, will be available until fourteen hundred hours after which off you go with your kit, bivouac equipment and individual 24hour ration packs. Now are there any questions.

Yes sir, called out the corporal, it all seems far too easy, there must be a catch. The catch, as you so neatly put it corporal, is that there is a troop of the Kings Royal Hussars having the very same briefing about a mile in that direction, he waved his arm towards the scrubland area, think of this as a tactical game, may the best team win.

The sergeant major called them to attention, saluted the captain, who marched away, then dismissed the soldiers, who broke ranks and headed for the tents. The Corporal stayed with Ronnie, bloody hell he said, us against the fucking Hussars, what chance do we have.

I would say exactly, the same, as them said Ronnie, you heard the Captain, we both have identical resources, and the same amount of time.

Except the bloody Hussars are highly trained front line assault troops moaned the corporal, whereas the Fusiliers are just Cannon fodder, charged with supporting artillery and tanks.

What is your name corporal, you already know I am Sergeant Lamb, but it will be fine for you to call me Ronnie, so what name shall I use when I speak to you.

Its Corporal Nash was the reply, Corporal Brian Nash. Well, Brian, we will get ourselves some grub, then work out a plan together, bear in mind that I am also being tested, not just C Troop.

One of the soldiers called out as they approached the food tent, come on the food`s not bad and at least we can get some rest before wasting a day getting muddy and probably wet for fuck-all.

Ronnie took bacon and egg sandwiches and a mug of tea, sitting on his own, he considered the options for the upcoming task, on the face of it equal opportunity for each side, but given the Fusiliers apparent lack of confidence in their own ability, possibly the odds were in the Hussars favour.

Calling Brian Nash to come and sit with him, Ronnie asked, so what would your plan be then Brian. Well, I guess we would need to get down to the lake edge unseen somehow, then paddle out and grab the flag, the problem of course is that the Hussar's will be doing something similar and will be trying to keep us off the island, and once the rubber dinghy gets punctured then we are finished.

Okay said Ronnie, let me get this straight in my head, our sole objective is to simply capture the flag and get it back to the officers. Yes, said Brian, do you have a plan.

I think that I do, Ronnie smiled, fetch me another fried egg sandwich and I will tell you what I am thinking. As Nash started to walk away towards the food tent he called back, it`s an egg banjo by the way. Pardon called Ronnie, but Nash was out of earshot.

Sitting together with sandwiches and mugs of tea, Ronnie asked about the egg banjo, only to be told that the nickname derives from the fact that when you bite into the sandwich, the yolk sometimes spurts out onto your collar, with the natural reaction being to raise the hand holding the sandwich and flick away the offending egg with the fingers of the other hand, imitating a banjo player.

I wonder sometimes what mentality of bored soldier makes things like that up said Ronnie, very gingerly biting into his egg sandwich, anyway here is our plan which will guarantee our success, not give us a chance but an absolute guarantee of winning.

But that's cheating said Brian as Ronnie stopped his explanation, we can't do that it's against the rules. Bollocks replied Ronnie, you told me yourself that technically there are no rules, and that the single objective is to claim the flag and deliver it to the officers, how we achieve that is up to us.

Fucking hell Ronnie, do you really believe that we can do it. Why not was the reply, they will be ardently concentrating their attention onto the island, and whilst keeping us occupied making their own attempts to get the flag, they will have no idea what we are planning, all we need to do is keep them thinking that we are playing the game.

Brian called C Troop to gather round saying, listen lads, our cunning sergeant has devised a plan that just might work, he will now tell you what we are going to do.

At thirteen forty-five hours they were called across to the tents and issued with Five Field Radios, Two tripod mount Machine Guns, One Mortar Launcher, a small inflatable rubber boat, with a hand pump and three short paddles, ten thunder-flashes, forty smoke grenades, forty Mortars, and composite ammunition comprising two hundred rounds per man, and five hundred for each Machine Gun. Four sheet style bivouac tents and fourteen 24hr field ration packs, one for each man.

At exactly fourteen hundred hours they were loaded up with the kit and Captain Adams said good luck and blew a whistle, they were off.

Carrying the equipment shared amongst them they jogged away from the clearing into the scrub, they kept going until Ronnie adjudged that they had reached a distance about 400 yards from their start, leaving on his reckonings about another 400 yards to the edge of the lake and then some 100 yards across to the island.

Finding a smallish area devoid of too much scrub and bush, he instructed the bivouacs to be erected, and told Brian to organise things, setting up as their base camp.

Get one of the lads up that tallish tree over there with field glasses to keep a watch on the island and the other side of the lake to see if we can get some idea of what the Hussar's are getting up to instructed Ronnie, and give him a radio, take one yourself and give me the other three, make sure all connect with each other.

Whilst Brian and C Troop set up base camp, he took two of the team away with him, each bringing one of the machine guns with ammunition. The three of them set off with Ronnie leading the two gunners forward through the scrub, which had become thicker and taller, making progress slower, but affording better cover.

After around 200 yards he stopped, and leaving one gunner to wait, led the other off to the left for about 100 yards, and finding a suitable small flattish clearing, gave the soldier a radio and instructed him to set up the gun pointing towards the lake which he guessed to be about 200 yards away. Returning to the other gunner they moved off to the right and set up the second gun in a similar manner.

Going back to a mid-point between the two guns he used the radio to speak with the gunners, telling them to set the gun trajectory to a range of six hundred yards with a fixed arc of fire of 45 degrees with the central position in line with the flag, which could just be seen over the bushes. Both of you are to fire 25 rounds rapid fire using the full arc, commence now.

The quietness was shattered by the deafening crack of small arms fire as the two gunners unleashed their fusillade, the radio crackled, lookout reporting sergeant, I had not originally seen any bushes or grass waving suggesting movement, but after our firing, there was evidence of the other side scurrying back away from the lake.

Good said Ronnie, they now know that we are here and have prepared, they will be more cautious about approaching the lake from now on, but keep a sharp watch, any signs of activity I need to know, you will all be relieved in two hours.

Back at the now established base camp, he checked his watch and saw that it was a little after fifteen hundred hours, good he mused to himself then asked Corporal Brian Nash to give him two soldiers able to use the mortar system.

He took them with the mortar and shells forward to the line where the gunners were concealed left and right. What is the effective range of this mortar he asked. About Eight possibly eight hundred and fifty yards sergeant was the response. Right stated Ronnie, so we can fire from here and land shells some four hundred yards the other side of the lake then.

Telling the Mortar team to set the range to seven hundred yards and load with heavy smoke munition, he spoke to the two gunners, lookout and corporal Nash at base camp explaining that some mortar fire would begin and that everyone was to relax and hold positions with the lookout reporting any activity visible from the other side.

They fired off four heavy smoke mortars in an arc at seven hundred yards, and the radio crackled with the lookout reporting activity in the other area with soldiers moving back away from the lake and out of the smoke, he smiled to himself thinking that so far it was good, the Hussars knew that they were active and not just going to sit back and watch, and that this was to be a real test.

Speaking to the Mortar team he instructed them to lift the weapon and drop back towards base camp about one hundred yards. Why sergeant was the queried response. Well, once the Hussars get their shit together, they will work out roughly where we were firing from and rain their response accordingly, and you two do not need to be sat here when the sky falls in.

About halfway back to base camp area he told the mortar team to set up again and fix the range to eight hundred yards loading with more smoke shells, he gave them his radio and trotted back to where the others had completed the base camp setup.

Taking Corporal Nash's radio Ronnie instructed the two forward gunners to load a full magazine of ammunition into each gun and stand by, looking at his watch he saw it was sixteen forty, so he gave instructions for tea to be brewed and scoff made ready for around seventeen hundred.

At sixteen fifty he instructed the forward gunners to fire their magazines sweeping their arc of fire fully side to side, after which the lookout reported quite a bit of scuttling around in the scrub the other side of the lake.

At seventeen hundred they ate from the ration packs, some soup and potato with greens mix, and a chocolate bar for dessert. Taking five of the soldiers he called the lookout down and replaced him, then similarly replaced the forward gunners and mortar team telling the five exchanged men to get their food.

He took the mortar team forward to two hundred yards from the lake and Instructed smoke to be loaded, he instructed the gunners to load a full magazine each and told all to fix the range at seven hundred yards and fire.

As the guns crackled, he had the mortar team fire off three more rounds, then pick up the mortar and trot back towards base camp, they were still making progress when the ground behind erupted as the Hussars rained shells on the position of C Troops fire.

That is good said Ronnie aloud, the Hussars believe that we are moving towards the lake, which is what we want, they will check their own progress a little to compensate, what can you see lookout.

Not a bloody lot sergeant, just dust and dirt in the air surrounded by lots of smoke, hang on wait, I see four of them carrying their boat towards the edge of the lake about fifty yards from water, our left side facing them roughly in line with the edge of the island.

Gunner One called Ronnie, full magazine, angle of fire set at four hundred yards, short arc firing at edge of island. A crackle of fire erupted then, they are running back sergeant, they have abandoned the boat.

Well done everyone, with a bit of luck they will take a breather and reconsider whatever tactics they are using before having another go.

Telling the lookout to keep watching and the mortar and gunners to await instructions he trotted back into the base camp area, tea would be good Brian he said, I think that now we have exchanged fire the Hussars might wait a bit until it gets dark before making their next move.

At nineteen hundred he had the Mortar team, gunners and lookout all changed, then at nineteen twenty hours he took the mortar team forward to one hundred yards from the lake edge where you could clearly see the flag fluttering on its high pole. Telling the gunners to load full magazines and set the fire range to six hundred yards then fire when ready using a sweeping arc, he ordered standard mortar shells and had the team fire three in a sweep arc at five hundred yards, and was pleased to hear the lookout report that movement was occurring away from the lake.

He ordered the mortar team back to about two hundred yards from the lake and Instructed them to set up and load smoke shells, taking himself back to base camp. At twenty-one hundred hours he ordered another personnel exchange, making sure that the new lookout had night vision field glasses, and once the exchange had been made and the returning soldiers were given a brew.

He then instructed the forward gunners to take three full magazines and using ranges at six, then five and finally four hundred yards, to fire off a magazine at each using a full sweep of their arc of fire. As this started, he ordered the mortar team to fire the loaded smoke grenade then immediately load flash bangs and fire off two at a range of four hundred then two at five hundred yards, then pick up the mortar and retreat to a position some three hundred yards from the lake edge.

Rewarded with incoming mortar and machine gun rounds zipping into the ground at around two hundred yards from the lake, Ronnie realised that the Hussars were also now set up and active, they had also plotted C Troops firing positions, so he checked the gunners were both okay, some close Incoming was the response, but both were fine.

Right then everyone, listen in carefully, Ronnie talked into the radio, Gunners I want you to fire off three magazines at a range of four, then five then six hundred yards using a full sweep arc of fire at twenty-two hundred hours then again at twenty-two thirty, twenty-three hundred, twenty-three twenty, twenty-three forty, and ammunition allowing, twenty-three fifty, ignore our outgoing mortars.

Mortar team you are to use all your ordnance, your current position is about three hundred yards off the lake edge, so fire a selection of flash bangs, smoke and standard shells, fix the range at five hundred yards, fire of several in an arc, then move forward about fifty yards and repeat, then back fifty and move to one side and repeat and so on, keep your firing sessions in between the gunners activities so that there is a reasonably frequent incoming for the Hussars to think about, when you get down to the last few shells try to land them on the island, and lookout, keep a close watch and if any activity is seen tell the mortar team where to land some shells.

What if we accidently manage to hit the flagpole site sergeant called out the mortar team, that is fine responded Ronnie, if or rather when the Hussars reach the island, some incoming might at least delay their progress.

Having issued instructions to the weapons teams he told the remaining eight members of C Troop to sort their kit and get ready saying, with any luck by the time our mortars start landing on the island it will all be over.

He ordered the Medic carrying the base radio unit to remain at the camp and to monitor all messages, remember there must be radio silence unless something occurs, and the call sign is simply base camp calling okay.

At twenty one fifty the eight men slipped quietly out of C Troop base camp and headed at a slight angle towards the far edge of scrubland where the real trees began, moving at a brisk trot they reached the main tree line just as gunfire erupted from their forwards gunners, twenty-two hundred said Ronnie, as the Hussars returned fire using flash bangs which lit up the sky with a slight orange tinged glow, let`s move, keep spaced apart and hug the edge of the tree line, do not go too far in and remember we are moving forward for about a thousand yards just over half a mile.

Movement through the trees and shrubbery was quite slow going particularly as they wanted to make as little noise as was possible, but at twenty-two thirty more gunfire gave some noise cover and they were able to quicken the pace, and when Ronnie had adjudged a thousand yards, he called them all to squat down with him on the very edge of the tree line and get their breathing back to normal.

Sending Corporal Nash alone to scout the area and see if he could locate the Hussars base, the others sat in silence keeping a sharpened ear for any sounds. It was somewhat after twenty-three hundred and the most recent exchanges of fire had taken place when Nash returned already within the edge of the tree line and well hidden.

The Hussars base is around one hundred yards farther on and something similar, maybe a bit more out into the scrub from the tree line, and it seems that there are eight soldiers currently posted there and all seem to be quite relaxed.

Well, they will not be relaxed for much longer grinned Ronnie, come on, quietly as possible lads, we need to retain the element of surprise.

They sneaked forward and inwards into the scrubland until firstly they heard murmured voices which became clearer and louder as they grew closer, then at about twenty-five yards from the tent area, the scrub flattened out and they could clearly see the Hussar`s. They waited and watched and finally agreed that there were seven Hussar`s at the location, meaning that the other seven were out capturing the flag.

Ronnie whispered instructions to C Troop to fan out quietly around the tents so that they could attack from three sides simultaneously. As the twenty-three twenty ordnance exchange ended a radio in the Hussar`s camp crackled into life, Alpha One calling Alpha Two over, one of the soldiers picked up a radio set from a small foldup table and spoke, Alpha Two receiving over.

THE CUP

The radio crackled again, Alpha one reporting, the stupid Fusiliers are just shelling randomly, they have no idea where we are or what our plans are, we are set to paddle to the island and recover the flag, you can expect to hear the Fusiliers next round of random fire around midnight, keep radio silence, over and out.

The Hussar`s within the tent area laughed amongst themselves, one loudly saying, sarge said that this would be a piece of cake, he could probably have done the job on his own.

The twenty-three forty passage of fire passed and as it died away, Ronnie signalled for C Troop to get ready, and as soon as the return mortar fire started from this side of the lake, they rushed the unexpecting Hussar`s easily overpowering them and seizing all the weapons.

Ronnie immediately used his radio, saying base camp calling, all secure here, mortar team fire on the island now with everything that you have left, and within seconds the crump of landing shells indicated that the Fusiliers mortar team were in action.

Just after midnight, the Hussars radio activated, Alpha One calling Alpha Two over. Covering his mouth with his hand, Ronnie pushed the transmit button and said simply in a whispered voice, receiving over. Alpha One have secured the objective, two casualties from stupid Fusilier Mortars, will need attention so get everything prepared, ETA around zero twenty over and out.

Oh, we will most certainly be prepared for you, Nash said out aloud as they finished binding the captured Hussar`s and gagging them with scarves. They sat them down together behind the tents, leaving one of C Troop to guard the prisoners, whilst the others hid either side of the most obvious pathway out of the tent area into the scrub.

A few minutes passed then distinctive sounds of approaching feet signalled the arrival of the other seven Hussar` with their sergeant leading the way carrying the folded flag and two soldiers behind him supporting a third with what appeared a foot injury, and a little farther back two more carrying the third who was seemingly dazed and had a bandage wrapped around a head wound.

As before overpowering the totally unsuspecting Hussar`s was far too easy, none had weapons ready and even the sergeant was taken by surprise. Ronnie snatched the Union Flag from his hands saying, thank you for getting this for us, we thought that it would be simpler to let you do the hard work.

While C Troop sorted the Hussar prisoners into the tents and allowed them to treat the two mildly wounded soldiers, Ronnie used the radio to instruct the remainder of C Troop to collect up the weapons and all the base camp kit then make their way along the side of the lake to the Hussar`s area.

Turning to Corporal Nash he said, well done Brian, get the lads sorted on prisoner watch, and get someone to make some bloody tea and get some scoff on the go, for the Hussar`s as well, I expect that they could use a cup of tea.

By zero two hundred, C Troops kit was stashed to one side of the Hussar`s area and C Troop were finishing some cocoa and sharing cigarettes around a substantial fire. The captured Hussar`s looked a dejected bunch and their sergeant said bitterly, you fucking cheats won`t get away with this, you broke the rules, we captured the flag not you.

To the contrary sergeant, replied Ronnie, you only took it from its flagpole, then handed it to us, I believe that the completion of the exercise is to pass it to the officers which we will do in the morning, as for breaking the rules, we had not realised that the Hussar`s saw the whole thing as a game with set rules, having been given the task, we simply chose to use our initiative, and resources as we saw fit, which I believe sits well within any so called rules.

The remaining night hours passed with C Troop doing stag duty over the Hussar`s and after a rather unpalatable breakfast of dried egg and bacon from the ration packs, and having allowed the Hussar`s similar niceties, Ronnie told Brian Nash to put on one of the Hussar`s jackets and go out towards the start point and when he could see anyone, call out that the Hussar`s requested officer attendance to accept the flag.

Some twenty minutes later a small group of officers led by a lieutenant Colonel entered the camp with him smiling and chatting away to the others, I told you that my lads had it in the bag, and that the Fusiliers would never be any match for them.

Whaat the, he stammered as Ronnie held out the neatly folded Union Flag and coming to attention saluted smartly. Good Morning Sir, C Troop Prince of Wales Fusiliers handing in the recovered flag as instructed. But this is the Hussar`s side not the Fusiliers hissed the officer, it is indeed sir, but it is the Fusiliers who have the flag and are handing it in as instructed.

Bloody improper, that`s what this is, a disgrace, he snatched the flag from Ronnie`s hands, you have not heard the last of this Lamb, mark my words, your card is well and truly marked.

As the officers stormed away, Ronnie told the others to free the Hussar`s, then collecting their kit they jogged back past the lake to their own side and out to the rendezvous area where Captain Adams and the sergeant major were already waiting.

I believe congratulations are in order said Adams, slightly out of the ordinary tactics, unconventional is the word I will use in my report, however they were nonetheless effective, so all of you well done a good team effort.

The truck will take you back to barracks for hot showers and some decent food. They loaded the kit and climbed aboard, as the truck started Captain Adams called out, sergeant Lamb, whilst your initiative is commendable, it is not what the British Army requires from its soldiers, compliance and following of procedures is the expected order of the day, and whilst the intelligence corps tend to operate a little outside of routine procedure, nonetheless establishing too many enemies could be an issue.

I will heed your advice sir, thank you, replied Ronnie. Lieutenant Colonel Critchley is not without influence, his father is a respected high-ranking official in the British Foreign Service, called Adams as the truck sped away, and for the record, the Hussar`s had one magazine with live ammunition out there, no one knows how it happened, but there could have been a tragic accident.

What the fuck was all of that about said Nash, and why would they have live ammo. To be honest I am not sure replied Ronnie, but it is beginning to look like my popularity in some quarters is not as good as it should be.

Well sergeant Lamb of the intelligence corps, you are top of the pops with us, isn't he lads smiled Nash, as the others asserted their agreement, you will always be welcome with C Troop.

Standing under the shower after shaving and toileting, Ronnie washed himself thoroughly, and as he rinsed the soap away thought back to what captain Adams had shared, particularly about the live ammunition.

What the hell is really going on he wondered.

Chapter Nine
Raising the Stakes

The next four days were taken up with map reading and orienteering exercises, speed marches in full kit and a rather testing assault course competition which set different troops against each other to measure physical ability. Ronnie spent the entire time with C Troop although he was not actually required for anything practical.

On the last day, Saturday, a final obstacle course challenge was the only task planned, with each troop working against the clock to get themselves and full carry kit through or over the various obstacles under the pegged-out cargo netting and into a wooden gazebo which signalled completion once all fourteen troop members were inside.

To provide the authenticity of combat, blanks were on constant fire over the cargo net, and the odd thunder-flash was thrown in for good measure.

Brian and Ronnie were the first of C Troop to clear the netting and reach the gazebo, immediately calling back to encourage and cajole the others to move it faster. Suddenly a zipping noise startled them both and looking at each other they guessed a stray blank round had passed close, bloody hell said Ronnie, I know that they are blanks but if the debris hit you, it could still do a bit of damage, and why are the firing arcs not fixed, someone has fucked up big time.

Brian was using the tip of his service knife to dig out something from one of the wooden support posts, and putting his knife away he looked hard at Ronnie holding out his hand to show what he had retrieved from the post.

Blank my arse, that`s a 7.62 SLR round, live ammunition spluttered Nash, what the fuck is going on.

I have no idea answered Ronnie ushering Brian farther inside the gazebo structure. Bollocks shouted the agitated young corporal, someone just tried to kill you, and you say that you have no idea why, I just don`t believe you.

Sorry Brian but it is the truth, I really do not have any idea why someone would be trying to shoot me, it must be a mistake.

Mistake, who the fuck fires a live round at someone by mistake, whoever you are sergeant Lamb, just stay the fuck away from me and my men, you are far too dangerous to be around.

A ride had been arranged back to Harrogate, and Ronnie spent the entire journey running all the week`s events through his mind, but whichever way he worked it no plausible answers came to the fore.

There was, in as far as he could see no connection between the Lieutenant Colonel Critchley and himself Harry or John, other than perhaps an Intelligence corps link, so was the shot destined for Brian Nash, then again Captain Adams had recounted a live magazine had been found in the Hussar`s ordinance, so if Nash were the target, then why had shots not been fired.

At the gazebo, Nash had been behind him making an impossible target and Nash had been genuinely shocked at recovering a live round from the post, so everything pointed to himself being the one that these attempts were aimed at, but why.

THE CUP

He considered what Harry had shared about other groups trying to obtain the cup being almost fanatical and willing to do almost anything to get it for themselves, but he had not yet been in contact with the cup nor even knew of its location, so any apparent enemies on that scene were either making assumptions that were untrue, or for some reason just wanted him out of the way.

For now, nothing made any sense, he just hoped that Harry or John might have some sensible explanation.

It was late afternoon when they arrived back at Harrogate, Ronnie considered going to see Sheila, but decided against this as he was tired and had a head full of unanswered questions which would have made their small talk difficult, so he chose to eat then shave, shower and sleep.

Sunday was spent washing ironing and cleaning his kit, then sorting out in his mind what questions he would ask Harry, and accordingly having taken an earlier breakfast then usual he was already brewing the tea on Monday morning when Harry and John arrived at the hut together.

Well, army exercises apparently suit someone said Harry chuckling, I think that Ronnie here should do them more often, what do you think John. Oh yes indeed smiled John, he needs to become a regular.

I would love to oblige you both, but I suspect that they would be the death of me, was Ronnie`s somewhat terse response, too which both John and Harry laughed, only to stop when they saw the expression on Ronnie`s face.

Oh, my word something has happened, said Harry and pulling stools out from under the workbench and taking the proffered mugs of tea, told Ronnie to tell all.

Phew breathed John when Ronnie had stopped talking, I never thought for one single moment that anyone would be willing to go that far, and we do not even have the cup yet.

Someone is starting to panic mused Harry, they obviously know what we are up to and are somehow keeping tabs on what we do, possibly they want Ronnie taken out of the equation, to make it a level playing field so to speak.

What do you mean asked Ronnie, who are they, and why should they need me taken out, as you so quaintly phrase their intentions.

Well for a start, if they are aware that you have the ability to discern the cups authenticity, they know that we have a distinct advantage, in that we are not likely to fall for some cheap replica scam.

They also know that you would not work for them, so getting rid of you gives them equality, and as for who they are, recent information shows that a Neo Nazi group calling themselves the Red Faction are allegedly seeking all of the three relics.

We believe interrupted John, that this Red Faction are highly professional, well financed, and have powerful people amongst the membership, including some living here in Great Britain. It is possible that they already have the linen grave cloth, known as the Shroud of Turin, so their interest in obtaining the cup cannot be ignored.

I am hardly likely to ignore people trying to kill me sighed Ronnie, but how do they know so much about our little operation, or even about me, and if they have the shroud, why is it not known that the one in the museum is a fake.

The experts who regularly examine the cloth, cannot even agree on its age sighed Harry, they bicker and counter argue over every conceivable part of the cloth its stains and alleged history, some claiming it to be a fake, manufactured specifically for the Roman Catholic Church, others believe it to be the real genuine article whilst a third group believe it to be part real and part fake, in that whilst the cloth can be dated back to the first century AD the stains are of human origin.

But surely exclaimed Ronnie, if my understanding of the Biblical telling of the crucifixion story is correct, Jesus was unable to die on the cross in his divine form, and it was only after God took away his supernatural authority that his human body was able to succumb to mortal death.

I am very impressed spluttered John, for one so apparently young innocent and naïve, your sense of understanding all things spiritual is amazing, but in broad terms your assumptions are correct, heaven removed the barrier preventing mortal death allowing Jesus in human form to become lifeless, presumed or to be more accurate technically dead as human understanding measures life.

So why do the experts examining the cloth expect to find non-human staining insisted Ronnie.

Because continued John in a somewhat exasperated voice as if explaining the obvious to someone slightly less intelligent, Jesus did not die, how could he, he was, rather is, a God, so any staining on the cloth as his life returned would hopefully show non-human make up.

So, if Jesus needed to regain his immortal life why did he die in the first place, I find it very confusing sighed Ronnie, I mean witness testimony records that he met people after coming back to life, they cannot all be liars, and not all were his supporters, some just historians who recorded events for posterity.

As we have tried to explain already when we had a similar chat last year, Jesus time on earth, an earth created by God, was a test to see if living a God-fearing blameless life, was possible, Jesus did exactly that, but God in his wisdom recognised that Jesus had advantages over all other humans, in that he had first-hand knowledge and proof of God the Father.

God`s answer to humanity`s inability to be sinless, was to self-sacrifice as a one-time payment for all the earths sin from beginning to end, promising that in doing so, all those who chose simple belief, essentially to trust and live life by faith in God would, on victory in the final battle between the angels be awarded places with them in Heaven for eternity.

Harry paused then added, anyone who expresses public belief and faith and personally asks God for his forgiveness will not only receive it, but be guaranteed a place for eternity, so as you can imagine the stakes are very high.

You must understand that while there are people across the world who believe all of this to be true, some have motives driven by support for the fallen angels as opposed to those who side with God, be very sure that where good resides, then evil is never far away, not every enemy of your enemy is necessarily your friend.

We represent a small group of traditional Jews, believers that Jesus was indeed part of the Godhead, and our aim is to protect the three known artifacts which are a direct link to creation and Gods overall plan from unscrupulous people who seek to obtain and use them for ungodly activities, personal gain and evil intent.

Harry paused to sip his rapidly cooling tea, we think that this Red Faction somehow exchanged the real burial cloth shroud during scientific testing sessions, we know that having found the cup by chance in 1942 the Nazis intended to put the cup and shroud together to support their attempt at global domination.

However, by fate or perhaps Gods intervention, the cup was taken out of Europe for supposed safe keeping, and we now believe that it has surfaced in Ireland.

If that is true, when do we go to Ireland and get it back asked Ronnie.

The Red Faction are linked, as so many terrorist organisations are, to the Irish Republican Army or IRA as everyone knows them. They are seemingly trying to utilise any power that the cup might have to assist them in their social and political struggle with the British Government.

It is likely that the cup is or will be in Belfast, and our intention is for you to go there and recover it, bring it back here where we can record its recovery and eventually return it to Jerusalem.

Right, all of this I now understand or at least think that I do, so who do I need to be looking out for, as possible enemies, and when will we get to go to Ireland.

We cannot answer either of those questions, sighed John, not because we are being secretive but because the truth is that we just do not know.

We can and will find out more about Lieutenant Colonel Critchley continued Harry, and hopefully that might give us some insight into who and what we will be dealing with, but for now, trust no one and keep aware of all situations.

if they really are intent on getting you out of the way, there is no guessing what they might do or even when they might do it.

Resorting to his Bibles, Ronnie tried to find something which could offer insight into the practical aspects of the three items but given the different timelines no real link could be established, he pored over both Old and New Testament text and was suddenly struck by the polarity of the Ark and the Cup.

The Ark was built to hold Gods written laws which man was to follow and obey, whilst the cup signified God`s forgiveness for not doing so. Then it occurred to him, that the burial cloth was the bridge between the two, the link.

Old testament teaching was obedience to Gods written Law as inscribed on the stone tablets known as the Ten Commandments which had been secreted into the Ark, New Testament teaching was God`s forgiveness for breaking these rules, paid for by Jesus sacrificial death, with Jesus himself using the cup to explain this new promise.

The Ark contained the old law, the cup represented the new promise, and the burial cloth linked both in that it represented the entire Godhead, old ways and new way.

Now into a new year, Sheila`s family particularly Mavis her mother, were earnestly beginning to make wedding plans, and they had chosen the date of November 25th the following year, with the wedding service to be held at Christ Church on the Stray and the wedding breakfast at the football club.

Ronnie was asked for a list of family and friends whom he would like to invite, so he gave his family details and added Harry and John with their partners as guests.

Back in the hut, Harry shared information about Lieutenant Colonel Critchley, being the son of Lord Critchley, which Ronnie suddenly remembered from what captain Adams had said, and that Critchley senior was a high-ranking diplomat with close connections to the prime minister and the Royal Family.

The Critchley`s owned several properties including a country estate in Hampshire near Andover where regular social events were held and well connected, socialite friends attended.

THE CUP

Apparently, Lady Critchley is from German descent, related to Eichman I believe said Harry. Well, that accounts for the Neo Nazi connection said John. Quite so continued Harry, and of course how they seemingly have no problem with money.

Talking of money interrupted Ronnie, might I ask who is footing the bill for our operation, I know that we are only three so far, but there must be costs involved, so who is paying.

You really do not need to worry about money said Harry, that side of things has been taken care of. That is fine for you to say replied Ronnie, but as I am now fully committed to the cup recovery, I think that I have a right to know who is paying.

The British Government, or to be more precise the Post Office said John. What, exclaimed Ronnie, why on earth would the Government give you money for such an operation.

Well, they didn`t exactly give us the money continued John, let us simply say that we borrowed it. Borrowed it cried Ronnie, where from, how, who.

From a Mail Train, chipped in Harry, an overnight Mail Train from Scotland to London.

Suddenly everything began to make sense, Mr Regenstein, the Train Robbery, Steiner and now here, he had been manipulated and groomed every step of the way, and without suspecting a single thing.

So, I presume that Mr Regenstein is the mastermind, Mr Big, he has been pulling the strings in secret all this time, when do I get to meet him again.

It has taken you some time to work everything out, but we knew that you would get there in the end smiled John, for the record I am his grandson, and Harry is his nephew, the family name is Steiner as you have probably already guessed, Regenstein was a useful alias.

Benjamin Steiner, or Reg as you so happily know him as, is a direct ancestor of Joseph the Jewish merchant from Arimathea, who using his fleet of ships transported Roman cargo to the garrisons and ports in Britannia, he was the very same Joseph who gave up his own burial tomb for Jesus.

So, you see Ronnie our family have been following and supporting Jesus since he walked this earth, and even now it falls to us to protect Gods interests like the cup, from improper use.

And what about me said Ronnie, we are not related so do I have such ancestry.

Yes of course you do smiled John, your ancestors are traceable back to the tribe of Levite, a direct line with Zachariah the high priest who was struck dumb upon the announcement of his wife Elizabeth being pregnant as they were both getting old when it happened, she gave birth to a son, whom they named John.

Are you trying to tell me that I am related to John the Baptist, Jesus cousin surely that cannot be true exclaimed Ronnie somewhat excitedly. Why not asked John, someone needs to be his descendant so why not you, at which both John and Harry started to laugh.

What is so funny, Ronnie bristled at them laughing seemingly at him. Well, laughed Harry, as we now understand congratulations are the order of the day, what with you having fixed the date to marry your young lady friend, it just amuses us that you Levites have poor taste where women are concerned.

Take a closer look at Eve, Jezebel, and Delilah, not exactly supportive of their men were they, perhaps your young Sheila will break the mould rather than your heart.

Very bloody amusing snarled Ronnie, angry with them both, I will have you know, that Sheila is kind and loving, she adores me and for the record not only has she no knowledge of our mission regarding the cup, she no idea of my Jewish ancestry.

Your support for the lady is admirable, if not entirely unexpected said Harry, but please be careful. Ask yourself how much you honestly know about her, the family, the extended family. Remember someone has tried to kill you at least once and presumably will try again, so do not take anything at face value.

As for your Jewish ancestry, wear that with pride after all if the Bible account is true, the early Jews or Israelites were Gods chosen people, so surely being one of them is an asset rather than a drawback we are what we are Ronnie, said Harry, and if you are so convinced that Sheila knows nothing of your ancestry, either you have not yet shared a bed, or as I suspect she has just taken it in her stride.

Whatever do you mean replied Ronnie, what on earth has sex got to do with who I am or rather might be.

Take a closer look at yourself the next time you have a piss, laughed John. And what should I be looking for murmured Ronnie. What is not there, giggled John, the little bit that is missing.

Later when he met Sheila Ronnie asked her why she had never mentioned that he was circumcised, to which she responded, don't be silly it`s not a problem and any way, I now have my own little Jew boy.

I am a real person not a bloody toy for you to play with cried Ronnie. Oh dear what a naughty girl I am she smiled, perhaps you should put me over your knee and spank me. Ronnie did not need a second invitation and proceeded to place the giggling Sheila over his lap.

By the time they were due to meet again, Ronnie had convinced himself that he might have been too harsh with her, so he took both flowers and chocolate, but she laughed and said, don't be silly, I adored you taking control it showed how much you care for me, please do not ever stop.

On his nineteenth birthday in February 1971, he breezed into the hut feeling on top of the world, but his euphoria evaporated when he saw the sombre mood enveloping both Harry and John.

It seems said Harry, that things across the water have taken a turn for the worse. He brewed the tea and continued, if it escalates and the Red Faction in cahoots with the IRA do have the cup, there is a strong possibility that it might get sent back to Germany where it will be so much harder to recover, we need to get preparations under way so that we can be ready to move at a moment's notice.

A Few days later a team of BBC outside broadcast engineers were killed when a booby-trapped car bomb exploded near a remote field transmitter in county Armagh, the device being meant for a passing RUC police vehicle, and further news reported that on the 6th February a young soldier, a gunner named Robert Curtis had been shot and died on the street whilst patrolling in the Shankhill Road area of Belfast.

As I suspected, said Harry over tea and biscuits, things are really escalating and will get totally out of control very soon, my London sources inform me that the Red Faction are actively working in Belfast trying to track down the cup's location, and they are offering one hundred thousand pounds for the genuine article.

Bugger me, breathed John that is a lot of money. A lot indeed replied Harry tersely, and we will have to match it at least, not that money is a problem, thankfully Her Majesty's

Postal Service were very generous with their contribution to our cause, the current problem is finding the cup before others do.

Surely using stolen cash to purchase the cup is both illegal and immoral, sighed Ronnie desperate to cling to at least some of the childhood ways that his parents had established for him to follow.

Well unless you have another source of money to replace it, then we simply have no choice retorted John, the moral high ground is a lovely place to preach from, but it also exposes you to attack from anyone looking at you, and from my understanding, using stolen money to recover a stolen object is poetic justice.

When you two have stopped waxing lyrical on the attributes of stolen money, you need to make some concrete plans instructed Harry, Ronnie needs to be given instruction on what to expect once out in Northern Ireland, the dangers and the obstacles that might need to be overcome.

You will both need good cover stories, and above all we need to consider the best way for you to get such a large amount of cash out there and keep it safe until the exchange, can you imagine the cash falling into the hands of the IRA muttered Harry.

And what will you be doing asked Ronnie. I shall be going undercover in Northern Ireland and possibly across the border, we are helpless without accurate knowledge of where the cup is and who is protecting it, as well as establishing if it can be purchased and if so, how much is wanted.

Daily routine was immediately set aside as Ronnie and John threw themselves into studying the coming mission in the province, they looked hard at the politics, the different groups and if or how they interacted with each other.

So called sectarian violence was increasing and the presence of the British Army rather than seen as helpful, was generally portrayed as inflammatory.

After one such intensive study session as John made tea Ronnie said, so it seems that we will be regarded as the enemy by just about everyone, civilian and paramilitary alike, bloody great he sighed.

And of course, we must always be dressed in uniform noted John, if we were to be compromised whilst wearing civilian clothes, at best we could be arrested as British spies, more likely shot as terrorists.

What a fucking nightmare snorted Ronnie, Belfast is a hotbed of intrigue and in-fighting, everyone will be looking for a legitimate reason to kill us, we will be carrying around thousands of pounds in cash whilst needing to meet with whoever has the cup, do the exchange, then get it out of the country without creating any suspicion or getting caught.

Quite eloquently put my friend, but I fear that you have omitted possibly the hardest part of the mission. Which is retorted Ronnie. Put simply continued John, the Army is rather particular as to who it is currently deploying into Northern Ireland, for lots of understandable reasons, and because we need to go there as service personnel, a weekend break is sadly out of the question, so whatever the challenges once on the ground, getting out there might just be the biggest one.

Through the spring and summer they spent days learning and perfecting their own and each other`s cover stories, which saw them as intelligence personnel sent by her Majesty`s government to establish if there was any basis for a lasting peace deal to be brokered.

Keeping to as much true detail as possible, with things that could be easily checked kept prominent, such as their positions within intelligence, based at Harrogate, the cover needed to be plausible while not so fanciful as to arouse suspicion or raise questions.

Life with Sheila continued much as normal with continued excitement about next year's wedding, which he found both amusing and tedious, after all anything might happen in over a year, he might not even make it that far.

He sat alone one evening in the bar considering both past and future events that could shape his life, he had without doubt become mature at a younger age than was the normal expectation, but then he had lost the mainstay of his life when only ten years of age, and while it was true that sister Christine had tried to be a substitute mother, she herself had suffered the same loss and was in reality not that much older than he.

His thoughts turned to Sheila, and the wedding, did he really love her he wondered, he knew for certain that he liked her a lot, would do almost anything for her, and looked forward to being with her, but did he love her, probably not in the true sense of the word, but then again, did he know what love was anyway.

Harry was away until early August, and upon his return they wasted no time in updating him on training, preparations and their cover stories, which once he had learned of the idea prompted him to disappear off to London, telling them to keep up the good work.

In the previous May, a known loyalist supporter called William "Billy" Reid had been killed by gunfire from British Soldiers and it was reported that he had been the terrorist who had killed Gunner Robert Curtis back in February, so the conclusion was a tit for tat execution had taken place which had been sanctioned by the British Army.

Tensions between the population and the deployed soldiers were running high, not helped by politicians stoking the flames of hatred for political gain, amongst whom a young female politician called Bernadette Davine was very prominent.

It is getting rather unsavoury out there, sighed John, I suspect we might be getting action sooner rather than later so we need to sharpen up, and a few days later some of his friends from the Intelligence Corps arrived.

Several days were taken up with urban warfare tactics and stealth training, they taught him how to kill effectively and almost silently, and that contrary to popular opinion a hard chop to the neck will not disable most fit men, however ramming your open palm up under the nose of the opponent is likely to force their nasal bridge bone up into the brain.

Questioned as to what they were training for John said a mission in Aden which seemed to satisfy everyone's curiosity.

Late afternoon on the Friday as the group were loading their kit into a Landrover for the long journey south back to Hermitage, one of them who called himself Hugh, hugged John very tightly and said, remember my friend do not let it be known that you are a Jew, all the world hates us, but none more so than the Arabs, hell, some of them even hate each other.

The group laughed at this impromptu ice breaker, and as the jeep sped away, John murmured to no one in particular, Yitgadal v`yit-kadash sh`mey raba, b`alma di v`ra hirutey, v`yamlihmal-hutey b`havey-hon uv`ha-vey d`hol beyt yisrael ba agalau-vizman kariv, v`imru AMEN

What was all that about then Ronnie asked as they walked away from the hut area.

Placing his hand onto Ronnie's shoulder John smiled and said, the truth is that the world hates the Jews, oh sure some people will say that they do not, but deep inside everyone holds us responsible for fucking up Gods gifts to humanity.

Not that any other race would have fared better but hey ho, you have to put the blame for life's shit onto someone, and that makes us Jews an easy target, quite apart from blaming us for crucifying Jesus, which was technically a Roman decision but who cares about mere semantics.

But cried Ronnie, surely God was here for the whole world, all of creation, not just the Jews, blaming us alone is so unfair. He suddenly realised that he had subconsciously included himself as a Jew and fell silent. Come on said John sympathetically, let's get some scoff then perhaps a beer in the bar.

What replied Ronnie mocking incredulity, you have never wanted to drink with me before, why now. Let us just say that we will soon need to depend upon each other, so the closer we can bond the easier that might be, and who knows we might not be coming back so why not.

Seeing the look of consternation on Ronnie's face John laughed, only joking mate, it will be fine, like stealing sweets from a sleeping baby.

In late September Ronnie took some owed leave, and he and Shelia travelled down to London. She had never been before and enjoyed seeing the tourist sites and travel on the underground. They stayed in a small bed and breakfast hotel in Bayswater and had diner each evening in a variety of different restaurants even going to see a theatre show in the west end.

On the Friday they caught a local train to Tring, and went to see Ronnie's sister Christine, who immediately taking a liking to Sheila said that she would be good for Ronnie, and they shared the wedding plans giving invitation for all the family who might be able to come.

After breakfast on Saturday, they walked to Kings Cross Station to catch the train north to York where Sheila's best friend Janet and her now Fiancé Peter were to meet them and drive them back to Harrogate. As they stood on the station concourse waiting for the York train to be called as ready to board, a scruffy man carrying a large, folded item stopped directly opposite them, and opening what Ronnie now realised was a notice board, showed what it said.

MY CUP RUNNETH OVER. Psalm 23. Ronnie looked at the man who was looking directly at him, and even whilst he closed the sign board holding the staring gaze.

With the sign board now closed the man used one finger to slowly draw it across his throat, then taking up the sign he was gone.

Looking nervously at Sheila to see her reaction Ronnie was relieved to realise that all her attention was apparently on the train departures board, and she suddenly grabbed his sleeve crying out platform eleven let's go.

By November incidents in Northern Ireland were becoming much more frequent with bombs being exploded at the Youth Employment Offices and again at the Red Lion Bar. Sectarian tensions ran high and the RUC and British Army who were working jointly were more than ever being cast as the enemies of the people and attacked at random.

Harry went back to Belfast only to return two days later in a very cheerful mood, sharing that not only had the cup been located, but the holders were keen to sell, and that he had already agreed to purchase it and would be arranging for the cash as well as getting both John and Ronnie out to Belfast in order to make the transfer.

Did you see the cup asked John, showing real excitement. No, sadly not, but it is on the absolute best authority to be true replied Harry, so we must plan accordingly.

John slapped Ronnie on the back, here we go mate its mission on and time we polished our cover stories together, remember this time it will be for real.

On the 4th December a massive explosion in Mc Gurks Bar in Belfast left fifteen dead with seventeen others injured causing total outrage in Parliament and calls for tougher action against what was rapidly escalating into civil war, and on the Monday 6th Harry met them in the hut and gave orders for them to make final preparations as they were to go to Belfast later that same week.

Wednesday morning saw Harry give them both rail warrants from Carlisle to Stranraer in south west Scotland where they would be catching the ferry to Larne in Northern Ireland. A Landrover would collect them from the hut on the following day Thursday late morning, driving them across country to Carlisle, where they were to take a train to the ferry port in Stranraer.

Once in Larne, they were to be met and driven to Belfast where they had been billeted in an old church in the suburb of Bantry now used by the army as temporary accommodation, they would be contacted by an ageing priest called Father O`Brian, who was a whiskey drinking sop, but who for some cash had agreed to provide some credibility to their cover story.

On the Thursday Ronnie and John took their kit to the hut using carry type hold all bags, rather than the more standard kitbag for ease and convenience. Harry was waiting and wished them both good luck and God speed, he said that the Landrover was collecting them at around Eleven Thirty, and that the Ferry sailed from Larne at Twenty-Two Hundred hours.

As Harry handed them both one way ferry tickets, John asked how they were to get home, to which the reply was by air, hopefully on Monday if you get the deal done. You just need to make your way to RAF Aldergrove, it is now also in use as a civilian airport, report to the flight office and they will sort a flight home.

Harry then gave John, a package tightly wrapped in brown paper which was slightly larger than a house brick saying, One Hundred Thousand Pounds in used twenties, for God`s sake do not lose it. Decimalisation had replaced the old pounds shillings and pence system earlier that same year and now the newer notes were smaller and took up less space.

Where shall we go Ronnie, do you fancy a long weekend in Blackpool laughed John waving the package. That`s just not funny grumbled Harry, this is bloody serious you two, just go and get the cup, ideally without either of you getting hurt or caught. Can you imagine the shitstorm if it were to be discovered that a covert British Army team were running around Belfast with thousands of pounds in cash apparently looking to buy supporters for a peace deal.

Who has the cup, and how do we make contact to set up the exchange asked Ronnie, suddenly switching into a serious mood. That information is given on a strictly need to know basis said Harry and I do not need to know it.

Father O`Brian will give you all the detail and information that you need, but remember he believes that you are out there to seek peace brokers, the details that he gives will be for a peace sympathiser as far as he is aware, he knows absolutely nothing of the cup and we need to keep it that way.

What is the expected timescale for everything, John asked Harry. The ferry docks in Larne early on Friday morning, you will get into Belfast around nine or ten, and

Father O`Brian will come to meet you sometime later that morning.

The timeline after that will depend upon what details he gives to you, but I suggest that before you make any active move, you check out everything thoroughly, including the handover area to minimise risks and give yourselves as much advantage as possible.

After they had loaded the bags into the Landrover they hugged each other with Harry wishing both a safe trip. Ronnie climbed into the rear to allow John the front seat and give himself more room to stretch in the back area, John had stayed outside and was close to Harry, and straining his ears Ronnie just made out what John was saying, bebkasha teii at hakdish basbili, but being Hebrew, he did not know what it meant, supposing it to be a family farewell.

As John settled into the passenger seat and the driver pulled away, Ronnie said, no secrets from each other, that is what we agreed, so what the fuck was that between you and Harry.

No secrets I promise said John emotionally, I was just covering all possibilities, it has nothing to do with us or the mission.

The trip to Carlisle was uneventful and the train to Stranraer was destined to stop at every station it seemed, so both dosed peacefully only waking as the train shuddered to a halt at the ferry port terminus.

It was just after twenty hundred hours and boarding did not start until twenty-one hundred, so they took seats in the café where Ronnie unwisely as it transpired chose a full breakfast while John settled for fish and chips.

On board they stowed their bags in the twin berth cabin and made their way up to the deck to watch as the ferry left port, the weather was slightly breezy but not too cold considering how close it was to Christmas.

The ferry did not seem that full and there were few passengers to be seen, so they made their way to the lounge and bar area where both ordered drinks of Guinness as a taster of the weekend ahead and sat talking for a while.

A little after midnight the gentle rocking motion of the boat started to become more pronounced, and John announced that he was going to bed as he hated rough seas. Sensing the wisdom in this action, Ronnie ordered a nightcap of double Macallan whiskey over ice from the lone bar steward as a voice over his shoulder called softly, buy a pretty girl a drink sergeant.

A short, raven haired girl, late twenties possibly early thirties was standing behind his stool hands on hips smiling, mines a large brandy. Perching herself on the stool next to him and holding out her right hand she said, it is always good to meet one of her majesty`s officers, I am Siobahn, Siobahn Flannery.

Shaking the proffered hand Ronnie responded with a simple sergeant Lamb at your service. So where might a sergeant in the Royal Corps of Signals be going this wild Friday night, she simpered.

Rather a silly question don't you think, laughed Ronnie, the bloody ferry only has one port of call. What I actually meant sergeant is where, in Northern Ireland, and what is your name I cannot keep calling you sergeant, her soft Irish brogue was somehow quite charming and put him at ease.

We are going to Belfast if you must know, just a brief weekend trip, and my Name is Ronnie.

Trying to recover what he considered was lost initiative he asked pointedly, how could you know that I am in the Signals very few ladies would know that. Oh that`s easy silly, I recognised the badge, the jimmy, it is a give away sign and in any case, I am a reporter for the Belfast Telegraph Newspaper, so I get to meet quite a few soldiers.

What are you and your friend over for, the lilting voice seemed so innocuous and friendly. Oh just some rather boring research into communications issues smiled Ronnie, pretty low key stuff but I guess someone has to do it.

So where does your Intelligence Corps friend fit in then, the soft voice was like warm whiskey filling his senses. Ronnie stopped himself talking with supreme effort, how the hell did she know who John was, or even that he existed.

His senses kicked in and downing the last dregs of whiskey from the glass he slipped from his stool.

As it happens, we just met on the boat and got chatting, decided to share a cabin, you know what it is like. Oh I do, she purred, even a brief chat can sometimes make a lot of difference. She too downed the last drops of brandy, put down the glass and kissed him hard on the lips, and walking away called back, thank you for the drink sergeant, have a good weekend, stay safe Belfast is not a nice place to be right now, and who knows we may even meet again.

As they went ashore in the morning, Ronnie shared the events at the bar with John who groaned, you and bloody women, you do realise that one day they will be the death of you. Ronnie scanned around for Siobahn, but there was no one to be seen anywhere, so they dropped their bags into the Landrover and were driven out of the port.

The Landrover was a standard model but steel mesh had been fitted over all the windows and so it was a little like being in a mobile prison. There were several concrete pillar checkpoints along the road to Belfast at which the soldiers on guard checked their identity`s and it was not until after eight thirty am when they pulled onto a cobbled square with a small church set along one side. Bantry barracks, said the driver pulling up to the side of the building where a door was open.

The church was a simple protestant chapel rather than a large mainstream church, it consisted of several rows of camp beds each with a small locker on wheels beside it, capable of sleeping twenty people, a kitchenette area, toilets and a stack of chairs to one end of the main room showing where the usual church furnishings had been set aside

There were three men already inside dressed in drab civilian clothes, who were already in the process of making breakfast. introductions revealed them to be United Nations Observers, who were on a fact-finding mission regarding human rights, and that they were flying to London that morning and would not be returning until Monday.

Selecting two beds to the opposite side from the UN personnel and having stowed their kit and used the washroom Ronnie said, I am famished let us see what the good Lord provides for weary soldiers in his barrack church.

The others had finished eating and even washed their plates and utensils, so the kitchen area was free. John took eggs and milk, some cheese and strips of bacon and was soon busily frying something in a pan. Ronnie boiled the kettle and brewed a whole pot of tea, then set two places at one of the three tables.

Just as he completed his little task a horn sounded outside and a taxi driver appeared in the doorway asking for his fare to the airport, and the three observers said curt goodbyes and left.

John came over to the table and set down two plates each holding a beautifully cooked cheese and bacon omelette and tucking in Ronnie found that it tasted every bit as good as it looked.

Where on earth did you learn to cook, he asked, this is delicious. Not cook exactly was Johns smiling reply, but I can knock up an omelette and I do a reasonably edible, fry up, so we will not go hungry, and they both laughed.

THE CUP

Around nine thirty a fat balding man in a black cassock with a ruddy face staggered through the still open door, and at first Ronnie assumed him to be short of breath but soon realised the man to be intoxicated, and as if on cue, the man pulled a bottle from inside his robe and removing the screw top, took a substantial swig from the bottle neck.

Replacing the top and secreting the bottle Inside the robe, the man burped loudly and said, so too be sure you two young fellas must be the very men who I need to introduce to Seamus Flannigan.

Tell the whole fucking world, why don't you growled John, we are supposed to be here in secret.

Now there`s a touchy fella if I do say so myself, and the priest burped again, this is Bantry my son, everyone knows everything here, why they probably already know how big your prick is. If that is true, spat Ronnie, they know that we are here to seek a peace deal, will they be happy with that.

The fat priest tapped his nose and replied, ah too be sure that's not very likely, you see any peace setup by the English would have strings attached.

So are we at risk from the locals continued Ronnie, will they cause any trouble while we are here.

Oh, bless me no, the younger colleens might have shown an interest in a couple of young handsome soldiers, but now they know at least one has such a tiny dick, they will lose interest.

The priest withdrew the bottle and took another hefty swig from the open top, burped again and as he replaced the top said. Seamus Flannigan, number six Caitsgill, it`s behind Eliza Street Market, Sunday evening at Nine PM.

Why Sunday, why so late and why at his home said John still visibly annoyed. So, the little prick speaks does he responded the priest, well Sundays are quietest and at nine it will be dark so there is much less chance of anyone being seen and I do not recall saying it to be his home

Retrieving the bottle once again he took an even larger mouthful or so it seemed to Ronnie, hiccupped then said softly, and make sure to use the back gate entrance. Then waving the bottle as he replaced the cap, he lurched out of the door and staggered away across the cobbled square.

John threw his plate into the sink with such force that it broke into pieces, Fuck, Fuck, Fuck, he almost spat the tirade, adding a final fuck for good measure.

Okay calm down said Ronnie, he is a bit of a liability I grant you, but we now have the information needed so have no reason for any further dealings with him.

A bit of a liability screamed John, your fucking priceless sometimes Ronnie. Understatement or what. No need to involve him further you daft twat, that fucking drunk knows who we are, where we are, what we are supposedly doing here, and above all when we will be doing it and where.

For Christ sake Ronnie we might as well wear Union Jack Fancy Dress, with signs around our necks reading, we are British Spies please shoot us.

Look mate said Ronnie trying to pacify Johns boiling anger, no one will take any notice of that piss-head, everyone can see what he is, and in any case in around seventy-two hours or so we will be laughing about it in Harrogate.

Maybe, conceded John still cross, but it is far too high a profile for my liking, and for what it is worth I don't believe that the tart who chatted you up last night on the ferry was simple coincidence either.

Ronnie collected the broken pieces of plate from the sink and threw them into the waste bin. Maybe he said, but then again, she could be genuine, coming home from a trip abroad after all she claimed to be a reporter.

Listen mate sighed John now much calmer, troops arriving in Northern Ireland are flown into RAF Aldergrove, not sent on a civilian passenger ferry in full fucking uniform, so if she is a bloody reporter then that alone would have set her thinking, I could kick Harry`s arse for being so stupid, fuck knows why we could not simply be flown in.

He considered sharing that Siobahn had known John was Intelligence services but thought it might set him off on another rant so chose to keep it to himself.

We can lie low here until we can safely go out and scout the area said John sourly. We obviously need to find this Eliza Street Market, but can hardly pop into a shop in full kit and ask for a fucking street map, and before you even suggest asking that fuckwit of a priest for help, his input so far has been a total disaster, so from now on we make our own choices okay.

Okay replied Ronnie, you're the boss. Its not about being the boss sighed John, it is about keeping us both alive and Harry gave me specific instructions to bring you back in one piece, not bring back one piece of you. They both laughed and suddenly the tension was gone.

Ronnie made some more tea and passed a mug to John saying, all we need to do is stick to our plan. We recce the area, find out where both the market and this Caitsgill are located, then work out a safe way to rock up unobserved on Yes, I actually agree with you smiled John we can still do this, he took a packet of cigarettes from his side pocket and putting one to his lips lit it. I did not know that you smoked gasped Ronnie. I dont replied John, but desperate times and all that bollocks might help me to think a bit more calmly.

Ronnie stood outside of the doorway on the cobbles drinking his tea, somewhat pointless in their pretending not to be there now he thought, looking across the square he was surprised to see Father O'Brian at the far side almost hidden under the cover of a shop canopy in deep conversation with two men, and strangely showing no sign of alcoholic impediment.

Abruptly the trio broke apart with the two men disappearing down a side street, Ronnie guessed, father O`Brian pulled the bottle from his cassock and after taking a drink, staggered out into the hazy morning sunlight just as an RUC patrol vehicle drove into sight. Waving the bottle at the two officers in the vehicle, the priest lurched away into the far street and the RUC patrol drove off.

Should he share this new information with John, he thought long and hard, John was still tense, and in any case what had he seen, perhaps what he had witnessed was nothing at all, just the priest chatting with people he knew.

But then again, he was now sure that the priest had been faking his drunken, Behaviour, but why and for what possible motive.

Was the priest a covert operative always acting the part of a drunken sop whilst all of the time being the watchful eyes and ears that no one suspected, and if that were possibly true then without doubt it was a great act.

He considered everything that he had seen, and his reasoning that the priest was a fake, but if that were true where did it leave them, and whose side was the priest on. Bloody hell he said to himself. Who is getting jumpy now.

Chapter Ten
On a Mission

After washing both of their tea mugs and realising that John was nowhere to be seen not even in the washroom area, Ronnie went outside and strolled round the little church, which was situated at one edge of the square.

Returning to the doorway he checked inside but there was still no sign of John, so he looked around for signs. To the far side of the square, he could see several streets leading away with the suggestion of shops and businesses being present whilst toward the lower area there was a flower shop and a bakery with a bicycle propped outside.

On the opposite corner to the church was a small public house ironically named the unionist, whilst behind the church and across the top edge shabby terraced houses with garish paintwork to their doors which opened direct onto the cobbles strongly suggested that a degree of poverty pervaded the area.

Apart from two older women both wearing headscarves and carrying wicker baskets near the bakers the square was deserted, then he saw the tramp partly hidden to the side of the pub.

Looking across seemingly at Ronnie he started a slow shuffle towards the church. Now tense, with still no sign of John and growing annoyance Ronnie went back into the church and switched the kettle on.

A croaky voice startled him, and he spun round to see the tramp leaning in the doorway. Spare a few coppers for an old soldier sergeant. Go away old man, the priest is not here. Surely you can give an old soldier something Bless you, croaked the old man, perhaps a mug of tea and some biscuits or cake.

Much against his better judgment Ronnie told the tramp to sit at the table nearest to the door, John will go spastic with me he thought, but then what harm is there in giving the old guy a mug of tea and biscuits, for he had seen a biscuit tin in one of the cupboards, anyway John is not here so I must take responsibility.

Placing the steaming mug of tea and the opened tin of biscuits on the table in front of the old tramp saying kindly, there you go old fella he stepped back outside the church and scanned his eyes around for any sign of John.

Fuck, he said out aloud but to no one in particular. Is everything okay sergeant Lamb croaked the tramp. Thank you for asking yes everything is fine, I am just watching out for someone they will be along any moment. Suddenly realising that the tramp had used his name he rushed inside and grabbed the old man by the hair which came free in his hands.

Johns wicked laugh replaced the tramps croaky voice, making Ronnie relieved and angry at the same time. You bastard he cried, this is no time to play fucking games, we have an important job to do here and all you can do is pull silly stunts and in case you wondered I was worried about you being missing. You are an arsehole Stott a fucking arsehole.

Maybe I am, replied John suddenly becoming serious, but if so, then I am a useful practical thinking arsehole Ronnie. He removed the outer clothing which had concealed his army uniform, and carefully placed them back on the bed of the larger of the UN Observers, saying I am sure he will not mind me having borrowed them.

I do not understand. Ronnie was not sure if he was pleased that John was safe, or still angry that he had tricked him but simply said, so what, if anything, did your little stunt prove, other than the fact that I am a gullible pillock.

Well, Father O`Brian said that Caitsgill was behind Eliza Street Market, did he not queried John. Yes, he did, replied Ronnie but neither of us know where they are, and as we have no maps and can hardly ask, finding out will possibly be the biggest challenge.

Not so dear friend, I know where the market is located, and it is less than a mile away from here, we can easily reach it by walking across the square and up the top street leading away. There are small shops along it and street lighting, but old-fashioned shit which will not give much illumination, so if we are careful, reaching it should be a reasonably safe move.

Well done John, I am sorry that I got annoyed with you, but the truth is I was worried that something had happened to you, I am so glad that it is you on the mission with me, I will try to be less emotive and more focused from now on.

I would like to tell you how clever I am and that I used my years of intelligence training to discover the location of Eliza Street Market, but the fact is that over on the far side of the square there is one of those information boards, you know the type with an arrow saying you are here, so as the great detective used to say, it was elementary Watson.

However, walking the streets even quiet ones, while dressed in uniform is not a good idea, so we stay here until it gets dark, say about twenty-one hundred, then carefully take a stroll up to this market and see if we can locate Caitsgill, now I am off for a shit shave and a shower, you just relax.

After sharing bacon sandwiches for their lunch which they made together, although John cooked the bacon, Ronnie did the washing up and said, I need to tell you something John, but first I need to know why me.

Why you what, replied John laconically. Why me on this mission, you are trained skilled and competent, whereas I am more a liability, some training but not to your standard, and more hindrance to you than helper, why not bring someone more suitable to help recover the cup, I could still have authenticated it back at Harrogate.

John laughed, and if it had proved a fake, everything would be fucked up, and we would be a hundred thousand quid poorer, whilst the bloody IRA would be on a spending spree, so the simple answer to your question is, you need to authenticate the cup before we part with the cash.

What if I cannot, asked Ronnie. Then we worry about that if, or when it happens, for now we have enough to concern us just to set up the meet.

For the record you are a direct descendant, the grandson of Jesse and Daisy Godliman, who Great Grandfather Steiner entrusted the cup to.

He would not have given just anyone the cup, so the Godliman family must be part of the trusted line, and legend states that a true Levite will know the cup by its familiarity when held.

To anyone else it will be a cheap looking rough wooden cup, but to you it will reveal its origin and glory, so you see I have a vested interest in being with you, thirty-nine years ago my grandfather passed the cup to your grandparents for safe keeping, now you are going to get it back for my family.

Now, what were you going to tell me. Oh, its nothing really, probably me being silly. Ronnie had wanted to talk about Siobahn, and the tramp neither apparently being who they seemed, but given Johns now relaxed mood did not want to spoil it, and in any case, he was not totally sure of what he had witnessed.

Try to get some kip said John, we might be out late tonight, and we must be totally focused and sharp when we go out.

Opening his eyes and taking a deep breath Ronnie smelled cooking and rolling onto one side, saw John busying himself at the stove, so climbing from the camp bed he wandered over and said, hmm, smells good, what is it.

Aha, sleeping ugly awakes at last, John smiled, this my trusted companion, is a Spanish Omlette and before you ask it has everything in it, bacon, cheese, onions, mushrooms, tomato, salt and pepper and brown sauce. It sounds disgusting laughed Ronnie as he made a pot of tea, you stick to what you are good at chuckled John, leave the culinary skills to the experts.

Well, you know what they say about experts replied Ronnie, No but I have an awful feeling that I am about to be enlightened sighed John. Ex translates as a Has Been whilst a Spurt is a drip, put under pressure chuckled Ronnie. Very funny, you are just a Spraycan countered John. Sorry, I do not get that connection quizzed Ronnie you will have to explain.

You like to talk posh, nothing wrong in that, but you posh, people call an aerosol a spraycan, air -o sole, get it now, arsehole. Oh you twat John grinned as he saw the smile on Ronnie`s face, just make the tea and sort the fighting irons.

John served up large portions of the yellow pancake. Amazing, quipped Ronnie, not only is it edible, but it also tastes good, you will make someone a good husband, speaking of which I do not know anything about you other than the basics, is there someone special.

Lowering his knife and fork, John reached inside his jacket and withdrew an envelope and passed it to Ronnie. It read, Anne

Raynor at an address in East Yorkshire. Is it serious, asked Ronnie, yes very replied John, we, she is expecting a little John around Easter. Wow that's brilliant mate, what do your family think, are they pleased asked Ronnie.

She is not a Jew sighed John, so you know what it is like, but we hope that they will come around before the wedding. Ronnie did not see why her not being a Jew mattered but said nothing and offered the envelope back. No please keep it said John, If anything happens to me I want you to promise that you will hand it to her personally, no one else but to her in person, do you promise.

Ok but nothing is going to happen to either of us said Ronnie, this is just a low-key operation, no real risk, just handover the cash and go home.

Maybe murmured John but I want your solemn promise, hand it to her yourself. Okay, I solemnly promise replied Ronnie. Good said John now we finish our meal and say no more.

Sitting on the edge of their beds finishing their mugs of tea, John said, give it until twenty-two hundred and then I think it should be safe to risk a trot along to the market. That girl on the boat began Ronnie, Ferry corrected John, to be fully accurate a passenger Ferry.

Whatever sighed Ronnie, but it is just that I have been thinking. Fuck me, he thinks too, smiled John, good humouredly. Funny man, it is just that she said that she recognised my Jimmy.

Did she indeed, John was suddenly alert. Yes, and she also knew that you were in the Intelligence Corps. Now that is interesting, I suppose that you told her we had just met by chance on the ferry.

That is exactly what I told her, was it wrong said Ronnie.

Ask yourself this question sighed John, what chance is there of two unconnected squaddies meeting on a night ferry to Northern Ireland in the middle of what is rapidly becoming a sectarian war.

Not much I suppose grumbled Ronnie acknowledging his lack of common sense and thoughtfulness, but maybe she did not make that connection.

My arse she didn't replied John, and if she is a reporter working for the Belfast Telegraph then I am a Klutz. So what do we do then asked Ronnie, who can she be. I am not sure muttered John, but what I am now certain of is that she followed us onto the ferry, targeted you for information and is watching us, so the other side, whoever they are, know that we are here and why.

Should we try to find her and see what she knows, Ronnie thought this idea might be exciting. I somehow think that she will find us groaned John, let us just hope that it is after we clinch the deal, just be on your guard all the time that is all we can do. And we are not even armed moaned Ronnie, surely that might turn out to be a mistake.

John fished around inside his bag and withdrew a black Sterling Machine Gun, with five full clips of ammunition saying, well, we do have this. Bloody hell mate, where did you get that from, what if your bag had been searched. Well, it was not, and I thought that we might need a little bit of something other than your gob to get us home safe.

At a little after twenty-two hundred they slipped quietly out of the church and hugging the edge of the square quickly entered the top street. As they had expected few people were about and those who were to be seen were obviously going somewhere and paid no attention to them.

Keeping into as much shadow as possible, and occasionally using a doorway for extra cover when anyone came into view, it took some twenty minutes to reach the outskirts of Belfast City Centre, and at a road junction John pointed out an arrow shaped sign on a post which read, Eliza Street Market.

Trotting along the narrow street it suddenly opened into a paved area, similar, to that at that church in Bantry, however this was a lot bigger and the square was covered by canopied market stalls, most with white canvas walls and trestle tables sat on the concrete inside.

Along one full side of the square was a greyish colour stone building with red painted double doors in three pairs set along one side which they presumed to be the access into a covered market hall area.

The square sloped slightly and in the lower far corner was a single storey brick structure with small windows and two entrances each with a yellowish lantern fixed to the wall above, and they instantly recognised this as public toilets.

Across the top edge of the square as in Bantry, shadowy buildings with lights glowing behind closed curtains indicated houses. In the same corner as the toilets and also on the opposite corner across the square were public houses, both with people spilled onto the street outside drinking and smoking the music and gabbled voices gave impression of a relaxed Friday evening drinking with mates.

The public house, or bar as the Irish tended to call them, in the corner near the toilets seemed to be the more popular, and in the dim glow of the lighting spilling from inside, a battered sign, seemingly advertising garage repairs, could be seen hanging by one corner from its wall fixings on the building opposite.

A thorough, eye scan of the entire area, showed no one, other than the drinkers to be in view, and checking his watch John said, twenty-two forty, we need to work our way around the market area to find this Caitsgill, it might be one of those streets at the far side where we can see house lights, we need to find the rear access and make plans to return on Sunday without causing any undue attention okay.

Fine said Ronnie, he found it quite exciting, his first mission, and they slipped silently into the open market area between the stalls. Moving along the rows and working upwards towards the far corner as quietly as they were able, they both stopped dead as the sound of an empty drinks can rolling across the ground drew their attention.

Straining their ears for further sounds, a shabby looking cat trotted past them, phew, breathed Ronnie, that wass..John clamped a gloved palm over his mouth, shh, he whispered. They crept even slower along the row listening for noise, and then heard feint sighs and moans, which got louder as they neared the end of the row.

In the final stall, which was open fronted, laid on her back was a young woman, her skirt was pulled up and bunched around her waist, and standing between her open legs which were hanging over the edge of the table, stood a man with trousers and pants around his ankles.

Fer fecks sake get on with it Liam, the feckin bar shuts soon. In response the man grunted as he thrust his hips forward.

John led him silently away, out of earshot and at the edge of the square he breathed a sigh of relief saying, see Ronnie, how careful you need to be, always on your guard, we do not want to see or be seen, but no harm done this time, just a couple of locals enjoying their Friday night out.

Ronnie gave him a slightly wry smile, John might be the experienced professional with all his undoubted training and experience, but he had caught a glimpse of the supposed local girl, skirt up legs spread, and he knew for absolute certainty, that he would recognise that mop of Raven hair anywhere.

Sliding through the shadows, they found their way out of the market into a side street, distant voices suggested that the bars were closing, and people would be making their way home.

Come on urged John, the priest said Caitsgill was behind the market, but that could be on any side, so we need to check every street around the square and then work outwards until we find it.

Taking the first street on the left side they quietly trotted past the gloomy terraced houses, some with a light still burning behind the curtains, and getting no sign of Caitsgill they took the next left and continued onward. The house has a back access, said Ronnie, so it must have a street behind it.

At last, he uses the brain that God gave him chuckled John, we need to be looking for back-to-back terraces, good thinking mate.

Constantly working left, it took them over an hour to get back to where they had started, and they had made no progress at all, so they worked outwards from the square and repeated the entire process, often having to retrace their steps as streets and alleys became dead ends.

By three am, they were both getting tired it was cold and Ronnie desperately wanted a wee, working their way down the edge of the square he was much pleased to see that the toilets were not closed, and slipping inside he checked both toilet cubicles, before gratefully relieving himself into one of the two stainless steel urinals.

As he headed out, his eye caught sight of a small scrappy card tucked into the top of the chipped mirror which was fixed to the wall above the single wash basin, pulling the card free, he tucked it into his pocket and trotted outside to meet John.

THE CUP

They made their way across the square to the alleyway where they had first entered and were startled by a commotion behind, turning back they saw two small vans had arrived and several people were already starting to pull boxes from the vehicles, whilst one man disappeared into the toilets.

Market traders wanting an early start suggested John. Ronnie nodded and they made their way on up the alley. if those traders had been a few minutes earlier the man in the toilet would have walked in on him Ronnie mused, how close had that been. And realising exactly what Ronnie was thinking, John said, gets the adrenalin flowing doesn't it.

Oh yes, there is never a dull moment with you, now can we please go back I am bloody knackered sighed Ronnie. Do not blame me for the fact that you cannot control your bladder mate, in the desert we shit into a plastic bag and carry it with us, after all if you leave it behind and someone sees it then your covers blown. Ronnie considered the idea of having a bag of his own excrement in his shoulder bag and suddenly felt quite sick.

I did say that your dick would get you into trouble laughed John, but I must admit that I had not considered a bog in Belfast might be the flashpoint. The jog back to Bantry was uneventful and after a well-earned mug of tea, the hard camp beds were much appreciated.

Ronnie was awake first and he filled and switched the kettle on to boil while he used the washroom enjoying the hot shower. Re-entering the main hall area wrapped in just a bath towel he saw John brewing a pot of tea and fussing over the stove. Looking up and seeing Ronnie John called out good morning adding, it will be a Stott special breakfast today.

And what if I may be so bold as to ask, might a Stott special breakfast be then chuckled Ronnie. Omelette of course was the giggled response and they both laughed.

Throwing his towel onto the bed and pulling on the uniform trousers Ronnie asked casually, can you cook anything else. Yes of course I can silly, pancakes, stir-fries, fry-ups, egg banjo's, you name it and Stotts the man to cook it.

Over breakfast they reviewed the events from the previous evening, agreeing that whilst it had not provided any practical results, nonetheless it had offered some live action on the job training especially for Ronnie who now understood the meaning of being constantly alert and observant.

Tonight, we must try much harder to get results said John, we must find Caitsgill and carry out a full recce in advance of the meeting tomorrow, otherwise it will all go for a ball of chalk, I cannot believe the place is so hard to find.

Well, said Ronnie withdrawing the tatty card from his jacket pocket as dramatically as he was able, I might just know how to solve that little conundrum.

Passing the card to John he watched as it was read aloud, Flynn's Repairs, Unit Two, Caitsgill, John stopped reading and looked hard at Ronnie, where on God's earth did you get this.

I would like to tell you that it is the result of my extensive training and observational experiences working with one of, if not the best Army Intelligence officer, but the truth is that I saw it stuck behind the mirror in that public toilet where I could have been spotted last night, so I popped it into my pocket out of curiosity, I did not read it until I was getting dressed this morning.

I also know where it is, or to be more precise I believe that I do. When we were scanning the square for the first time, down in the far bottom corner nearest to the toilet block was a pub, and I think that I saw a garage sign on the wall opposite, if I am correct then there cannot be that many garages in the area, so it must be worth a look.

We will make a proper surveillance sneak out of you, yet my friend chuckled John, good stuff mate we can go straight there tonight and if it proves to be the correct place it will give us much more time to sort out our plan and our escape route.

Ronnie spent the next few hours idling on his bed, constantly running and re-running the previous evenings events through his head, like watching a video cassette over and over again. He kept seeing the black hair and was certain beyond doubt that it had been Siobahn there in Eliza Street Market, but how, and more importantly why.

If it were her, and he was almost positive that it had been, then who was the man, how had they found them, what were they doing there, or were they simply locals enjoying a Friday evening as John believed and just by chance it had been her.

Having enjoyed a somewhat late breakfast or more accurately brunch they skipped the actual midday scoff and made just tea instead. Ronnie tried to talk to John about Anne Raynor, but the topic was seemingly taboo.

He wondered if he should have written something for Sheila, just in case anything happened, perhaps soldiers going on missions always did it, but then this was not really a mission. There would be no interaction with the enemy, no fighting, no one would die, and in any case what would he have written.

Perhaps that he loved her, would miss her, miss the sex, wished that they had been together longer, wished her well for the future, it all seemed so blaise and contrived to him.

In truth he did not spend every waking moment thinking about her, in fact he had spent so much of the time trying to get the mission right that he had hardly given her a second thought.

Still not suffering pangs of real hunger, and eager for the night`s action, John fried up some eggs, bacon and made eggy fried bread from three eggs that he cracked into a plastic bowl. As usual Ronnie made the tea and set the table, a proper little couple he thought, then immediately chided himself, he had heard about men who seemingly preferred other men to women, and the very thought repulsed him. But he did like John, much like having an older brother, and he knew that John would protect him.

As they sat and ate, Ronnie considered mentioning the black hair and how he thought Siobahn might be involved but guessed that John would just chuckle and tell him that he had her on his brain, and that it was highly unlikely that he would ever see her again.

Considering this he realised that he really might like to see her again, it was as if something both mysterious and enchanting surrounded her, exciting and possibly dangerous at the same time. But then again, she was just a woman, how dangerous could she possibly be.

As on the previous evening it was agreed to wait until twenty-two hundred hours before going out, and while they waited for the minutes to slowly tick past, John placed a steaming mug of coffee in front of Ronnie.

I do not drink coffee complained Ronnie, I prefer tea. So do I replied John, but coffee is more of a stimulant, it will make you more attentive and less sleepy.

We need to be at our most observant and keep fully alert, even the smallest error might compromise the whole thing, and for fucks sake Ronnie, have a piss before we go out.

Retracing their movements of the Friday evening, they stood in the shadows looking across Eliza Street Market, the stalls were all empty, and whilst the frames remained, the white canopies and sides, along with the tables had all gone, presumably packed away until the next market was held.

Bollocks, hissed John, much less cover for us, so we work our way around the edge all the way down until we get behind the toilets, no talking and for fucks sake stay close behind me.

As they started to slip across the edge of the square they noticed that here were more people gathered outside the bars and it seemed more lights in the window of the houses.

To avoid the bar in the top corner, it meant traversing the street behind it before making their way back into the square, and as they did so, John suddenly dragged Ronnie onto the floor into an open gateway.

He spluttered, what the f.. then looking up as the passing RUC Patrol Vehicle edged away realised how John`s observance had saved them.

He had not even seen or heard the vehicle, would he ever be good enough to call himself a real spy. Sitting next to each other in someone`s front garden breathing heavily John confided, that was close, they had no lights on the vehicle, even I did not see them until they were right on top of us, we were fucking lucky there mate.

In the shadows secreted between the back wall of the toilet block and the bushes hanging over what was a retaining wall for the buildings beyond, they could quite clearly see the bar and six people standing outside chatting smoking and drinking.

They could hear them talking but not quite make out the actual words, except an occasional louder phrase usually an expletive.

From the frontage of the bar, it was only about twenty-five yards to where they were sat watching, but even though the nearest street lamp was thankfully inoperative, the light spilling from inside the bar added to that emitting from the wall mounted street light on the building opposite, was more than enough to make any sort of movement across the open area to the relative safety of the shadows beyond the far side impossible.

Killing ground muttered John, not a fucking chance. So, now what do we do, asked Ronnie, create a diversion. You read far too many books or watch too many spy movies mate, sighed John sitting down with his back to the wall of the toilets, we wait is what we do. Wait, fumed Ronnie, we might be here for ages.

I did not know that you had a date, sit your arse down and wait, the bar closes in a while, so we wait.

Some twenty minutes had passed when active movement on the bar forecourt stirred them, last orders I guess whispered John, let us hope that they all go inside, two of the women and two of the men took all of the empty glasses and disappeared inside the bar, damn exclaimed John, as the two remaining men exchanged cigarettes.

Suddenly one of the men lurched away from the bar towards them calling out clearly, I am going for a piss, at which the second responded good idea, and followed.

Rising to his feet John instructed Ronnie to follow, saying do not speak, be as light on your feet as possible and keep up with me, we only get one shot at this and if we fuck up, it will be game over.

As the second man disappeared around the front of the toilet block, John grabbed Ronnie by the arm and leapt out of the shadows bouncing on the balls of his feet across the illuminated space and into the comparative darkness of the far side across, and to one side from the front of the bar.

Breathing very heavily Ronnie almost fell against him just as chattering voices declared the return of the drinkers.

That was close wheezed Ronnie. Not at all, piece of cake grinned John, but tomorrow might be a different story, if this is the place, then we cannot come this way, the meeting is at twenty-one hundred, and we cannot be late. We need to find another way in and out or we will find ourselves up shit creek without an oar. Paddle, corrected Ronnie, it is paddle not oar.

Listen you out of breath shit for brains moron hissed John, we need to get in and out tomorrow without getting caught, remember I will be carrying a weapon.

And one hundred thousand pounds in banknotes added Ronnie I can just imagine you trying to explain that away. No dip shit, you will be carrying the money, I will need both hands for the weapon, so let`s cut the banter and see what we can find.

Edging forward into the darkness in what was little more than an alleyway, they quickly came to a dead end and realised that with the side wall of the bar and its rear garden wall and access gate accounting for one side of the alley, the end and other side were solid brick walling running from the end nearest the front of the bar.

Creeping back towards the voices they could make out the garage sign hanging from one remaining wall fixing, Flynn`s Garage was the fading lettering. At least we are in the right place chuckled John, well done mate, all we need now is to find our way around, lift me up.

What said Ronnie. Cup your hands and give me a lift so that I can see over this wall said John.

Why do we not just go round the front and work our way down asked Ronnie. Good luck with that replied John, we have almost been caught out once tonight, and that lot outside the bar will surely see you.

Sorry I was not thinking replied Ronnie lamely. Well then, it's a good job that you are only here to authenticate the cup, leave the thinking to me, now lift me up ordered John.

The rear area was, as John had guessed a concrete yard behind the garage, with a narrower concrete driveway running away into the gloom, which he presumed to be the rear access to the properties alongside of the garage.

There were no lights showing excepting one from an upstairs window somewhere further down the block. Hefting himself up onto the top of the narrow brick wall, John reached down and helped Ronnie scramble up with him, and then both dropped somewhat noisily onto the yard surface below.

Making their way along the rear alley which had a continuous high wall to the left side and the rear garden walls of several houses each with a wooden gate to the other, they came to slightly better lit road junction.

Peering around, they could see that the road which traversed their alley location went away to the left into what was obviously more houses, whilst opposite them the roadside was bounded by a low wall, with thick bushes rising from behind and above, and to their right the road seemed to curve around the front of the row of terraced houses which they were currently sat behind.

Probably goes back past the garage into the square, said John catching Ronnie`s eye sweeping the road, this was where those two vans came from last night, so off to the left there must be other ways to get here.

The road was only dimly lit, with the occasional lamp posts with their fishbowl shaped lanterns glowing a deep orange and creating shadows between each pool of light.

Silently crossing the junction and hugging the scrub covered wall, they made their way to the right and around the front of the terrace, which as they had suspected led up to the bar and square. There were five little houses plus the garage at the end nearest to the bar. Ronnie assumed that originally six houses had been built, but at some time in the past, the end one had been turned into Flynn`s Garage.

All the properties looked tatty and rundown, and several had broken glass in the windows. Ronnie felt sorry for anyone who had no choice but to live here.

There are six properties said John, assuming the garage is not the meeting place, logic says that number six is therefore the end terrace, and as that appears to be the only one with any lights on, my guess is that the others are empty, but we need to check, so come on, keep quiet, we are going back to the rear alley.

Crouched in the alley against the wall opposite to the end house John told Ronnie to stay put and keep quiet while he did some checking, and he slipped away into the gloom.

Some time passed and Ronnie was getting nervous and fidgety when he saw John on the other side of the alley silently open the wooden gate of the end house which creaked slightly, as he vanished inside the garden.

We will be going in the front door tomorrow night said John tersely as he re-joined Ronnie crouching in the rear alley. But we were told to use the back entrance spluttered Ronnie, why change it.

Ask yourself why we need to use the rear garden gate and back door Ronnie, Who, would benefit from it. Maybe the occupier this Seamus Flannagan, doesn`t want anyone seeing us enter, so wishes us to use the more concealed rear entrance suggested Ronnie. Possibly, acknowledged John but I just don`t like it, so we are going in at the front okay.

Surely the front door has a much higher risk sighed Ronnie, anyone watching would be more likely to see us there than round the back here. Exactly said John, so they will then probably try to catch us in a trap when we leave, their problem will be not knowing which way we will exit, whereas if we are committed to entering and exiting the premises by the rear garden, they can ambush us as we leave, we would be unlikely to go in the back secretly, then brazenly trot out of the front.

And so that we have no arguments tomorrow, when we come out the rear exit, we wait where we are now in the shadows to be certain that our visit has not been compromised before we make our way back.

And we go in at twenty-one thirty, half an hour later than planned, that way anyone watching will hopefully get pissed-off and reveal themselves.

Now we need to find a new way back to the church and remember it needs to be registered backwards so that we can use it to get here safely tomorrow.

A stealthy trot through the deserted streets always taking left turns soon bought them out onto a recognised street only a hundred yards from the square in Bantry.

John took a thin black cable tie from a pocket and tied it around a post at the junction, then they made their way silently into the church. Tea biscuits and sleep followed, and Ronnie dropped off quickly.

Sunday was at least for Ronnie a tense and frustrating time, worried that he might somehow make a mistake, or be unable to authenticate the cup, and constantly thinking about Siobahn Flannery.

He tried to convince himself that even if she were somehow involved, what harm could a single young woman possibly do.

At twenty-thirty, John handed him an oversized coat, borrowed from the UN teams clothing, here you are put this on over your

THE CUP

uniform. But we are supposed to be in uniform not disguise moaned Ronnie. And we will be when it matters scolded John, but for now that is far too dangerous.

If we get noticed, most of North Belfast will be out looking for us, and if the RUC do not pick us up first, we will be at the mercy of the IRA and that does not even bear thinking about.

They slipped from the church with coat collars turned up, heads bowed and walked purposefully across the top of the square into the top street, then along until they saw the cable tie where they turned into the side lane and started to reverse the route taken the previous night.

Reaching the entrance to the rear alley behind Caitsgill terrace, having only seen eight people none of whom had paid them any attention, they stood together to take stock and catch their breath. I guess that this sectarian violence makes people nervous said John, did you notice how the few people that we saw actively tried to avoid us.

Yes, replied Ronnie, perhaps we look like IRA thugs. Of course, chuckled John, two men in overcoats, probably concealing weapons, who would want to challenge them, violence or threats of violence makes people extremely nervous.

Well mate, said John as they crouched in as much shadow as possible between two of the cars which were parked to the rear of Flynn`s garage, so far all seems well, let us trust that it all goes according to plan.

At Twenty-One fifteen he stood up and removed his overcoat, gesturing for Ronnie to do the same, and showed for the first time the machine gun he had been concealing.

From the pocket of his overcoat John removed the brick of money and gave it to Ronnie, quipping, and don't spend it all at once, especially not on wine women or song.

Folding the two coats and placing them under one of the vehicles, John started to move away saying, come on Ronnie its time for us to do this.

Remind me to buy you a watch that shows the correct time muttered Ronnie as they quietly made their way back along the rear alley and round to the front of the end house.

A dim light showing through the closed curtains suggested that someone was home, whilst the rest of the row of terraced properties were in total darkness.

Checking the sterling and popping a full clip of ammunition into his belt, John scanned the area, all quiet he breathed, lets go.

Standing directly in front of the front door with John cradling the loaded weapon across his chest stood to one side, Ronnie tapped on the door.

With no answer forthcoming, John used the butt of the sterling to tap louder and they were rewarded with noise of movement from inside. John tapped again, louder this time and the door opened sightly a shaft of light illuminated what they supposed to be a small passageway.

Turn the fucking light off you twat, hissed John, and was rewarded as the hallway was plunged into near darkness. Stepping in front of Ronnie and into the hallway John raised the sterling to waist height and said calmly, good evening paddy Jehovah's Witnesses, and he edged forward ushering the occupant to move backwards.

Calling for Ronnie to follow and close the door behind him, they made their way along the short hallway into the small front room which was lit by a single lightbulb dangling from a short flex from the centre of the ceiling.

Two old armchairs, a small table with two upright wooden chairs pushed underneath, a tiny black and white television on a pedestal in one corner and a two-bar electric fire fixed to the wall made up the entire contents.

John used the gun barrel to push the man backwards into one of the armchairs, saying simply sit the fuck down. You were supposed to be here at nine o`clock and come in by the back way moaned the man. What`s your name paddy said John scanning his eyes over the middle-aged overweight man, who was shabbily dressed in a worn pullover, check shirt and stained, torn at the knee trousers.

Flannigan, Seamus Flannigan, now for the love of Mary Mother of God put the feckin artillery down, guns make me nervous. Do you have it paddy, snarled John. Yes of course, but for fecks sake I am not armed, so put the gun down.

John lowered the weapon slightly so that it pointed more at the man`s groin rather than his chest. Right then let me see it, and just to be clear, if you try anything stupid, I swear that this shithole will need more than a thorough deep clean to remove any little bits of you which remain and are stuck to the walls.

There`s no need to be nasty, the man reached down and slowly withdrew a brown paper bag from under the chair he was sat in. Careful said John raising the weapon again, I warned you.

Open it carefully mate, said John, and Ronnie taking the bag from the man slowly opened it withdrawing a small purple velvet cloth drawstring bag which he then held up for John to see.

Moving behind John, so as not to block his line of fire to the now sweating fat man, Ronnie took the bag to the small table and untying the drawstrings removed the small wooden cup. A greenish blue colour with a short stem and circular base the cup was in its own way fascinating but probably of no real value, not even to a collector.

Is the cup genuine, Johns voice gave indication of the sense of tension each of them was feeling. I do not know said

Ronnie beginning to panic, I cannot feel anything sorry. You bastard, John shouted at the man, you think we are fucking stupid, trying to flog us a fake. I swear that it's real sobbed the man, honest, I stole it myself from Mengle's house, it's real I swear.

Try taking your gloves off mate. Ronnie did as John had instructed instantly being rewarded with a strange tingling sensation running through his whole body, almost like minor electrical pulses. He put the cup down, and the sensations stopped immediately. Picking the cup from the table he replaced it into the bag and tied the strings tightly saying, it is genuine, we did it we really have the genuine cup.

We have not finished yet said John tersely, we still need to get out of here. What about my money, cried the now trembling man. Ronnie took the package from his jacket and threw it into his lap. Feck me was the instant reaction, mind me feckin nuts.

Ripping open the top side of the brown paper to reveal the stacked twenty-pound banknotes, the man put the package to his face and kissed it, saying thank you, I am made for life shall I count it.

Be my fucking guest snarled John, but we will be long gone by the time you even reach the first thousand fuckwit. Turning his head slightly towards Ronnie John said, go out quietly by the back door now and wait in the garden. Unlocking and opening the door from the little kitchen into the rear garden Ronnie stepped outside leaving the kitchen light switched off.

He stood anxiously waiting, but John was only seconds behind him, and closing the door quietly he moved along the garden path and opened the gate holding the top hinge under his gloved left hand so that the squeaky sound was almost inaudible.

Slipping outside and closing the gate behind them they knelt against the wall opposite to the gateway just a few yards from the street junction. I do not trust that man Flannigan one tiny little bit whispered John.

For pity`s sake what have you done to him moaned Ronnie. Nothing that a couple of Anadin and a good night`s sleep will not cure hissed John, now keep quiet and stay alert.

After nearly five minutes crouched there against the wall, apparently satisfied that no threat was present, John stood and motioned for Ronnie to follow. Creeping to the junction of the alley and street, they were about to step out when a sneering Irish voice called out from the darkness.

Well dear Mary Mother of God, what have we got here then, British soldiers hiding outside Seamus Fuckin Flannigan`s house late on a Sunday night, do you think that they have been praying together or might it just be something else.

As Ronnie started forward, a shove in the back sent him sprawling onto the street, and he heard a loud crack.

Everything seemed to happen in double quick time, John also fell to the floor sprawling across his legs with the sterling clattering to the ground in front of them, and the little purple velvet bag which Ronnie had been clutching lying a few feet away. He heard John whisper, shoot them you fucking moron don't just lie there. Then two more sharp cracks followed, and a Raven-haired head appeared in front of Ronnie`s face as she bent to pick up the velvet bag.

Typical of you Jews, I wonder why you always send boys to do a man`s job, it started with David and Goliath I believe, but then of course he was successful, and I am afraid that you are not, oh well to the victor the spoils it seems.

Ronnie looked directly into her face as she tucked the cup away inside her zippered jacket. Thanks for this and all your help, and for what it`s worth I really am truly sorry about your friend here.

Bitch snarled Ronnie bitterly. That might well be considered to be true, she smiled as she put the 9mm pistol into her handbag and hooked it over her shoulder. But always remember Ronnie I am the Bitch who saved your life, and if your famous wartime songstress was right, who knows, maybe we will meet again.

Chapter Eleven

Aftermath

It was after two in the afternoon when Harry arrived at Bantry barracks, accompanied by two other uniformed men, one a captain in the Intelligence Corps.

Sitting at one of the tables with a mug of tea, and Harry having introduced the men as Captain Aldridge and Warrant Officer Miles both Army Intelligence the de-briefing began.

Ronnie slowly and seemingly factually, recounted his and John`s arrival on the Friday morning and the subsequent encounter with father O`Brian, the priest`s information about a British Government sympathiser, who wanted assistance in pulling together an influential group who might be able to broker a lasting peace deal, and how the meeting needed to be held in total secrecy given the current level of sectarian dissidence.

He shared details of how John had led the two reconnaissance evenings and then the fateful evening meeting with Seamus Flannigan, his provision of a list of potential peace sympathisers, which John had suggested Flannigan keep for now as this was a simple fact-finding mission, and any future contact would negotiate at that level.

He explained that after saying their goodbyes, Flannigan had requested them to leave by the rear garden, as in his words, you never know who might be watching.

He gave details as best as he was able. How, as they made their way along the rear alley, shots had been fired and John returned fire before falling to the ground. Then of course the arrival of the RUC followed a while later by soldiers from the Parachute Regiment who had secured the area and transported him back to Bantry church barracks.

Captain Aldridge asked how much Flannigan was asking for the list of alleged peace sympathisers, to which Ronnie replied he was not sure but a figure of five thousand pounds had been suggested by Flannagan, to which John`s response had been. Not in my remit, as I have said this is an initial factfinding exercise, if it goes forward money will be discussed then.

Warrant officer Miles asked who had been carrying the sterling, to which Ronnie replied truthfully John, and when asked how many shots had been fired, he again truthfully replied that he had heard only three.

What about your own weapon sergeant Lamb, asked Captain Aldridge. To which Ronnie replied, that as a fact-finding mission only, they had deemed it inappropriate for them both to carry weapons, and in truth they had hoped for a totally discreet meeting, which had it gone to plan might have been useful to encourage future peace progress.

That was a bloody stupid decision in my opinion snorted Warrant Officer Miles, Belfast is hardly Blackpool, any number of situations might have arisen where a firearm was required.

You are obviously correct sir, Ronnie tried to sound as contrite as he possibly could. But having been instructed to keep the entire mission as low key as possible, it was a decision that we both agreed with, albeit that even if I had been carrying a weapon nothing would have turned out differently.

As a matter of interest, why were you not hit sergeant Lamb, said Captain Aldridge. Because John Stott shoved me out of the line of fire almost certainly saving my life replied Ronnie, he deserves a medal.

One final question sergeant said Aldridge as he closed the small folder that he had been scribbling into, I understand that you are in fact Signals Corps rather than intelligence, was there a particular reason for your inclusion on this mission. Yes sir, John Stott had suggested that I might be suitable for Intelligence work so we trained together, and he included me for the trip as he believed it to be just routine, a low level intelligence gathering with minimal risk, as instructed and sanctioned by Lieutenant Colonel Critchley.

Colonel Critchley sanctioned the mission, well in that case I believe that we are all done here said Aldridge, goodbye sergeant and please accept my regrets at your loss of a colleague and friend.

As the others made their way to the door Harry pulled Ronnie aside. That was some bullshit son, even by my standards it sounded almost true, but including Critchley`s name might have been a mistake, what if they check. I doubt that they will, replied Ronnie and even if they do, he is up to his fucking neck in this shit, so chances are that he will simply accept the responsibility for a mission gone wrong.

We need to talk, you fly home from RAF Aldergrove this evening, a Landrover will collect you so be ready, we can meet tomorrow in the hut and before you even think about keeping to the same story, the two dead Irishmen were both only carrying 9mm pistols, and they and the dead Flannagan were all shot by a single bullet between the eyes also from a 9mm pistol.

John was carrying a fucking sterling, which incidentally had not been fired, so I want to know exactly what happened and who killed fucking who, okay.

At the airfield Harry was already there with John`s coffin which had been draped in a Union Flag, and once Ronnie had climbed from the vehicle, six dress uniformed para`s "quick marched" to the side of the RAF Hercules transport plane and after carefully lifting the coffin, solemnly "slow marched" it aboard.

Harry motioned for Ronnie to board and carrying both his and John`s holdall`s he climbed into the cavernous open area of the huge plane and took a seat along one side of the fuselage, Harry sat next to him whilst the six paras sat opposite, and John`s coffin was secured on the floor between.

Doors closed, engines roared and what seemed ever so slowly, the huge cargo beast lumbered into the night sky. We need to talk one to one, murmured Harry, tomorrow morning but say nothing to anyone about this until we set our stories straight. Ronnie said nothing, and simply nodded his understanding, and the eighty-minute flight passed in total silence.

After watching the Para`s carry John`s coffin from the plane and load it into the waiting hearse, saluting as it drove slowly away, Ronnie climbed into the waiting Landrover to be greeted by the driver offering his condolences. Sorry I do not want to talk about it said Ronnie, and after the soldier muttered his understanding, the journey was completed without conversation.

Blythe bought his morning tea and similarly offered his regrets, asking if there was anything Ronnie needed, to which he somewhat tersely replied no, with a belated thank you, mentally noting to apologise to Blythe later.

After making a pot of tea, he was drinking his second cup when Harry arrived, make mine bloody strong was the growled instruction, we have some serious discussions ahead.

Taking a sip of the steaming brew Harry spoke. Right then, forget all the crap that you so convincingly ladled out to the debrief team, this is me, us, I need to know exactly what happened, the truth. Even if it was your fault I need to know and leave nothing out however seemingly trivial, I want both chapter and fucking verse okay.

Ronnie dutifully recounted everything from their boarding the ferry in Stranraer, the meeting with Siobahn, Father O'Brian, John's expert subterfuge skills, the two reconnaissance nights including the tart in the market with the Raven hair, and all the events of the fateful Sunday meeting, including how he believed John to have saved his life by pushing him.

Harry listened intently without interrupting him even once, then sat silently as if digesting everything that he had just heard.

Okay firstly, whatever guilt that you currently feel, John's death was not, I repeat for clarity not your fault, so you stop feeling guilty and sorry for yourself right now and focus on the problem okay. Yes, sighed Ronnie.

Good, let us review the events and try to put some sense to what appears to be a series of disconnected happenings. As John shared with you, this Flannery woman meeting with you on the ferry was obviously no mere coincidence.

However much you see yourself as a magnet to a pretty woman, she had targeted you as a means of getting information, the question being not why, but who was she working for, or as I suspect, was she the opposition, working alone or with a single accomplice.

Everything had gone apparently according to John's planning, and you had the cup, already authenticated, in your possession when the two Irishmen accosted you. if as suggested John had incapacitated Flannigan temporarily, where did they appear from, was it just chance, or were they tipped off and if so by whom.

There were three shots heard by you, all similar sounding, which concords with the evidence of three 9mm rounds being fired, but as John was carrying a sterling, you were apparently unarmed and the two 9mm pistols carried by the Irishmen had not been fired recently, then by a process of elimination it suggests that this Flannery woman fired all three shots.

Each of the three were killed with a single shot to the head, so assuming that this woman was responsible, then she is an extremely good shot, professional marksman level maybe even better. Whoever fired the shots, it seems clear that they did not want witnesses left alive, and that of course included Flannigan, who arguably did not even see the Irishmen.

So, you are saying that Flannigan was shot as well, exclaimed Ronnie, John told me that he had knocked him unconscious. Yes, and I have no reason to doubt John's version sighed Harry, sadly for Flannigan someone else was doing the cleaning up operation.

But I only heard three shots, insisted Ronnie, if Flannigan had been shot, we would have heard the noise. Not necessarily if as we suspect, the gun was buried in a cushion, after all Flannigan was not going to resist, John had seen to that.

So, what you are saying is that after we left the house, Siobahn entered, killed Flannigan, then came outside and killed the two Irishmen as well as John before taking the cup.

That is about the size of it, and do not forget the money, the black-haired lady now has both the cup and one hundred thousand pounds in used banknotes, we have been well and truly fucked over.

I guess that is the end of it sighed Ronnie, I am sorry that John died and that we were so close to success but we can do nothing now, the cup has gone, the money has gone, and we have lost John, we lose.

Fuck that shouted Harry, no way are we giving up, that woman killed John and stole both the cup and the money, so you owe it to John, if not the rest of our group to appease his death and get the cup back.

But where do we start moaned Ronnie, she is probably long gone, and the only thing we know for certain is that the cup is genuine.

Are you totally certain about that encouraged Harry, I mean one hundred per cent, not ninety or more but as if your life depended upon it.

Yes, I am sure, Ronnie recounted how the tingling had surged through his body once he had removed his gloves, and Flannigan told us that he had personally stolen it from the house of someone called Mengele.

Mengele, breathed Harry, bloody hell, so that bastard hid himself in Ireland did he, it is a pity that Flannigan only stole the cup and did not think to execute him, but then I guess he had no knowledge.

Ronnie desperately wanted to ask what knowledge Harry had referred to, and who was this Mengele, but considered this was probably not the right time.

You mentioned John giving you a letter for Anne Raynor, give it to me and I will see that she gets it said Harry. That is kind replied Ronnie, but he made me promise to hand it to her personally. But I know her and we would have been family replied Harry, I am sure that John would not mind me passing it on.

You are probably right sighed Ronnie, but a promise is a promise and I owe John at least that much, and to be honest after everything is considered, he saved my life by pushing me out of the way.

He did not save your life snapped Harry, he fell into you when the pistol shot hit him in the side of the head, and because it was a side of the head strike, he lived for a few seconds, just enough to tell you to use the sterling and save yourself, whereas the Irishmen were hit between the eyes, dying instantly.

As I have already acknowledged this was some marksmanship by anyone's standards, and in the dimly lit conditions with only a 9mm pistol at around twenty yards, my guess is an expert professional, be aware Ronnie this woman is certainly dangerous.

Why was my life spared asked Ronnie, as if suddenly understanding the enormity of everything that had recently happened.

That, I am not sure about, sighed Harry, but from what you have said the woman obviously thinks that you might be useful in the future. Perhaps they have no one to authenticate the cup, who knows, but one thing is for sure, we find her and exact revenge for John, as well as recovering the cup.

John's funeral is at his local family church in Yateley Hampshire, on Friday afternoon at thirteen hundred. A driver will collect you from the gatehouse at seven am, he will have directions.

You are to wear full dress uniform, any questions asked of you are to be given vague answers, John was the professional and you were just the backup, and communications expert, nothing more.

One last thing said Harry as he left the hut, pack all your personal stuff and bring it with you, leave a change of clothes on the top. Leave all the army kit folded on the bed in your bunk, this part of our mission has run its course.

Okay said Ronnie, and I am really sorry about John.

We all are sighed Harry, but as I have already explained his death was not your fault, we simply totally underestimated the level of professionalism and cold calculated planning that the opposition had managed.

We were as the saying goes, caught with our trousers down, or as your black haired lady friend explained so succinctly, using boys to do a man`s job, and that analogy is no disrespect to either of you, quite simply you were going to lose even before you started, the opposition was too well organised and too ruthless.

What happens now then, I mean to me and the mission. We were fucked over this time said Harry, stepping through the now open hut door, that will not happen again I promise, and as for you, we stay on the trail of the cup and the woman, I will be sorting everything, we can chat at the funeral.

Looking smart in his dress uniform and carrying his beige colour suitcase and leather holdall, Ronnie was waiting in the cold when the dark green army staff car pulled up at the gatehouse. Hop in sergeant said the uniformed driver, I suggest the rear so that you have the room, it will be a long journey.

The big car with red leather upholstery purred away and soon they were on the A1 heading south. At Doncaster they switched to the M18 then onto the M1 and continued southward. At Trowell service station near Nottingham, they stopped for tea and a toilet break, but were soon back on the road.

From the M1 near Northampton they took the A43 across country to join the main North to South A34 arterial route which went to Southampton, eventually pulling into the entrance of Upper Heyford RAF base where Harry was waiting at the gate.

In the car Harry appeared deep in thought and did not even acknowledge Ronnie`s good morning. Passing the Harwell Nuclear Facility just south of Oxford he spoke.

You are to be as formal as possible Ronnie instructed Harry tersely, we have no idea who might be present today.

Surely now that they have both the cup and money, possibly the shroud as well they will have no interest in us replied Ronnie.

What they know, Harry was seemingly part emotional and part angry, is that we will do everything within our power to recover the cup. The money is probably not going to be reclaimed, but fortunately for us the guys managed a decent heist, so money is not one of our worries.

They also know that they got lucky this time, and as I have promised that will not happen again. For whatever reason they still need you alive, at least for now, remember that you can identify the woman, she will want that loose end tied up at some point.

So then, I am some sort of bait then to lure her out of hiding. From what limited detail I already know of the woman muttered Harry, she is unlikely to be hiding, unless it is in plain sight, and she will know where you are and what you are doing all the time. You must be constantly on your guard, no one and I repeat no one should be accepted at face value.

When we find her, or she finds us, what then asked Ronnie. Then my friend, we show her exactly how pissed-off we are at her ruthless actions, and ask her, where we can find the cup said Harry. And if she will not tell us, queried Ronnie.

Then we persuade her, and once we are certain that we have all the information she has to offer, you take revenge for John`s execution.

Ronnie was not sure that he could kill the woman, whatever she had done, he was not even sure that he could kill anyone, but today was certainly not the time to share such thoughts with Harry.

THE CUP

Perhaps sensing some of his thoughts Harry touched his arm and said, that woman murdered four men in cold blood. However you want to wrap it up, even if the two Irishmen and John were collateral damage, the seller of the cup whilst a thief, was just a greedy prat, did he deserve to be executed for that.

And please do not kid yourself that for some romantic or sexual reason she let you live. She would have, and will kill you as and when you are no longer useful, so for fucks sake make sure that you never let her get the upper hand again.

Did you bring your personal belongings asked Harry. Yes, they are in bags in the car boot Ronnie replied. Good, after the wake, the driver will take you back to Harrogate. When you stop, get changed into civvies and leave your uniform in the car, the driver will return it.

Harry passed Ronnie a vanilla envelope. Name and address of your new lodgings in Harrogate, introduction letter to your new employer, interview is next Monday 18th December, plus a thousand pounds in cash to tide you over, and the army will honour your final pay.

So, I am no longer in the army, or a soldier said Ronnie a little shocked. Harry laughed out aloud, no, certainly not, none of this ever happened, no pension, no one-off payment, nothing, except that your university course continues, and of course we keep moving forward with the mission.

What is my new job, Ronnie asked in a somewhat excited manner. Sorry I truly have no idea replied Harry, but I am sure that you will soon fit in. And remember we will always keep our eyes on you and find you when we need to act, meanwhile get on with your life, now "heads up" we are here.

The Funeral was being held in the village where John's family had their home, and the little church was packed. Smartly uniformed soldiers from the Intelligence Corps carried the flag covered coffin into the church and set it across three wooden trestles before taking their seats, and Ronnie, looking around could see that a lot of those present wore uniform of some description.

A Brigadier also from Intelligence delivered a rather touching eulogy ending with the poignant statement that John had as always been willing to put others first and in so doing had laid down his own life for his country.

Ronnie considered this and thought it to be both pious and in John`s case untrue, at least as far as Queen and country went. But then he supposed John`s past service must have counted for something. John`s siter Hannah gave a moving tribute to her brother and shared happy memories before the congregation stood up and sang "abide with me", as the soldiers took up and slowly marched the coffin outside.

The family were understandably gathered closest around the open grave, and Ronnie was grateful to be almost at the back of the mourners. As the Vicar gave his prepared statement about dust and ashes it began to rain. How absolutely perfect thought Ronnie, John would have liked the idea of everyone getting soaking wet through just to say goodbye to him. He had once said to Ronnie, everyone else gets the glory, it always seems to rain on my parade.

The wake was a buffet affair held in the church hall, and the rain had stopped meaning that people were able to spill outside to relieve the squash in what was quite a tiny room. Ronnie carried his plate of sandwiches and sausage rolls around trying to work out which of the several younger ladies present might be Anne Raynor, but no suitable candidate was to be seen and he felt it would be inappropriate to ask.

John's sister Hannah suddenly appeared next to him and asked quite brusquely, if he were the soldier who had been with John in Belfast.

Confirming her guess to be true, he was suddenly slapped hard across the side of his face as Hannah shouted, you bastard, I hate you, why are you alive while John is gone, why could you not have saved him.

Several guests put their arms around her and ushered her away, and Ronnie suddenly felt that everyone was looking at him. Seeing Harry deep in conversation with the Brigadier, he slipped away found his driver and was soon starting to breathe more easily as they headed back north.

When they stopped at another motorway service station, Ronnie used the washroom to exchange his dress uniform for civilian clothes before having something to eat and drink, although he felt neither hungry nor thirsty.

The car sped north and sometime after twenty-hundred they reached the outskirts of Harrogate from the Knaresborough road side. Passing the driver the address for the lodging house Ronnie was rewarded with a, sorry sergeant I don't know Harrogate. Reading the address again, and from the word Bilton, which he knew to be an area he rode through when he cycled back to camp from Sheila's, he directed the driver along the same route. As luck would have it they found it quite quickly.

The house was a three storey Victorian dwelling along the main road, and while the driver waited, Ronnie trotted up to the front door and rang the bell.

A reddish faced plump woman who he guessed to be in her fifties opened the door immediately saying, hello you must be Ronnie. He waved to the driver who jumped from the car and fetched the two bags, then said goodnight.

Well come in, said the lady, we do try to keep the house warm. Stepping inside and putting his bags onto the floor Ronnie held out his hand, which she took. Nice to meet you, and yes, I am Ronnie. She gave a broad smile, Mrs Hughes, but Doreen to my friends and of course my guests.

Nice to meet you then Doreen said Ronnie, I apologise that we are late, but we have been to a funeral in Hampshire. Yes I know, she smiled again, it must have been a long journey, anyway I will show you the room then make some tea.

His room was on the second floor overlooking the front, the top floor being an attic style area with just one bedroom. His room was furnished with a double wardrobe, three quarter size bed, chest of four drawers, a soft based upright chair and a small china washbasin fixed to the wall with a narrow glass shelf above it and a wall mounted mirror.

The toilet and bathroom are just along the passageway said Mrs Hughes, now I will pop into the kitchen and make some tea, do you like fruit cake, and not waiting for an answer she started away down the stairs calling out, just come down in a minute love.

Ronnie used the toilet, swilled his face with water and then went downstairs, the kitchen was at the rear on the ground floor and Doreen was standing by the worktop brewing tea while an attractive, thin, blonde-haired woman sat at the large farmhouse style kitchen table eating some fruit cake.

Amanda meet Ronnie, and Ronnie meet Amanda my other guest. Doreen placed a mug of tea and a plate with a large slice of fruit cake onto the table, gesturing for Ronnie to sit, she placed a mug of black coffee in front of the blonde woman then said, right I am off to bed see you both at breakfast, and then as if an afterthought rummaged in her housecoat pocket and handed a set of two keys to Ronnie, small key is your room the other is for the front door, goodnight. And she was gone.

THE CUP

They sat for a few awkward moments with Amanda sipping her coffee and looking at him. Who lives here then, he finally broke the silence. Just me and Mrs Hughes, Doreen, and of course now you, oh and the two Siamese cats, the chocolate colour one is called pepper and the grey is called salt said the young woman. Oh, how very original chuckled Ronnie, so just the three of us, no Mr Hughes.

She, Doreen, was widowed some years ago. Apparently it was an accident at the factory where he was working but I don't know any details. I do know that she is keen to rent out the other two rooms, as while we do okay, money can be tight sometimes. No big pay-out from her husband's accident then asked Ronnie, surprised at his seeming callousness. No, she said that there was no insurance and the company deemed it to be his own fault, why do you ask, are you in that line of work.

Sorry, no I am not, just plain inquisitive I guess, what about you, have you lived here long, what do you do for work. Well, I must say, you are certainly very forward, but if we are going to live together, I suppose we need to know something about each other. After all you might be a serial sex maniac who will regularly come to my top floor attic room and ravish me, its small but quite cosy.

An interesting concept conceded Ronnie, but for tonight my libido is I am afraid, overpowered by tiredness, it has been a long and somewhat emotional day.

I have been attending the funeral of my best friend. Ronnie considered adding only friend but on balance decided this would far too truthful and demeaning.

Yes I know, Doreen told me that you were coming here straight from a funeral, a fellow soldier I understand. Ronnie knew that Harry had arranged this lodging but was still surprised how much they, or at least this Amanda knew about him. The funeral was okay I guess but as you can imagine the family were quite upset, and it was in Hampshire so a long journey.

You said that Mrs Hughes, Doreen was keen to rent the other two rooms, is no one interested asked Ronnie. There has been a little bit, but no one suitable, she does not want unemployed people however clean looking living here, after all that would only mean even more drain on the household`s meagre budget.

She was so grateful that you paid six-months rent in advance, and in cash. We will certainly eat well for Christmas, and for the next few weeks afterwards at least, and Christmas is of course only next weekend

Bloody Harry thought Ronnie, he certainly seemed to cover all eventualities. Sipping his mug of tea Ronnie looked directly at Amanda saying, you have not yet told me how long you have lived here and what you do for work.

Well Mr nosy parker, I am called Amanda, Amanda Collier, I have lived here nearly a year, I work in the Midland bank in the town, and before you ask, no, I don't currently, have a man in my life.

Do you know Harrogate well, asked Ronnie, it`s just that from your accent I guess that you were not born locally. Yes, I know it reasonably well now, Amanda smiled at him, certainly the town centre area, and as you guessed I am originally from Newcastle.

The Geordie accent was the giveaway smiled Ronnie. Moron, she smiled back, Geordies are from Wearside, the areas around Sunderland. I am a Newcastle girl and proud of it, so come on mystery man, what about you, where do you hail from.

Oh here and there, everywhere, and then of course nowhere, you know how it is said Ronnie. Aha a mystery man, I quite like that, I guess I shall just have to discover your hidden secrets, what do you do for work.

Ronnie was somewhat taken aback, she had already suggested him to be a soldier, so immediately on his guard replied, I work for a company called Maxon, just down the hill.

How marvellous she giggled, they bank with us isn't that amazing, what a coincidence and I am their account manager.

Of course you are Ronnie sighed, Harry could sometimes be such a pain in the arse.

Do you have someone special in your life she cooed or are you available.

Ronnie was certain that she already knew of Sheila, probably where she lived, worked and the type of knickers she wore, even how often she washed them, but he was dammed if he was going to sit and play silly games, he was too tired.

I am engaged to a local girl, hence the reason for being here in Harrogate, but in truth I am not sure that marrying her is what either of us want, now if you will excuse me, it has been a tiring day and I still need to unpack my toothbrush, so I will bid you goodnight.

Goodnight mystery man, breakfast at weekends is between 8am and 9.30, during the week between 7am and 8.30, so I expect I will see you tomorrow, but I work some Saturday mornings so will have left by 9.30. I will wash the crockery so don't worry.

It took him only a few minutes to unpack his clothes and put them on the steel wire coat hangers in the wardrobe, with socks and hankies into one of the drawers, he stowed the suitcase on top of the wardrobe and the holdall under the bed, then taking his wash things trotted along to the bathroom.

The bed was surprisingly comfortable, and he slept well, rising at half past seven he used the bathroom before dressing and going down into the kitchen. Mrs Hughes and Amanda were already there with Amanda making tea or coffee whilst the landlady had the toaster going and was grilling bacon. Good morning, the two women said almost together, and added Tea or Coffee, is a full English breakfast okay.

Amanda left around twenty past nine for her job in the bank, and while washing up Mrs Hughes asked if he would be needing evening meals. He had not even considered that requirement, as so far in his life things like that had been simply available, now he realised, things might be different, so he said yes please.

Well normally Amanda arrives home from work around half past five, so I try to have dinner on the table for six thirty will that suit you, tonight we can have some gammon steaks with fried eggs and fried potatoes if you like. He said thank you and that he would be back later then taking his coat walked to Sheila`s house.

Hugs, kisses and a few tears later, she confessed that knowing he was to be in Northern Ireland, and after hearing on the radio news that a soldier had been killed in Belfast, they had telephoned the camp to get information, but had been told that whilst it could be confirmed that a soldier from Pennypot had tragically died whilst on duty in Belfast no further details were available at that time.

Well, it is all done and dusted now said Ronnie, I have left the army and have a job here in Harrogate at Maxon on the Ripon road. I have a room in Bilton, but before you ask, the landlady frowns upon lady guests, possibly male guests as well, but she didn't mention that.

Sheila smiled and hugged him, we don't need your room she said, we have here, and this time next year we will have our own home, wont that be wonderful, this is going to be the best Christmas ever. Shit, muttered Ronnie to himself, I need to go shopping for Christmas presents.

THE CUP

On Monday morning at nine am, he presented himself at the Maxon factory and was interviewed and then shown around by John Apsom the factory production manager. You will start tomorrow in the electrical department and then staedily work your way through all departments so that you have a broad understanding of all processes that make our equipment work, your role then will be as our field commissioning and service engineer.

You will be given a vehicle which you may use privately and a card to purchase fuel, although you must keep receipts and you will be on-call to attend any client across the country from Scotland down to Cornwall which will mean staying away sometimes is that all ok.

Yes of course, thank you said Ronnie, but one small thing, I can drive as I was trained in the army at Pennypot but I do not have a civilian license, will that be a problem. Not at all, we will get it sorted, eight thirty am start tomorrow, and wear suitable work clothes.

Walking into town he felt exuberant, he now had a job, hopefully with a certain amount of freedom, a vehicle, van he guessed but that was fine, and what seemed to be an interesting role to fill, perhaps his life was finally going to settle into what others called normality.

He spent several hours in the shops buying what he hoped were suitable gifts. Purchases included a selection of assorted chocolates for Mrs Hughes in a posh box with pull out drawers, and on impulse a gift wrapped bottle of expensive "Rive Gauche" Eau de Parfum, for Amanda.

In the Library he was greeted by a warm, More Religious Studies. Not this time he smiled do you have anything on the Maxon factory here in Harrogate. What is it that you wish to know asked the librarian.

Oh, the usual sort of thing he said, what they make, how long have they been here, is it worth trying for a job there.

That factory caused quite a fuss when it opened two years ago said the Librarian, what with Menwith Hill being just up the road, everyone was up in arms saying that the Americans were taking over. In any case why might you want a job, I thought that you were in the army.

Just keeping all my options open Ronnie said, adding and why should people think the Americans were taking over. Well now, what with Menwith being a secret radar tracking station run by the Americans and Maxon being a specialist gas and off-shore exploration systems manufacturer also owned and run by the Americans what else were we locals expected to think.

I mean Harrogate was a sleepy market town before this all started.

Ronnie had never heard of Menwith Hall, but if the local librarian knew all about it, he doubted that it had any real level of secrecy, but Maxon being owned by an American company might prove useful.

Lost in his thoughts the librarian added, and of course Fylingdales is not really that far away either so everyone thinks that they are all somehow connected.

Heavens, he thought to himself, first it is secret societies trying to obtain ancient religious relics, now American secret operations, why can I not have a normal life, his life was stranger than fiction, you simply could not make it up, and if you did, then no one would ever believe a word.

In the market hall coffee shop with the requisite mug of tea, he was pleasantly surprised when Amanda sat down opposite him. I thought that you worked, in a bank wasn't it he chuckled.

Likewise, she responded, as it happens, I often pop in here at lunchtime, it is much cheaper than the posh coffee shops and contrary to what you probably think, I am a humble accounts clerk, so I have to watch what I spend.

A humble bank clerk who wears expensive designer clothes thought Ronnie, but said aloud, Well that makes sense, as for me I have taken some time out to do my Christmas shopping. he indicated the bags on the floor near his feet.

You never did tell me what you did at Maxon, I bet that it is something secret and exciting simpered Amanda. Not at all replied Ronnie, I am just a helping hand for whoever needs it, you know the sort of thing, a bit of this and a bit of that to help the experts.

Finishing her sandwich and drink she stood up, that`s my mystery man, I shall have to work much harder on you I can see, but I must go, as I too have Christmas shopping. She walked away then turned her head back towards him saying, I do hope that there is something for me in your bag`s mystery man, Shalom Ronnie.

Finishing his tea Ronnie considered things, everyone knew that Shalom was the Jews word for peace, and they often used it to each other as a parting expression, but not, as far as he knew with non-Jews, and why would a non-Jew use it.

Amanda Collier did not sound Jewish, but as Harry had said trust no one. Had he placed Ronnie in that house so that Amanda could keep an eye on him, was she working for Harry or someone else.

She might of course be quite genuine, but if so, what reason did she have for being in Harrogate, and was she really from Newcastle. Not for the first and probably not the last time in his relatively short life Ronnie felt totally confused.

Tuesday saw Ronnie waiting outside John Apsom`s office, which was in one corner of the factory area, he was dressed in a plain shirt, grey trouser`s and black oxford brogue shoes. A tall thin gangly man with a receding hairline ambled across the factory floor and introduced himself as Rob Milland the Electrical supervisor, adding you are starting with us in the sparks department, so if you come with me, I will get you sorted.

The electrical department was a smallish room with six workbenches in two rows of back-to-back formation. Racks of cable and shelves stacked with all types of electrical items adorned the walls, and on some of the workbench sets, stood steel control panels each part completed, with wiring diagrams pinned to the back of the bench or taped to the wall.

A much larger panel stood on the floor, with open doors and a steel base plate propped against it, this will be your first job said Rob. You will be laying out the various parts onto the baseplate, adding the plastic cable trunking between each row to allow wiring interconnection, then fitting it into the panel. Later you can drill and install the lamps into the panel fascia, and we can start wiring it to the drawing.

They stepped across to one of the benches where a young curly haired man was working on one of the panels, drawing cable into the installed trunking. This is Peter, he is our panel wiring expert, he will give you any pointers that you might need.

Ronnie simply stared at the man, he was dressed in tight leather trousers, a fancy brightly coloured shirt with a frill down the front, which was open to mid-chest topped off with a large gold medallion hanging around his neck.

Ignoring the stare Peter held out his hand and shook Ronnie`s firmly, ignore Rob, I am the only panel wirer, and as you will find, we no only wire the panels, we then mount them onto the equipment which the fitters build, wire the panels to all of the electrical kit installed on the equipment, before finally testing that everything works as it should before it gets shipped out.

Ronnie was still staring, and Peter laughed, don't worry Ronnie, you aren't my type, I prefer older more mature men, like Rob here, he gestured at the tall supervisor. In your dreams you fancy little ponce, chuckled Rob seemingly good humouredly, now let me show you around Ronnie.

They walked around the factory and he was introduced to the factory supervisor, Brian Wild, the Machine Shop supervisor Charlie, and the man who hand built the control valves Pat Bayle.

They looked at the washrooms, the small kitchen with a table where they could eat lunch, and the free vend machine which dispensed tea, coffee and chocolate.

Walking back towards the electrical room Rob said, Peter is Italian, he is a bit loud and "in your face", but he is harmless, just ignore him if he gets too personal, or speak to me okay. In the room Rob asked Peter to sort drinks for the three of them, and Ronnie asked for tea with one sugar. So, a white coffee then replied Peter, trust me the tea is undrinkable, and certainly does not taste like tea.

Bringing the three drinks on a small cardboard tray which had been the lid of a box at some time, Peter asked, where are you from. The home counties a little way north of London replied Ronnie.

And is it true that you are going to be our mobile commissioning engineer continued Peter. That is the plan agreed Ronnie, but first I need to learn the basics in all the various stages of equipment manufacture, so that I will be able to fault find out on site.

I would have loved to have been given the chance at that job moaned Peter, no one here even knew that we were looking for someone.

To be honest the projects we have completed so far are all part of a big installation in Scotland, something to do with North Sea Gas. But the plant is not due to start work until later this year, so perhaps that is where you will be going first, that large panel is part of the job.

Rob interrupted them, school's not out boys, it's time we did some work, and as for you being the company commissioning engineer, do you seriously think that our American owners would want a shirt lifting fairy like you as their ambassador, you can see why they chose Ronnie, smart, well-spoken and polite, so get over yourself and get back to work.

The large panel had various drawings folded inside it, one of which said, baseplate layout, and Ronnie concluded that it was not difficult to follow. The various items needing fixing to the baseplate were stacked in boxes to the side, and the trunking, screws, and nuts and bolts were to be found on racks along the back wall, so by the end of the day using the comprehensive tools on his two bench area, Ronnie had completed the baseplate installation and Rob told him that it was a good job, well done.

After washing and changing his clothes he joined Mrs Hughes and Amanda in the kitchen and enjoyed the Lancashire Hot-Pot which she had cooked, even the dumplings or dough-boys as she called them. Rather than paying for your evening meals would you perhaps do some maintenance jobs around the house asked Mrs Hughes.

Ronnie had agreed with Sheila that they would see each other Saturdays and Sundays, sometimes for Sunday lunch, then on Tuesday and Friday evenings, leaving Ronnie free for football training on Mondays, and with Wednesday and Thursday for anything else that he needed, so he readily agreed to try and fix any odd jobs.

So are you visiting your lady friend tonight asked Amanda, yes replied Ronnie, Tuesdays and Fridays plus weekends, but I will look at jobs on the other days.

Oh good, does that mean that you could have a look at my radiator asked Amanda, it is cold and with even colder weather due it would be nice to have some warmth in my little room. Yes of course I will, after dinner tomorrow if that is convenient replied Ronnie.

The following morning, he asked Rob if he knew anything about radiators, who replied that he did not, but suggested Ronnie speak to Brian the factory supervisor. Brian suggested that if the other radiators on the system were working then it was probably air in the radiator stopping the water flow, and he took Ronnie to one of the radiators in the works office and showed him how to vent the air, lending him a vent key to use.

Dinner was roasted chicken with potatoes and carrots followed by apple pie and custard, and as he sipped his tea, Amanda said, give me ten minutes or so before you pop up to look at the radiator as I must get things tidy.

Amanda`s room was in the third-floor attic area with the stairs ending outside the door on a small landing. Ronnie tapped on the door and was answered with a "come in" the radiator is on the wall. Pushing gently the door swung open and he could see that the room itself was a little smaller than his but had its own bathroom area with an open door.

Amanda was standing outside of the small shower enclosure stark naked and drying her hair with a large white fluffy towel, and he could see a toilet and washbasin to the side. Apparently lacking any embarrassment, she continued to towel herself and Ronnie confirmed his earlier suspicion that despite her blonde locks she was in fact naturally dark haired.

She walked into the bedroom area dressed in just a transparent nylon nightgown with a small towel wrapped around her head, and removing it started to blow her hair dry with an electric drier.

Ronnie knelt alongside the radiator, which was only lukewarm. He inserted the vent key and was rewarded with a thin spurt of water and no air, so locking off the vent and placing the small brass key onto the bed, he checked the radiator valves only to find that the main inlet valve had been turned off, and opening it found the radiator got quite hot very quickly.

There you are he said, all working fine now, I do not think that it will give you any further problems. Amanda had picked up the brass vent key and was twiddling it between her fingers, thank you mystery man, I do so admire a man who has a quality tool and knows how to use it.

Christmas Eve Sunday was spent with Sheila and her family in the Claro arms pub, and it was after midnight when he turned his key in the lock of the lodging house.

Amanda was standing outside his bedroom door wearing just skimpy panties depicting a Father Christmas riding his sleigh across the front, and she was holding a bottle of MaCallan Whiskey.

Happy Christmas, just a wee nightcap perhaps she simpered, gently pushing him into his room.

On Christmas morning he gave her the gift that he had purchased for her before she disappeared up to her room to get washed and dressed for breakfast.

In the kitchen she grabbed him and kissed him passionately saying thank you for her present. Now you two, none of that, this is a respectable establishment said Mrs Hughes smiling broadly.

THE CUP

Christmas, New Year and the ever increasing preparation for the forthcoming wedding in November, together with committed hard work in the electrical and then fitting departments at Maxon saw the winter dissipate into spring.

Despite explaining to Amanda that he fully intended to honour the wedding plans made with Sheila, they still somehow managed to end up coupled in each other`s beds on a regular basis, and he began to understand that not all women were simply seeking a husband, children and a home.

Some were much more confident within their own personality and happy to seek out and take whatever their fancy rested upon.

Late spring, and a football cup game saw him seriously injured, stretchered from the pitch and taken straight to hospital, where he remained for almost six months in full length leg plaster after a complete knee operation.

Sheila and Amanda both visited regularly somehow managing to avoid accidently meeting each other which Ronnie perceived to be more Amanda`s caution rather than pure luck, and it was October before he returned to the house.

He had been paid in full by Maxon, so money was certainly not a problem, but with only weeks until the wedding he had many things to sort out, not the least of which was to find a suitable home for Sheila and him to live in, and of course choose a best man.

Over dinner one evening he shared his thoughts with Mrs Hughes and Amanda saying how much he wished that he might find a way to contact his friend Harry, and Amanda let her guard slip by saying, oh perhaps I can help, before hastily adding, if you can give me some details.

By the end of October, he had purchased a two bedroomed terrace house less than half a mile from where he was currently living so it would be ideal for both his work and Sheila`s office job at the local office of the Milk Marketing Board.

The property had a small low walled front garden and a garage to the rear, with one sitting room, a kitchen and a bathroom downstairs, and he agreed a price of two thousand two hundred pounds, with Amanda sorting a mortgage after he had given a five hundred pounds deposit.

Amanda had been as good as her word in contacting Ronnie`s friend, and Harry duly arrived in the first week of November, and they sat in the kitchen chatting over tea and some of Mrs Hughes homemade scones with jam and cream.

Ronnie invited him and a partner to the wedding and asked him to be the best man, to which Harry replied that he would be honoured. So raising the stakes Ronnie told him that he knew Amanda to be part of the group somehow, but just did not know exactly where she fitted in, and that he was annoyed that Harry felt him to need watching.

Laughing softly, Harry replied, that`s my Ronnie, always assuming the wrong reason for something to happen, she is watching you to protect you not monitor what you are doing silly.

Harry smiled then continued saying, believe me she is more than capable of taking care of most situations, and we thought that it would be better for you to be living with friends rather than total strangers. Something which Ronnie fully agreed.

Before Harry left Ronnie asked if there had been any news on the whereabouts of the cup to which Harry replied, as it happens there has been, it would appear, that there is a plan to bring both the shroud and the cup here to England where they are to be auctioned in private to the highest bidder.

At the moment we only have sketchy, outline details of the plan, but rest assured Ronnie, after me, you will be the first to know.

As Harry climbed into his car he paused, 25th November you said, right then I must get working on my speech, I will arrive on Thursday 23rd and stay in a hotel, or perhaps even here as Doreen has a couple of empty rooms. We can sort all the finer details together then okay, by the way my guest for the wedding will be Amanda is that all right with you.

Ronnie stared open mouthed and then managed, Amanda, is that sensible. Sensible for me, or for you my young friend responded Harry, she is a rather sexy little thing isn`t she.

The boys stag night went surprisingly well if that is, you discount Ronnie`s brother in-law John being thirsty at the end of the evening, drinking what he believed to be a pint of water, which in fact was neat Pernod, which Harry had been using to ensure that Ronnie only got merry rather than totally pissed.

Apparently, John took some time to find his lodging house, and in the end, resorted to climbing over garden fences to get there.

The wedding itself was grand, Sheila looked radiant in her full white gown and the bridesmaids in matching purple created beautiful photographs. Harry amused the guests with tales of Ronnie`s military exploits some a little too close to home for comfort, but all in all a good day.

A honeymoon week followed, spent at a guest house in Rhyl, then back to Harrogate to start married life together.

As promised John Apsom had sorted the driver`s license for him and he was given the keys to a new Ford Escort van, bright red with white lettering showing the company name.

A fuel card and details of how to claim expenses were included and that evening he drove home proud as punch and after the evening meal he took Sheila for a drive.

Life moved on a pace and Christmas came and went quickly with them still having dinner with her family, New Year allowed them to have a small party and Sheila invited Janet Peter and some work colleagues while Ronnie invited Amanda, Rob and Peter with their partners.

Peter of course became the talking point as he came alone explaining that he was currently between lovers as he needed to find one less volatile.

In February 1973 as a birthday present to himself Ronnie purchased a green mini cooper which he spent hours cleaning and polishing, and in the spring they used it to drive back to Wales.

This time it was for a week long holiday at Butlins in Pwllheli, where on the Friday which was their last evening, sitting in the Pig and Whistle Pub on the holiday camp, Sheila dropped the bombshell that she was leaving him for another man when they returned home.

Ronnie was totally shocked as this was so unexpected, he had considered their life to be happy, but obviously it was not, at least not from Sheila`s viewpoint.

Saying that her new man was planning to pick her up from the house on the Sunday, in just two-days, Sheila begged him not to start a fight with the other man whom she called Stuart, saying that she was sorry but that she loved this man and that his wife was leaving this Stuart so the two of them could be together.

Ronnie felt strangely indifferent and gave his word that he would not attack this Stuart person, and whilst the journey home was a little strained, the parting was amicable, with him helping to load her belongings into the car.

He asked if she had told her family to which she said no, but she would soon, which he thought to be very callous, and hoped that they would not need to find out from him.

Now alone he suddenly remembered the letter given to him by John. Searching through his belongings he found it and tapped his open palm with it. He felt angry with himself that he had let John down by not delivering it, rather forgetting it until now, so he decided to go that very afternoon, and being a Sunday there was less traffic.

He drove across to Thirsk and found the address, where a thin woman probably in her sixties he guessed, and perhaps Anne`s mother answered the door. Told that Anne would not be long and invited to wait, he sat and exchanged pleasantries with the woman until Anne arrived with a small boy and pushchair.

How old is your son Ronnie asked, Fifteen months, and before you ask his name is John of course. He passed the sealed letter to Anne who opened it, read it then began to cry. Comforting her daughter, the mother motioned for him to leave which he did quietly. Later via Harry he discovered that John had deposited ten thousand pounds in a bank account in Anne`s name, with all details included in the letter.

When aloud in front of Harry he wondered how John had accumulated that amount of money, the response was simply.

I don't suppose Seamus Flannagan would have been best pleased had he ever got chance to actually count that money, mind you who could he have complained to. I am glad for John and Anne and the child, that crooked bastard Flannagan did not deserve the money anyway.

At home Ronnie settled into a regimented lifestyle, eating sleeping and working. Even though his leg had healed the injury would always haunt him and football at top level was out of the question.

Whilst he would miss playing competitively, in truth he was pleased that this also meant little or no contact with Sheila`s family, as they had been disgusted by her actions, particularly breaking up another marriage where children were involved and thought that Ronnie should be doing more to win her back.

He had of course considered that option, as she was only living some ten miles away in a small village called Darley, but after deep inner searching, he had managed to reach the conclusion that he had never loved her anyway.

Her assertion that Stuart`s wife was leaving him to allow the two of them free rein to set up home together was slightly inaccurate, as the truth was that he had beaten her senseless and put her in Leeds Infirmary where Ronnie had visited her out of sympathy, so Stuart and Sheila deserved each other in Ronnie`s opinion.

Still friends with Peter, although Janet kept her distance, they shared a few boy`s nights out in pubs on the moors and in the dales, and Ronnie periodically slept with Amanda although apart from the sex he knew that he really did not like her that much.

Sheila had requested a divorce almost as soon as she had left him, and Ronnie saw no reason to deny this and readily agreed to a so-called quickie arrangement.

In November almost a year since the marriage he was at a popular nightclub in Leeds with Peter, sitting in the VIP area which his previous playing career had facilitated when he met Linda.

Bottle blonde and recovering from her broken engagement to a well-known national radio station presenter and charity fund raiser, she was a beautician and qualified pharmacy dispenser working for the Mary Quant brand under the umbrella company of Myram Picka.

An only child Linda lived with her widowed mother in Ripon, and Ronnie spent Christmas with them both. He soon grew fond of Jean her mother who was quite young and sexy in her own way and with Sheila pushing him to sell the home he was forced to take what he considered a low offer, so after giving her the agreed share of the six hundred pounds profit, he moved into Linda`s home permanently.

In February 1974 Harry contacted him via Amanda and shared that new information linked the RAF to the cup coming back to England, and that he was arranging for him to be given security clearance to enable access when needed, covering both home and European bases. Adding that Ronnie needed to get himself back into shape and ready for some action.

Here we go again he said to no one in particular, I promise not to fuck it up this time, for John if no one else.

Chapter Twelve
Conspiracy

By the beginning of March 1974 Ronnie was the proud holder of a high-level security pass which would see him admitted to almost any RAF, Army or Naval establishment in both Europe and the UK.

After being called into John Apsom's office on 08th March which was a Friday afternoon he found himself southbound on the A1 heading for RAF Wittering, apparently to fault find on the latest gas fired turbine test facility, which was being trialled, but really to meet with an RAF sergeant who apparently needed to speak with him about some important information.

Flight sergeant James Appleton was a time served NCO whose role was the overall management of the Hawker Hunter, long range attack bombers of 58 squadron, which along with 45 squadron also based at Wittering, were part of the RAF strategic Strike Command.

A dedicated family man, married to Joanne for over twenty years, with one child a daughter named Rose who was away at Durham University studying to be a Lawyer, Appleton was an old school type of man who believed in fairness and second chances.

Ronnie had been allocated a room within the sergeant's mess on the base, with the use of all normal facilities and meals provided, and although a civilian was afforded the rank equivalent to warrant officer second class which raised some eyebrows given his youthfulness.

However, the word went around that he was in fact Intelligence corps with time spent in Northern Ireland, after which he was treated with courtesy and respect.

Meeting over a coffee in 58 squadrons hanger mess room on the Saturday morning, James Appleton explained that RAF Intelligence had been investigating illicit smuggling activities between Germany and the UK, which surprising as it might seem were not that uncommon.

Seemingly air crew were regularly bringing home cigarettes, alcohol, perfume and small electrical items to take advantage of both the service discounts and lower prices in Germany.

However, said James, although we knew that several crews were undertaking such contraband trafficking, undercover locker searches have revealed some interesting paperwork with an address just outside Stamford, and a note instructing that basic provisions be placed there on the Tuesday after next.

Explaining that the RAF Intelligence had considered this to be more than just simple smuggling and accordingly they had contacted British Intelligence, hence Ronnie`s presence he handed Ronnie the copy of the note.

Ronnie read aloud, Tuesday 19/3 Stamford House address as previous, supplies to be dropped, Ready Meals for one, Toilet Rolls, Instant Coffee, Fresh Milk, Yoghurt. Key under mat.

This is very interesting sighed Ronnie, feeling disappointed as he had hoped for some news on the whereabouts of the cup, but I fail to see what any of it has to do with me.

In another locker continued Appleton, they found a second note, he again passed a copy across the table. Ronnie eye scanned the brief note which read.

Hunter Six to collect Jaguar 2100hrs, 1903, and deliver to nest.

I might have intelligence connections said Ronnie, but I still have no idea why you have contacted me.

Please come to my house tonight for dinner, you need to meet someone who can explain everything I hope, now go and spend the day playing around the turbine test facility and for Pete`s sake don't break anything, or we might have to call a real engineer.

Over dinner with James and his pleasant but rather plain wife the chat was social and mundane, after which whilst Joanne cleared and washed the dishes, the two men sat in the small but cosy sitting room with cigars and whiskey, not McCallan but still a rather tasteful malt.

With Mrs Appleton having discreetly retired for a bath and early night the knock at the door was soft and Ronnie might easily have missed it but James was up like a shot and after exchanging a few words in the front hallway he led the visitor into the room and made the introductions saying, Ronnie this is Eugene.

The man was about 25 years of age a little short of six feet in height and being neither thin nor overweight gave the impression of fit well maintained perfect masculinity. He was dressed in trousers, jacket, white shirt with a light blue tie, and with a tousled mop of blonde wavy hair and a smiling face his overall appearance gave the suggestion of an over age public schoolboy, but looking closer at the grey eyes, hard and steely, Ronnie instantly recognised that this was not a man to be trifled with.

James provided whiskey and a top up for Ronnie and handed both cigars saying, Castella brand, not top notch but still a decent smoke. Eugene sipped his Malt and carefully placed the cigar into his jacket breast pocket, and patted it saying, company for the journey home.

THE CUP

Now then Ronnie, If it is acceptable to call you that rather than Mr Lamb, or perhaps Godliman, James tells me that you believe that we have called you here by mistake, and that you have no interest in the little smuggling operation he has shared with you.

Why would I have any interest smiled Ronnie, after all I am simply a civilian contractor here to check out some reported issues with the turbine test facility.

Eugene smiled broadly, that is such a good story, but with the probable timescale being so short I suggest that we cut out the normal inter-service tap dancing routine and get straight down to business.

I am sorry sir, whoever you are, but as I have already explained I believe that someone has made a terrible mistake and that whilst you believe me to be part of your team whatever that is, in fact I am just a civilian.

Ronnie started to rise from his chair, so I will bid you gentlemen goodnight, and thank you for dinner.

Sit down hissed Eugene with authority, as Ronnie sank back into the armchair, then added more softly, please.

We know who you are, all about your mission in Belfast and the unfortunate death of your colleague John Stott. We know that despite your protestations to the contrary you have been involved with Mossad since such a young age, and we know of the overarching mission to recover the cup of the last supper.

Believe me Ronnie we truly know everything about you even down to your taste in whiskey and women, who thus far have not met your expectations.

We know which ones you have slept with, where and when, and best of all we know that your current overriding passion is to take revenge for Johns death which you still rather precociously blame yourself for, when the reality is that you were outwitted and out manoeuvred

Now that my character assassination is complete, might I ask who you are, and why I am here asked Ronnie, certainly not for a simple smuggling racket, unless of course British Intelligence is really that short of projects.

To answer the first question, we will agree to my being just someone with connections to her Majesty`s Intelligence Services, and with regard to the second, on the face of it absolutely nothing at all.

However, despite what you may believe we are not all faceless morons who cannot see the tree because it is hidden in the wood. Our investigations have led to suggestions that a certain well organised German group are behind at least some of the smuggling operations, possibly bringing items into this country which would be of massive interest to HM Government.

And for the record asked Ronnie, might I know the name of this alleged German group who you believe to have some involvement.

They are known as the Red Army Fraction said Eugene simply.

You really mean Faction, Ronnie smiled, trying to appear more knowledgeable than he actually was, on that particular subject.

Sadly not, Eugene returned the smile but with pursed lips, Red Army Fraction, from the fact that they are a smaller but nonetheless powerful breakaway part of the Bader-Meinhoff Gang. It seems that clever as Mossad undoubtably is, even they are not always correct.

Anyway he continued, we must get down to business, this groups apparent involvement has flagged up strong interest within government, as it would seem that previously gathered intelligence suggests a plot against the life of a member of the Royal Family, and Bader-Meinhoff are mentioned.

Surely the Royal Family are too well protected for any such plot to have a chance of success cried Ronnie.

That is as maybe, responded Eugene but we simply cannot take any chances, even a failed attempt would create a national outcry, scandal and possibly the fall of the government.

Given the current political status of the country no one wants another election, as continued lack of support for any one party could lead to cries for Nationalism, the current Labour government are limping along but a fall would be disastrous for everyone.

James refilled everyone`s glass as Ronnie said, I still fail to see how I can offer any assistance, I obviously know of the group, but very little, in fact next to nothing about them.

Their plans are being arranged and controlled by a woman member of the group who is called Denise Proshyn, and we need to find her and detain her for questioning which is why we need your help said Eugene.

But you are mistaken said Ronnie, I do not know this woman, why should I.

No one we have connection to knows her Ronnie, sighed Eugene, her secret identity is her strongest weapon.

We do know for certain that she is single minded, strong willed and utterly ruthless, certainly not afraid to kill, and she is allegedly a superb marksman.

We believe her to be in her late twenties, possibly early thirties, with shoulder length or longer jet black, hair and a disarming captivating charm which disguises her cold heart, and that she also has links to Northern Ireland where she was born and was known as. Siobahn Flannery spat Ronnie.

Now perhaps you can see why we need your assistance smiled Eugene. We need you to work with us on this and be our means of identifying the lady. Do you think that you would recognise her again, assuming her to be the woman that you encountered in Belfast, and are you willing to cooperate.

I will do everything and anything that you ask replied Ronnie, just to get my hands around the neck of that murderous bitch. And for the record she is certainly not a lady.

Her Majesty`s need to question this woman must I am afraid, take precedence over your understandable desire for retribution and revenge murmured Eugene. So we will need your guarantee that whatever you reason to be fair justice, you will allow her to be taken into our custody as and when that time arrives.

Downing the scotch Eugene said. We have the basis of an understanding I believe which is good. But given such a limited time period before we believe action will need to be taken, we need to convene again tomorrow, even though it is a Sunday.

So, James will arrange a room to be put at our disposal for the next week or so within the sergeant`s mess, and I will see you there tomorrow afternoon around two pm.

Laid on his bed Ronnie ran through the evening`s discussion, it seemed so unlikely that Siobahn would be interested in low key smuggling, so if it really where her, what was the real motive. And was the implied threat against the Royal Family both real and credible.

In the meeting room, there were already three people sat around the table with both coffee and tea in pump action flasks available on a side table along with some assorted biscuits, and Eugene provided the necessary introductions.

Eugene introduced the woman as Alison Roper from special branch and the man Alan Sedgewick from British Intelligence, Ronnie being introduced simply as Ronnie.

Before we begin said Eugene, please all understand that everything discussed within this forum is classified within the general meaning of the official secrets act and as such must not be shared with anyone who is not directly connected to this project or who has a need to know, in order to allow the provision of information where further progress so dictates.

It may also be necessary to add persons to this group if we deem it to be advantageous, however for the time being we need to work on the premise of the fewer people who know the better. And for the record this investigation shall be known as Jaguar.

Eugene handed out copies of the two notes which the RAF intelligence team had discovered and added, as both Alison and Alan have already been advised, your role here Ronnie is to help us with any detail or information about this Siobahn Flannery that you can provide.

Hopefully in due course you will be able to identify her in the flesh, if and when we get her on UK soil, and therefore as the only known link to the identification of Proshyn you will remain an integral part of our group.

If I might ask sir, Alison Roper smiled thinly at Ronnie, and with no disrespect to our newcomer here. Whilst Alan and I are aware of each other's status and ranking, we know nothing of Ronnie and do not even know what rank he might hold.

This mission might well involve the lives of members of the Royal Family growled Eugene, so from a government perspective any help that we can obtain and from whatever source is valuable.

For the record he is ranked as a junior commander in the Israeli secret service, although for the purposes of this operation each of us has something unique to bring to the table and so I therefore think that rank is not important. For what it is worth, without Ronnie`s identification of this woman there might not be a satisfactory conclusion.

Ronnie spent the next two hours recanting everything that he knew about Proshyn or Flannery including the real or simulated sex act in Eliza Street Market which Alison apparently found to be slightly distasteful.

He took time to dispel her moral considerations by pointing out that if the woman in the Market had indeed been Flannery, it added a new dimension to her character showing a complete lack of any moral compass and total disregard for others, but most of all it showed a coolness of behaviour in stressful situations.

Ronnie concluded his talk about Siobahn by adding, whatever judgements regarding her that you individually make or how dangerous you consider her to be, I can assure you from personal first- hand experience that she is ruthless to the point of being pure evil.

And she is in my belief, more than capable of doing anything to achieve her goals, please remember that she murdered four people in cold blood.

Thanking him for his comprehensive report, Alan Sedgewick said. What I do not understand is why this alleged cold-blooded killer chose to spare your life. Perhaps she liked me, offered Ronnie lamely.

Please do not flatter yourself snorted Alan, even though your attraction to the fairer sex precedes you, this woman whatever name we care to give her, had already killed four men in the space of a few minutes.

Allegedly she was carrying a 9mm automatic pistol, presumably with a six-round magazine, and even allowing for the extra safety of leaving one chamber empty she still had a round left. Which suggests by the evidence so far known and added to what you have just given, that the last bullet should have had your name written upon it, so please explain why she chose to spare you.

Eugene came to Ronnie's defence, by saying, there is an ongoing separate mission being run by the Israeli's in which both Ronnie and the woman we need to detain are interlinked.

However, because the details of this mission cannot be discussed within our group and with British Intelligence fully satisfied that there is no common link between the two missions, we cannot expect Ronnie to divulge details of something that might compromise him personally.

And for the record, although unconfirmed at this moment, it appears that the lady we are interested in is somewhat unconventional where her sexuality is concerned.

I think that we need to break now for the washrooms, some coffee or tea, and perhaps fresh air, when we come back in say fifteen minutes at sixteen-hundred hours we need to get down to business, what we know, and perhaps more importantly what we need to know said Eugene.

I suppose getting any detail of what Flannery took from you that night in Belfast is out of the question, simpered Alison Roper, but as our job in special branch relies on having as much information as can be gathered it is my responsibility to at least ask.

I am sorry replied Ronnie, but as Eugene has already shared, I am not at liberty to discuss anything to do with other operations but can assure you that whatever might have happened in Belfast, it does not have any connection to anything that might be occurring here.

That is just typical of bloody Mossad snorted Alison, always happy to share when there is something in it for them but strangely reticent when they have no vested interest.

Corporate protocol and decision making are way above my pay grade smiled Ronnie, but I promise to give as much as I can to help with this project and believe me, I do have a vested interest in that bitch.

Okay then people, Eugene called them to sit, If you would refer to the notes which I gave out earlier, let us discuss what we know first.

We know that a house has been rented or borrowed somewhere near or possibly in Stamford, presumably to offer some sort of bolthole or meeting place.

We further know that one of the groundcrew members based here at RAF Wittering has been instructed to sort provisions and deliver them for Tuesday 19th March, which is a week Tuesday.

We also know from the same intelligence sweep that a member of the aircrew also based here has received a cryptic note instructing him to collect the Jaguar and deliver it to the nest also on Tuesday 19th March, and not being a believer in coincidence, I am happy to go with the idea that these two notes are indeed connected, even if the recipients are unaware of that fact.

Separate intelligence has given an indication of a plot to either kidnap or execute a member of the Royal Family, and whilst seemingly disassociated, the link, albeit at this stage somewhat tenuous, is the Red Fraction based in Germany.

Those are the known facts. Sadly, we have no way of discovering what each of the two airmen who received the notes knows about the other or whatever the plan might be without destroying the operation.

Nor indeed do we have any real reason to link these notes with any suggested or inferred plot against the Royals. However, there is enough in the notes when linked, and I do believe that we must link them, to assume that Jaguar is in fact a person rather than animal or object.

Indeed, the mention of toilet rolls and particularly yoghurt plus meals for one, suggest in my mind a female.

If as we then suspect, this person entering the UK illegally and under cover of such planning might be the woman Proshyn, AKA Flannery, then I suggest that we have a major problem, in as much as all that we currently know, is of her impending arrival and nothing more.

So then, what do we need to find out people, please kick us of Alison.

Obviously exactly where this house is located and get it under surveillance, what Jaguars movements are likely to be, how long she / he will be staying and of course why is she here replied Alison.

Good said Eugene, Alan you must get your entire resources focused on finding that property and fast. What are your thoughts.

I totally agree that we need to locate the property and get it watched which I will arrange. We also need to find out how it might be possible to fly someone into the country illegally, especially onto a tightly controlled airbase, and we need to "kick the shit" out of all known anti-royal sympathisers, to see if we can get a handle on any possible real time threat to HM or the family.

Good work team, Alison you use everything that you have to turn over stones and see what crawls out concerning the Royals. Ronnie as you are here on base, you must do your best to discover how it might be possible to bring someone in undetected. Alan and I will collectively motivate the intelligence services to discover the property and its paper trail.

We meet here at fourteen-hundred tomorrow and I suggest that we make any necessary plans to stay here for as many nights as we feel are needed, I will make the arrangements for rooms, right then thank you people see you all tomorrow.

Good afternoon everyone, Eugene called the quorum to order adding a thank you all for being so prompt particularly as time is not on our side.

As everyone now understands he continued, HM Government are treating this potential threat as a highest-level priority, and it therefore falls upon our heads to resolve the incident as quickly and smoothly as possible.

Currently information to hand is at best sketchy or limited. There is too much assumption and conjecture filling in the missing pieces, so each of us needs to share anything new so that we all know where we are, and then we can have a round table discussion on where we go from here, perhaps we can start with your report Alan

My team have worked through the night and all this morning to get a handle on the property which we believe to be part of the Jaguar drop plan and which they refer to as the nest.

I am extremely pleased to say that we are confident that the property currently under surveillance by our specialist observers is indeed the one which is to be involved in whatever the Jaguar team intend.

The property is a small extremely isolated cottage literally in the middle of nowhere, with the nearest dwelling, a remote farm being over half a mile even as the crow flies, and there is no ground cover for almost as much distance in all directions.

So, whoever chose the location certainly did not want anyone watching or seeing things, even by accident.

The property is a two-bedroom cottage named Carpenters Lodge outside an isolated hamlet called Barnack, just a hundred yards, maybe less from the southbound side of the A1, and about a mile north of RAF Wittering where we now sit. It has been rented for a period of six months, from the beginning of March until the end of August by a seemingly endless trail of shell companies.

We will of course keep tracking these shell organisations, but this is unlikely to provide any information on the person who booked and presumably paid for the use.

The property is currently empty, and we have highly specialised observation teams already in place watching the entire area twenty-four hours, but so far no one has been anywhere near.

From the note we can deduce that unless further shopping is planned, the cottage is just a bolthole, perhaps to kick off the action and retreat to in the event of need.

If there were to be any more than short stay planned, we would have expected more provisions up front, why risk a second shop.

The first note indicates that the provisions are to be in place on or before Tuesday 19th March which as I am sure you realise to be one week from tomorrow, and the second note instructs that Jaguar is to be delivered to the nest, which we now presume to be Carpenters Lodge the same evening, possibly some time after twenty-two hundred hours.

Therefore, the assumption must now be that whatever is planned, it is scheduled to take place or at least start on or around Wednesday 20th March.

Thanking Alan for such excellent work in so short a time period, Eugene asked Alison Roper for her input. She looked hard at Ronnie but said nothing. Please Alison we need your report coaxed Eugene, Ronnie has a higher level of intelligence clearance then even you, so please do not be concerned about anything sensitive being misused.

Alison coughed to clear her throat, and still looking directly at Ronnie began her report. After yesterday`s quick briefing and whilst driving back to London, I made some telephone calls from a service station where I had stopped.

One of those calls was instructions to my team to search for anything remotely linked to anti royal or far right activity which had been flagged within the last year, and if nothing was found to keep going back in six-month intervals, and that this was to be top priority, code amber with round the clock research.

From today`s update reports, it would seem there have been five notable interactions with right wing groups within the last year, although none of these gave any indication of an anti-royal leaning, with ethnic and Jewish hatred being the foremost issue.

She continued to look hard at Ronnie, who remained passive and unmoved by the implied third-party hatred. However last year in November, the Met Murder Squad arrested an Eastern European Man in his mid-forties and charged him with the murder of a London prostitute.

The man, in exchange for leniency of sentence offered information about a right-wing plot to kill one of the royal family in the hope of destabilising Mr Wilsons fragile minority government and bringing anarchy to the streets.

I personally interviewed this man in prison earlier today, and for a promised, look at his conviction for murder, which he claims was an accidental death as the prostitute agreed to rough sex, he volunteered that the alleged plot was scheduled for this March.

Sadly, he has no other useful information excepting that the planning was being done in Germany which we already know.

For the record, irrespective of any supposed agreement to rough sex, A knife being forced into her vagina and twisted before being throttled is unlikely to have been on that sex workers agenda. So, before anyone even asks. No, I will not be looking at the conviction, he can rot in jail as far as I am concerned.

Ronnie said thank you to Alison and asked if there were any real evidence to suggest that Siobahn Flannery was indeed the most likely suspect in the Jaguar mission which prompted Eugene to speak.

When the Met arrested the man who Alison referred to, as a matter of protocol they told special branch of his allegations regarding the Royals, and therefore British Intelligence were also notified as a matter of course.

We appreciate that Mossad have a belief that Britain's various services including the Military, Police and Intelligence agencies all have their own agendas and do not share information, this is not always strictly accurate.

It is true however that unlike the autocratic Israeli government machine, our modus operandi here, is structured by the individual needs of ministers who form a democratically elected government. Nonetheless, and despite this somewhat "Old boys network scenario" at least some of us strive to see the bigger picture and act for the so called greater good.

What Eugene is trying to explain Ronnie, interrupted Alan, is that a few of us, and I specifically include those around this table actually do believe, that if we all pull together then we can make a difference and keep our country more secure.

Spare me the politics, smiled Ronnie, I am British remember, and quite aware that our politicians all have their own particular, hobby-horses to ride, the question is not whether anyone here knew of the alleged plot, but rather, did anyone do anything about it.

Yes of course snorted Eugene, once we had word of the alleged plot, we instructed all departments to make it a top priority. With the suggestion of foreign involvement specifically focused within Germany our team there established that a Right-Wing fundamentalist group known to be a splinter faction of the Bader-Meinhoff Gang were planning an attack in London.

It was discovered that this was being organised by their leader a woman called Denise Proshyn, who it seems is wanted in several countries on suspicion of terrorism.

Closer investigation into Proshyn, reveals her to be of Irish descent, born Deidre Borchene, a farmer's daughter from Londonderry. Convent school educated, with a strict father who believed that sparing the rod does indeed spoil the child, young Proshyn was by all accounts certainly not spoiled.

Her mother passed when she was a young teenager, and at eighteen Proshyn's father was murdered in a cross-border gangland incident. Left alone as an only child and responsible for the failing family farm, she took up with one Ewan Bale a known IRA sympathiser and supporter. After a few "run-ins" with the Garda she left the farm in the dubious hands of her uncle on the mother's side.

He, one Michael Flannery still manages the land, whilst Borchene and Bale disappeared not re-surfacing until 1970 in West Germany, as supporters of the then highly feared Bader-Meinhoff group, where she became close friends with Ulrika, even sharing a sexual liaison if gossip is to be believed.

So, we now know where the name Flannery fits in, with it theoretically being part of the family heritage so to speak, and furthermore how she fits so neatly into the Irish question said Ronnie. But why the German connection and where does the cup fit in.

Realising that he had inadvertently mentioned another mission, Ronnie tried to cover the slip up by adding, sorry I meant current operation, slip of the tongue.

The look on Alison Ropers face was priceless, and she smiled broadly at him saying, so you are human like the rest of us after all, we all make slipups occasionally.

Eugene broke the tension by saying. This woman took herself off to West Germany, linked up with one of the most well lead and dangerous terrorist groups then known, with a distinct purpose in her mind. We now believe that purpose to be revenge for her father's murder. We think that she was, and perhaps still is, seeking to extract retribution on those who killed him.

But I thought that you said he was quite strict with her insisted Ronnie, surely, she hated him for that. Accepting discipline from someone who loves you, does not make your love for them any less strongly bonded sighed Alison, and whilst I do not condone her need for revenge, I can see her reasoning in joining a group who she believes will help her achieve it.

The bigger question here is continued Alison, If and how, this Ewan Bale fits into our current investigation, and if he does, where can he be found.

We know next to nothing about him, even if he is still alive. Not what he looks like, or where he is, and obviously we have no way of knowing if he has any connection to this plot groaned Alan.

I believe that we can make a link to him suggested Ronnie, it is possible, although nothing more, that he was the person assisting Flannery during the Belfast incident which I outlined to you, and if that is true it tells us that he is still alive and working with her.

Okay people said Eugene, summing up what we know as fact, what we reasonably presume to be fact or part fact, and what we have as conjecture.

Fact. A potential threat to the Royal Family from a German based terrorist organisation, has potential links to the RAF base here at Wittering.

Fact. We know of two airmen involved at some level in smuggling being given instruction to stock a safe house and deliver a package, and we know that this is planned for Tuesday 19th March.

Presumption. The safe house is part of the alleged threat against the Royal Family, the package to be delivered is in fact a person, and that given the limited provisions being left, the safe house is not being used much.

Conjecture. The package is a woman named Proshyn, AKA Flannery, she may be assisted by a male friend called Ewan Bale.

Conjecture. The plot against the Royals is being orchestrated by this woman, who has somehow managed to rent the cottage for the purpose of this plot, and that the attempt on the Royals, if indeed an attempt it is, will happen either in March or possibly April.

There it is people, our prime suspect in a plot of undetermined activity is a black-haired female whom we nickname the Jaguar, after the vicious big cat. I think that we need to enjoy dinner here in the mess, and then retire to our rooms to think.

THE CUP

When we meet here at 0900am tomorrow I want everyone to have not only listed what we know, but a priority list of what we need to know from our own organisation's perspective.

As they made their way from the meeting room Alison whispered, are you going to tell me what the cup is, to which Ronnie simply smiled and walked away.

After a reasonably good dinner, with the Lamb, even if slightly undercooked to Ronnie's preference, nonetheless tender and tasty, and the homemade trifle superb, they retired to the bar for a drink although as agreed there was no discussion of the project given its secrecy and sensitivity.

It emerged that Alan was married with two young children, Eugene was a confirmed bachelor, and Alison was single, and as she put it married to the job, as they headed upstairs, she whispered room nine, give me half an hour.

Popping back to the bar, he asked the barman for two bottles of Guinness with the tops removed, then showered and shaved, before dressing in an open necked shirt with trousers but no socks or shoes.

Tapping on the door he was greeted by Alison, who had also showered and changed into a short vee necked pullover dress and like him was bare legged.

Offering her one of the bottles as he closed the door behind him, he said you look nice, but your hair is still wet. Ignoring the comment, she scowled beer, what happened to champagne or at the least a decent wine.

Take it or leave it he replied, placing the open bottle onto the chest of drawers, it is your choice. She picked up the bottle and took a swig from the open neck, resulting in bubbles running down her chin, and he laughed.

Are all Jews so bloody arrogant she said whilst wiping her face with the towel presumably used to part dry her hair. Only the wealthy ones I believe replied Ronnie, and they both laughed.

Sir told us to keep ourselves focused on the job in hand I believe, whispered Ronnie putting his arms around her shoulders and pulling her into his chest.

Yes, indeed he did she sighed, so we had better get ourselves focused.

Good morning, Eugene called them to order. Now that we have all benefitted from a night of rest, we need to get down to some serious brainstorming, so Alan do you want to kick things off please.

The house that we have under observation has still not been visited, and we still have no handle on the person who rented the property or indeed the intended occupant, other than the assumption it will be this Proshyn character.

Alison please, said Eugene. Well, for our part, special branch suspect that this German group, possibly lead by Proshyn or Flannery, might be involved in a plot to undermine the government, possibly by instigating an attack on the Royal Family.

However, most if not all, of our information is at best third hand and we have no hard evidence that such a plot exists, or idea of who might be involved in any such plot. Furthermore, we have no information on where this Proshyn woman can be located, for all we know she may already be here in the UK but she might just as well be on the Moon.

Okay said Eugene, as I have already reported, HM Government is taking this threat at face value and accordingly all assets are available. We have therefore raised the threat level against the Royals to Amber and the close protection officers have been instructed to be more vigilant than usual with a shoot to kill authorisation expectation, being given to the armed protection team.

As Eugene finished, Ronnie interrupted before anyone else could speak. Look I know that you are all top professionals within your respective department`s and I am just an outsider looking in. But if I might be allowed to say so, several things trouble me.

If the note found in the airman`s locker does indeed refer to his collecting Flannery or anyone else for that matter, then how is the pilot of an RAF Hawker Hunter on a routine flight to RAF Bruggen in Germany going to bring them back.

Surely these flights are crewed by two pilots, so if our assumption is correct both would need to be involved, with one remaining behind in Bruggen which would surely arouse questions.

Secondly if somehow, they can bring someone into the UK illegally, how do they get them away from what is a high security base.

Thirdly, on such a high security RAF base, how was it possible to get the notes into the aircrew lockers unnoticed, someone working here must also be involved.

Fourth and finally, why Wittering and why a property near Stamford, are there any planned Royal activities happening in the area, or are we perhaps focusing on the wrong target and is the base itself to be attacked.

Bloody hell, groaned Eugene we have nuclear missiles here. I did not know that hissed Alison. Neither did I added Alan, another striking example of the so called "Need to Know" protocol. Talk about trying to do the fucking job with your hands tied behind your back, this government wants us blindfolded as well.

Technically, the missiles are not ours said Eugene, let us just say that we are looking after them for our American friends. But we should have been told said Alison and Alan almost in unison, surely this changes everything.

Actually, it changes nothing said Ronnie, and they all looked at him. From what you have all just shared even if a little emotively, my understanding is that the American use of Wittering as storage for missiles is a close secret, and irrespective of my opinion regarding British Intelligence secrecy capabilities, if you two did not know, then it is highly unlikely that a terrorist group in Germany know.

Furthermore, even if that information had been leaked secretly by someone from the base with such knowledge, it sure as hell would have found its way to others. So, whilst we cannot discount the base as a target, I believe the plot is against the Royals.

Eugene having regained his composure, added, he is right we need to be constructive, examine all possible motives and possibilities but quickly discard those which just don't fly, if you excuse my metaphor.

I suggest, offered Ronnie, that we must find out how the notes were placed into the lockers, and how it might be possible to fly someone into here from Germany in secret. And of course, what makes the rented house so important, why it is where it is, if any plot seemingly revolves around London.

You are absolutely right Ronnie, replied Eugene. I suggest that as we have time before lunch, the four of us drive over and look at this property for ourselves, meanwhile I will get someone I trust here on the base, to draw up a list of everyone who conceivably had access to those lockers.

Barnack was only a mile from the airbase, and as Alan had described it was an isolated Hamlet surrounded by fields and open countryside.

They drove through the small cluster of cottages then on, out into open countryside pulling up at the end of a narrow track with grass growing centrally to the wheel ruts either side.

Pointing along the track Alan said. Carpenters Lodge, two bedrooms, bathroom and toilet upstairs, kitchen and parlour downstairs. No heating or hot water other than open fires in all rooms and an AGA wood or coal burner in the kitchen, but there is no fuel stock, and none listed to be provided on the note discovered.

Reminding you of the secrecy regarding this operation continued Alan, I can tell you that we have placed a listening device in the kitchen, which is being monitored around the clock, as well as the visual observations being carried out by the team here.

I see no one, nor any possible location for covert observation to be undertaken from, said Alison. That is indeed a compliment then replied Alan, I will tell the team.

So where are they mused Eugene, the land is so flat you can see for at least half a mile in every direction, anything out of the ordinary would be obvious immediately, even a parked vehicle would be easily noticed.

Smiling broadly Alan pointed to a sizeable pile of rotting hay to the edge of the field nearest to the property about fifty yards further along the track. That pile covers a team of two doing twelve-hour shifts. And before you ask, access both in and out is by crawling through the dirt along the edge of the field to that bank over on the right side where surprisingly the A1 passes.

Then shuffling up the bank they can access and take away, the vehicle that the incoming team has left for them.

What do you think Ronnie, asked Eugene, you are very quiet, are you not impressed by Alan`s teams surveillance.

I think that we have a serious problem Ronnie replied. Explain please, surely the surveillance is exceptional said Alison. Yes it is and full credit to everyone concerned, but ask yourselves what is being watched, the answer being an unoccupied cottage with nothing happening, and nothing is going to happen here replied Ronnie.

So, you believe this place to be unimportant then said Alan. On the contrary replied Ronnie, it is of the utmost importance but not because anything will happen here, rather what will be exchanged here.

This elaborate charade has been specifically created to throw anyone who might take an interest from the scent. No one can arrive unnoticed, so we must assume that whoever comes will expect to be under surveillance and have a get-away plan.

Any self-respecting terrorist would assume that the property had been compromised, and as we can see, any escape attempt provides zero cover making capture almost inevitable.

I see what you are saying said Eugene, and of course any attempt to storm the cottage unnoticed would be similarly disastrous, killing fields I believe the Americans call it.

Exactly sighed Ronnie, which is why this property has been chosen. Something important will be exchanged here and not documents because there are easier ways less elaborate to achieve that, so something physical with a specific purpose. A bomb perhaps suggested Alison.

Maybe replied Ronnie, but whatever it is, we need to be prepared to apprehend whoever leaves this property with it and be bloody certain that we do.

Back at the mess they enjoyed lunch whilst Eugene disappeared yet again, and when they reconvened at 2pm in the meeting room he had a broad smile on his face. I have some good news team, as part of the ongoing smuggling investigation the base commander gave the RAF investigations team permission for some covert filming of the locker areas. Not within the hangers or other possibly sensitive parts of the base, but in so called common use locations.

The good news is that whilst he is not actually seen interfering with the lockers themselves, a male cleaner is shown on film clearly holding a small piece of folded paper in his hands just a few yards from the lockers.

As we speak the base RAF Police are questioning him with regards to this, and the alleged smuggling operations.

When they have concluded their enquiries, he will be bought straight here to us and perhaps Alan will ask him some pertinent questions.

Nico Vlladus was a middle-aged Greek, a Cypriot whose family still lived in Larnaca on the south side of the island, where Nico had previously been employed on the RAF Akrotiri base just along the south coast from the town.

Under questioning Nico had apparently claimed that that he had gained a job at Wittering from his trusted service working there.

Alan made short shrift of the Greeks protests that he knew nothing of any smuggling, and the guarantee that he would be sent back to Cyprus, jobless, penniless and to be charged with smuggling gave his tongue free rein.

He had become friends with an airman based at Akrotiri, and for small amounts of cash he had smuggled cigarettes and perfume plus some alcohol onto the base, believing them to be for local use.

Later he had also carried in, some wrapped packages although he denied knowledge of the contents.

A second, flying crew airman, had then befriended him and suggested that he go to the UK to work at RAF Wittering, and whilst he was not keen to leave his family, the threat of being named to the Cypriot Authorities as a smuggler persuaded him to come.

Being hired here at Wittering was apparently a formality, as the supervisor in charge was expecting him, and they had helped with local accommodation.

He had been here just over six months now and had not seen his family in that time.

He had linked up with the airman from Akrotiri, and now frequently passed messages to and from a Greek man called Stefan Haledes who owned a local "truckers stop" services on the A1.

He claimed to have no knowledge of any plots or plans, but when Alan, guessing that this Nico had in fact read the notes before placing them inside the lockers, threatened jail for him and his family if he did not cooperate, the man broke down in tears and said that a pilot was bringing someone here to Wittering next week secretly,

This plan was apparently as a surprise for another long serving officer, and that to assist with that, the man would be secreted away overnight in a place outside Stamford.

Alison interrupted the questioning asking, and when did you deliver the latest message to Mr Haledes, to which the response was simply yesterday evening.

And what did it say Nico pressed Alison, he looked from face to face for sympathy but found none to be forthcoming. So sighing loudly he blurted.

It simply said. All as arranged Jaguar delivery to Carpenter around twenty-two hundred hours as planned, meeting with Falcon Ten am following.

After instructing the RAF police to make sure that the man was monitored carefully and given orders to maintain his usual work schedules until the supposed threat had passed, after which they must deal with him as they saw fit, he was allowed to leave.

After Nico had gone Alan spoke. Well, that confirms someone is being bought into the UK illegally in secret next Tuesday, and then being taken to Carpenters Lodge at least overnight. And that whoever they might be, they are meeting somebody else there, presumably the following morning at ten am.

Not someone said Ronnie, Siobahn Flannery or your Jaguar, the real question is though, why come here in person just to complete a delivery drop, surely anyone trustworthy could do that. And using an RAF Jet to be smuggled in by is not a ruse that might be repeated frequently, so why the elaborate cloak and dagger setup for what is presumed to be a simple drop and pickup.

Because it is not just a simple exchange said Eugene agitatedly, whoever is coming in, is teaming up with another who is already here, and together they plan to carry out the attack whatever it is.

Of course, sighed Ronnie, Flannery will kill without compunction, but she will almost certainly need local assistance to help her get in and out of the target zone. Plus, she will only want to be here for the shortest possible time, so I think we must assume the attack will be next week, and she has probably already set plans in motion to return to Germany possibly in the same way as she arrives.

I need to get back to London said Eugene I need to know all, and I do mean all the Royals movements for the next three weeks, and I need to see Mr Wilson and get authority for a shoot to kill warrant regarding any events at Carpenters

Lodge. Me too responded Alan we need surveillance on that café now and we must raise the imminent threat of attack from Amber to Red.

We meet here again next Tuesday 19th on the morning of the events "kick off" said Eugene, two pm okay. Meanwhile we keep each other abreast of all and any developments, nothing is to be kept secret agreed.

As the two men left the room, and with Alison packing her papers into the bag that she carried, Ronnie asked, are you not running away back to the big city as well. Yes, I am, but I will be back she replied, there are some things that I need to check out here, what about you, have you plans.

Oh well, I am not sure, maybe a greasy burger at a local truck-stop, and a visit to an estate agent in Stamford.

But most of all I need to know how the pilot of an RAF Hawker Hunter, on a planned flying mission can apparently bring in someone from RAF Bruggen without raising any suspicions, it seems too far-fetched to be true.

Do you mind if I share that greasy burger said Alison, it might make your visit less high profile and in regard to the someone flying in secretly, even if it is possible how can they leave the base without being detected.

That's what I intend to discover said Ronnie. If you are back tomorrow, we can share that burger. I could stay over if you like she said. I will look forward to that he smiled, and she was gone.

Wednesday morning found him driving north along the A1. He passed the busy truck stop services, continuing to the first Stamford Junction, where he left the northbound carriageway and re-joined on the southbound.

Taking his time and looking ahead across to the other carriageway he saw the truck stop coming up, so pulled into a small layby at the roadside. Getting out of the vehicle he walked around the van and peered through the hedgerow.

As he suspected Carpenters Lodge was clearly visible about fifty yards from the hedgerow and some fifty to eighty yards further south almost opposite the services.

Driving straight back to the base and then out to the 58 squadron, aircraft-hanger, he sought out James Appleton who immediately insisted that he join them for dinner again that evening. Ronnie said thank you, of course he would be delighted to share dinner with them, but that he urgently needed some information.

Anything that I can do to help said Appleton. Please remember everything we discuss is classified said Ronnie, and whilst I know that it sounds terribly dramatic, it is important okay.

Your smuggling racket is almost certainly part of a wider smokescreen, to cover any interest in what we see as a bigger picture operation. What I need to know by tonight please is, how difficult it might be for a Hunter Pilot to secretly fly in someone on a routine return flight from RAF Bruggen undetected.

Not at all difficult, replied James Appleton. Absolutely fucking impossible, the Hunter is a two-seater Jet Fighter, Bomber and there is zero room for anyone else.

Quite apart from the lack of oxygen at altitude causing death by suffocation and assuming the temperature did not kill by hypothermia, there simply is not any physical space.

I will invite someone else to dinner who will convince you that this is genuinely impossible, do you need anything else. Just to borrow your car tomorrow please just for a few hours.

What's wrong with your van then asked James. Nothing at all but I need that for a different journey replied Ronnie. Well okay but it is my pride and joy so please do not scratch it murmured James

Dinner as before was an affable affair, with Spaghetti Bolognese followed by some more of Joanne's homemade trifle, however this time there were two other guests. A chief technician called Colin Davies with his wife a bubbly Welsh lady called Glady's.

Have you been to Wales Ronnie she purred. Yes, a few times but only the North, Rhyl, and Pwllheli. Oh, you mean the Butlins Camp, was it with your wife. Yes, it was but it is not something that I choose to remember, we are no longer together.

After dinner, leaving the ladies to clear and wash-up, the three men shut themselves into the parlour where James took out his whiskey. But stopping him from pouring, Ronnie produced a bottle of Mc Callan saying, try this and let me know what you think. What do you have with it, enquired James opening the bottle.

The only thing that goes with a good shot of Malt, is another shot, anything else is sacrilege said Ronnie. They chuckled at this together, then Colin spoke.

James here tells me that you want to smuggle someone into Wittering from Bruggen on a routine Hunter flight is that so.

Yes, that is the basic plan can you help. Colin laughed, I would love to be able to my friend, but the truth is, that what you are suggesting is not just impractical but totally impossible, and before you ask questions allow me to explain why.

There are only two seats in a MK2 Hawker Hunter, these being for pilot and co-pilot. There is no storage, or small compartment other than the missile tubes which when the plane is not armed are fitted with simple artificial inserts.

The routine flights to and from RAF Bruggen, and indeed other locations are not a joy ride but are planned and plotted exercises involving both ground and aircrew as well as radar and communication teams.

Each flight route is carefully plotted in detail, both ways, and is constantly monitored for any issue or deviation. Mostly the two aircrew are known to each other and whilst one is designated as the lead pilot, both are more than capable of flying the aircraft.

Finally, and certainly not least. All the locations where we fly Hunters into and out of, are covered by the HM Secrets Act and admission to any such base is strictly managed and monitored.

Accessing the high security areas such as the apron, or hangers is restricted to only fully cleared personnel, and there is simply no chance of dodging the tight security.

As an afterthought, even if everything that I have said could be somehow overcome, taking a Hunter on a routine flight without a co-pilot would not happen as the ground crews at both airfields would clearly see the plane to have just one occupant and take the appropriate actions.

But what if they were all involved said Ronnie, realising as he spoke how unlikely the suggestion was. Colin laughed loudly saying, the number of people who would need to be involved at both airfields makes such a suggestion impractical.

There would be no secrecy under such circumstances Colin continued, and whatever the joke or jape the higher-level staff would never risk careers for such a thing, as the RAF would certainly come down heavily on the misuse of both systems and security.

Taking a sip of his whiskey Colin added, this is indeed a good malt, I am just sorry that I could not be of any help regarding your project it really is quite impossible.

Smuggling perfume cigarettes or other small items in flight bags or tucked into tunics, yes of course, and we all know that it does happen, but a person, not a chance.

They sat together for a while chatting, then Ronnie said. Tell me again Colin, there are two seats in a Hunter is that correct. Yes, replied Colin for the pilot and co-pilot. But what if the smuggled person was dressed as the second aircrew the co-pilot might that work suggested Ronnie.

I do not think that you understand sighed Colin, these flights are strictly controlled at both ends, two aircrew climb aboard and fly out or fly in, and if you are suggesting that a swap were to happen out in Bruggen what happens to the co-pilot left behind he can hardly hitch a ride home to the UK.

Quite apart from which the ground crews know the pilots, they would spot an imposter straightaway, I can see where you are coming from Ronnie said Colin but trust me, what you are suggesting is just not possible, in a spy novel maybe, but here in real life no, not a chance.

I admire your confidence Colin, and respect your professionalism but in my experience the totally impossible can often be what happens sighed Ronnie. Please tell me, what time is the last flight out to RAF Bruggen and then back to here at Wittering on any given day.

Weekday routine flights are kept to a planned schedule with the last return flight leaving here at Sixteen Hundred hours GMT arriving at Bruggen Eighteen Fifteen GMT but Nineteen Fifteen local time. The aircrew refresh while the plane is checked and refuelled, taking off for the homebound flight at twenty-one hundred local time stated Colin.

So then, touchdown here would be around twenty-two hundred hours on any given night for an inbound flight from RAF

Bruggen said Ronnie a little excitedly. That`s correct sighed Colin, but as I have tried to explain, excepting small items nothing, I repeat nothing can be bought in secretly.

Last question please smiled Ronnie, thank you for your patience. Would the ground crew who saw the flight leave, be the same crew as those on duty when the plane returned.

Yes of course said Colin. James interrupted by saying, that`s not strictly true, with the recent cutbacks and cost saving ideas new late shift rota`s have been introduced starting from next Monday, with only batman attendance to the hanger apron for the last flights in, with those incoming crews needing to fill out the returning flight log themselves.

When did you get told of this spluttered Colin I have not heard even a whisper. I have not heard anything yet either said James, however Joanne does a few hours typing for wing commander Brownlow and she overheard him talking on the telephone.

Ffffing socialists spat Colin cost cuts indeed, they will be rationing the bog paper next. Mind you that still does not help you Ronnie, because you would still have that surplus flight crew member stuck in Bruggen which is a nonsense, and of course your secret passenger would need to be able to fly a Hunter.

Do the pilots always fly the same plane asked Ronnie. Usually, but not always answered James, sometimes if there are faults with an aircraft, they use a different one of course but why do you ask.

Is it possible for a single pilot to fly the plane by himself continued Ronnie. Technically the answer is yes, for example if the other pilot is taken ill, but in any normal circumstance it would be totally against RAF protocol said Colin.

Fuck your protocol spat Ronnie, if someone could take off from Wittering no questions asked and land at Bruggen again with no questions being asked could he do that without a second pilot.

Yes, sighed James, the Hunter is a two seat Jet designed for pilot and assisting co-pilot, but as Colin has intimated it is possible to fly the plane alone, as already mentioned this usually being in medical emergencies, in fact we do simulate such an event by one man crew short flights.

They are known as circuits and bumps added Colin, the pilot takes off circles the airfield then comes in as if to land but just bumps the tarmac then lifts off and circles again, they are dummy runs for a crew emergency.

Oh, my word of course shouted Ronnie excitedly, it is a dummy run, he leapt up from his armchair and hugged Colin, you have cracked it my friend, how clever but how cunning, let us have more Mc Callan.

After swearing both of his new friends to complete secrecy, Ronnie outlined how he believed a real person was to be flown into RAF Wittering next week and how he needed them both to assist him by carrying out some discreet checks.

They were both astounded by the audacity of such a plan and sceptical that it might even succeed, but they both agreed to get the information he requested.

Back in his bed, Ronnie ran through everything that he now knew or at least suspected to be the plan, there were gaps of course and these needed to be filled in, not the least being where this Stefan Haledes character from the café fitted in, but all things considered they were getting somewhere.

In the morning he contacted Eugene and passed the information that it was apparently possible, at least in theory to fly someone into Wittering from Bruggen. This meaning that the plan that they had uncovered must be considered viable and therefore probable. Eugene thanked him and promised to get things ramped up requesting that he be kept in touch with any further developments.

Ronnie walked across to the married quarters area and knocked upon the Appleton's door which was opened by Joanne. Oh, I am sorry, but James is already at work you can find him in the hanger I expect. Yes, I know but it was his car that I need smiled Ronnie, he offered to let me use it but only for as long as I took good care of it. Oh yes, said Joanne I remember now, he did mention something wait and I will fetch the keys.

The car was a Humber Hawk with bench seats in both front and rear covered in blue leather with veneer panels and wooden steering wheel. Being "column change" which Ronnie was unused to, driving it took a little practice, but all in all a nice motor and Ronnie could see why James was justifiably proud of it.

Ronnie drove out of the base and turned onto the A1 heading north, he pulled up the slip road to the truck-stop and parked in the spacious but rough potholed hard standing outside the cafe where there were already several lorries and vans scattered around.

To the side rear area of the café a small porch jutted out and parked near to it was a black motorcycle, one of those sporty looking types which had spikey tread tyres, similar in appearance to autocross motorcycles.

He toyed with the idea of going into the cafe for a mug of tea but looking across the A1 dual carriageway at the thick hedgerow opposite, reasoned that his time might be put to better use.

climbing back into the car he drove on up the road to the Stamford south junction, where he intended to head south, but on impulse took the Stamford road and parked in the town.

Wandering around the streets he looked in the windows of the "real estate agents" and made a mental note of them, fortunately there were in fact only six that he deemed worthy of note the other being sales only and not rental properties.

Of the six, he discounted two of these quite quickly, on the basis that they seemed to have more higher end value properties, leaving four to begin with.

Having set his mind upon a standard question system, he entered the first estate agent's and said hello, I am moving into the area in about six months and am looking for a small out of the way place which I can rent where I can write a book, ideally "well away" from any urban noise.

The negative response was a bit disappointing, but he carried on to the next agents and only began to consider it a waste of time when only the fourth was left.

The same response saw him somewhat dejectedly walk towards the door when the agent said, wait a moment please, did you say in around six months. Ronnie turned around and replied yes that is correct, maybe seven.

Well, I might just have something suitable simpered the woman, a remote cottage, only accessible from a rough track, no modern comforts I am afraid, open fires and no telephone service, just two bedrooms, but very private.

It sounds interesting, offered Ronnie is it far from Stamford. Not at all replied the woman, you will need transport of course but just five minutes of driving from the property would get you to the outskirts of the town.

The property might be ideal said Ronnie, when might I have a look at it, he asked. It is currently rented I am afraid replied the woman, but only until August, so if you are interested, I can ask the owners if they are happy for you to take it on.

Smiling at Ronnie, she continued, It is owned by one of those wealthy land-owning families, but they never use it themselves, we only have it on the books because it sits on a larger parcel of land that they own, and we manage for them.

In fact, she hesitated slightly, thinking about it, we did not arrange the current rental it was a private deal between the tenant and the Critchley family, all we did was handle the keys. a Greek gentleman has taken use of it for the period.

What is this charming place called asked Ronnie, Carpenters Lodge replied the woman, although as I said it is really more of a cottage, but I suppose Lodge sounds more grand. Who knows it might have been the lodge gate cottage of the estate in years gone by offered Ronnie.

Yes, I had not considered that was the reply, shall I make enquiries about renting it for you, but Ronnie was already out of the door before she had finished speaking.

Back onto the A1 southbound he pulled into the same layby he had used previously, he climbed from the vehicle and bending down, forced one of James beloved car wheel trims from its fixing. Tucking it under his left arm he walked along the grass verge towards the café which was on the opposite carriageway.

After about half of the way he casually dropped the trim onto the grass and continued walking until he was exactly opposite the café.

He immediately noticed there to be a sizeable gap in the otherwise continuous thick hedgerow, and he stepped through.

At the foot of the banking which the hedgerow sat upon, a bridleway ran away from where he stood, across the fields to what looked to be a cluster of farm buildings in the far distance probably a half mile away.

Ronnie realised that because its path ran alongside the hedges bordering the fields, it had not been apparent from the end of the track from where they had viewed the cottage, which he could now clearly see, below and directly in front of him around fifty yards away.

Shit, he said aloud, there is a second way in and out of the place. Thinking to himself he decided, Alan needs to know about this, or we will really fuck up, and it explains to some extent the involvement of the café.

Walking back towards the layby, a police car with blue lights flashing pulled up next to him and with window lowered the uniformed officer in the passenger seat asked is everything all right sir. Yes, thank you officer I am just searching for a wheel trim is that a problem.

Not at all sir, was the reply, is that your car in the layby. Ronnie affirmed that it was. We understand your actions sir, but it is dangerous to walk along the verge with the oncoming traffic travelling so fast, might we suggest that you get back to your car and purchase a new trim, rather than place your life in danger. Thank you, officer I will do just that, it was stupid of me not to think said Ronnie. Have a safe journey replied the officer as the car pulled away.

Ronnie walked on and picked up the trim, waving it high in the air for the policemen's benefit, then carefully placed it back onto the wheel before looking again at the nearby hedgerow. If a close look were made some evidence of a hole at the bottom could be seen, carefully concealed by a bunch of removable twigs, the access hole for the surveillance teams smiled Ronnie.

Back in the Humber he drove south to the next junction. Finding a petrol station, he topped up the fuel tank and returning to the base, drove back to the Appleton's home and parked the car on the drive before handing Joanne a bunch of flowers that he had purchased when fuelling the car.

THE CUP

Collecting his van, he drove to the "45 squadron" hanger in search of chief technician Davies, who he found doing some paperwork in the small office. Have you managed to find out anything useful yet Ronnie asked, more in hope than any expectation.

I am not sure if it is part of your alleged charade or not replied Colin, but in the washroom here, there is a full-size shop window manakin, dressed in RAF flying gear, with a sign and collection tin saying "RAF Benevolent Fund please give generously".

So then, our theory is correct a dummy flight out and the bitch bought back said Ronnie aloud but to no one in particular. Pardon said Colin abruptly. Oh, nothing, sorry, sighed Ronnie. It is a bad habit of mine thinking out aloud, I really must try to stop doing it.

Look Colin, I will take full and all responsibility for everything, in writing if you need it, but you must make sure that whichever airman is booked to fly out to RAF Bruggen next Tuesday on the last trip, he is not prevented from flying alone with that dummy, and please keep the ongoing smuggling searches low-key at least until after next Wednesday okay.

I understand replied Colin, and therefore I am aware of what you are suggesting, but honestly there is no way it can happen, no one could pull a stunt like this without being caught and expecting to be caught.

Maybe smiled Ronnie, but if he is likely to be found out and caught, you must make sure that he is not detained but allowed to fly. For what it is worth, the actual security of the country might depend upon it, and before you ask, no I am not joking.

Back at the mess, Ronnie was pleased to see Alison taking her room key, and suggested they meet for dinner, over which he updated her on his investigations and findings. You believe that the café is involved somehow then she asked, I mean other than this man Haledes being a message taker.

Yes, I do said Ronnie, in my limited experience, when analysing a situation, chance is about as likely as being struck by lightning, not impossible but certainly not top priority.

The cottage is located almost directly opposite to the café, the café is being used for message drops, there is a hole in the hedgerow within fifty yards of the cottage making access in and out quick and probably undetectable.

None of that is chance, which reminds me I must inform Alan of the hole in the hedge and the bridleway access. I will do that now, she smiled, I have his home telephone number.

Returning to the table she offered Alan`s thanks for the information, then blushed a little when sharing that he had also asked what she was doing at Wittering. And what did you say smiled Ronnie.

Oh, that I was following up some leads with you she giggled. To which Alan just replied, Be careful Alison, you know what those Israeli agents think about women.

The following morning after breakfast they took the van up to the café and parked on the rough surface facing the road. That opening in the hedgerow is only fifty yards from the cottage, which makes the cottage less than five minutes on foot from where we sit said Ronnie to Alison, pointing out the gap in the hedge.

Someone could leave here, go there and be back unnoticed in less than fifteen minutes, then away up the road almost uncatchable.

They entered the café and ordered two mugs of tea and some toast. Looking around they saw that the place whilst slightly grubby and in need of decorating, was obviously well used, and not just by truckers, as there were several businessmen in suits as well as van drivers, even a family of four having breakfasts.

Sitting at a Formica topped table, the two of them sipped their tea and ate the toast whilst scanning the room for staff. There were several men who appeared to be of foreign origin rather than white British born working to serve customers and clear tables, and Alison whispered that she could not identify which might be Stefan Haledes.

Ronnie asserted that neither could he, and it would be unwise to ask as they did not wish to alert suspicion in anyone at the café. Outside Ronnie noted the black motorcycle was where he had seen it previously, however being slightly closer could now see that there was no number plate attached.

Back at the base, there was a message for Ronnie informing him that both Alan and Eugene would be arriving that same afternoon and would require rooms for the Friday evening with dinner, which he arranged straightaway.

I wonder what the reason for this might be exclaimed Alison, normally Alan would not want to be away from the family at a weekend.

After lunch Ronnie drove her up the A1 and as before, stopped in the small layby, showing her the concealed access and the general area as visible through the hedgerow so that she could see for herself how easy access was to the A1.

Alan and Eugene were already in the meeting room when they returned and Eugene looked distinctly worried, asking them to sit and listen. Confirming that the Royals close protection squad had been updated and given a shoot to kill mandate for any real time event, he added that there were apparently no scheduled Royal engagements until May and that this was concerning because thus far the premise had been an attack on the Royals, which if seemingly now less likely, left them nowhere.

Alan chipped in with details of the observation team who were covering the cottage and local area, adding that scraping the barrel, the only remotely possible person of interest, had been a passing motorist driving a Humber who had apparently stopped briefly to recover a missing wheel trim.

Ronnie gave his detailed report including the wheel trim incident adding his impressiveness at the surveillance team checking him out. You have been busy said Eugene congratulations, you must be pleased. To the contrary replied Ronnie, I am deeply worried.

Why asked Alison, we have achieved such a lot in so little time why be worried. Let us assume replied Ronnie, that it is Siobahn Flannery or Denise Proshyn as she might wish to call herself now, being secretly flown into Wittering next Tuesday, which is in a little over one hundred hours.

Now let us also assume that she is somehow spirited out of the base and taken to Carpenters Lodge arriving sometime around ten thirty pm under the watchful eyes of the observation team.

With what we now also know, the expected meet at the cottage will be the following morning at ten am when we are going to be outsmarted I fear.

Nonsense blustered Alan, my team have eyes on the property around the clock, a cat could not get into that place without being seen. Undoubtably Alan sighed Ronnie, but ask yourself why the property has been chosen, and I mean this particular property not just any isolated place but this specific cottage.

I am sure that you are going to tell us sneered Alan. But ignoring the barbed sarcasm Ronnie continued. It is because they simply do not care if they are seen, they know that they can make a clean getaway without fear of capture making British Intelligence look foolish.

Now look here began Alan, but Eugene silenced him, saying, that is a bit strong after all our efforts Ronnie, please justify your comments. I believe said Ronnie, that they have anticipated being discovered, at least to some extent.

The person meeting the cottage inhabitant will arrive on a motorcycle from the A1 café via that gap in the hedgerow. They can be at the cottage in less than two minutes, and if needed, both can be spirited away back to the café in the same amount of time. And gentlemen as things currently stand, we would be able to do nothing about it.

Shit, shit, shit, exclaimed Alan, sorry Ronnie you are right, and if they were to do that, we would have no intelligence on what vehicle or where they were going, and because of the location of both the café and the cottage heavier surveillance is totally out of the question.

Fucking hell, snorted Eugene, here we are on the Friday before it kicks off and rather than being on top of things, we are back in the shit, it seems that we are just dancing in the dark.

The three of them Alan, Alison and Eugene returned to London to see what mitigation might be possible to counter the new threats, leaving Ronnie to kick his heels alone at Wittering.

He spent all of Saturday and into Sunday in the mess dining room, setting up possible scenarios using salt pots as people and the cruets as the two buildings.

Whatever way he arranged it, there were always two trapped covert observers, one terrorist in the cottage a second travelling the short distance between the café and the cottage, and who knows how many backup persons within the café.

Fucking outnumbered again, he sighed to himself. What had Harry insisted for the future, never to allow himself to be outwitted again, a point well taken.

But how could they counterbalance the opposition without obviously revealing their presence and thereby defeating the objective, which whilst stopping any planned atrocity, must also include the detention of those involved.

Working with his condiments, wherever he placed extra resources, these became highly visible and would compromise the observation. He considered storming the cottage late on the Tuesday and capturing whoever had arrived but reasoned that would delay but not necessarily destroy any planned attack and could in fact drive any such plot even further underground.

He was fully convinced that the café was involved and therefore might provide the answer, so he telephoned Alison and shared his thoughts seeking suggestions from her. Leave it with me she said I might have an idea, see you on Tuesday afternoon.

More and more Ronnie knew that they needed experience on the ground, but he also knew that he and he alone could identify Siobahn, if indeed it was to be her, and therefore he needed to get close to the cottage.

The very thought of lying in the damp field under a pile of manure disgusted him and he immediately discounted being part of the undercover observations team.

Tuesday arrived more quickly than he would have liked considering what he perceived to be their lack of overall control, and not for the first time recently, his thoughts turned towards John and what he might have suggested that they do, but nothing obvious came into his mind.

It was after four pm by the time all of them had arrived at the meeting room, and Eugene in his usual straight forward manner got down to business.

All right people this is it, we will go round robin for updates, but be under no illusion if tonight and tomorrow go tits up, some, or possibly all of us, will be receiving our P45s. And make no mistake, whatever mitigating circumstances might be presented. Great Britain does not expect nor indeed sympathises with intelligence fuckups.

Alison your update please. Well, Ronnie called over the weekend to discuss his thoughts, with which incidentally I readily agreed, these being that as our plans currently stand, we are outnumbered, with only two covert observers effectively trapped under their cover.

Thinking about this said Alison, I have made provision for two, armed officer, police cars plus two unmarked police vehicles to be deployed from nine thirty this evening.

One pair at each of the road junctions on the A1 both north and south of the café. In the event of anyone needing to be apprehended or followed we will have the available resources to do that.

Alan could add little that was not already known, and Eugene confirmed that as things currently stood, they were reliant on the surveillance and Alison`s recently added stop or follow teams. He concluded by asking Ronnie, when he thought it likely that a positive identification of the person being bought in might be possible.

That is going to depend on a number of different factors, replied Ronnie thoughtfully, I am hopeful that as they climb from the Hunter Jet, I might get a close enough look, but of course if they keep their helmets on that may not be possible.

I will of course covertly follow them to see if I can get a visual as they leave the base, but again if this is a secret exit, the person will be out of sight. All things considered it just might have to be a knock on the cottage door after the meet and hand over tomorrow morning.

Oh yes, and you think that they will simply open the door to you. Alan`s sarcasm was palpable.

Why not countered Ronnie coolly, they will not be expecting anyone, and as far as they are aware their plan has not been discovered so why not. And I will simply say that as the next prospective tenant I was looking around at the cottage, and unsure if it was occupied, knocked the door out of politeness.

And if your Flannery woman answers the door breathed Eugene. Then I really do not know sighed Ronnie, but she has had one chance to kill me and did not take it, so such an unexpected meeting might cause panic. And if she decides to kill you, we will be left holding the can said Eugene, no way is that going to happen.

Okay said Ronnie, I have an idea or to be more precise my best friend John has a plan, and before you ask it is not a risk and will guarantee identification whilst preserving my cover. Are we to be told what this new wonder scheme is said Alan still showing his sarcasm.

If, or rather when it has worked you will know chuckled Ronnie, and to be frank we have no other options. What I will need though, is radio contact with Alison just one-to-one, not open band.

Right then said Eugene, we all know what we are doing, Alan and I will get back to London and keep things moving at that end, Alison and Ronnie will remain here with Alison controlling the police response and Ronnie covertly trying to get real time identification of the person or persons.

We will liaise throughout as required concluded Eugene, and share full updates by telephone tomorrow, by which time if everything goes to plan, we will have both under close surveillance. Or as our "worst case" option, in custody.

After the two men had departed for London Alison asked, what Ronnie`s idea to get a close look at the suspect entailed, and could she help in any way to which he simply replied. How long will it take for one of your armed response vehicles to get to the café from either static location.

About five minutes I guess she replied, maybe more. Dammit Alison we may not have five minutes certainly no more, so make it five as a worst case muttered Ronnie.

And regarding the armed police officers, if you need to call them out, I guarantee shots will need to be fired so forget Gold Command Protocols, they shoot to kill on sight if required is that understood.

Yes sir, giggled Alison, I will be sure that we meet sir`s expectations, are there any other orders sir wishes to give me, have I really been that naughty.

That is just not remotely funny sighed Ronnie, I know these people, they do not care about anyone or anything, and if it is Flannery, we simply cannot let her get away, she has no scruples and will kill without even taking a breath.

And if it is not her what then asked Alison. Well, then I guess my involvement will become no longer required replied Ronnie, and you and the others will sort out whatever needs to be done.

And when this is over, I mean fully over, will we still see each other she asked. I would like that Ronnie said, taking her in his arms as they kissed, who knows maybe British Intelligence might have a slot which I can fit into.

I doubt that there is a slot, as you so quaintly put it, anywhere in the world that you could fit into whispered Alison. You are who you are, which is why people bristle in your presence, no one likes to admit that others are smarter and more professional, ignore Alan his pride hurts that is all, he secretly admires you.

Bollocks, said Ronnie laughing, let us share dinner and some time together before we kick off around twenty-one thirty to go over to the "45 squadron" hanger area. Or perhaps, time together then dinner then more time together giggled Alison. You are such a naughty girl he smiled, come on.

At nine thirty pm they drove across to the hanger and parked his van out of direct sight behind some mobile access platforms, whilst keeping a basic line of sight across the front of the hanger with its doors part open.

The Hunter is due to land around ten said Ronnie. Alison produced a radio handset and speaking into it said, Gold One to ARUs one and two and pursuits one and two over, to which four simple responses of receiving over came back

Alison spoke into the radio set again. Gold commander here, sit tight all four of you, Jaguar is expected around ten pm, I will keep you updated. only move on my command out.

What is your plan then Alison, said Ronnie. To which she responded. We will follow them as they leave the base, keeping a good distance away so as not to suggest anything even remotely suspicious. When they come off the A1 at Stamford, the northern unmarked patrol will follow to make certain the Lodge is the destination.

Then I guess it is some stand down time until an early breakfast tomorrow for us, the vehicles will remain overnight with shift change every four hours.

Just after ten pm they heard the distinct sound of approaching aircraft and some five minutes later two Hawker Hunter Jets taxied onto the concrete apron in front of the hanger and rolled to a stop. Two pairs of ground crew wheeled out mobile steps and with aircraft canopies opened, both flight crews climbed from the planes. Five of the six had removed their helmets but the sixth who was carrying two flight holdall bags kept it firmly in place.

Shit, muttered Ronnie, I should have realised that with the other crews knowing each other, the fake crew member would need to retain their flying helmet. Carrying the gear is good reason for that.

We need to be around the rear of the hanger but cannot take the van because of the engine noise, so you wait here I will not be long. Ronnie silently climbed from the van as the crews walked towards the hanger entrance.

He trotted as quietly as he was able to the rear corner of the hanger and patiently waited and watched as eventually the first crew came out into the gloom and climbed into parked vehicles then drove away.

Several minutes elapsed and he thought that he had somehow made a mistake, then they appeared together still in flying gear and both wearing caps on their heads, as they were walking away from him Ronnie could not be fully certain that one was a woman, the walk suggested it to be so, but he simply could not be certain.

He trotted back to the van and taking a longer route, but at some speed, towards the main gate he exited and was able to park outside the base, along the road in the small layby reserved for visitors and vehicles to be checked over.

It was nearly fifteen minutes later that a single vehicle exited the base, an RAF liveried Landrover, passed them, and he was relieved to count two persons inside both still in uniform.

They allowed the vehicle to set off along the deserted A1 road, heading north towards Stamford before following at a lengthy distance. Alison radioed the waiting police teams that two suspects, currently unidentified, were heading north along the A1 in a marked RAF, Landrover, and were expected to exit at Stamford South Junction then take the road towards Barnack. The northern unmarked police car was to follow discreetly with lights off to confirm the suspects destination.

At the Stamford junction Ronnie and Alison left the northbound A1, re-joined on the southbound carriageway, parking in the layby and turning off the lights and engine. They climbed from the vehicle and peered through the thick hedge and were rewarded after some five minutes by the lights of a single vehicle approaching from Barnack hamlet. The vehicle pulled into the track and drove slowly down to the cottage.

Ronnie raised the night vision goggles that Colin had thoughtfully loaned him and focused on the cottage as the Landrover turned around and stopped. A single uniformed figure emerged from the passenger seat, closed the door and the vehicle drove away. The figure walked the few yards to the door of the cottage and disappeared inside. A few seconds elapsed and a light from the ground floor window confirmed occupancy by one person.

Well, said Alison as they drove back to the base did you get a close enough look, was it her. Ronnie considered his answer, he did not want to deceive Alison but then he did not want to be wrong.

In all honesty he replied, I am simply not certain. I believe that the person was, or should I say is female, but cannot be certain, and even if it is a woman, it might not be her.

He was showered and ready for bed, when the soft knock came at his door, Alison was carrying two bottles of Guinness each with the top removed, pushing past him into the room she said. Here mystery man this might be our last chance, after all you might well be gone tomorrow.

Eight fifty AM saw Ronnie and Alison pull up into the car park at the café, he lifted and propped the bonnet as steam rose from the engine compartment. Inside the cafe Alison ordered two cooked breakfasts with tea and toast whilst Ronnie used the wall telephone booth to seemingly contact the breakdown service.

Then popping back outside apparently to check the engine, he was relieved to see that the motorcycle was still there.

Back inside the cafe and sat with Alison he tucked into breakfast explaining to the waiter about the van and that the breakdown team were coming but it might be a while.

Just after nine forty-five AM, a silver, Fiat 124 Spider sports car pulled up near to the motorcycle, and a fit young white man, dressed in denim jacket and matching trousers climbed out. With no interaction to anyone at the café, he kick-started the motorcycle and pushed it out of the parking area to the side of the roadway.

As the approaching traffic thinned, he jumped onto the motorcycle and roared straight across both carriageways, disappearing through the hole in the hedge.

Catch yourself a lift Ronnie said to Alison, I have things to do, and saying that he dashed outside to the van. Bundling up a pair of tatty old boots with no laces, a frayed felt hat and a grubby oversized overcoat from the back of his vehicle Ronnie tucked them under his arm and trotted across the road before disappearing through the gap in the far hedge.

Less than fifteen minutes later as he shuffled along the edge of the yard outside the cottage, the door opened and a man and woman emerged, the man carrying a backpack. Clear off you "dirty old bugger", shouted the man.

No, called the woman, I will leave the door open, there is some food old man, help yourself. The mop of blonde hair, reddish cheeks and white framed sunglasses meant absolutely nothing to him, but that soft lilting Irish voice was unmistakable, he would recognise it anywhere.

As the man and woman climbed onto the motorcycle, and with his head bowed low he touched the brim of his hat in gratitude and started towards the open doorway. Why do that, he heard the man chide the woman. Because Ewan my darling boy, the Hobo will mess the place up and there will be no trace of us whatsoever, if anyone were to ever come looking.

Inside the small kitchen Ronnie yanked the radio from inside his jacket as he heard the motorcycle roar away. Come in Alison, he shouted, come in Alison, for God`s sake woman, where are you come in.

The radio crackled and her cockney voice responded, okay keep your hair on, what`s wrong do you need help with your makeup.

Listen you stupid woman, he shouted. Both, I repeat both suspects have left the cottage on the fucking motorcycle. They are heading back to the café, and within a few minutes they will be long gone. it is confirmed, and I repeat it is confirmed that the woman is Jaguar. They must be apprehended or at worst followed, they must NOT be allowed to get away, and remember these are dangerous people almost certainly armed so sort your shit now.

Dragging off the overcoat and boots he pulled on a pair of training shoes which were stuffed in the coat pockets and set off at his fastest sprint towards the gap in the hedge where he could already see the two suspects pushing the motorcycle up the bank.

Out of breath, he had to wait seemingly long seconds for a safe gap in the busy traffic, before running to the middle and having to wait again. As he sprinted across the northbound carriageway to the sound of blaring car horn's he heard two very distinct cracks.

Reaching the car park area, he saw the silver sports car racing off towards the northbound slip road in a cloud of dust, then turning to look back across the car park his full attention was taken by the sprawled body lying face down on the rough ground.

Checking for a pulse, he gently turned her in his arms and saw the two reddish brown holes in her forehead, knowing instantly that she was gone. He sat on the ground gently cradling her head on his lap, as for the first time in his memory, real tears poured down his cheeks.

Wailing sirens greeted the arrival of the police armed response unit, and as one of the officers gently lifted him away, saying come along sir, we are here now, he could only reply. But your too late you are too fucking late, as he sobbed.

De-briefed, and on his way back to Harrogate, he wondered why all of the women that he came into contact with ended up as a complete disaster.

Alison had been a great person and probably a good policewoman, but she had simply been out of her depth where Siobahn Flannery was concerned.

Her death should not have happened, but, yet again, the Irish bitch was to blame, first John and now Alison. There and then, he swore to avenge them both by killing her himself.

Eugene had explained that despite the tragic incident intelligence had everything under control, and that it would only be a matter of time before both Flannery and Ewan Blake were picked up and charged. He thanked Ronnie for his valued input and said that with confirmation that Proshyn was in the UK, anti-terrorism units would swing into action and take full control.

Concluding that all things being considered, the operation had been a resounding success, and that in return for his services Eugene would assist where he could, with the matter of the cup, Ronnie had shouted at Eugene that if he considered the operation a success then he hated to think what failure looked like, and simply stating Alison's murder as a tragic incident was both crass and unforgiveable as apparently, she had not even been armed.

Ronnie considered everything carefully and wondered if he might have done anything differently, but then concluded that until you had dealt with Flannery in person it was hard to see any threat from her, to be any greater than from another person, this woman was it seemed pure evil.

The following morning the main newspapers carried a picture of Alison with the heading, OFF DUTY POLICE OFFICER SHOT BY SUSPECTED ROBBERS , the main headline news was however.

CLOSE PROTECTION OFFICER SAVES LIFE OF PRINCESS , with the story telling how an armed Royal protection officer had foiled an attempt to kidnap or possibly kill the Princess, and that in recognition he would be awarded a medal.

So, they captured Ewan Bale Ronnie sighed, big deal he was always expendable, but what about Siobahn. There was no mention and presumably she was long gone. And was Alison getting a medal, even posthumously, no, like John, just a couple of bullets marked her term of service for Queen and country.

What a total fuckup he said pulling up outside Linda's home, will I ever get another chance to meet up with that bitch.

Chapter Thirteen
Another Chance

By the early summer of 1977 Ronnie and Linda had moved out of Mothers home in Ripon, and were living in Milton Keynes New Town, near Northampton.

The work being undertaken by Maxon in the UK was apparently concluded and as had always happened in his life, he found himself working for a Jewish owned company specialising in furnaces and industrial ovens. The company had premises in Bletchley, which was now a suburb of the New Town, and a second at Andover in Hampshire. And Ronnie divided his working time between the two locations and customers premises.

His morning break in the Andover works canteen, was rudely interrupted early in August by a Tannoy call, requesting him at reception, where he found Eugene waiting. Hello Ronnie, it is good to see you again and before you ask, Harry has, as I am sure you know, been keeping a watchful eye on you and helping where he is able, to make life go smoothly.

You mean go in the direction that he requires replied Ronnie, rather than worry about me too much. You really do need to see the bigger picture sometimes Ronnie Eugene sighed, can we get a coffee and have a quick chat.

Ronnie fetched a coffee for Eugene and a fresh mug of tea for himself and asked. Why is Harry not here then, am I no longer his good little boy. Harry is unwell replied Eugene, he has been diagnosed with cancer of his lungs which sadly is in its terminal stages, all they can do is offer some comfort and pain relief.

I am genuinely sorry to hear that replied Ronnie, whatever else he was, Harry has always been a good friend to me. Despite what you might wish to think he speaks very highly of you as well muttered Eugene, which is to some extent why I am here.

Because of the illness his mobility is not what it was, and with the families search for the cup and possibly the shroud still a priority, someone else needs to lead the project. The family and I have held discussions in Harry`s presence resulting in my being given instruction to do whatever it takes to bring this project to a satisfactory conclusion, and of course to fulfil that obligation I will require assistance.

You can fuck right off, you are a cynical, self-protective bastard spat Ronnie. For three years you have hidden under a rock, only interested in your own needs, oblivious to the fact that you fucked up big time in Stamford. It is because of your pathetic self-interest that Alison died. You do know that I hold you solely responsible.

Yes, I do know that sighed Eugene, but the truth is that she was her own woman. Fiercely competitive in a man`s world, and constantly angry at the so-called glass ceiling, which she saw as, us men trying to keep her where we could control her and keep her obedient. But despite those beliefs she was still determined to somehow break through and reach the very top.

We will never know if she would have succeeded will we said Ronnie bitterly. The truth is that none of us can take any credit or kudos from that episode. In our own way we all fucked up and contributed towards Alison`s death. My biggest regret is that I let that bitch Flannery, or Proshyn as you prefer to call her get away. I have vowed to find her and take revenge for both John and now Alison, but who knows when or even if. I will get a chance.

Your Irish lady shot Alison in that carpark when, unarmed but still fearless, she attempted to stop the two of them getting away. Shot twice in the head in cold blood. So, despite my nurtured "stiff upper lip" work ethic, I too wish her to be brought to justice responded Eugene.

I doubt that you have come all the way here from London just to update me regarding Harry`s health issues, or to chat about our past failure said Ronnie so cut the bollocks Eugene and tell me why you are here.

Are you aware that Denise Proshyn was arrested in France last year suspected of being involved with the Bader-Meinhoff organisation, queried Eugene. Yes of course replied Ronnie. It was well covered by most of the newspapers, and it was also reported subsequently that somehow she had managed to escape from custody, which hardly came as a surprise.

I have some good news for you, which as you so kindly asked, is indeed the reason for my being here mused Eugene. A certain landowner who as it happens has a country estate a few miles from here in Andover, is holding a summer ball at that very estate in August we believe.

For fucks sake Eugene, get to the point, probably most or at least three quarters of wealthy landowners, the so called "English Gentlemen hold summer events on their estates quite often charity related said Ronnie in exasperation. It is apparently good for their image quite apart from being a tax write-off.

This particular "wealthy landowner" just happens to be called Lord Critchley smiled Eugene. And we already understand he has strong connections to the far-right, Neo-Nazi group called the Red Fraction. We also know that this particular summer ball, will be held over three evenings on a Friday, Saturday, and Sunday with the Saturday event being a Masquerade Ball.

The great and the good from afar will be invited continued Eugene, but we believe it to be a smokescreen for a small group to meet in secret, to view this cup of yours and possibly even the shroud.

Ronnie sat bolt upright. Do you mean that the items might be bought here to the UK. Yes, indeed we do, Eugene was still smiling. We have it on good authority from our American cousins, that an Arab State wishes to purchase the items at no expense spared.

For Heaven's sake, hissed Ronnie, we cannot allow that to happen, if it does then possibly the entire course of world history might be changed.

Forgive me if I do not share your Zionist beliefs Ronnie, Eugene was now in his fully professional mode. However, I do commit to give you every possible assistance within the bounds of legality and law. And if you are successful, with the recovery of the items, they will be treasured by the British Museum, and Herr Critchley and his cohorts will be detained at Her Majesty's pleasure.

And "when", not "if", we recover the items and they suddenly go missing, what will happen then smiled Ronnie. Then Eugene paused, British Intelligence will know exactly where to look for them, starting at your front door. But of course, if we recovered the items only for the Experts to discover them to be fakes, elaborate replicas but nonetheless fakes, then we would all have to assume that Critchley had been trying to pull off a huge scam by selling fakes as the genuine article concluded Eugene.

THE CUP

Point taken, and understood responded Ronnie, and I for one would certainly believe "that family" would see such a scam as well justified. What happens now, is there a plan.

You will of course need to be close to the estate leading up to and during the event, and to that end we have booked a room at a nearby country pub, giving you a genuine reason for being around the area.

The pub owners are both fully security cleared. As a retired cryptographer, the wife was at the ministry`s code breaking centre at Bletchley Park during the war, whilst he was a Navy veteran, Normandy beaches and all that, their security is now only lowest level clearance, but more than adequate for your needs added Eugene.

What about me being able to access the estate, can HMG manage that asked Ronnie. We will try of course but being honest I do not hold out much hope responded Eugene. The place is pretty much self-contained, tight security, with all the suppliers closely vetted, even down to the local butcher. There is also gate lodge security and patrols so any uninvited visit will be out of the question.

A genuine invitation to the Saturday Masquerade Ball is not likely to be forthcoming either then I guess sighed Ronnie. Final question at least for now. When exactly does all of this occur, and will I get any support other than your occasional input.

I think, smiled Eugene, that if you get your arse into gear, there will be plenty of time for you to prepare everything needed. Today is June 15th, you are booked to stay at the pub from Monday 18th July with the events scheduled for Friday 29th July as a Jazz Dance evening, the grand Ball on Saturday 30th July and a wind down buffet dance on Sunday 01st August.

Eugene passed over an envelope saying. Inside there are details of the pub, some contact name`s and some cash, if you need more let me know. I now have access via Harry, to your group`s considerable funds, into which I will not enquire, other than to say that I will need some evidence of expenditure.

They stood and shook hands and Ronnie escorted him to his car, I will keep in touch with you Eugene said, but please be careful and stay safe, from what little I know or wish to know about this mission, it has danger written all over it.

In the envelope Ronnie found details of the pub, The Portsmouth Arms Hurstbourne Priors with its owners being John and Glenda, plus the name of a Rabbi with a telephone number, and cash which he counted out carefully and amounted to three thousand pounds in used banknotes.

Using the office telephone, he dialled the number for the Rabbi and a soft voice answered. Reuben Kravitz speaking how may I assist you. I have been given your name by a friend as someone who might be able to help me with my work on some ancient religious artifacts said Ronnie, namely the holy shroud and the covenant cup.

I think that you have made a mistake, I am Reuben Kravitz a retired orthodox Rabbi, not a shop owner and as there are no shops here in Yardley Gobion, you must have been given an incorrect number and the telephone line went dead.

Ronnie was just on the point of completing the redial, when his brain kicked in. The Rabbi had given the name of his home or at least the location from where the call had been answered. Why do that unless he was telling Ronnie something, he wanted him to know where it was, he wanted Ronnie to go in person.

He asked Carol, his trusted work planner, and the company "service help desk coordinator", to research all villages called

Yardley Gobion within the UK, and if necessary, to try spelling variations, after all how many villages with that name could there be.

I need to go back to Milton Keynes tonight Carol he said, I will be at the Bletchley works tomorrow as there are some tests that I want to try, do I have anything urgent booked.

As it happens, she replied. Research and Development at Bletchley called, and would like you to pop in tomorrow to discuss some new ideas. Apparently, it needs to be Thursday, because Mr Bird their design director is working to a tight schedule so it will fit nicely for you with R and D tomorrow and your tests Friday, so I will probably see you next Monday, but I will let you know about this Yardley place as soon as I have something.

Over dinner that evening he explained to Linda that towards the end of July he would be away for at least a week, possibly a few days longer to manage a special project in Andover, which judging by her mute response, was either disbelieved or showed her total disinterest.

On Thursday afternoon Carol telephoned him at the Bletchley factory to give an update on the Yardley Gobion search, which had apparently revealed there to be two possibilities, one in the Islands of Scotland and the second just a few miles from Bletchley near Towcester.

With Linda apparently working, at least for the morning, the Saturday found Ronnie in the quaint little village of Yardley Gobion on the main road between Towcester and Newport Pagnell, enjoying a morning coffee and a slice of homemade cake in the small but clean café aptly named the coffee pot.

Asking the young waitress if there was a synagogue nearby, he suddenly realised to his dismay that she had absolutely no idea of what he meant, so he asked instead if they had a telephone directory.

There were few names listed under the letter K and the Rabbi had "Little Copse" shown as his address. Asking the waitress again, if she knew where Little Copse might be found, she simply pointed across the road to a small, thatched cottage hidden behind tall bushes.

Leaving his van in the café car park, Ronnie walked across the road and through the wrought iron gate which was set into a low wall above which bushes sprouted. A short, block paved pathway led to a white painted door with a stained-glass window set into it.

Before he could knock, the door swung inwards and a grey-haired wrinkled face old man said, good morning Mr Godliman please do come in I have been expecting you, and before you start asking silly questions, my friend Isaac Rabonitz said that he thought it would be today, you of course know him better as Harry I believe.

Ronnie wondered if he could ever get the hang of all this cloak and dagger stuff, but said simply, I think that I need your help Rabbi, or at least my colleagues think that I might. Yes, yes of course chuckled the old man, sit down, we have many preparations to make and not much time.

The cottage was tiny, and the old man presumably lived alone. The cramped parlour was filled with shelves of books plus a small table and two wing backed armchairs, heavy curtains blocked most of the morning sunlight and Ronnie considered that the room might have not been out of place a century earlier.

Krabitz shuffled in carrying a tray with teapot cups saucers and a small milk jug, and, gesturing for Ronnie to sit he stirred the pot then poured two cups. Always add the milk to the tea Ronnie he said sagely, that way you get to choose its strength, after all it is a cup of tea as opposed to coloured milk.

Now down to business, I understand that you require a copy of the Turin Shroud and a copy of the Cup of the Covenant neither of which will be easy. Particularly the cup as few people have ever seen it, and I personally know of no one who has, excepting present company I am told, so you will have to detail exactly what it looks like said the Rabbi.

I will do my best, but I am no artist sighed Ronnie. He had not considered that any picture or painting was likely to be an artist's idea, rather than a picture of the real thing. Reuben had pulled down a large book filled with engravings and pictures, several showed various images reputed to be the cup, but all were hopelessly incorrect either ornate and majestic or pewter and tarnished.

Do you have any pictures of the everyday cups used at the time of Jesus that I might take a look at please, Ronnie suggested to Reuben. The Rabbi took an old lithograph showing the last supper depicted and gave it to him.

The wooden table had three simple cups scattered across it whilst the ornate gilt goblet was central, held high in Jesus, hand. Do you have a magnifying glass Ronnie asked, and focusing on the simple cups said, like that in shape made from a very light wood about six inches tall three inches diameter across the top and the same in depth of cup.

It is pale blue almost greenish in colour with a thin stem as thick as a standard pencil, and a slightly concave base the same size as the diameter of the cup top.

Reuben took a sketch pad and began to scribble earnestly just with a single pencil as Ronnie sat and sipped his tea watching.

Some five minutes later he turned the pad towards Ronnie and showed a remarkable likeness of the cup.

The cup was hand carved but smooth and stained rather than painted, almost as if the wood were coloured, offered Ronnie. Some type of Woad I expect responded Reuben, I will get working on copies of both items, but I cannot guarantee them to be exact replica`s we can only hope that they will pass casual inspections.

What about money asked Ronnie, how much will this cost. Psh psh, money money, how much he asks, not how long will it take, but how much will it cost, my boy always ask the important questions first.

Well then replied Ronnie, how long will I take you to make these replicas for me. About Five Thousand Pounds, came the sardonic reply.

What exclaimed Ronnie, Five Thousand Pounds. Psh Psh, Funny Money, Five Ten, who knows when, Oy Vey, tomorrow is another day. Listen my young friend you wish for copies of possibly the most iconic and unique items anywhere in the world, do you think that these can be purchased as trinkets from some Aladdin`s Cave of ancient artifacts. I will need all my skills to make these items, and if it makes you feel any better Harry has instructed there to be two of each item made, just in case you lose them, and he has already made payment.

Oh of course he has, I sometimes wonder why I bother sighed Ronnie almost to himself, talk about sorcerer`s apprentice. Thank you for your time old man can you tell me how long these replicas might take you.

Sorcery he says, never confuse fictional magic with the real thing Mr Godliman Angels and Demons do not always appear as winged beings, and we do not always see them in the flesh so to speak, but that does not make them less real or less powerful.

As for how long, who knows, I have never created such things before, but let us say six weeks. Make it five weeks maximum, smiled Ronnie, the summer Ball is Six weeks tonight and I must have them before then.

Over the next three weeks Ronnie researched Lord Critchley and in particular his country estate of Hurstbourne Park in Hampshire which was close to the small hamlet of Tufton. The estate dated back in part, over seven hundred years, and had in fact been used as a country lodge by King John when hunting in the Savernake Forest.

When Critchley had purchased the estate, he had arrogantly changed the name to Critchley Hall, and the estate held an assortment of functions and events.

Sir Henry Critchley was a prominent socialite who lived for most of the year at a London, Belgravia home with his German born Wife Lady Greta Critchley. They had a long list of wealthy friends and hangers-on including banker`s industrialist`s, politicians and even nobility.

Greta Critchley was born Greta Mendal in Bavaria, and she had met and subsequently married Henry Critchley in Berlin in 1938 aged twenty-two. Henry who was the only child of land-owning gentry and an ex, Rugby School Student, had been twenty-six at that time and a junior attaché at the British Embassy there.

In 1939, at the outset of war the newly married couple came to London, and over the years Henry worked his way up through the ranks at the Foreign Office. Today he was a highly respected personal advisor to the foreign secretary with the ear of the prime minister, whilst Greta was a wealthy socialite chairing various charities and hosting numerous events, with Royalty included within her circle of friends. They had two children, a married son serving as a lieutenant colonel in the army intelligence corps, and a daughter, Pandora not yet married and who owned her own property development business.

Late one morning Ronnie drove his van out of the Andover factory towards Whitchurch. Coming into Hurstbourne Priors he saw the pub where he was to stay and noted its location. He drove on through the village towards Tufton, then left and past the huge Critchley Estate, with uniformed security at the gate. Ex-military I expect he mused, the question is, what they believe to be of such value. The question is of course, are they trying to keep something in, or maybe keep someone out Ronnie wondered aloud.

He turned around after driving past three quarters of the estate, which was all well hidden behind twelve feet high eroded brick walls, and slowly returning towards the gate he stopped about fifty yards short.

Ronnie casually pulled a map from behind the passenger sun visor and pretended to study it whilst carefully checking the security and noting the closed-circuit camera installations. The roar of an engine made him look up and along the road, as a bright yellow open top sports car raced towards him then with a squeal of brakes swerved into the open gateway. The two security officers deftly stepped aside in an apparently well practiced manner as the car shot off along the driveway. Probably, heading towards the house, he thought.

The incident had taken only seconds he guessed, but it had been enough time for him to establish a decent mental image. That of a youngish woman early to mid-thirties, bright ginger hair and pale skin, wearing white rimmed sunglasses and a pale orange headscarf.

Parking on the frontage outside the pub in Hurstbourne Priors, rather than the designated rear car park Ronnie went inside and perched on a high bar stool in what was called the public bar. A pint of Guinness please he asked the ruddy faced barman, an overweight figure smoking a small cigar who was wiping glasses with bar towel.

We only have cans, came the gruff response, and if you know anything about Guinness it is nothing like the same taste. The rough looking unshaved face wheezed and then coughed, but I can do you a poor man's black velvet if you like.

Without waiting for a reply, the barman took down a chunky pint glass with a thick handle and half-filled it from a bar tap which read Bulmer's Cider, then placing the glass mug down he opened a can of Guinness and tilting the glass onto one edge slowly poured the black stout beer into the cider.

Putting the cream headed brew onto the bar in front of Ronnie he said that will be one pound and fifty pence, and Ronnie handed over the correct money,

This is nice thank you Ronnie said after tasting the drink. I am pleased that you like it, if you are wondering we can, and do make the real thing using champagne of course, but that tends to be only when the Toffs from the big house come in to show off replied the barman

Ronnie looked around. Excepting a scruffy looking man, possibly a gardener judging by his clothes the public bar was empty. Wipe clean tables, upright chairs with plastic covered seats, a dartboard, pool table, a wall mounted jukebox, and linoleum floor covering, all hard wearing and easy to clean.

Taking his drink Ronnie climbed from the stool and walked across to a door marked lounge. He went through and was greeted by a smaller red and green carpeted room with four tables. The chairs were upholstered, and faux leather bench seating ran around the walls. Laminated menus, salt pepper and vinegar adorned each table, and an unlit open fireplace gave a semblance of homeliness.

The barman had also moved around behind the bar and was still polishing the glasses. Ronnie realised the bar served both rooms and that by doing so, one person might keep up with any orders from either area.

Were you interested in lunch enquired the barman. No thank you, not today, maybe another time replied Ronnie, adding, do you have rooms for visitors. Just the four singles, no doubles. We do not get visitors as such, just the odd company representative and spill over from the big house when a large event happens.

Does that happen often then enquired Ronnie, I mean events at the big house. The barman coughed, took a long draw on his cigar and blew out a ring of blue smoke, wheezed, coughed and wiped his mouth on the back of his hand before speaking.

Your room is not one of the four we offer to our guest`s, it is one of our own private rooms so it should offer you some privacy and freedom for whatever it is you need to do.

As your cover story, we will be looking after our nephew called Ronnie. The barman held out a podgy hand saying I am John my wife Glenda is around somewhere. How, did you guess who I am, Ronnie said. After all, I hardly have a label hanging around my neck.

Twenty-eight years spent alongside David Ben-Gurion counts for something I guess murmured the barman. As to how I knew that is easily answered, firstly you are not a local, you are inquisitive yet not pushy so not a reporter. Any genuine traveller would have no interest in local issues, so you are not a representative or salesman.

Taking a large draw on the last of his cigar before stubbing it into an ashtray on the bar John said. If you had been any type of authority such as police or intelligence you would have been comfortable with saying so, but it seems that you only want a rough background on the pub and particularly the big house, and then of course there is your van.

My van queried Ronnie. It happens to be sign written, and as we already knew the name of our forthcoming guest`s employer, the deduction was hardly difficult smiled John. Two plus two quite often make four, at least in my experience, so it was nothing amazing, now what do you want to know.

Basic stuff said Ronnie. As you already know I will be staying with you before and during the planned, Summer-Events weekend, at the big house, which happen toward the end of July, and anything that you can think of which might be useful would be much appreciated.

May we be permitted to know what you are particularly looking for as it might help us focus our information search asked John. I cannot say for certain sighed Ronnie, not because of any secrecy but simply because I am not sure myself.

In outline terms we believe that one of the events probably the Saturday Ball, will be a cover for a subversive group to meet and maybe exchange things.

I need to be there continued Ronnie, and as things stand, a formal VIP Invitation is most unlikely, so knowledge on how to get in, and ideally out again would be nice, some idea of guests or at least numbers, the same for entertainers and caterers.

Leave everything to us then smiled John. Quite a few locals work on the estate and others as temporary staff for the special events, and of course the landlord of the local pub gets to hear all the gossip and tittle tattle.

One last thing before I go back to work said Ronnie, when I drove past the Critchley Estate, I saw a young woman in a yellow sports car do you know who she is. That my young friend is the right honourable Lady Pandora Critchley, his Lordship`s blue eyed daughter, she can do no wrong in his eyes. She is the one who manages each of the events and believe me, from what they say of her she can be a vicious vindictive young madam to anyone who displeases her.

Oh, dear me then I had better not upset her laughed Ronnie, which might be difficult as my record with the fair sex is not brilliant, I will see you in two weeks and we can get our heads together to run through what we know and what else we might need to know.

The following week Ronnie had been booked for several days site testing and pre-commissioning at the Main "Gas Liquifying Plant" at Glenmavis, not far from Glasgow in Scotland which he was gradually bringing on stream as the various parts were completed.

This work being an obligation taken over from Maxon as it required Ronnie`s capabilities. The plant allowed gas in its vapourised gaseous state to be pumped ashore from beneath the North Sea and stored in huge tanks as a liquid having been cooled down be cryogenics, then when required it was heated in huge water tanks to return it to a gas for delivery into the gas network distribution system.

On the Friday afternoon as he travelled home his pager beeped requiring him to stop and telephone the office.

Ronnie pulled into a Services on the A74 near Dumfries and telephoned Carol, let me guess I have left something behind he said. No, nothing like that and even if you had, I would not have called you to stop and telephone for something unimportant. A man has telephoned for you and allowed me to take a message. A Mr Crabbies says that your copying is now complete, but you need to check it over so would you please call him.

Yes of course thanks Carol you are my rock, I could not do the job without you. Flattery will get you everywhere Ronnie Giggled Carol, see you next Monday, do not be late it is the annual Directors and Employees meeting and it begins at ten am sharp.

On the following morning a Saturday, Ronnie drove to Yardley Gobion to see Krabitz, smiling to himself at Carols mispronunciation. The items were finished, and he admired the workmanship. Holding the cup and turning it over in his hands he realised that it was not as heavy as the real item, and was too blue, needing to be slightly tinted in a greener shade. Reuben clucked away but said that it would be done and told him to return the following week and collect the items.

After the meeting on Monday, Ronnie fetched coffee for both him and Carol and asked her what she knew about the Critchley Estate in Tufton, to which she immediately replied nothing at all, it is far to "upper crust" for the likes of me but talk to Anita in accounts, as I believe that she and her husband live in one of the Estate Cottages.

Anita was a tallish long legged blonde haired young lady he guessed mid-thirties, but with the accounts area open plan he reasoned that any form of private chat would be impossible, so late afternoon found him waiting in the works car park to chat with her as she left for the day.

At half past five the office girls began to trickle out and leave but it was almost quarter to six when she appeared walking with Colin the finance director, they chatted as they walked to her small white Fiat 500 where she climbed into the driver seat and almost casually, Colin leaned down and they kissed.

Well now, who is a naughty girl and for that matter a naughty boy too Ronnie mused, as he knew both to be married. Waving to Colin she drove out of the works car park and turned towards Hurstbourne Priors with Ronnie following at a discreet distance, she drove on into Tufton and then along past the turning to the Estate pulling up outside a row of four terrace cottages.

Climbing out and locking her car she started walking towards the door of the near end cottage. Ronnie was considering going to the door and knocking when a dishevelled young man hurried up behind her and slid his arm around her waist ushering her along the remaining pathway to the front door.

The following day Ronnie resolved to get a chance to talk with Anita, but at every seeming opportunity she got called away, so in desperation he popped the bonnet of her car and removed the HT cable supplying the distributor ensuring that the car would not start.

It was again well after five thirty when she rushed out to her car, this time alone, and seemed flustered when the car would not start. Ronnie trotted over casually and asked if he might help, to which she almost cried oh yes please, if I am late Stuart will kill me.

If time is that important, let me drive you home and I will sort the car tomorrow, is that okay Ronnie smiled. During the short journey he took the opportunity to chat, discovering this evening to be a dinner dance event for employees at the Critchley estate, where her husband Stuart worked as part of the grounds team. Apparently, the estate was giving a free dinner for the employees, as several large events were due which would involve quite a bit of extra work.

Dropping her outside their cottage he checked the time, seeing it to be after six and the drive back home took over two hours, he went to the Portsmouth Arms and asked John if he might stay. He telephoned home and spoke to Linda who seemed far from pleased, but he reasoned needs must, and he had already agreed to pick Anita up again in the morning around half past eight.

Over a rather good homemade steak and ale pie he chatted with Glenda who whilst partial to red wine in substantial quantities, was nonetheless extremely charming, and she promised to give him as much assistance as possible with his project.

It seemed that Stan the local butcher provided all the estate's meat and being a friend, she thought that he might be able to offer some details, at least the numbers expected.

Apparently Maurice the baker and Raymond the grocer also supplied the estate and she had strong links with both men, so felt sure that at last some useful information would be unearthed.

I have not seen any shops said Ronnie, heavens no said Glenda, not here but down the road in Hurstbourne Tarrant, a lovely little village with a decent pub called the George and Dragon. John and I go there sometimes on our night off a sort of busman's holiday.

Wednesday morning, Ronnie picked Anita up as promised and drove her to the office, taking her car keys he sent her inside then popped the Fiat bonnet and restored the cable, checking the car started he locked it and returned the keys to Anita.

After checking work schedules with Carol, he drove back out to the estate where without warning Anita's husband stepped into the road and threw a large rock at the van.

Stopping and climbing out Ronnie saw that a house brick had bounced on the bonnet and then shattered the windscreen, next time I will kill you shouted the irate husband as he started to walk away, just keep away from my wife.

Ronnie was so angry that he considered beating the man senseless, but fortunately common sense prevailed, as he realised that any action would result in unnecessary publicity. And being so close to the estate could and probably would, put an end to the current project.

Back at the office he explained to his technical director Peter, that a lorry had thrown up a huge steel bolt causing some severe damage to his van and was instructed to take the vehicle to the garage always used and get a loan car for the duration of the repairs, and nothing too flash Ronnie, called Peter as he left the office.

At the garage, Joe the head mechanic simply did not believe the lorry and steel bolt story, any more than Ronnie suspected Peter had, and made mutterings about panel beating and paint spraying, finally saying it would take two possibly three weeks, adding I suppose that you want a car to use.

We have a nice clean little Ford Fiesta over there that you can use said Joe, I will get the keys. What about that one asked Ronnie pointing. The Granada said Joe surprised, your boss will never sanction that. Well, he would have to, if it were the only one available smiled Ronnie.

But like I said we have a couple of Fiesta`s, groaned the mechanic, as Ronnie tucked a twenty-pound note into his overall`s pocket. But the Granada is the only one available now I think, said Ronnie and ready to go I believe, can you get the keys.

At home Linda was impressed by the car and after they had eaten dinner, she insisted on him taking her for a drive, so they went to one of their favourite canal side pubs on the Grand Union called the Three Locks at Stoke Hammond.

The car is nice she said as they drove home can you keep it, I doubt it Ronnie sighed, I expect I will get the van back once it has been repaired, this is hardly suitable for carrying my equipment. But we will have it for a couple of weeks at least so we can make the most of it.

Take me to my Mother's at the weekend she said, we can go up on Friday evening stopping for food on the way and come back after Sunday lunch, she would love to see us both and it has been a while. Okay said Ronnie but I must see someone before we go as I have some bits that I need to collect.

I will work from the local factory tomorrow and Friday said Ronnie, then take the afternoon as leave, picking you up from work so that we can go straight off. So, pack a bag for us both and I will take you to work on Friday morning.

Reuben ushered Ronnie into the tiny parlour and disappeared, only to return a few moments later with a tea tray and some biscuits. Instructing Ronnie to pour the tea reminding him that it was tea first, he went out of the room and Ronnie did his best to pour two cups of strong looking brew.

Reuben reappeared and handed Ronnie a rectangular parcel wrapped in brown paper about the size of a tailored shirt box which he then placed on the small table and unwrapped. Inside was indeed a box and removing the lid he saw the folded shroud wrapped in some type of polythene covering and the small wooden cup wrapped in white tissue paper.

Removing the tissue wrapping Ronnie saw the blue velvet drawstring bag and taking out the cup he examined it carefully. Marvelling at how genuine it looked although he had only held the real thing for a short time, Ronnie knew that this would pass any casual inspection, indeed he would take it for the genuine item if he did not have the ability to feel it.

Lifting the shroud, he examined it through the wrappings, the cloth was gently pinned to a backing board, with only the front top exposed to immediate view, showing a greyish white almost threadbare linen cloth with brownish streaks.

The image of an old artist's overall, sprang into his mind, and he suddenly wondered what the international fuss was about, only to realise that the cloth was an irrelevance, it was the staining which made it both unique and priceless.

The cup is amazing, he said to Reuben, but I have no knowledge of the shroud having never seen it, so how do we know if it will pass muster when inspected. Reuben smiled and passed him a colour lithograph which showed the shroud unboxed and he was surprised at the close similarity of linen texture and positioning of the staining.

A second picture showed the shroud boxed for public display and from Ronnie's perspective the copy he was looking at would pass as the real thing.

Thanking Reuben and locking both items into the boot of the Granada he drove home, deciding that it might be safer to keep them in the car rather than at home.

Collecting Linda direct from the local pharmacy in Stony Stratford where she was helping to demonstrate cosmetics, the drive north to Yorkshire was uneventful and the weekend with Jean quite relaxing.

After lunch on Sunday when Jean had openly asked about their future and might she expect wedding plans soon which Linda somewhat neatly sidestepped, they drove home in warm sunshine and enjoyed the luxury of what was a top of the range motor car.

Nearing the motorway exit FOR Milton Keynes and home, local radio gave a newsflash about the sad death of a retired Rabbi who had been trapped in his cottage after a suspicious fire had ripped through it.

THE CUP

Shit said Ronnie out aloud, that is down to me not being careful enough. Pardon replied Linda, what is down to you.

Oh, the engine warning light just flashed on and off again and I suspect I need to top up the oil, I should have checked it over the weekend, but it will be fine.

On the Monday morning a rather sombre Carol greeted Ronnie with the news that their Director Peter had passed away after suffering a massive heart attack at his home on the Saturday and Ronnie gave her twenty pounds to organise some flowers and a condolence card.

He then checked through the work schedules for the next few weeks to see if he needed to rearrange anything, but apart from a request to "help out" in the research and development department there in Andover, nothing of importance was booked which suited him well.

After lunch he was called to see the managing director Guy Henwin, and after exchanging mutual expressions of sympathy regarding Peters sudden demise which in Ronnie`s case at least, was quite genuine, the managing director told him that with immediate effect he was to be promoted to service manager, he would use Peter`s office and assume all the daily responsibilities of managing the department.

They would not be replacing Peter as a director therefore it was seen by the board as Ronnie`s opportunity to work towards future advancement.

Thanking the Managing Director for the promotion he returned to the service and engineering department office to tell Carol, who was thrilled. Ronnie then explained the situation to Brian, the factory foreman and asked him to consider promoting one of the employees to the position of mobile service engineer, and back in the office he boxed up Peter`s personal belongings.

Ronnie spent a while rearranging the office to his own liking during which time Carol bought coffee and some biscuits, after which they checked all forthcoming work requirements and arranged with Brian for the chosen new mobile service engineer to meet with Ronnie and Carol the following Monday morning at 9.30am in the office.

After finishing at the office around six pm in the evening he checked in at the Portsmouth Arms, unpacked his clothes, then telephoned Linda to share the good news about his promotion, and the likelihood of keeping the car.

Over dinner alone with his drink of black velvet he considered the most recent events and decided that God was indeed in his Heaven and all was right with the world.

On the Wednesday evening he was perched on one of the public bar stools chatting with John whilst a small group of locals played pool, when a young woman entered the bar and sat on a stool at the far end of the bar to him.

Might I have a half pint of lager and lime please she said in an upper-class accent.

Put it onto my tab please John said Ronnie and slipped from his stool, saying to the young woman, let it be my treat, it is not every day that we get the pleasure of an attractive lady from Devon in here, are you staying locally.

Taking a sip from her glass she looked him up and down then said. They did tell me that you fancied yourself as a lady`s man, and they were not wrong, I presume that you are Charles.

At your service, my lady. Ronnie offered mock subservience to her, what gave me away. You mean apart from the boyish good charm, the cheap chat up lines and the mop of fair hair, I think it was the eyes that clinched it, they said piercing blue, and again they were not wrong.

THE CUP

Well now it seems that you know who I am responded Ronnie, but for the moment you have me at a distinct disadvantage, as I have no idea whom you might be, or for that matter why you have picked me up.

Hmm, that is an interesting viewpoint, considering it was you who bought my drink as a treat I believe you said, but for the record my name is Heather, and I am here to offer whatever assistance that I can towards your forthcoming project.

Is this yet another Harry intervention Ronnie smiled, because if so, it is most definitely one of his better ones. I do not know any Harry Heather replied, I was asked by a distant relative, Eugene, to contact you and see what if anything I might do to help.

Have you eaten yet, Ronnie asked her to which she responded no she had not, and that of course she would love to share dinner with him. So over plates of steak and eggs, each had time to share some details of their life.

Heather was a full time Ladies Maid, or Lady in waiting as she so quaintly put it working for HRH Princess M, at which Ronnie laughed and said what a load of bollocks, we all exaggerate to some extent, but a bloody lady in waiting to a princess what the fuck does Eugene take me for.

Rather than being angry Heather simply smiled, they also told me that when nervous or taken by surprise I could expect some strong language from you and a fair amount of scepticism. However what mileage would I achieve from telling you lies. And given the short amount of time that I now understand you have at your disposal, suggest that any help should be valued rather than sneered at.

I am in a unique position to offer some help although exactly how much is not yet clear, as HRH Lady in waiting, I have unconditional access to the Estate when she is staying, and for your information as things currently stand, we are here through the three evening events scheduled for the end of July.

Ronnie took his time and weighed his words carefully, but in essence explained the Shroud and Cup to Heather, leaving out the gruesome deaths in Belfast and totally omitting the most recent sad RAF Wittering incident. She listened attentively without interrupting and waited until he had finished before asking what he thought she might be able to offer him in the way of assistance.

He asked if she recognised the description of Siobahn, or knew either her or Denise Proshyn`s names, the answers to all of which were no. She did not know any details of numbers attending any of the events and had no way of either attending herself as a guest, only being in waiting should she be summoned.

On the Friday she called into the Pub and told him that the Critchley`s had arrived from London for the weekend and were taking dinner with HRH in Alton, as guest of the Lord Lieutenant of Hampshire so as she had a free evening, he could go back to the estate with her for coffee.

In the huge farmhouse style kitchen, Ronnie was standing by the sink, watching Heather percolate coffee after crushing Arabica Beans in a small hand grinder, when the door opened and HRH resplendent in a turquoise evening gown with a white fur stole around her neck partially covering the sparkling necklace stepped into the room. A lit cigarette dangling from her lips.

Oh good, fresh coffee, just what I need, well done hag, bring some to my rooms and fetch something for my headache. Heather bobbed a small curtsy, yes of course maam she replied, then sweeping her arm towards Ronnie added, this is Charles a friend. HRH turned and looked him up and down, then turning on her heel swept out, calling loudly as she departed. Coffee hag NOW.

When Heather returned to the kitchen Ronnie still in awe, asked if that really had been HRH the Princess . Of course, silly, she developed a headache so has returned early, I have given her some medication and she will be fine tomorrow.

Ronnie asked why she was so rude to her maid calling her hag, Heather laughed, it is my initials, Heather Ann Gamblin, Heather is too informal and Gamblin seemed a little coarse and so she settled on the initials, it seems to amuse her.

Is she always so ignorant, even downright rude, Ronnie asked. Heather giggled, I can see that you do not know anything about Royalty, they live in a totally different world from the rest of us, so what you perceive as rudeness or ignorance is neither of those things.

The reality is that their entire lives have been privileged and pampered, gold plated some would say, and therefore within the circles that they move the likes of us hold no worth other than as servants. Therefore, why waste time on conversation with persons who can offer nothing, it would be such needless exertion.

But would it have been that hard or demeaning to at least acknowledge me sighed Ronnie. Oh, trust me Charles, she did acknowledge you, she held your gaze for several seconds, and believe me several seconds of eye contact with a princess is acknowledgement.

I do however have some news for you continued Heather. HRH told me that she and the Critchley`s, are spending Saturday and Sunday with Lord Salisbury on his Estate leaving the staff here to carry out initial preparations and cleaning in readiness for next weekend`s events.

Much to his disappointment Ronnie did not see how this information helped, as he had no access to the estate, but every piece of information was needed to create the bigger picture.

Ronnie was eating his breakfast on the Saturday morning when Heather walked in, I thought that you were away for the weekend on the Salisbury's Estate he said.

Her Royal Highness does not want me along, she smiled stealing his toast. You mean that she has dismissed you he queried. No of course not. It is just for this weekend, sometimes when we are staying away from her usual home, she meets someone in secret so as you can guess the fewer people who know the better.

Anyway, it is good news for us, as we can now spend the next two days on the estate together, you get to look around the place and I get the company. Tell your uncle John that you will not be back until Sunday afternoon so that he does not worry about you.

Critchley Hall was not as luxurious as Ronnie had imagined. The bare stone walls of the main entrance were hung with tapestries and the wood panelling gave an overall grim and cold feel. There were fourteen bedrooms plus two small suites each with its own little bathroom, one of which was the Critchley's own and the other for special guests such as HRH. Four separate bathrooms served the other bedrooms.

There was of course the requisite library, a study and drawing room as well as a smoking room and a huge dining room. An orangery, and garden room, completed one wing, whilst an ornately decorated ballroom the other, with the main central staircase leading off both ways at half level to a first floor, galleried landing.

The lower level to one wing of the house was made up of storage rooms and a huge kitchen which Ronnie had already seen and a couple of staff offices and steps leading to the wine cellar.

Across the cobbled courtyard was a coach house with stables underneath, the rooms above, being occupied by the grooms and chauffeur, a further block across the end provided four more bedrooms for the servants of guests to use, one of which was currently occupied by Heather.

The other wing housed a large basement area with the wood burning boiler and hot water system together with all its pipes and pumps, and behind the boiler room area was a large, detached garage housing several high-class motors.

Heather opened the door to her room revealing a bright if old fashioned style bedchamber with a three quarters size bed, dressing table, small wardrobe and a china basin, small chest of drawers and a single chair.

She flopped onto the bed patting the cover for Ronnie to join her which he did, and taking her in his arms he kissed her, to which she responded passionately.

We will sleep here tonight she said, we can eat cook`s dinner together and tomorrow, I will cook you some breakfast. I did not bring a change of clothes said Ronnie, I need to go and fetch some.

You will not require clothes as you will be sleeping in what you are wearing, Heather smiled, I may have agreed to help you, but I am not that sort of girl. Come on let me show you around the estate before we get some lunch.

Walking around the grounds with Heather, Ronnie realised that the cup and shroud would not be displayed in any public area, so somewhere more private whilst still accessible, seemed to be the most likely showing area.

But from what he had seen, everywhere was to some extent open access, so he asked Heather if there were areas of the estate he had not yet seen.

They were sat in the kitchen whilst she brewed coffee. No, I do not think so she said thoughtfully, of course there is the old icehouse, but it is small and not used because of the dampness, and there is no other area.

Scuse me maam, a young maid was cleaning the large stove, forgive me for intruding, but there is the summerhouse and chapel.

Thank you, it is Molly I believe said Heather. Yes maam. Well thank you Molly, I did not know that the estate had a summerhouse or a chapel. Oh yes maam, over on the far side of the estate among the small trees, the summerhouse is posh I gets to clean it sometimes after Lady Pandora has been entertaining if you know`s what I mean.

And the chapel asked Ronnie getting excited. That`s a cute little place sir where the family holds special services like Christmas and Easter. Exactly where can we find these interesting places said Ronnie handing Molly a twenty-pound note.

Oh, dear me thank you sir, she folded the note and placed it into her apron pocket, they both be over the far side of the estate, you goes down the little drive to the helicopter landing area and you will see the chapel, the summerhouse is a bit farther on just in the trees.

In Heathers little car Ronnie could hardly contain the excitement that he felt, a chapel and a helicopter pad he chuckled, how simple, they can fly the shroud and cup in, show them and then fly them back out with no one being any the wiser or even knowing that they were here.

That goes for people as well said Heather, your infamous lady perhaps. Yes of course, how stupid of me, if I am lucky that bitch herself will bring them replied Ronnie.

So, my suspicions are confirmed cried Heather, you do intend for us to steal them, I thought you to be a little better than a common thief.

Thank you for that character assassination sighed Ronnie, the truth is we intend to recover the items, and you need to consider how they came to have them in the first place before assigning either legal or moral guilt to my motives.

And for what it is worth you are not getting involved, so there is no US, just me, all I need from you is to get me in and hopefully back out on the night in question which I still think will be Saturday.

And how does Mr smarty-pants intend to find out which day this alleged exchange is going to happen if it occurs at all, or maybe it is just another of his fantasies Heather snorted, rather indignantly.

Look Ronnie sighed, I do appreciate what you have volunteered to do but I will not let you be placed in any danger nor risk your job with HRH, so I do this alone. What I do is my choice hissed Heather, not yours, we do this together or not at all.

The chapel was quite small and consisted of just the one worship area with a small vestry area concealed behind a floor length curtain. The only way in or out was by the main doors, and looking around Ronnie said in a disappointed voice, there is no obvious hiding place or display area here, let us go and have a look at this summerhouse.

The so-called summerhouse was in fact a full-size log cabin, just yards from the chapel but almost totally concealed behind overhanging fir tree and willow branches. Consisting of a spacious sitting area complete with television, sound system and drinks cabinet with a bar top. There was a double bedroom with blue satin sheets and pillowcases, a sizeable bathroom with shower cubicle, and a small but nonetheless well-equipped kitchenette. The cabin provided comfortable and discreet living, well hidden from any prying eyes.

Is Lady Pandora staying here at this moment, Ronnie asked Heather. No, she has returned to her flat in London, but she will be back next week to manage all the preparations for the events weekend. When she does return here, she but will take one of the rooms in the Hall rather than stay out in this cabin, at least that is what she has done previously replied Heather.

Back in the car, Heather's annoyance with Ronnie showed, as she raced the car along the narrow drive only just missing a gardener pushing a heavy looking wooden wheelbarrow, who shouted, Hoi Miss, slow down where's the fire.

I have it, shouted Ronnie as the car screeched to a halt in the courtyard outside the kitchen. Whatever have you come up with this time, sighed Heather, I suppose it to be yet another one of your brilliant schemes.

The helicopter will fly in whoever is bringing the items and they will hide out in the summerhouse, only going to the chapel at a pre-arranged time to show the items to whoever has been invited.

Then after the showing they will either go back to the summerhouse or be flown straight out, said Ronnie smiling. And when and how will you get an opportunity to steal them if your suppositions are correct sighed Heather. I am hopeful that nighttime flying will be an issue so expect the flight out to be the following morning continued Ronnie, giving me overnight, to sneak into the summerhouse and do the deed.

If I am correct the incoming helicopter flight will be late afternoon and the flight out the following morning, all I need now is to know for certain which days, Ronnie was quite upbeat.

Lord and Lady Critchley are scheduled to fly back to London on Monday morning after breakfast and probably HRH will fly with them, so unless you expect other helicopters, my guess is the Saturday event will be the one you are interested in, said Heather. Will you not, fly back with them asked Ronnie. Heather laughed at his naivety, no silly, I am expected to drive, I get all the costs paid but never travel with HRH, she values her privacy too much.

And are they all, staying on here then, from now until the events happen, I mean, asked Ronnie. No, replied Heather. They are all flying back to London on Monday afternoon and returning Friday Morning then staying the weekend. Friday`s event is in aid of an RAF charity which HRH is patron of so she will need to be present for it.

Tell me about the Saturday event urged Ronnie. The summer masquerade ball is a formal dinner for VIP guests said Heather. Canape`s at seven on the terrace followed by dinner at eight pm then dancing until Midnight, I believe that the RAF are providing the music with their dance band group, the "Squadronaires".

Can you imagine all those people here, milling around, wearing fancy face masks, mused Ronnie. What better cover could there be, to obscure a secret meeting from any casual observance. The planned showing must be during the Saturday Ball, at some pre-arranged time during the dance, those invited to view the items will slip away to the chapel.

Can you take ne back to the pub please Heather, I need to collect something and bring it back here to the chapel said Ronnie, and an hour later, with a black refuse sack carefully hidden behind the chapel they were in her room listening to music, but whilst Heather was happy to kiss and cuddle, she was not in any mood to allow anything further.

Later after sampling cook`s tasty chicken dinner they slept side by side on her bed, where true to her word, Ronnie had to sleep on top of the covers fully clothed, or rather minus shoes and tie. After breakfast she dropped him back at the pub saying that she needed to prepare for the princesses return and probable journey back to London tomorrow, so she kissed him, wished him luck, and said that she would see him later in the week.

It was Sunday evening in the bar when John answered the telephone then spoke to him Your lady friend has been called back to London with her employer from tomorrow morning. She will be required full time, at the Estate next week once they return here, and will therefore be fully occupied during the various events. However, she hopes to be able to see you before they return to London after next weekend.

Does this cause you any problems, asked John. To the contrary smiled Ronnie, it is perfect as she knows nothing of my plan and need not be involved in any way. I understand and totally agree but how do you propose to get in and presumably out again undetected without her assistance said John, adding, security will be tight everyone will have VIP passes, and no one gets in without one.

Glenda will arrange the way in, and hopefully the RAF will bring me out if everything goes according to plan. If it doesn't then getting out again might be the very least of my problems sighed Ronnie.

At half past ten on Saturday morning, Ronnie resplendent in butcher's apron and straw hat with ribbon, walked behind Stan the Master Butcher into the estate's large kitchen.

Both were carrying boxes of meat, and putting his boxes down onto a worktop, Ronnie trotted back to the van. He quickly removed the apron and white coat wrapping these around a half pig carcass which he sat on the passenger seat.

Topping the effect off with the straw hat, strategically tilted downwards, he closed the passenger door. Finally taking his holdall from the rear of the van, he closed the doors and had just darted into the bushes when Stan and the cook emerged from the doorway.

He waited in the bushes for several minutes to establish that Stan had left safely, and no one was wise to the deception, then reasoning that his plan had worked thus far and shouldering the holdall, he slowly and covertly made his way round the edge of the estate towards the chapel.

Checking that his concealed plastic sack was still in place Ronnie secreted himself in the bushes and lay down in the warm summer sunshine allowing himself to doze.

Around half past three in the afternoon, he was wakened by the beating rotors of an approaching helicopter and peering through the shrubbery towards the landing pad he was pleased to see the Critchley`s, and HRH along with Heather and four other unknown persons exit the helicopter, climb into the two waiting motor cars then slowly drive away towards the Hall.

The helicopter departed and everything was peaceful as before, then just after five pm, he again heard the distinct sound of approaching rotor blades and looking out saw the yellow sports car parked at the edge of the landing pad with the ginger haired woman waiting.

The helicopter touched down and a single figure jumped out and head down hurried towards the waiting car as the helicopter lifted away again.

As the summer dust, churned into the air by the departing helicopter settled, he stared at the two figures by the car, identically dressed both with ginger hair cascading over their shoulders either could be mistaken for Lady Pandora, at least from a rear view.

The two women exchanged hugs then walked together into the summerhouse, and it was almost six pm when one left and climbing into the car drove away towards the Hall.

Knowing that he needed to identify the mystery person in the summerhouse, Ronnie carefully made his way to the building, slid along the wall, and peered in through the living area window, just as a black-haired woman entered from the kitchenette carrying a mug of something.

Bitch, he hissed to himself, I have you this time. And I have the advantage, as you are blissfully unaware of my presence. He spotted the ginger wig on the seat of the couch and smiled, saying softly to himself, what a clever bitch you are, copying Pandora, anyone seeing you from a distance would simply assume that they were watching her.

Keeping a watchful eye on the summerhouse door Ronnie slipped back into nearby shrubbery and rested again, and it was around half past nine in the evening, with strains of music from the hall floating across the summer air when two cars pulled up by the chapel.

Five men and a single woman emerged and went inside the little building, and a few moments later Siobahn, still dressed as Lady Pandora and carrying a package, emerged from the summerhouse, and followed them into the chapel.

With only the single entrance and exit it was not possible to get close to the chapel, so Ronnie waited until the seven figures came out, the last closing the doors behind them. The lady Pandora lookalike, still with her package, went back to the summerhouse whilst the others climbed into the waiting cars and drove back towards the hall.

Retrieving the plastic sack that he had hidden beside the chapel Ronnie slipped back to the summerhouse and peered through the living area window again. Siobahn, resplendent in her ginger wig was slouched lazily in one of the armchairs a drink in one hand and cigarette in the other.

Removing his tie, he worked his way quietly to the door which she had conveniently left partly open presumably for cooler air flow, then checking and double checking all round to be certain that no one was anywhere within sight or hopefully earshot, Ronnie removed his shoes and slipped through the door.

Tiptoeing silently towards the chair behind the seated woman it was an act of seconds to drop the tie as a noose over her head and yank hard, placing his sock covered foot against the back of the chair for leverage, and pulling the tie tighter as the body kicked, and struggled with its fingers to loosen the grip.

It seemed an age for the body to stop struggling and become lifeless. but was in all probability less than two minutes. Ronnie let the body fall naturally and quickly put the tie loosely back around his neck. Spotting the bag on the floor and opening it he was thrilled to find both items, with the cup in its velvet bag wrapped in blue tissue and the shroud in a dress box.

Collecting his sack from the doorway he removed the replicas and swapped the wrappings and boxes so that the fakes were in the same packaging as the real items had been, he put the replicas into the bag and closed it placing the genuine items into his plastic sack and tying the top.

Sniffing the air, he detected a faint burning smell, and investigation revealed that Siobahn`s dropped cigarette had burned a small hole in the carpet before extinguishing itself. On the small table was a box of tissues several of which Ronnie took and unfolded, placing them over the burn hole, then taking the loose arm cover of the chair he pulled it sideways so that it dangled above the tissues. Blowing on the semi extinguished cigarette he was rewarded with a glowing tip which he gently placed into the tissues and watched them spurt into a small flame.

Pulling the lifeless body upright in the chair and checking for any pulse he waited until the flames caught the chair covering and started to burn properly, then taking his sack he exited and closed the summerhouse door.

Ronnie quietly slipped through the grounds and into the kitchen courtyard where, as he had hoped and expected, a large blue van in RAF colours was parked, the logo on the side declaring Squadronaires. Climbing into the unlocked rear and hiding himself behind unused equipment he used the sack as his pillow and settled down to sleep.

Movement of the vehicle bought him awake and he looked at his watch, it was nearly one-thirty am, so he reasoned that if the band had stopped playing at midnight, given half to three quarters of an hour to demount the equipment and load up the van, they had been travelling for around three quarters of an hour, so he idly wondered where they were.

The van came to a stop and he heard chatter outside, which gradually seemed to fade into nothing and after a few minutes he climbed from the vehicle. He was inside a large building, possibly some sort of garage or hanger which, from what he could see in the gloom was almost empty, so carefully finding his way to a small pedestrian door he pushed it open and stepped outside.

Quietly trotting across the concrete apron in front of what was now apparent to be an old hanger, Ronnie found his way to the main gate of the compound, where a single security guard from a private company was snoozing in the small gatehouse. Sliding quietly by the guard post, he was quickly out onto the main road, and looking back saw the sign which read, RAF Upavon Logistics Depot. Looking around

THE CUP

for reference points, he could see streetlights along the road, so made his way towards them.

Do you know what time it is, snorted an obviously sleepy and irritated John, It is nearly half past two in the Morning. Stop nagging and just come and get me, you old goat, chuckled Ronnie, I will wait here by the telephone box in the village.

We heard sirens a little after midnight said John as they drove back to Hurstbourne Priors, I take it that was of your doing. Certainly not sighed Ronnie, but look I am totally knackered and just want to sleep, we can talk about it tomorrow. You mean today snorted John far from impressed.

Ronnie shuffled into the kitchen a little after eleven am, John was brewing fresh coffee and Glenda cooking bacon and eggs. I want to share something with you both he said and placed the sack onto the table, briefly outlining the history of the shroud and the cup he carefully began to open the sack.

Gently removing the boxed shroud and tissue wrapped cup revealing the small velvet bag, Ronnie opened it and withdrew the little wooden cup. Feast your eyes my two friends what you are now looking at, few people have seen or will ever see and even fewer have touched.

Are you seriously telling us, gasped Glenda, that these are the genuine, shroud of Turin, and the cup used by Jesus, to offer his disciples wine at the Last Supper.

Yes, both are the real genuine items confirmed Ronnie, but please, while you may look as much as you like do not unpack the shroud. You can of course hold the cup, but again please try not to drop it, I have a telephone call to make.

Back in the kitchen after using the telephone he sipped the mug of tea John had provided. A courier will collect the items in a while, so if you have seen enough, I will pack them away. Ronnie picked up the cup and popped it into the velvet bag then placed both items into the plastic sack. Picking up the mug of tea he suddenly frowned, put the mug back down and took the velvet bag from the sack and opening it removed the cup.

Turning the cup over in his hands he started to laugh. What is wrong, said Glenda seemingly concerned. There is nothing wrong really, he chuckled, let us just say that whatever you do there is always someone as smart or perhaps even smarter than you. To be fair, Siobahn Is one very clever woman, I never even considered she would do that.

The courier is here, called John from the public bar, and after checking him to be genuine by asking for the codeword agreed over the telephone when he had called Eugene, Ronnie handed over the sack containing the items. What is Kaleidoscope supposed to signify, asked John as the courier departed. Oh, just Intelligence being childish again replied Ronnie.

On the Sunday evening he was perched on one of the stools in the public bar enjoying a black velvet and a small cigar which John had kindly provided, when a pale looking Harry arrived and pulled a stool alongside his.

This is not a friendly social meeting Ronnie, wheezed Harry, what the heck are you playing at, apparently the shroud is a fake. They are both fakes smiled Ronnie, and sadly it is not a game, the bitch had fakes to sell or at least to show, she came prepared just as we did.

So, you are saying that all you managed to do was exchange her fakes for our own sighed Harry, order me a pint of lager. Not quite smiled Ronnie, I did manage to revenge John`s death, that bitch will not be causing any further trouble, now be a good fellow drink your lager then go back to bed.

THE CUP

On Tuesday Ronnie was somewhat surprised to see Eugene pull up outside the Andover Office seemingly in an anxious mood, and ushering him into his new office, Ronnie asked Carol to fetch them both mugs of coffee. To what might I owe this unexpected visit he asked.

Flannery, or Proshyn or whatever the fuck she chooses to be called, is far from deceased, in fact she is very much alive hissed Eugene.

What, exclaimed Ronnie, that is not possible I choked the bitch to death myself and checked for a pulse afterwards, she is dead, and in any case the fire…

Would have destroyed most, if not all the evidence had there been any, added Eugene. Exactly muttered Ronnie so what is this rubbish about her still being alive.

The fire brigade discovered the body of Lady Pandora inside the remains of the summerhouse sighed Eugene. She was identified by her dental records and the cause of death was that she had been stabbed through the heart.

The police have arrested one of the estate workers and are currently not looking for anyone else.

But how can this be, I am certain that I choked her to death sighed Ronnie.

As you say how can it be, said Eugene, but one fact is indisputable, the stabbed body is Lady Pandora for certain, and intelligence have confirmed Proshyn, to be in Germany alive and well.

For what it is worth Pandora was stabbed before the fire as there was no evidence of smoke in the lungs continued Eugene.

So, whoever did this, intended either to simply cover up the supposed death of Proshyn, or to use the attempt to get rid of Pandora for other reasons, or perhaps a bit of both.

Whatever the motivation, we have been outsmarted yet again and are no nearer retrieving the genuine articles than we were before any of this began.

Always one step ahead of us, groaned Ronnie, they make us look like amateurs. Compared to them we are exactly that, replied Eugene, and remember we do NOT run around killing people, as they seem happy to do.

So, for what it is worth, consider yourself fortunate that your skills as an assassin seemingly need to be sharpened.

At least with her still alive they will try another sale for certain, said Ronnie, if at least one group or buyer is interested they are sure to make another attempt to make the exchange.

We are already working on that assumption replied Eugene and I promise that whatever and whenever, we will not fuck it up again.

You can add this little fiasco to your memory bank Ronnie, get back to your normal life and await further instructions. We expect it will not be that long before we need to go again said Eugene as they shook hands.

Chapter Fourteen
A New Plan

The fire, and death of Lady Pandora, were reported in just about every newspaper and it became clear that she had been having a relationship with someone and had frequently used the summerhouse for illicit liaisons.

The handyman from the estate who had been arrested, was not charged with any offence, and returned to his job with character unblemished. The police then issued a new statement suggesting that one of the guests attending the ball was now a suspect.

The guest had allegedly been dressed in a harlequin outfit and had been seen coming back to the Hall from the direction of the summerhouse late in the evening. However there had been several Harlequin Costume guests, present at the ball, all of whom denied being outside of the Hall at any time during the evening and checks cleared each of any involvement.

The knife used to stab Lady Pandora was from the summerhouse kitchenette but had no fingerprints, and the only evidence, if it could be called such, came from the originally arrested estate worker who insisted that he had seen smoke near the summerhouse and the Harlequin dressed figure heading back to the Hall.

Lady Pandora`s death had been placed at between eleven pm and midnight, with the body being partly consumed by the localised fire, which the brigade had quickly gained control of.

Ronnie read and reread this statement and concluded that as he had strangled Siobahn and set the small fire sometime after ten pm, for the fire to have been discovered well after midnight, it indicated that his fire had either been extinguished then re-lit or had gone out of its own accord only to be restarted after Pandora's body had been placed.

The burning question in his mind was why. Had Lady Pandora's death been planned anyway, and his bungled attempt on Siobahn used as a diversion.

Or had she been used as collateral so that a fire consumed, unknown woman's body, would have been reported, which he would take as Siobahns demise.

If it were the former, then the question was, who had wished Pandora dead, if it were the latter, then almost certainly Siobahn had to be seriously implicated.

Ronnie was aware of his growing anger of himself for allowing Flannery to outsmart him yet again and at her callous indifference to life, but he forced himself to put the incident to the back of his mind and concentrate on work issues.

Asking Carol to attend Peter's funeral with him, he took the opportunity away from the crowded office environment to ask her about Anita and the Critchley Estate, she told him that she knew nothing about the estate, and that Anita had left suddenly last week without giving any notice period which had annoyed everyone, particularly Colin.

He asked if she knew about Anita's relationship with Colin to which she truthfully answered only what the gossips chat about, so he suggested that with Anita gone she might ask the girls about it.

Two days later Colin walked into his office and closed the door. Now you listen to me Ronnie, I do not know what you believe might have happened between Anita and me, but trust me whatever it is, then I can assure you that it is wrong. I am very happily married and would never do anything to hurt my wife, so kindly stop whatever you are trying to start.

Taking a huge gamble Ronnie said, so it was you who gave her husband that huge payoff, to keep him from telling your wife. Certainly not, and like you I was surprised that they left so suddenly, it seems that Anita`s husband was given a long service cash bonus and severance payment combined, and as they needed to quit the estate cottage both have simply moved on.

Look Colin, said Ronnie, Anita`s husband knew that she was seeing someone, whether he had worked out it was you, I do not yet know, but he was intent on finding out and she was terrified of him doing something to whoever he suspected.

I for one know that you were fond of her and can only assume others were knowledgeable as well. What is more important from your position, is that the husband may have been either directly or indirectly involved in the death of Critchley`s daughter Pandora. And if he was somehow involved, and the police begin delving into the marriage you may well come up as a connection.

Oh, dear God, I cannot let Jane find out, it will ruin my marriage what shall I do. Nothing Colin, I will sort everything, but I suggest that you forget her, as I do not think she will be coming back at least anytime soon. But what can you do, bleated Colin. Let us just assume that I have connections, replied Ronnie, and we will leave it there.

Considering all the information pieces available, Ronnie thought that his presumptions were probably as close to the truth of what happened as could be achieved without eyewitness confession. His botched attempt on the life of the

Flannery woman had resulted in her realising that she was under surveillance and therefore needed to get out, and what better cover than being a corpse, so she used the opportunity to kill Pandora as a stooge.

He stopped himself, that was bollocks he reasoned, after all he had seen the two women earlier and there had been no hint of issue between them. To the contrary they had been bosom pals. So, Flannery had left the estate on the Saturday night but how, and then it came to him. She had needed to leave the estate quickly to avoid being caught up in any police investigation, so she had dressed again as Pandora and taken her car to drive away from the estate.

But who killed Pandora and why, and then as if a light had come on inside his brain he understood, whoever killed Pandora thought that they were killing Flannery, Pandora had gone to the summerhouse late on Saturday evening to meet with Flannery, where she had been killed by someone assuming her to be Flannery but dressed to look like Pandora.

Everything made sense, except that only a handful of people had known Flannery had arrived dressed as Pandora, those being himself, Pandora herself, the helicopter pilot and probably Lord Critchley, the incoming disguise presumably being conceived to confuse anyone seeing a woman in the grounds near to the summerhouse.

If, he was correct, and he was now sure that he was, and as it was Pandora who had been murdered and he had not been responsible, either the pilot, Lord Critchley or most likely someone acting on his Lordships instructions was the killer, and of course none of them knew it would be the real Lady Pandora in the summerhouse, how could they.

Telephoning Eugene he cut short the others moaning about the botched mission saying that he needed answers to just two simple questions, firstly was Pandoras car found at the estate or not and secondly was she either an open or closet Lesbian, putting the receiver down before Eugene could ask any questions.

Eugene returned his call only an hour later stating that Lady Pandora had indeed a tendency towards liaisons with her own sex and her car had been found near Andover station, presumed to have been stolen. Now certain of the sequence of events Ronnie explained everything to Eugene asking him to give the police whatever they needed to move their investigation forward although identifying the actual killer might prove difficult as Ronnie suspected him to have been paid to go away from the estate.

Eugene asked if Ronnie might be more forthcoming perhaps naming the killer as he obviously knew who it was, but thinking of Anita and her sorry life, decided that being married to a brute and killer was one thing, knowing him to be a killer was something different, and some secrets were best kept as secrets.

In October and with his new managerial position confirmed which included keeping the Granada, salary increase, and much higher expenses account, on impulse he bought chocolates, flowers and a bottle of Vodka which was Linda`s favourite drink. And decided to surprise her by going home early.

Parked on his driveway was a red Ferrari Dino, with Linda`s Tiger parked in front of it, so pulling up alongside the kerb he got out and quietly let himself into the house. Slipping into the main hallway he found a trail of clothing leading into the split-level lounge diner area and on the upper- level Linda was almost naked wriggling away under the body of an Olive skinned, male who was still wearing his Shemagh scarf.

In the local pub, over a glass of whiskey, Ronnie weighed up what he had seen between Linda and the other man, and what his options were. And after giving the barmaid the bunch of flowers he drove home. Over dinner dispassionately and quietly, he explained to Linda what he had seen and instructed her to pack her belongings and be gone by the Friday evening when he arrived home as their relationship was over.

After a pub meal on the Friday evening, he slept well and spent Saturday doing housework even cooking a meal for one and then spent the evening evaluating his next moves. So, on the Sunday morning he decided to drive around the local area to see if he could find a new home.

Just off the main A5 past Towcester, he saw a signpost saying Astcote, and on impulse turned down the narrow lane into the small village, where a large stone farmhouse had a FOR RENT sign outside. The owner lived in the village and deal done, with the house being empty, he decided to move in sooner rather than later. So, with the farmhouse keys in his pocket he popped into the tiny pub for a drink.

The Queen`s, was indeed tiny, with a lounge bar area containing eight tables with upright wooden chairs and a large open fireplace. A second smaller room to the rear, held a skittles table and a dartboard. The toilets were outside and basic, and the bar was a hole in the wall into the owner`s area from where they served drinks.

The pub did not serve food, just crisps and nuts which disappointed Ronnie so chatting to Anne and her husband who owned the pub, he was pleased when after hearing that he would be moving into the village and using the pub regularly she offered to cook his evening meals.

That afternoon and back in the Stoney Stratford house, he decided upon a new start, and after weighing up the positives and negatives he spoke to the young couple who lived several doors away, who he knew had been struggling with payments.

He offered them a rent free, share of the large farmhouse in exchange for them to live in and obviously keep it safe when he was away.

Ronnie briefly explained that he and Linda had chosen to part, and with the young couple's bubbly enthusiasm spilling over he drove them over to Astcote to see their new home.

They agreed to divide the rooms in the farmhouse, whilst sharing the bathroom and the huge kitchen which came with a full-sized pool table included. They also shared a removal van with Ronnie having given a lot of furniture away to charity, and the three of them moved in on Saturday 28th October 1978.

On the following Monday Carol came into his office and closed the door. You asked if I could check what information was available regarding a young lady called Heather Gamblin, may I ask if you have some personal interest sir.

I met the lady in connection with the Critchley Estate replied Ronnie, and please do not call me sir, Ronnie is fine.

Well, the young Lady was tragically killed in a road accident after her car veered off the road and rolled over several times crushing her, with no explanation for the accident the police investigation has determined that she probably fell asleep.

They killed her as well, the bastard's, spat Ronnie. Pardon said Carol who killed her, the police are saying that it was just a tragic accident. Sorry Carol, I must stop thinking aloud sighed Ronnie, can we have a drink please. While she went for coffee he sat down and considered everything.

Eight people had died dead so far, four in Northern Ireland, Alison at Wittering, Rabbi Reuben in the cottage fire, Pandora on the Estate and now Heather, all related in some way to both him and the search for the cup, he really was a walking disaster.

In early November he was in his new Village pub on a Friday evening playing dominoes with one of the locals, when a young woman came in alone. She was well dressed in fur collared, top-coat and dress or skirt with heeled shoes.

Ordering a half pint of lager with a packet of crisps, she sat on her own and talked to no one, which he found strange.

It was six weeks before she came in again, however this time before she could leave the pub, Ronnie bought her another half pint of lager and asked for her name, which she gave as Beverley and added that she was married.

After she had left, the landlady Anne spoke to him, warning him to stay away from the woman as not only was she Married but her husband was the local tough guy dressing in denim's and with both motorcycle and shotguns. Moreover, he was the possessive type who would frown upon Ronnie chatting to his woman.

Relishing the implied challenge, he was determined to get to know her better and up to and even after Christmas, she came to the pub a number of times allowing him to buy drinks and crisps, then in late January 1979 she stopped coming in.

Discreet enquiries revealed that she had been involved in a car accident where the vehicle she was a passenger in had skidded on some ice and rolled over, throwing her from the car and crushing her underneath.

She had been taken to Northampton Hospital where it was discovered that she had fractured her pelvic bone and would be in hospital for a short time. However, whilst there had been others in the vehicle no one else had been injured.

Once she was discharged from the hospital, she and Ronnie started to meet outside of the pub, and over the next few months Ronnie realised that this woman was the one person who he wanted to share the rest of his life with.

He was accordingly overjoyed when she told him that she intended to leave her husband and return home to her family in Devon, where Ronnie could go and see her.

It was the late May, bank holiday, and Beverley had told her husband that she was going home for a visit to her family, whilst secretly she had given Ronnie all the things that she wished to keep from the home for him to take to her parents. So, she caught the train to the nearest large station at Rugby, from where Ronnie collected her and drove them both to the family home in Newton Abbot.

Immediately welcomed by her family, Ronnie knew instantly that this was the real thing. In both of his previous relationships he had liked Sheila`s parents and Linda`s mother, and believed them to have liked him, but what made this real was the feeling that he wanted to be with Beverley all the time.

Sometimes when he left after staying for the weekend, he wanted to just forget his job and start a new life in Devon.

Beverley`s husband was hardly thrilled to discover that his wife had not only left him, but that she had done so after a short romantic liaison with a man from their village, and one Saturday morning he knocked on the door of Ronnie`s rented farmhouse with his arms concealed behind his back.

Opening the door and confronted by the man, Ronnie asked what he wanted as a game of pool was ongoing which he was part of. To which the husband bought his hands into view holding a shotgun, which he then pointed directly into Ronnie`s face.

You stay away from my wife, snarled the man, or I will blow your F...ing head off. I am sorry I cannot do that replied Ronnie, as we love each other and will eventually get married, so either shoot me or piss off, as I am playing pool.

The irate husband departed, and Ronnie returned to his game, only for the doorbell to sound again some minutes later. Again confronted, by the husband who was holding his hands behind his back, Ronnie said, what now, I have said that I am playing pool.

Bringing his arms into view the husband held up a six pack of beers saying, playing pool you said, can I join you.

Over several games, Ronnie and the husband discussed things, and when asked why he had not shot Ronnie the man simply said. That was the first time anyone has ever stood up to me.

Later, the husband drove one of the self-hire removal vans for them when Ronnie and Beverley left Astcote for their new life together.

With Beverley`s divorce now under way and after discussion with her, Ronnie looked at the practicalities of getting a new job in Paignton or nearby.

Together they looked at potential homes, but after much discussion they decided to live near to Ronnie`s work and just visit her family occasionally, so using his contacts he arranged a new house in Andover, and they moved in on Saturday December 14th 1979.

In May 1980 Ronnie was called to see Harry at the home he had shared with his wife of over thirty years, and he was shocked to see how poorly he now was. A young man was also present whom Harry introduced as Neil Smith, from the RAF Police, who he totally trusted, and that Neil was to be the new link between Harry and Ronnie, as Harry`s illness had made getting around especially outside of the home almost impossible.

New information had been received suggesting there was to be another sale arranged, where the cup and shroud would be effectively auctioned to the highest bidder, seemingly with this event being held under the cover of a summer event on a private estate in Monchengladbach in Germany.

Harry instructed Ronnie to make whatever plans might be necessary with Neil`s assistance, to go out to the event and do whatever he deemed to be required to get the two artifacts, explaining that the replica`s would be returned to him in due course, and an envelope containing five thousand pounds was handed to him by Harry who wished them both the best of luck.

Neil explained that he had a fair degree of autonomy in his role investigating smuggling issues within the RAF and Ronnie quietly groaned, not again, but said aloud, that`s great we will need to get out to the nearest RAF base to Monchengladbach then.

I have already carried out some checks and RAF Bruggen is the nearest, only three miles from the estate where the event will take place and around eight miles from the town, when we are ready we will fly out under the cover of investigating smuggling between UK and German RAF Bases.

Ronnie`s Ministry of Defence Pass was still in date and he had no difficulty in gaining access to RAF St Athan in South Wales where Neil was currently stationed, so taking Beverley along as company and because she was not yet working, they drove down to Wales.

Neil was it transpired, a third generation Jew, yet another Steiner relation although he did not speak Hebrew or attend the Synagogue, nor did he follow modern Israeli politics or Judaist principles so Ronnie`s first question was how and why he was involved.

The response was abrupt and quite terse, with Neil explaining that he was a nephew of Harry on his Mother`s side and that he had reluctantly agreed to work with and for Ronnie to assist wherever he could to facilitate the recovery of the shroud and cup.

Before we get anything started said Ronnie, I must warn you that everyone involved with me in this venture tends to end up dead, usually rather suddenly and callously.

Yes, I have been told about that replied Neil, but having made my promises to the family I intend to keep them, so you need not worry about me. I will be as committed as you need me to be, and as far as your being a jinx, I simply do not believe that rubbish so let us get down to it.

Neil told Ronnie, that the intelligence mentioned by Harry regarding the possible auctioning of the two items had been received from a Mossad source who were based in South West Germany. The information which they had received apparently giving details of a group representing the Red Fraction led by a woman called Daniela Klette, and she was the person making the arrangements to hold the auction.

Furthermore, recent information revealed that the location of the auction was to be at a country estate called Schloss Adler which was the home of a German Nobleman, Count Von-Richston, who was a distant relative of Heinrich Himmler.

There were several groups that had expressed an interest in the artifact sale with the three main bidders being an American Consortium, a group from Japan and scariest of all an Arab group based in Dubai.

The latest intelligence suggested that a late July event at Schloss Adler would be the cover for these groups to meet and examine the items, and that a starting bid of five hundred thousand Euros was required.

Neil suggested that they needed to spend a few days out in Germany at RAF Bruggen, so that they could assess the local situation and hopefully get sufficient details and information to enable them to establish a watertight plan to recover the items.

Explaining to Beverley that he needed to go to Germany for business reasons, Ronnie and Neil flew to Germany and were billeted in the NCO`s Mess at Raf Bruggen, using Neil`s cover story idea of their presence being due to suspected smuggling issues.

On the day after arriving, the Base then held an exercise which involved part of the RAF service personnel defending the base against others who were playing the part of terrorist attackers, with the defending group being mainly made up from RAF Regiment who rather than being aircrew were the RAF foot soldiers whose role was base protection.

The day long exercise seriously restricted any movement and as seemingly almost everyone on the base was involved in some manner or other it left Ronnie and Neil at a loose end, and both were enlisted as casualties with labels pinned to their clothing detailing the extent of injuries.

Ronnie`s card read, shrapnel impact, deep lacerations, concussion, probable internal bleeding, likely result fatality.

Around midday, whilst laid on his back across the pathway leading to the officer`s mess dining entrance Ronnie was accosted by a uniformed Air Commodore, who bending down to peer into Ronnie`s face said. You there, why are you blocking my pathway. Ronnie simply pointed to the clearly printed card adorning his chest which the officer read out aloud and barked, well go and die somewhere else you are making our mess area untidy.

Recounting the event to Neil in the bar later, Ronnie was told that the Commodore was not only a senior RAF Officer on the base, but a respected friend of both the local Burgermeister and Count Von-Richston. To which Ronnie scathingly replied, well if he is the epitome of Britain`s Air superiority, I hope that we stick to land and sea warfare from now on.

As it happens said Neil, the commodore is hosting an RAF Charity dinner here on base this Saturday and Count Von-Richton has been invited. Adding that when the guests arrive Ronnie might get a close look at both the count and his lady companion.

On the Saturday evening and from a concealed vantage point on the medical centre roof, Neil pointed out the Rolls Royce Phantom as it pulled up outside the officer`s mess. Resplendent in dinner dress with medals adorning his chest the tall blonde haired athletic looking Count waved away the chauffeurs proffered hand and he himself then held the car door for the emerging woman.

As she coyly climbed from the vehicle Neil whispered, I believe that is Daniela Klette. Staring hard at the raven-haired woman in her glittering evening gown and white fur stole, Ronnie hissed through gritted teeth. That my friend is public enemy number one, Daniela Klette, Denise Proshyn or Siobahn Flannery, you may call her whatever you like, but she is top of my kill list.

Well, all that I can say is that she looks quite sexy and harmless to me chuckled Neil. Do not ever be fooled where that woman is concerned snarled Ronnie, if she smiles at you look for the weapon because as sure as hell there will be one, she is I can assure you the most ruthless and cold blooded of killers.

With the information that Flannery was again the mastermind behind the sale of the items they went back to the UK, and Ronnie arranged to get the replica items in readiness for a second chance at exchanging them for the real thing. That of course being dependent upon Flannery having the real items, rather than another set of replicas.

With the Schloss Adler event being scheduled towards the end of July on Saturday 26th, timing was going to be tight as Ronnie and Beverley had booked their wedding for early August in her own hometown of Newton Abbot, but as things worked out the event went ahead without the showing and auction, as the American Consortium had apparently worked out a private deal with the Count and Daniela Klette and whisked the items out of Germany and away to America.

De-briefing at Harry`s home Ronnie was sad to see even further deterioration in his health, not much improved by what had been another disappointment regarding the recovery of the cup. The agreed way forward was for Eugene and Neil to work together to see if they could somehow purchase the items from the Americans although little hope of that was expressed.

Ronnie was to get married to Beverley, then move on with his life, on the understanding that if his services were to be required anytime in the future then he would always be available.

Ronnie`s terse question regarding Siobahn Flannery, was met by Eugene with a, let us deal with her, we owe you that much, not to mention John and the others.

Friday 01st August found Ronnie and Beverley gathered in Newton Abbot along with Brian who was Best Man, John and Glenda, Eugene and Neil plus their families and friends. Separate Hen and Stag Night celebrations were held on the Friday evening with the wedding at Highweek Church the following day and a reception at Highweek Inn afterwards.

The newlywed couple settled into married family life in Andover, with Beverley starting work in the accounts department of a Medical Supplies Company so that they both worked normal day time hours and shared evenings and weekends together.

And of course, with the added plus factor of Ronnie being away from home less often now, they joined a local Ten Pin Bowling Team, and the couple were seemingly content and decided to plan a family.

In the spring of 1981, the newspapers carried the story of a private jet crashing in the French Alps. The Gulfstream Jet had been on a flight to Paris from Germany and all of those aboard had died including the pilot and the passengers named as Count Von-Richston with his female companion who was believed to be Daniela Klette, reports suggested engine failure or possibly pilot error might be to blame.

In September 1982 news reached him of Harry`s passing, and Ronnie attended the cremation in Salisbury although he did not go to the Synagogue service. But the buffet wake held at Harry`s home gave him the opportunity to chat with Eugene and Neil.

Eugene explained that the Arab group who had been an interested party in the Schloss Adler auction were still keen to get possession of the items, and as the Americans had apparently not been able to prove the authenticity of either item, there was a slight suggestion that a resale might be arranged, currently doing the rounds in intelligence circles.

Eugene said that the Americans were secretly of the opinion that Daniela Klette had sold them fakes and they were looking to cut their losses by at least recouping the sale value.

Towards this end, they had already tested the strength of the Arab interest and it seemed with money being no object, a deal looked highly probable.

Neil added that while there were no hard details yet, RAF Intelligence sources revealed that for the purchase, the American group had used an experienced smuggling ring working inside the United States Air Force to take the items back to the United States and would most probably use the same setup to transport the items for any sale, which was likely to be within the UK as both American and Arab attendances at USAF bases were not unusual.

Eugene added that the next major American Air Force Event in the UK was to be held at USAF Lakenheath in Suffolk in 1983 and that they would be working on a plan if the items were indeed to come back into the UK.

In February 1983 Ronnie Junior, was born who they named Nathan. The birth was a traumatic experience for Beverley who struggled to deliver the baby due to the road accident damage to her pelvis, and after an extended and painful labour in Winchester Hospitals maternity unit, the unborn child went into foetal distress.

Now in an emergency situation, and with no time to spare staff called the hospital senior registrar, and the baby was virtually dragged from Beverley's womb causing severe blood loss and with her coming close to death.

Standing alongside the bed in the delivery room, with the surgical registrar in his dinner jacket and bow tie having delivered the baby, and a nurse kneeling on Beverley's chest slapping her face and giving CPR Ronnie prayed aloud, openly promising a lifetime of service if God would save her.

It was September before Neil met with him and shared the updated intelligence which pointed towards the Americans planning to bring the two items back to the UK via the airbase at Lakenheath, for a sale to the Arab interest headed by a Prince Khalid, and it was assumed, although not yet confirmed that the transaction would be, off base, but somewhere local to Lakenheath.

Assuming the sale event to be away from the air force base, further searches had revealed that the Critchley family owned yet another country property called Wetherby Grange close to Thetford, which seemed more than simple coincidence so even more checks were being undertaken.

It transpired that a Halloween ball had been planned by the Critchley Family to be held at Wetherby Grange, this being highly unusual as they rarely spent time at the property, preferring to be closer to London. The event was being tagged as an invitation only, VIP Halloween Ball with fancy dress mandatory.

Ronnie asked how the Americans might bring the items into the UK undetected, at which Neil chuckled saying, if Ronnie thought that the RAF smuggling was out of control, the American Airforce had taken it to a whole new level where even cars and large items were smuggled both ways.

Neil arranged for the two of them to be billeted at RAF Mildenhall, a former RAF Base now operated by the Americans with a small retainer of UK personnel managing the base security and services.

They met in the sergeant's mess on 23rd October a week before the ball only to be given the terrible news that a major suicide bombing in Beirut had killed over one hundred and sixty US Marines.

The Lebanese militia were widely considered to be a terrorist organisation financially supported by some of the Arab countries including Iran, so Neil suggested that after such an outrage the selling group of Americans might call off the sale meaning yet another dead end.

However by the 28th of October it became apparent that the items had arrived in the UK and were already presumed to be

THE CUP

at Wetherby Grange after covert surveillance had seen a USAF vehicle making a delivery.

With the event now seemingly planned, Eugene provided both Ronnie and Neil with passes to the ball as part of the security team being provided by special branch because of the presence of the Arab Prince.

Both Neil and Ronnie dressed the part in bow tie and dinner jacket and Eugene had arranged for Ronnie to receive the replica shroud and cup.

Wetherby Grange was situated in the village of Weeting, to the West of Thetford, and Ronnie and Neil arrived in the early evening, relieved to be granted access and shown where to meet the special branch unit commander.

Senior Officer Stella, was in the kitchen giving an overview to the special branch team, explaining that the event had its own private security paid for by the Critchley`s and the special branch presence needed to be covert and low key and was purely to ensure the safety of Prince Khalid, nothing more.

Mingle discreetly, stay alert and never allow the prince or his entourage to be isolated or alone. But always maintain a respectful distance from the guests, and report anything suspicious directly to her.

As the small group dispersed, Ronnie and Neil introduced themselves to Stella, who looked them over and somewhat sarcastically commented, so you are the two stooges that I am expected to babysit, just what the minister is playing at I have no idea, I hate this cloak and dagger crap, but must do as I am instructed.

As you can tell she continued, I am not exactly thrilled at having you two wandering around and most probably getting in the way, whatever the Minister wishes. So, whatever it is that you need to do, just make sure that you don't shit on my parade, because if you do, Minister or no Minister I promise that I will cut off your balls.

I am Neil, this is Ronnie smiled Neil, Stella looking Ronnie directly in the eye snarled you were at Wittering, her cold green eyes boring into his own. Yes, I was there murmured Ronnie. Alison was a friend spat Stella, as well as a bloody good officer she did not deserve to die, it was your fault, you fucked up.

For what it is worth we all managed to do that, Alison included, replied Ronnie, but if it helps, the bitch who shot her is dead. However, nothing can bring Alison back and I was also very fond of her, so you are not alone in your mourning.

Just don't be planning any mass murder here gentlemen, said Stella, as I have no urgent desire either to lose my job, or meet with my maker.

Nothing is further from our intentions Maam, smiled Ronnie, we are just here as casual observers, and we are not armed. Stella walked away calling over her shoulder. Your boyish charm may have turned Alison`s head but not mine, I am a totally different proposition, so I suggest that you stay on my good side.

What is it with you, grinned Neil, all of the women that you meet either want to bed you or kick your arse, why do you never have normal relationships like other people.

That my friend, is a long story sighed Ronnie, I may just decide to tell it one day who knows I might even write a book. Well let me be the first to know if you do chuckled Neil as it will be a best seller.

Reaching inside his jacket Neil withdrew a 9mm Browning pistol and handed it to Ronnie, six slugs already in the magazine, and here is a box of thirty more, he passed the small box across adding, I have the same. Ronnie popped the magazine and removed one bullet putting into the box. What on earth, queried Neil.

A six shot Browning, notoriously jams if you have a full magazine, so always leave one chamber empty, it might just save your life one day, and with Neil following his example Ronnie realised exactly how much he owed to John. Pocketing the weapons, they left their bags in a corner of the kitchen, then went off to look around.

Guests began arriving from around seven-thirty pm and they were greeted with music playing both inside and out, a small band offering a mixture of ballroom and modern dance inside whilst more upbeat Jive dancing was offered from speaker units set along the terrace.

A constantly topped up, buffet was arranged along one wall of the large dining room and two bars one in the main stairwell lobby and the second at one end of the terrace provided every type of drink that could be desired including cocktails.

To one side of the sweeping gravel driveway across the front of the house, a firepit area and hot food barbecue were cooking fish wrapped in tin foil and the more traditional steaks and beefburgers which seemed to please the American contingent.

By nine pm most of the guests had arrived including the Prince and his entourage in a limousine, with a minibus following packed with personal aids and bodyguards.

Looking around Ronnie calculated there to be, something in excess, of two hundred people present, not including staff and security, although within the sizeable grounds it did not appear crowded.

Two of the guests, obviously American, despite their British style fancy dress, of pirate and robin hood costumes, seemed to be quite anxious. They were constantly looking around as if waiting for someone or something.

None of the Arab party were dressed up, except for the two females, who were in veiled costumes and Ronnie wondered if they were designed to be fancy dress or just what the prince usually chose for them to wear.

Having identified the American and Arab interests, Ronnie wandered around in the shadows looking for either Lord or Lady Critchley but found neither.

Passing the study and trying the door he was amazed to find it both unlocked and empty, even more unbelievable was the shroud and cup laid on the polished mahogany side table under a deep red woven cover.

Deciding not to be caught out yet again, he quickly withdrew the cup from its small velvet bag and turned it around in his fingers. Thank you, God, he breathed to himself as the weird sensations flowed through his body.

Retracing his steps to check quickly on the Arabs and Americans he was surprised to see Lieutenant Colonel Critchley chatting with both groups.

Presumably, Critchley had called them together in advance of showing them the items Ronnie guessed, so he quickly retrieved his bag from the kitchen and slipped back to the study.

Lifting the red velvet cover he exchanged the real artifacts laid on the table for the replicas that he was carrying. Satisfied that everything was as he had found it, Ronnie closed the study door and returned his bag to the kitchen.

Coming out from the kitchen into the main stairwell Ronnie bumped into Neil who seemed to be a little on edge and agitated. What is it mate, Ronnie asked, and Neil explained that he believed two men were acting suspiciously in the parking area, so together they went outside to find Stella, and shared Neil`s observations with her.

The three of them walked around the house and through the arched opening cut into the hedgerow into the gravelled car parking area, where they could see two males squatting behind the Princes Limousine.

Shit exclaimed Neil, I think that they are planting a bomb.

Leave this to me said Stella officiously, do not move or do anything is that clear. Moments later she returned with four armed officers and issuing them instructions to fan out and surround the vehicle she drew a handgun and stepped forward.

As she stepped from the shadow of the hedgerow cover, she called out. Stop what it is that you are doing, we are armed British Police officers, put your hands up in the air where we can see them.

One of the men appeared from behind the vehicle with his hands on the top of his head and started to walk towards her.

Movement in the far corner of the car parking area caught Ronnie`s eye, and he was surprised to see the two Americans, one of whom was pointing a firearm at Stella who was oblivious to his presence.

Sensing the danger Ronnie leapt up, ran the four paces between his position and Stella throwing her to the ground as a single crack echoed across the area.

Two further shots rang out and looking up Ronnie realised that both Americans had disappeared, and the two men who had apparently been planting the bomb were both laying immobile, prone on the ground with armed officers stood over them.

Looking around he saw that Neil was lying on the gravel and running back to him looked at the small red blotch in the centre of his white dress shirt.

Holding Neil`s hand Ronnie looked towards the sky calling out, how many more God, is anything, really worth this.

Stella knelt beside him and placed her arm around his shoulder, and he suddenly realised that a fireworks display was in progress.

Everything is under control Ronnie, the bomb has been dealt with, both suspects are still alive and along with the Americans will be taken into custody, although I suspect each of them will claim diplomatic immunity.

After the body had been carefully taken from the car park, Stella caught up with Ronnie who was somewhat aimlessly wandering around the grounds.

We are most grateful for your assistance in dealing with the attempted bomb plot beamed Stella. Without Neil`s observations we may have had a tragic and serious diplomatic incident on our hands, and the truth is that none of the guests are even aware of what has occurred here this evening and we will be keeping it that way.

They had carried Neil`s body into a garage and covered it with a sheet waiting for a suitable opportunity to remove it probably after the event was over.

So, you simply see Neil`s death as just another piece of collateral damage fumed Ronnie, what is it with you people, does human life not mean that much anymore, does the greater good always trump the here and now.

No of course not, replied Stella, any death is a sad waste, but we all have a job to do, and know the risks, your friend gave his life for the cause and his family will be justifiably proud of him for that.

They watched together as the Arab contingent climbed into their vehicles and drove away followed by the Americans, and not for the first time he felt a great sadness, even though he had completed the mission.

Chapter Fifteen
Running on Empty

With the artifacts safe in the expert hands of the British Museum Ronnie rightly presumed that his somewhat chequered but nonetheless eventful career in Israeli Intelligence was over, and that as such his services would no longer be required. However, Eugene contacted him and explained that he might be required to undertake just one final mission, that being assisting in the cup authentication

Ronnie attended Neil`s funeral and was both surprised and pleased to see Stella, and whilst she made no acknowledgement of him during the service, at the wake she sought him out, and kissing him on the cheek said simply, I never did thank you for saving my life.

It was my pleasure maam he replied, I remember Alison complaining that with so few women holding ranking positions in the service, the promotion Glass Ceiling would never be shattered. Given her passion for female recognition within special branch, I thought that I owed it to her memory to make sure that another one was not taken out of that number. After all who knows maybe, just maybe mind you, one day you might be head of intelligence.

I do not think so she smiled, there are still too many male dinosaurs around for that to happen, the so called, glass ceiling has in fact never been more concrete.

That may well be true conceded Ronnie. But speaking from the viewpoint of both chauvinist, and lover of women, which I agree is by any standards a conundrum.

Women fall into three basic categories. Those driven by the inner desire to succeed for their own satisfaction, not that of others. Those who seek position to satisfy the desires of others most often family. and those who just see life as a day by day journey, and who let whatever happens wash over and around them either being buoyed by it or drowned under the weight of it.

I had not measured you to be a philosopher Stella chuckled, which category do you place me within. The first without a shadow of doubt replied Ronnie.

Not only do you have a fierce belief in yourself, others, are starting to share that belief. So, whatever you do, giving up must never be an option. in fact, that hard concrete ceiling is just waiting to be smashed open and you are the woman to do it, so go for it, if not for yourself do it for Alison.

Christmases came and went, and Ronnie settled into routine family life again concentrating on work and Beverley and Nathan. In May 1986 Eugene contacted him with the news that the British Museum were nearing the end of the testing they were doing on the artifacts saying that his sources had told him the items were believed to be genuine.

They are genuine, exclaimed Ronnie, I know that to be true. Yes of course murmured Eugene, but the question now, is what happens to them. There is a suggestion that the government offer them to the Israelis for display in the museum of Hebrew History in Tel Aviv.

They cannot do that hissed Ronnie, we both know that there are too many people who want them for their own use, personal power, and authority, if they get shipped to Israel they could be lost forever.

Well, that is some turnaround in attitude snorted Eugene, I was under the impression that you were at best, a reluctant participant in the pursuance of these items, and probably give no credence at all, to any power that they are purported to have.

Times and opinions change Eugene, sighed Ronnie, I have seen first-hand how intense emotions can become in respect of the shroud and cup, even down to cold blooded murder.

And whilst I accept money is the root cause of the sellers reasoning, what motivates the purchasers, if it is not a belief in whatever they expect the artifacts are able to deliver.

Okay then responded Eugene, from what you say I am happy to trust you to help me stop this happening, but we need much more information before we can take any action, I will start looking into it and get back to you when something has been confirmed.

Early in October Beverley gave birth to their daughter who they named Natalie. It was for her a much easier birth and they now had a complete family. All that Ronnie wanted now was a final resolution of the Cup and Shroud issue, possibly getting all three items of Ark, Cup and Shroud together in a safe environment.

In July 1987, to be both closer to Beverley`s family and for ease of Ronnie`s work travel, the family moved to Taunton, purchasing a new house on an estate situated on the Eastern fringes of the town close to the motorway.

It was February 1988 before Ronnie received a call from Eugene, and a meeting was arranged to be held at a motorway services on the M4, where much to Ronnie`s surprise, Eugene introduced Ursula, a leggy, bottle blonde, who was apparently a serving officer in the Israeli armed forces.

She lived in Swindon with her husband Tom, a Lieutenant Colonel in the Intelligence Corps who were based at Hermitage near Newbury. Ursula was currently stood down from active service and listed as a reserve, although she still retained her regular service status authority as a ranking officer.

We have positive confirmation that the artifacts are to be shipped secretly to Israel in April said Eugene. The government are not making this an official donation, possibly to avoid any public outcry, although as far as is known, only a handful of people even know that the British Museum has the cup and shroud.

So, is this an official gift then, or yet again someone trying to make a quick monetary killing asked Ronnie. To be honest, we do not know replied Eugene thoughtfully, and we cannot make enquiries of the people in positions of seniority who might be privy to such information without alerting them to the fact that Britain does Indeed have the items.

Catch 22 sighed Ronnie. What is that queried Ursula. A novel and later an American made film about the Vietnam War in which war weary GI`s who do not want to fight anymore start to attend at the medical centre displaying signs of mental instability, as mental health issues are a reason for medical discharge from the army.

However, as the number of soldiers trying this angle increases, a senior medical officer points out that whilst mental angst is seen as a reason for discharge, anyone who was in fact normal would be expected to display such mental angst as part of a normal behaviour pattern. Damned if you do and damned if you don't, and this logic was incorporated into the army medical regulations as item number 22.

I see replied Ursula, you could display mental health issues relating to the war which should have allowed your discharge, however the catch, was that such issues were only to be expected in a normal person because the war was mentally challenging, hence catch 22.

You have a clever lady here Eugene, Ronnie found it hard to conceal his sarcasm. Yes, I know replied Eugene evenly, that is why she will be assisting you in making sure that the real items do not get transported to Israel.

Assuming that this is another get rich quick scheme, what do we know so far asked Ronnie. Well, replied Eugene, the main official at the museum who has been dealing with the items is a professor of ancient history who specialises in religious artifacts. We cannot discover who else has any knowledge of them either inside or outside of the museum staff, so if this is a money sale then the professor almost certainly must be involved.

You said that the items were to be transported to Israel said Ronnie, do we know where from and when. That we can be certain of, responded Eugene, there is a combined Israeli and UK air defence exercise due to be held in April, with the main flying to be from RAF Valley which is north west Wales on Anglesey.

With Neil gone, how do I gain access to the base asked Ronnie. We have that under control replied Eugene, the question is how you manage to swap the real items for replicas which we still have and will get to you.

Here we go again sighed Ronnie, I just hope that no one gets killed this time. After Eugene had left them, he asked Ursula how and why she had become involved and was only mildly surprised to discover that she was related to Reg and like the others had developed the mentality that made the claiming of the cup a family expectation.

Before we get involved in any way said Ursula firmly, I already know of your history in this mission, the number of deaths and of course the numerous women, and you need to know from the start that I have no intention of joining either group.

So then, you see me as a ruthless killer and womaniser smiled Ronnie how quaint. To the contrary, she smiled back, I see you as a bit of a clown, stumbling through life with a complex oversized ego, especially where your attraction to women is concerned, whereas in fact, it has been the needy women, who have cultivated that opinion of yourself.

I see replied Ronnie flatly, so our relationship is going to be purely platonic. Not even platonic muttered Ursula, just purely professional. Far too many people around you seem to end up in a box, and as I have already said, I most certainly do not intend to be yet another.

Now that we have established the ground rules continued Ursula, perhaps we can discuss how to intercept the transport carrying the items down to RAF Valley from the science museum in London and both safely and discreetly make the exchange.

And what does superwoman consider to be a feasible plan, Ronnie simply could not hide his annoyance at this woman's apparent confidence and suggested capability. Ignoring the barbed comment, Ursula responded with.

Any sort of hijacking or intervention will be so high profile that it would defeat the purpose of the exchange, as we are supposed to be discreetly swapping the items so that they can be sent off to Israel with no one aware that they are now fake.

So, what then, we break into the museum or RAF base and make the exchange there said Ronnie. Not exactly tough guy, she smiled again, ask yourself this question. If the powers that be, knew that this country held the genuine Shroud and Cup of the covenant, do you seriously believe that they would just give them away.

No, I do not, Ronnie replied, this is something being arranged secretly by another money mad criminal. The point is Ronnie, these items are in fact either priceless or worthless, depending upon your perspective on what they represent. Surely anyone purchasing them would need to have a reasonable expectation that they had some intrinsic value, not necessarily of a monetary nature, and of course that the items were genuine.

Of course, muttered Ronnie, the Israelis would know the history and perhaps even believe that with the items in their possession, any actions undertaken by them would be guaranteed success under the influential power given by the items, you are quite a clever girl after all.

Firstly, please do not ever call me a girl, I am NOT, and never will be your girl, Ursula, is fine thank you. Secondly, if this sale as we now suspect is just for money and not as Eugene has suggested on behalf of the British Government, then it is reasonable to assume that the receiving group may not be representing the Israeli government either.

The logic is undeniable I agree, but what difference does it make to what we need to do asked Ronnie. When I was serving in the intelligence wing at Al Harad north of Tel Aviv, there was a lot of gossip about a splinter military group planning to force an invasion of Lebanon to clear out the hostile politically motivated terrorist groups for once and for ever said Ursula.

Obviously, most of the comments were along the lines of, in your dreams, but I did hear one chap saying, "who knows, the ancients carried the Ark before them into battle as a guarantee of success, what if it could be found".

So, you think that this group who you have some knowledge about, are the ones who are now trying to purchase the Shroud and Cup, and that they may already have the Ark.

Possibly replied Ursula, but if they do not have it, then they have a plan to get it, and once they have all three items who knows what power might be unleashed.

I see murmured Ronnie, and if you are correct and this group can assemble the three items and use them somehow to start hostilities against Israel`s near neighbours,,, he tailed off sighing to himself. Then God help us all, completed Ursula, we must stop this exchange somehow.

So, we are in total agreement then said Ronnie, the Shroud and Cup must not be allowed to leave this country. However, before we make any firm plans, we need to check out exactly how RAF Valley fits into this exchange.

It is highly likely that the Israeli group are simply using their security cleared access into and out of the base to facilitate secret transport of the items, after all they can hardly send them by conventional means. But we must check that to be the situation just in case there is more to it than the base being a convenient way for the air crews to fly the items out.

It was not practical to take Beverley, as she was now working part time hours in a gateaux making factory, and the children needed to be looked after. So, after leaving his car at Strensham Services on the M5 Motorway, he allowed Ursula to drive across Wales and over the Menai Bridge onto Anglesey.

RAF Valley was a high security fighter command airbase, with aircraft permanently patrolling the English Channel and coastlines around the UK as they played a cat and mouse game with various Russian submarines who constantly entered UK waters.

Pulling into the layby just outside of the main gates at RAF Valley, Ursula said here you are, passing him a small plastic wallet with the identity card inside naming him as Charles Godliman a warrant officer in the Israeli Defence Force (IDF)

Asking to see hers he read aloud, Lieutenant Colonel Ursula Renik IDF. Oh, that is simply great, he sneered, you are a high-ranking officer and what, ??, I get to carry your bag as a junior NCO.

Can you fly a fighter Jet, No. Can you speak fluent Hebrew, No. Can you distract men by just lifting your skirt hem a few inches, No. So just shut up and be a good little boy, put your ID around your neck and let us go and play smiled Ursula.

Before we go onto the base and for your information, there are quite a number of IDF personnel based here almost permanently, as the terrain is ideal training for the plains of Armageddo and the Lebanese borders, so do not be surprised if I know some of them.

Their tour of the base was guided by Captain David Henshey who Ursula already knew from previous service in Israel and their warm embrace made him feel left out and perhaps even jealous. They were given an extensive look around, and over coffee when Ursula mentioned that she was interested in possible smuggling operations David laughed and said that of course things like that happened, just as they did in all air crew services probably across the globe. Guys took home perfume and other items for wives, girlfriends, and others, and for as long as things were kept low key, the authorities deemed it to be a perk and turned a blind eye.

Ursula pursued her point and continued by asking him if he knew anything about the smuggling of ancient relics, particularly those of religious significance. David looked hard at Ronnie and then babbled away in Hebrew with the two of them chatting that way for some time, after which they exchanged another embrace with a kiss this time and Ronnie and Ursula left the base.

In the car Ronnie sullenly asked her what the secret conversation had been about, at which she giggled and said, I do believe

Godders

that you are jealous. Not at all he lied, but if we are to undertake this thing together, then we should not keep secrets.

Quite right she said somewhat breezily. David and I were an item back in Israel, I broke it off when I met Tom, but we remain friends and trust each other completely. When I queried him about other types of smuggling, he asked if you spoke Hebrew and when I said that you did not, he told me about a current operation that he is involved in.

It seems that senior Israeli Intelligence has an idea that a small group of hard-line Zionists are planning some sort of incident, presumably to generate support for action against anti-Israeli countries notably Palestine and Lebanon possibly even Egypt, all of whom have a deep-rooted hatred of the Israeli state. David did not know what might be planned, but it is likely to be carried out somewhere within the UK with the blame being pinned upon foreign insurgents concluded Ursula.

Does he have any idea as to who might be involved asked Ronnie. Israeli security services are watching several guys based at Valley but have nothing concrete yet replied Ursula. So, we now have two plots on the go muttered Ronnie. Ours, which is to somehow swap the artifacts, and theirs, seemingly some terrorist action on UK soil, which of course must take precedence, so we need to tell Eugene as soon as possible.

We went to RAF Valley to gain information which might be a help with our mission and have come away with the terrifying prospect of a terror plot being launched within the UK and with no useful information to help us exchange the shroud and cup moaned Ronnie.

That is not quite true responded Ursula. David gave me the name of the suspected leader of the RAF Valley group, a pilot office named Reuben Gorash, who is taking some leave next week apparently to visit distant relatives who live in North London.

THE CUP

I do not suppose that you also know the name of those supposed relatives, Ronnie asked. Sadly not, replied Ursula, that will be for us to discover, but for now you really do need to get over your childish jealousies and pointless pride and work with me to sort this. You may be the expert when it comes to the artifacts, but according to the reports that I have seen, you are not yet a patch on James Bond. So please let me do what I am good at, and I will keep you safe to authenticate the items when we retrieve them.

A telephone call from Eugene received at his office provided Ronnie with an update, telling him that after extensive research they had discovered that a small but wealthy group of Zionist Jews living in Bethnal Green, a suburb of North London, planned on hosting a party next week and it was possible that Reuben Gorash had been invited. This event was being held at the home of someone named Aaron Berkowitz, who they were still researching.

Later Ursula called him to say that she had an invitation to the party, and she hoped to get some further information asking him to wish her good luck, which he did and for the very first time he felt isolated and left out.

She called him the day after the party had been held and he agreed to meet with her at Chieveley Services and on arriving was surprised to see Eugene was also present.

Ursula explained that from the outset the organisers of the event had made no secret about their Zionist beliefs and that she had been loosely interrogated about what she believed by several people present, mainly in a gentle interested way rather than any hostile aggressiveness.

Later in the evening a slide show about the Ark, Shroud and Cup had been shown, with a running commentary suggesting that soon the true believers could be celebrating ownership of these sacred and treasured symbols of their God "Yaweh" along with the real prospect of restoring Israel to its former power and glory. All of which had been an awful amount of hype, but of little substance.

But Ursula paused. Late into the evening after quite a number had left the party a second presentation was given. This was much more radical, with the speaker openly citing the UK as being a fundamental stumbling block in the way of any Israeli power moves in the middle east.

The speaker continued by arguing that whilst Britain still sees its creation of the new Israel in May 1948 as a gift that all Hebrews should be forever grateful, the reality is that five thousand years ago Canaan was the Israelites home given by God himself, and so far from being a gift from the British, the small part of land now occupied, was in fact just a token gesture.

The speaker went on to say that the time was near when true believers would need to stand up against such archaic tyranny and that Britain's apparent soft relationships with Israel's sworn enemies demonstrated their intention to maintain the status quo in the middle east just to suit their needs.

Finishing by saying, soon my friends these British Autocrats will see that appeasement can sometimes bring wrath, and what better way to demonstrate this than friction between Britain and its Arab cohorts.

There were no specific details or references to anything planned said Ursula, but I gained the impression that anyone with a particular interest, already knew some if not all of whatever is planned. Eugene thanked her for such useful work and in his usual philosophical manner added, that we now knew everything and yet in reality knew nothing.

Frustrated at what seemed meaningless and disconnected events Ronnie asked them both. This information may be of some interest to the intelligence services, but I cannot see any link to the transporting of the artifacts out of the country, excepting that the slide show event purported hope for the future.

Whatever motivates these partygoers including some fanciful suggestion of future power, it is hardly a ringing endorsement of a plan already in action, nor can I see how tension or friction between Britain and any of the Arab countries might be involved sighed Ronnie.

I think that you Ronnie, are both correct and yet incorrect in your assessment, said Eugene as if thoughtfully. Let us assume that the transfer is indeed yet another illegal sale. If it were to be discovered that Israel had effectively stolen the items from Britain a huge diplomatic row would ensue, and the Museum director would almost certainly lose his job.

But if it were to be discovered that some Arab group had stolen the items, perhaps to use against Israel in some way, the shock waves would reverberate around the world, with international support for Israel being offered suggested Ursula.

Britain would never admit to "not knowing" that they had the items said Eugene tersely. Some story would be cooked up for press consumption about Britain only holding and authenticating the artifacts in readiness to make some sort of surprise offering to Israel.

Wait a moment said Ursula more excited than Ronnie had previously seen her. What if the sale to the Israeli group is just a money grabbing scam by someone who has access to the items, and that as a diversionary tactic some incident is planned to make the UK Intelligence services look elsewhere for a short time. You know, to cover any eventuality they had gained knowledge of the planned sale and transportation out of the country.

The upshot would be that some fanatical Zionist group gets the items while Britain is in diplomatic disarray with the Arab states, and is therefore likely to see any Israeli actions against these states in a less hostile way than would normally be the case sighed Eugene

Eugene, who really, knows that Britain even has the items here in the UK Ronnie asked. And by that, I mean people that you are certain know. After all there has been no publicity, so how many people are there that have that knowledge. I personally handed the two items over to the Director of the British Museum instructing secrecy until authentication had been completed at which time we would make a formal public announcement replied Eugene.

Therefore, in answer to your question, obviously us three, the Director at the British Museum and possibly my personal assistant whom I trust completely.

So, the truth is that if he wished to do so this Director could himself sell the items and then claim to you that they had been stolen. Or even replace them with fakes and give them back to you as such, and you could do nothing about it, having told no one that we even have the genuine relics stated Ronnie.

For pity's sake, sighed Eugene, Andrew Neilsen is a highly respected Oxford professor of archaeology specialising in ancient religious practices, he is hardly likely to flog off the company silver for a few shillings.

That assumes he is what you believe him to be and that he is not being coerced smiled Ursula.

Just wait a second, said Ronnie. Eugene my friend did you not tell us that the director had told you that he believed the items to be authentic.

Well, yes but what has that got to do with... How, did he authenticate the cup continued Ronnie, cutting off Eugene in mid flow. I believed it to be only specific individuals who could do that myself included.

But surely if his intention were to sell the items, then telling Eugene they were fakes would be the better option, less outcry if they were then stolen, murmured Ursula apparently thinking aloud.

Yes, that is true sighed Ronnie, but if he were somehow being coerced to sell or even give up the items, by informing Eugene that they were genuine perhaps he hoped that the resultant publicity might make such a transaction impossible.

Possibly not a happy ending for our professor though said Ursula. Maybe, or maybe not grinned Ronnie, but if knowledge of the items were to be made public, more credibility to a theft might be given, after all how can you steal something that nobody even knows exists.

All of this is simply preposterous sighed Eugene, Andrew Nielsen has established a reputation as a world expert on artifacts. Indeed, it was his assertions that it was the Templar Knights who removed the Ark of the Covenant from Jerusalem and secreted it away somewhere in Southern France before it was taken to French controlled North Africa, that have inspired countless books and films. I find it impossible to accept him to be anything less than honest and forthright.

But after discussing this with you two cynics, we need to find out one way or another and soon, so I will do what checking I can without raising suspicions and report back said Eugene.

And whilst you are doing that, I shall go back to RAF Valley to see how much more if anything I can find out about any plots or plans smiled Ursula, we can meet here again next week at the same time okay.

As Ronnie and Ursula walked towards their respective cars he asked, do you want me to come to RAF Valley with you, but smiling broadly she replied thank you but that would not be a good idea. I think that it is better if you stick to what you do best with your engineering and leave the spying to the professionals, at least that way fewer people might end up dead, and yet again he felt disappointed that he was being left out of the action.

Sipping a mug of hot chocolate, Eugene sighed, it hurts to admit it but everything seems to point towards Andrew Neilsen being involved, at least in some way. Firstly, even though I was discreet no one has any awareness of the items in question ever being in Britain, let alone under scrutiny at the British Museum. Furthermore, Neilsen is related to the Berkowitz character from Bethnal Green, although their association is I believe, not the warmest of relationships.

May I please get things straight in my own head snorted Ronnie. I gave you the genuine items for safe keeping and you immediately passed them over to a radical Zionist group, hell bent on world domination, starting with Holy War in the Middle East.

You do not need to point out my failings sighed Eugene, those I am already far to painfully aware of, however the good news, if indeed anything we discover is such, might be that as far as we are able to establish Andrew Neilsen still has the items in his possession, so keeping them in this country must still be our priority.

What about your trip to RAF Valley, how did that go Ursula, asked Eugene. Well, apart from confirming that Ronnie is not the only person trying to get into my knickers, she smiled at him saying, just my idea of a little joke Ronnie. David told me that, a three-way exercise is planned for the end of April with fighter Jets from the RAF, Israeli IDF and the Saudi Air Force involved. The exercise is designed to test a combined air defence strategy, if successful this being followed by a long-term RAF deployment to the Middle East with RAF Air Bases to be located within several different countries.

Bloody hell exclaimed Eugene, we are currently negotiating an extremely lucrative arms supply deal including new Jet Fighters with the Saudi government, if there were to be an incident it would almost certainly make the negotiations difficult if not scupper the deal completely.

What can we do then, asked Ursula, all we currently have for evidence is speculation and supposition, nothing that even comes close to a reason for action. I will speak to the Ministry of Defence said Eugene. But I will have to tread carefully as if I even raise the slightest amount of suspicion, I will be forced to tell them what I know.

Assuming that the items are not yet handed over and are presumably still with Professor Neilsen which might just be the only good news, perhaps I can find out where he is keeping them and where and when he intends to show them or indeed hand them over said Ronnie.

And how, might one ask, do you intend to accomplish that sneered Ursula, he is hardly likely to meet with you to discuss them. You can finally leave that job to me replied Ronnie, although sadly I fear that I might require your input at some stage but for once I can be useful.

Sneaking into the private areas of the British Museum was far too easy as no one even looked at Ronnie in his boiler suit carrying a small toolbox. He made his way downstairs to the basement area where, as he had suspected the boiler room, electrical switch room and maintenance workshops were located.

Godders

He quickly discovered floor plans showing the electrical services layout and was pleased to see that they detailed individual rooms and offices as well as the larger areas and public spaces.

The rooms were only numbered and did not name their occupants, but from studying the drawings it was clear where the main group of offices could be found.

Taking up a hand tray holding spare lightbulbs Ronnie decided to work downwards from the sixth floor, top of the building to find the professors room and was rewarded for his efforts by finding a small brass plaque displaying Director Neilsen fixed to an office door on the fourth floor.

Taking one of the lightbulbs and a pencil he wrote Director FLR 4 on the cardboard packaging, knocked upon the door and stepped inside. Yes, what do you want, cannot you see that I am busy.

The speaker was a shortish plump man Ronnie guessed to be aged around sixty-five years or maybe slightly older. He was dressed in a cheap looking brown linen suit of the mass production style rather than hand-made tailoring, a white shirt and colourful tie which he recognized as Eton old Boys.

Sorry sir offered Ronnie, I have come to replace the failed lightbulb, holding out the new lamp clearly written as Director FLR 4. Gesturing at the ceiling in annoyance the Professor said, as you can see, the lights are just fine thank you, so please go away.

Leaving the lightbulb on a table near to the door, Ronnie apologised again adding that his supervisor must have made a mistake and stepped out of the office and closed the door behind him.

As he made his way across the ground floor concourse towards the stairs leading down to the basement, he was called out by a uniformed security guard who was speaking into a two-way radio handset.

THE CUP

Hey maintenance man you are in real trouble. Resisting the urge to run, Ronnie turned towards the guard, who immediately said, you are new I have not seen you here before. No responded Ronnie, it is my first time I am just helping the guys who work here for a short time because of sickness, is there a problem.

You bet that there is pal, grinned the security guard, it seems that you have left a lightbulb in the Professor of Antiquities Office and he is not amused. Okay, sorry about that I will collect it the next time that I am up there said Ronnie. You will get it right now replied the guard, the Professor is an important person, and no one wants him to be annoyed.

Back outside the director's office Ronnie tentatively knocked but received no answer, so he opened the door and found the office empty. To his surprise the filing cabinets as well as the small cupboards were also unlocked and in the top drawer of the desk, he found a diary with notations against passed dates as well as future events. Skimming through the pages he found the drinks at the Berkowitz had been listed so he had presumably been present when Ursula had witnessed the slide show and presentation. Moving forward and backwards through the pages he found identical entries, noted as Miss W 8pm each of which were for a Friday evening generally once every month with the next being later that week.

In August, an underlined entry read, Ingleby Hall Summer Party with Greta and Friends, so he jotted down details and replaced the diary closing the drawer. He moved over to the door picking up the lightbulb on his way and as he opened it, a small two door cabinet in the corner of the office caught his eye.

He gently closed the door again and stepped to the cupboard, it was unlocked and opening it on impulse, he was amazed to find the shroud and cup wrapped just as he had passed them to Eugene seemingly untouched. To be certain he gently unwrapped the covering and removed the cup, thrilled to feel the now anticipated feelings pulsing through his body.

Rewrapping the items precisely as he had found them, he noted the printed business card next to the parcel with the professor's name shown on it as Director of Antiquities British Museum and underneath in small but elegant handwriting it read, Quality Copies but nonetheless fake examples of the Turin Shroud and Last Supper Cup.

Closing everything and returning the tray of lightbulbs to the basement workshop he left the Museum still wearing the boiler suit and spoke to Ursula from a nearby telephone box. She was quick to congratulate him on his exploits, adding that she would discuss the Ingleby event with Eugene to see what could be discovered.

Ronnie explained that they needed to find out what the mysterious meetings with Miss W were all about especially with the next shown as being that Friday and, that as the professor already knew him by sight, following the man to see where he went for these meetings, was not something he felt able to undertake. Ursula was more than happy to do the surveillance and report to him and Eugene next week at Chieveley again.

Saturday's newspapers were filled with stories about a spectacular air crash over the Irish Sea where two English Electric Lightning Jet Fighters had apparently flown into each other. One being piloted by the RAF the other by the Saudi Air Force resulting in the loss of both aircrews and with the initial suggestion that the on-board navigation systems had malfunctioned rather than it being down to pilot error.

The mood of the meeting with Eugene and Ursula, had as Ronnie expected a sombre start with Eugene explaining that the suggestion of controls failure was being hotly disputed by the plane manufacturer, and there was now a faint whisper that pilot error might have been involved.

But whatever the eventual explanation, British and Saudi relations were being increasingly strained with the arms deal also in jeopardy.

Ursula spoke up saying that David Henshey had telephoned her at home, to tell her that pilot officer Gorash had been overheard, bragging to his cohorts that he had personally tampered with the two separate navigation systems by altering the onboard giro-compass settings.

Adding that with the explosions and near total destroying of both Jets, any subsequent investigation would be impossible.

Ronnie wanted to ask her why, Henshey had her home telephone number but instead commented. When they recover the flight recorders, all that will be shown, is instrument malfunction rather than sabotage, so Gorash is right in his assumption that no one will suspect any plot.

They have always made the point that whenever YOU are involved, people tend to end up dead hissed Ursula how many is it now, Ten or more. That is enough, cut in Eugene, not all of the deaths are his fault. Not ALL thought Ronnie, he did not feel responsible for any of them, but seemingly others disagreed.

He accepted that he had tried to strangle Siobahn but had failed at that, and the fact of her being a homicidal maniac could hardly be placed at his door. Ursula interrupted his thoughts by giving her account of the professor`s assignations saying that she had followed him to his home and waited outside to trail him wherever he went, only for a woman visitor to arrive and be let in. After about three quarters of an hour the woman left so I followed her to a nearby shopping area and stopped her with a small lie suggesting that I was police.

Convincing her to come for a coffee, even I was quite surprised to find out that she, was in fact male, a crossdressing trans-sexual I believe to be the correct terminology. So, our professor is in fact a homosexual, retorted Eugene that is something he cannot afford to become public knowledge even in today's enlightened times.

I thought that we now lived in a more tolerant society where people can feel free to express their sexuality as they choose without fear of legal persecution said Ursula. That's as maybe snarled Eugene but I doubt that the Governors of the British Museum would share your apparent modern ideology regarding such practices.

Well, you two can discuss our charming professor and his sexual preferences all day if you like but what possible linkage can there be to our issue with the sale of the items quipped Ronnie. Really, you cannot see the implications, Ursula was giving him that, I am disappointed in you smile. Surely open to blackmail, he would give anything to keep his sordid secrets exactly that secret, so keeping the possession of the artifacts to himself ensured that he had the wherewithal to meet the blackmailers demands and still retain his job and lifestyle.

Money might not then be the motivation said Eugene, self-preservation is after all the greatest of the incentives in life, and therefore preserving his character and job must figure high on Neilsen's list of priorities.

So then if what you suspect is in fact true, then who might be blackmailing the professor and for what reason if they have no knowledge of him holding the two items asked Ronnie. I think that I can help there said Ursula, the transgender chap who I chatted with, also told me that he is not paid by Neilsen but by someone else.

And this person just offered that information voluntarily scoffed Eugene. Well not exactly voluntarily, smiled Ursula, but outside the café in a side alley when I had his balls squeezed in my hands, he remembered that he gets payment from a uniformed chauffeur outside Earls Court Tube Station at Ten am the day after his trysts with Neilsen.

Oh hell, sighed Eugene, if we had known about that we could have traced the car to its owner now we will just have to wait until their next meeting to do so. Not at all, responded Ursula you really should have much more faith and trust in me Eugene, the car is registered to a Fredrick Schwimmer who lives with his wife at their home in Hampstead North London.

Patting Ursula on the knee Eugene purred, see Ronnie, I told you that she was good, such a talented and resourceful all round, clever girl, all we need now is to watch the Schwimmers and find out where they fit in, but my guess is that we are getting close to the head of this snake.

We meet here again in three weeks, same time and day does anyone need anything asked Eugene. Just that you get me the replica items so that I will be prepared if we suddenly get an opportunity to do a swap requested Ronnie. That is indeed a good idea I will arrange for it to happen replied Eugene.

The replicas of both cup and shroud arrived via his office a few days later, and as before Ronnie was impressed by the close likeness to the genuine articles, they were indeed high class quality fakes that even those with some knowledge would be unable to distinguish as such without very close scrutiny.

Now that he had the replicas, a plan formed in his mind. For too long he had been on the back foot just responding to events as they happened, it was time to change that.

Repeating his cover ruse as a maintenance operative working on site he returned to the British Museum. He had a fright and somewhat heart pounding moment when he met two of the real maintenance team on the stairs leading down to the basement workshop but thinking on his feet, he said good morning to them and added I am part of the telephone services crew, which they happily acknowledged and told him to help himself to tea or coffee in the workshop just not to eat all, of the chocolate biscuits.

Professor Neilsen`s office was empty, and the small cabinet still unlocked so it took less than two minutes for him to neatly make the exchange and close the office door as he left. Smiling to himself, he made his way downstairs to the main concourse only to see one of the maintenance men he had spoken to earlier, chatting to a uniformed, post office telecoms engineer and a security guard.

The guard abruptly spoke into his radio handset saying, suspicious activity, find and detain a male maintenance person dressed in a blue boiler suit carrying a dark holdall bag. Shit. breathed Ronnie. just when it was going well, what to do now.

Reading the sign on the nearest door which said, Cleaners Room. a quick plan formed in his head. Stepping into the small room he donned a brown work coat and flat cap both of which carried the logo Trident Cleaning and putting his holdall into a green rubbish sack he picked up the waste sack and a cleaning cloth then went out onto the concourse again.

Checking around to ensure that no one was watching, Ronnie used his elbow to smash the fire alarm, break glass in case of emergency, and was rewarded with the immediate wailing of sirens, and as people began to spill out into the concourse and make their way towards the exits, pulling the cap lower over his face, he jostled himself into their mix and in seconds was outside.

Using the chaos of people milling around outside, Ronnie slipped over to his van and slowly drove away considering himself to be a lucky chap, musing that whilst his plan had been foolproof in his own mind, it demonstrated that a fool's plans could indeed prove to be foolish.

When they met, Eugene was buzzing, explaining that the Schwimmers were in fact Neo Nazi's who had been living in London since the late nineteen forties having come to Britain via Austria. The husband Fredrick was a banker employed by Deutschebank, and the couple are, surprise surprise, part of the Critchley's social circle, which also includes Berkowitz.

The bigger discovery however, being that Christina Schwimmer had been formerly Christina Mendel, sister of Greta who is now Lady Critchley and was as a young woman a close friend of one Eva Braun. Indeed, Braun had been Maid of honour at Christina's wedding to Fredrick.

Good lord, gasped Ronnie, are you seriously telling us that Hitlers Mistress was this woman Schwimmer's chief bridesmaid. Exactly that my friend but there is more. After the discovery of the bodies in Hitlers Berlin Bunker, a search was made at Berchtesgaden the Nazi hideaway nicknamed the Eagles Nest, where a note in neat handwriting, was discovered.

I do not have a copy, but that note read something along the lines of. We were not successful, this time, but the struggle must continue, and next time with the Jews own covenant symbols in our possession again, to protect us, we will prevail.

The note was catalogued and filed as of no particular significance however the signature was just two initials rather than a name, C.S.

Christina Schwimmer breathed Ursula, so even back then she was part of the fanatics who wished for world domination.

That I fear is an oversimplification of what the Neo Nazi's believe, but for the purposes of our mission is sufficient to place her right at the heart of any plot said Eugene and for that reason alone they will be kept under surveillance.

You mentioned that the note said we will have the items again queried Ronnie, does that not suggest possession of them during the war. Yes, indeed replied Eugene, certainly pre-war, and in the early years we believe that they had at least the cup and shroud possibly all three items.

There are photographs of Hitler holding a small wooden cup at rallies as a symbol of how something basic and unvalued could become sought after and successful with hard work and effort.

And as he frequently quoted, not by mere Gold or Silver but riches born from rags.

Allegedly a Jewish manservant and his wife stole the cup along with some silver from Hitler`s home and disappeared, in panic the entire state was put on highest alert with the instruction to find the stolen items at all costs leaving no stone unturned and no glass unbroken.

Krystalnacht, breathed Ronnie. Quite so continued Eugene, as you already know the cup was entrusted to your relatives eventually.

Of course, there have been many claims made that the Third Reich had possession of the Ark of the Covenant which is why Hitler placed so much belief in Germany`s infallibility. However, given that Ronnie has authenticated the cup if not the Shroud, it would seem unlikely for that to be so, as why would they retain the Ark but sell the other items queried Eugene.

Maybe they were not intending to sell the real items after all said Ronnie thoughtfully, did Flannery not bring fakes to the Hampshire estate. After her murderous spree in Belfast there would have needed to be some dramatic turnaround for the group to want to sell. No, all these events have been scams simply to raise money.

But the Americans did have the real artifacts I believe added Ursula. Yes, they did smiled Ronnie. Presumably they were shown the real items in Germany, but my guess is that Flannery's group switched the real items being kept by the count, for the replicas also held by the count before the exchange, not realising that Count Von-Richsten and Klette had already swapped them for the copies. The group then sold the Americans the real items not knowing that what they kept were fakes.

But why then try to do a deal with the Americans to buy them back at Wetherby Grange if they believed that they had sold the Americans fakes asked Eugene. They were not trying to purchase them said Ronnie, just facilitating the Americans recouping seemingly lost money after the Americans had assumed, wrongly as it happens, that they had purchased fakes.

So, the Neo Nazis still believe that they have the real items in their possession queried Ursula. Yes, they do said Ronnie, and they also believe that what professor Neilsen is holding are the replicas which they sold to the Americans, with the intention of perhaps making one last money spree by getting him to sell them to the Arabs.

And when the Arabs discover the artifacts to be fake, asked Eugene, what then. Who can they complain too replied Ronnie, certainly not the British Government as they have no knowledge, Professor Neilsen, yes, but he will not have the money so while he will be expendable, his demise will not offer any fiscal recovery for the Arab group.

All, of these exchanges are driven by money muttered Ronnie, a couple of sets of replica items doing the rounds of greedy power hungry, wealthy individuals and groups with only one winner, that being the cheating Neo Nazi idealists who have turned the search for these items into a money making, circus.

What now then asked Ursula, we must at the very least prevent the items being taken out of the UK, why do we not just announce publicly that the items are currently in the possession of the British Museum for authentication.

How many valid reasons would you like said Ronnie, for a start everyone and his wife would want to know where they came from, who gave them to the Museum, why did no one else know.

For certain Eugene loses his job and the shake up inside Intelligence would have cataclysmic consequence, not that it would necessarily be a bad thing but that is another story.

We must exchange the items at the British Museum for the replicas which you have Ronnie said Eugene, and I will then arrange for the real ones to be returned to where the Templar Knight stole them from, and that will be mission accomplished, and case closed.

You mentioned return to where the items were taken from, said Ursula to Eugene, can you expand that please. Well, no one can be certain of course, but some educated theologians believe that after Christ's Resurrection, the Shroud was entrusted to Mary Jesus close friend and the cup to Joseph the Merchant who had lent Jesus his family tomb, as the immediate and closest followers expected to be rounded up and killed.

Joseph took the cup and kept it with him as he journeyed, and during one such voyage on his merchant ship, whilst taking supplies to Britania, one of the far flung, outposts of the then Roman Empire, legend tells that he fell gravely ill and fearing death he buried the item at the foot of a nearby grassy hill for safe keeping.

Miraculously he became well but decided to leave the cup buried until his return, which of course never happened as he died of heart failure on the journey home. Some thousand years later with the Persians besieging Jerusalem a call went out for fearless Knights to band together and march to Jerusalem and save the Holy Temple from the Muslim Hordes.

One such Knight was making his way Eastwards through Britannia, to join the growing army when being thirsty, he stopped to find water for both him and his small band of followers and the animals.

There was no water to be found anywhere near, so using the hilt of his sword as a cross, he knelt and prayed to God for guidance. In front of their eyes the ground became soft, and a small spring of pure water bubbled up, then opened a little more to reveal the cup lodged on a stone under the earth.

That Knight`s name was Hugo De Payen, and the year was 1096. He prayed some more for new guidance and placed the item into his saddlebags explaining to his men that were to take the item with them to Jerusalem, place it in the Holy Temple and thereafter establish a trustworthy group of followers who would dedicate themselves to its protection.

The cup remained in the temple, until Jerusalem was virtually destroyed by Saladin`s invading armies and with the defending knight`s being given safe passage away from Jerusalem in exchange for giving up the city itself, they left taking the cup amongst other relics with them.

Back in France, opinion was being turned against these so-called Holy Knights of the Temple, and the King under strong pressure from the religious leaders eventually instructed that they be rounded up and executed.

In Fifteen Thirty Six, a Bavarian Monk living at an Abbey near Roissy in Southern France where Mary had eventually fled too, discovered the shroud and cup items, which the Knights had presumably hidden for safe keeping, taking them back to Bavaria his home country unaware of what they were. And it was here that they eventually came into the hands of the Nazi ancestry.

So, there you have it said Eugene softly, the complete history of the items, what we need to do now is ensure that we get them back, and I believe that I know how.

The Critchley home in Wales, is as you have already guessed Ingleby Hall, and yet another summer Ball has been planned with our Professor, the Berkowitz's and Schwimmers, all on the VIP guest list.

However, we have it on reliable authority that a small Saudi contingent will also be attending, led by a member of their Royal Family secretly flown in via RAF Valley.

I thought that the Saudi and British Governments were currently diplomatically distant snorted Ursula. Yes, they are officially, sighed Eugene, but this arms deal means a lot of British Jobs as well as a great deal of money, so this is one way the government can facilitate restoration of reciprocal friendship.

And just how do you propose that we attend this Ball said Ronnie sarcastically. That has already been taken care of growled Eugene, Ursula is one of the catering supervisors whilst you will be a porter fetching and carrying, that should give you both, enough freedom to find the items and to make the exchange.

Just one small thing said Ronnie. Let me guess sneered Ursula, he is not happy being a porter while I am his supervisor. To the contrary, porter suits me well thank you, no, my query is to Eugene, as I have yet to receive the replica items and without those, attending the Ball will be somewhat pointless.

What, cried Eugene I assumed that to have been sorted, I will get onto it straight away, heaven knows what has happened, fortunately we had two sets made as you know.

With the new set of replicas in his possession Ronnie met with Ursula and the owner of the Anglesey based catering company, who stated from the outset that he was happy to have them as part of the team but did not wish to know anything about their purpose, as it had been promised that his business would be awarded the outside catering contract at RAF Valley if he agreed.

The company owner introduced them to the events catering manager, as RAF Valley staff, who needed to be at the event and would cover as catering team members no questions asked. The manager fully accepted this at face value, and as both Ursula and Ronnie held RAF Passes, access to the event would be simple, as the events manager would notify the estate security that two of his team were coming from there.

The party was scheduled for Saturday 27th August, and Ronnie was annoyed at having to deceive his darling wife, explaining that an overnight testing job would mean him not being home on the Friday or Saturday evenings, returning home on Sunday.

On Friday 26th he met Ursula at Strensham Services again and drove with her to RAF Valley where she was booked into the officer's mess, with him billeted within the sergeant's mess, not even sharing dinner together.

Saturday morning after breakfast, Ronnie and Ursula went together to Ingleby Hall and helped with the setting up of tables and chairs and the decoration of the marquees.

Some of the guests including the Schwimmer's and Berkowitz's were already staying at the hall, but professor Neilsen was not amongst them.

During the afternoon, Prince Haasan arrived with two other men, who Ronnie presumed to be his personal protection and by early evening as more guests arrived the event began to develop more of a party atmosphere.

Professor Neilsen finally arrived a little after Eight Thirty pm accompanied by a slim, blonde haired, effeminate youth who Ronnie assumed to be a familiar companion, and with drink and food in abundance the party was soon in full swing.

Just after ten pm, Ursula shared with Ronnie that she had seen the professor coming from the Library and presuming that to be where the items were being kept, instructed him to make the exchange as soon as he was able.

Offering a mock salute to her in response and saying "Yes Maam" Ronnie turned and walked away smiling to himself.

Around half past midnight as the catering team were clearing things away and he was checking around the outside for discarded glasses. Through the part open wooden doors leading from the garden into the library, Ronnie overheard the Schwimmer woman talking to Sir Henry Critchley, asking if everything had gone according to plan with everyone happy with the result.

Yes indeed, Christina was the reply, the Arabs have in their possession what they believe to be the Jews most prized artifacts, whereas in fact, we now have all three items. And of course, once plans are finalised, we can and will use them to bring forth the rise of the Fourth Reich, we will be unstoppable, invincible.

I will drink to that, a third voice, female smooth and silky, Ronnie peered through the crack in the door and was stunned to see the long Raven Hair. Resisting the urge to rush in and strangle the bitch with his bare hands, he continued to listen.

The three of them were joined in the library by Lady Critchley and the Berkowitz`s and all six of them began sharing a bottle of champagne.

Raising their glasses Christina said, to the glorious Fatherland, to our future and to the future of our young Eva here. They clinked glasses and drank the toast saying in unison TO THE FATHERLAND.

What happens now, asked Reuben Berkowitz, to which Sir Henry Critchley replied. The cup will be flown from RAF Valley to Saudi Arabia which will complete our agreement with them and at the same time conclude our little entertainment.

And the real items added Berkowitz. They are held safely in Germany by Greta's Uncle and will be reunited with the Ark once we return it to Germany from North Africa. Once all three are together, we will raise young Eva here to her rightful position and her parent's dreams will finally become reality smiled Critchley, and they all made another toast this time to "Eva and the Fatherland".

Oh, my dear God, exclaimed Ronnie to no one in particular, the bitch, is Hitler's daughter. As more chinking of glasses sounded the other side of the door Lady Critchley said, and what about that ghastly professor fellow, with his sordid little life will he not pose some threat.

That my dear Lady has been taken care of, soothed Lord Critchley, we have taken the necessary steps to ensure that sufficient harm comes his way. More laughter and glasses chinking followed.

Now I must lock the items away until the Saudi RAF Pilot comes to collect them, after all he needs to see them safe under lock and key as would be the real items said Sir Henry.

On the way back to RAF Valley Ursula queried his quiet, broody mood. Why so glum Ronnie, did we not make the exchange successfully she simpered. Eugene will be so pleased with us, where are the real items.

In the holdall behind your seat, replied Ronnie sourly. You keep them, and give them to Eugene, I am done with all of this.

Dropping Ronnie back at Strensham services to collect his car on the Sunday morning Ursula kissed his cheek and said well done, and with a wave of her hand through the open window of her departing car, drove away to meet up with Eugene, whilst Ronnie went home to his family.

As arranged, the three met again at Chieveley Services some weeks later with Eugene all smiles and Ursula looking as if she was going to a fashion photo shoot.

Well done team said Eugene, the British Government now has the genuine artifacts which will be announced to the public at some point in the future when the time is judged to be right, and this time, no one died.

That presumes you to believe the professor's road accident to be just that, an accident sighed Ronnie. And you do not, asked Eugene sharply.

Ignoring the question Ronnie asked what happens to the items now. We keep them safe until we can get them to Jerusalem for authentication, and possibly they might stay there, after all surely that is where they belong.

But what if they were to be used to wage war against the Arab world hissed Ronnie. Then we of course would be victorious, smiled Eugene broadly.

I am sorry Ronnie but there really is no place in the modern world for idealists and compromisers, you are indeed a nice person, and we all love you, but you are also a romantic and far too trusting, the entire purpose of the mission was to gain the items for the state of Israel.

Well fuck you, snarled Ronnie, I have given over twenty years of my life to this cause and for what, just to be "mugged over" by the very people that I placed my whole trust and belief in. That is, I am afraid about the size of it said Eugene, but in the end, I do believe that you will come to see that the actions that we have taken are in fact justified.

You calmly sit there and tell me that I have simply been your stooge cried Ronnie. A clockwork toy, that you periodically wound up and pointed in the right direction, making sure that I went exactly where I was needed to go. What about the lives of those who were also involved, were they just expendable stooges.

Far from it said Eugene, everything that you have experienced has been very much for real, real people, real events, and sadly real deaths, including John and later Neil. They were real people and both was family members, and there were sad, but necessary deaths of others, none of which were planned or wished for, but what you might call collateral.

For pity`s sake I tried to kill someone for this cause, for you cried Ronnie angrily. Which is one reason why you will never share any of this with anyone, after all attempted murder is still a criminal offence in this country sighed Eugene. He held out his hand for Ronnie to shake saying, no hard feelings. Bollocks, said Ronnie pushing his way past them both and out of the café area calling back, I hope that I never see either of you ever again.

Epilogue

Keeping the Artifacts secreted away, Ronnie started to build his family life expecting that any day Eugene would appear for them, but days passed into weeks and then months and years.

The far-right wing in German politics started to become more mainstream and for a short time it was a possibility that one of Europe's governments might succumb, but everyone was relieved when centre stage politics prevailed.

In 1994, with his family, Ronnie visited Glastonbury and the aptly named "Chalice Well" which used the ancient Legend of the cup to its advantage as a tourist attraction.

Not being able to either confirm or disprove the Chalice Well location to be that of the Legend, if indeed the Legend were true, Ronnie had decided to do what Eugene had suggested and accordingly taken the two artifacts with him on the family outing, so unseen, he hid the items inside the small well area, and simply continued with the day.

Despite the earlier years of involvement, Ronnie felt surprisingly unburdened and hoped that his life with family would be for everyone what it should have always been, and as their two children grew into adults, married, and had children of their own life was indeed satisfying.

Seven grandchildren were added to the family and despite the passing of close family members, life had become what he had always expected it to be. He absolutely adored his beloved Beverley, although justifiably she sometimes questioned his sincerity and faithfulness even if perhaps in secret and within her own mind, but he contented himself in the knowledge, that since meeting her, she had been the only woman in his life, even if he did enjoy the company of women rather than men.

In 2008, news reached him of the death of Reg Steiner, he did go to the funeral, but as an onlooker, not wishing to meet with anyone. It was an elaborate affair with the coffin inside a glass panelled horse drawn carriage and he estimated over two hundred people attending.

The years continued to roll by and then in 2019 Eugene made a totally unexpected appearance at Ronnie's workplace in North London.

How did you get access here he snarled at Eugene, I never wanted to see you again, please go away, these are private premises.

Don't be silly Ronnie, I am MI6 remember, I can go anywhere that I choose there are no exceptions. Then what do you want, I am done with you and your lies. To say goodbye, actually, replied Eugene, I am being retired, slightly earlier than I might have wished, but I do get to keep the pension.

I am trying to tie up the loose ends of my life and of course you are top of that list. So, you see me as one of your loose ends smiled Ronnie. Indeed, I do, replied Eugene, can we get a coffee somewhere as I want to tell you a story.

Once upon a time, in the small village of Nazereth, in what was then the Northern Territory of Judea in the land of Palestine, a young virgin girl found herself expecting a baby, you know the story I am led to believe.

Anyway, as a grown man this baby named Jesus carried out miraculous healings, changed water into wine, walked upon water, and fed thousands of people with small amounts of food, he was a Legend in his own lifetime.

Godders

In fact, his popularity and associated power over people was so great that the authorities at the time both Jewish and Roman decided that he had to go, the Jewish priesthood terrified that their lavish lifestyles at the expense of the common people would come to an end, the Romans concerned that he might insight rebellion.

The Jewish High Priest at the time was a man called Caiaphas who publicly denounced Jesus as a fake and fraud, therefore being by definition a blasphemer, which required a death sentence under Jewish Law.

Look I obviously know all this hissed Ronnie, you did not come here to give me a lesson on Biblical History.

As I was saying continued Eugene, Jesus was Crucified using three nails one through each wrist the third through his crossed ankles, and as far as both Jewish and Roman leaders were concerned that was the end of it.

Even when the body went missing three days later, it was passed off as a stunt undertaken by Jesus followers designed to create support for the idea that Jesus was indeed the son of Yaweh the Hebrew God.

I do know all this snorted Ronnie, what suddenly makes you a bloody expert on Jesus.

If you will let me finish the story sighed Eugene. despite Caiaphas and the other Jewish leaders attempts to shut down this growing band of "Jesus believers" who called themselves "THE WAY" groups began to spring up.

These new bands of believers were seemingly everywhere and not just in Palestine but Greece, Sardinia, even Rome itself. And both the Centurion called Longinus who supervised the crucifixion and Herodius the Governor's wife, acclaimed Jesus to be God's son.

THE CUP

Look Eugene, I really do not care what you may or may not believe about new testament Bible History muttered Ronnie. For me Jesus was, and is real, and will in his own time show the world that to be true, although at that point it will sadly be too late for unbelievers to acknowledge that fact.

Precisely, smiled Eugene, we do agree on something, I did think that we might, so having agreement on Jesus being of a divine nature and not of this world we just need to understand exactly where we all fit in.

Oh, for pity's sake, not Aliens again please groaned Ronnie. Not at all, sighed Eugene. Like you I believe Jesus to be God the creator and that is why I am here so let me complete my story.

After the resurrection, the grave clothes or what we now call the shroud, together with the cup were secretly taken away, and you already know how they travelled across Europe and their subsequent history right up to today.

Ever since then different groups have searched for the items in the hope of using them for their own ends and I believe that you have first-hand experience of how much evil has been committed in their name.

The Steiner family got together in the 1950's and made a promise to collect the items in preparation for the second coming, and historically we knew that only male descendants from the house of Levite could authenticate the items.

The tribe of Leveite which is one of the twelve named Hebrew tribes were it seems, gifted by God, to act as the guardians of his Holiness on Earth, rather than owners of land or treasure, that of course is where you came in.

None of us IN THE Steiner Family were sure that you would even be able to authenticate anything, but of course only time would tell. In the event it took over ten years, but worth all the waiting, as your sincerity in confirming the cup to be real was overwhelming, so we knew it to be true.

Others of course including Ursula have held the cup but felt nothing, but that only increases our belief in what you have told us.

Anyway, after several costly attempts to get the item`s we were finally successful and took grateful possession of them. And with both Arab and Neo Nazi groups believing themselves to have them, whilst the real genuine articles are safely held in Jerusalem, everything is just about perfect, and the right and proper end to what is an incredible story.

Quite so old friend, the perfect ending as you say, smiled Ronnie. Except that it is not, muttered Eugene.

I warned everyone, Harry, John, Neil, even Ursula that you were not as dim witted as you pretend to be, and that we should not trust you. Sorry I have absolutely no idea what you are talking about replied Ronnie, I have always done whatever was asked of me.

Yes, I know that Eugene sighed hard, the problem is that somewhere along the way God got to you didn`t he. What was to be a simple authentication and handover responsibility, became something personal, and we never saw that coming. In the end it was all just "smoke and mirrors" wasn't it.

Did you not say yourself that everyone was now happy, both the Arabs and the Nazis think that they have succeeded so tell me, just what is your problem growled Ronnie.

Eugene reached into his pocket and drew out a 9mm pistol, the problem my friend is, as you say the Arabs and Nazis are happy but the Jews, as you well know have been tricked.

THE CUP

We considered of course, that somehow either the Germans or Arabs had ended up with the genuine articles, but of course you were far too clever to let that happen, and at every stage it all simply comes back to you.

Foolishly I believed your tale about not receiving the replicas sent to you and provided you a second set, my guess is that you switched the genuine articles for replicas at Ingleby Hall but handed Ursula the second replica set.

You are not quite right said Ronnie, but your logic is certainly on the correct track, but what of it, are you going to shoot me because I did what you instructed, which was to return the items from whence they came.

Eugene sighed heavily again and putting the gun back into his pocket said, what good would that do, I know that you will never tell me where the items are, so shooting you achieves nothing.

Anyway, my superiors have deemed me to be surplus to their requirements, apparently spying and surveillance is best undertaken these days by computers and drones not shabby old men dressed in long coats.

I know the feeling Eugene believe me smiled Ronnie, we are both dinosaurs in our own way, but we were there when it mattered, and a fucking machine can never make a sound judgement whether to pull the trigger or not. So, I guess that it`s time for both of us to go. Well, said Eugene rising to his feet, I really did come to say goodbye even though you tricked us out of our expected inheritance.

In fairness Ronnie whispered, I did have a good teacher, two in fact in Harry and then you. Ronnie stood up and they shook hands and Ronnie watched as Eugene walked away up the path. Eugene, he called out, and the ageing British spy half turned back to face him.

Two things my dear friend. Firstly, the artifacts are where Joseph wanted them to be, but then you have already worked that out. More importantly, that Bitch Flannery tricked us all, even the mighty British Secret Service. Not only is she still alive, but for what it Is worth she is Hitler and Eva Braun`s daughter, so in my book it's a bloody good thing that they did not get their hands on the Artifacts.

Smoke and Mirrors sighed Eugene, turning away, and walking off, then he stopped again and turned back. Who knows he called out maybe one day someone will find them again just like the Templar Knight did and the cycle will be repeated.

Oh, I do not think so called Ronnie, one day, soon I hope, every eye will see, and everyone will have no choice but to believe, after all even some of the authorities had confessed a belief at the time of his death.

Take care my friend smiled Eugene, I fear we will not meet again, not in this life anyway, ha, smoke and mirrors, it was all smoke and mirrors after all, and he was gone.

Ronnie and his son often travelled to work together and during those trips discussed all things Biblical, and whilst Nathan was not a student of theology, like his sister he had a belief in God which for their generation was significant.

Ronnie tried to offer proof to Nathan, that God as creator, would eventually reclaim his creation in all its decadence and decay, just as it was written in the Bible. He explained about things like the Essene Scrolls found at Qumran in the desert which had been carbon dated to around the time of Jesus, giving detailed eye-witness accounts of Jesus ministry. Which Nathan countered with sound disbelieving logic and scepticsm, all which Ronnie found most agreeable.

THE CUP

They did agree however, that in any situation such as a faith-based ideology, the seeker should consider all the evidence available, evaluate and discount the plausible and possible, until if only left with the impossible then that must be the truth, or as Nathan somewhat crudely explained it. If it looks like a Duck, walks like a Duck, and Quacks like a Duck, then there is a high chance that it is indeed a Duck.

Discernment and evaluation are life`s stepping-stones, Ronnie told Nathan, and there is nothing wrong with that, but the words of Jesus spoken over two thousand years ago were true than and are still true today, discover the truth and the truth will set you free.

As Pandemic swept across the globe, Ronnie wondered, perhaps even hoped that this might be the start of God`s second Judgement. Would Christ return in Glory during his lifetime, after all technology had advanced to such an extent, where wars and atrocities happening across the globe could be watched as live action. Sitting in your favourite chair watching people suffer, thousands of miles away, would God use such technology to announce his coming.

No, he smiled to himself, his God was not in need of Man`s tools, no matter how advanced and clever. Mankind might well be able to put people on the Moon, or remote controlled, craft on Mars, but it could not breathe human life into anything.

Artificial intelligence no matter how sophisticated could never replace the human God given ability of discernment. As he had told Eugene all those years ago, a machine can pull the trigger and rain hell fire onto people, but it cannot now, and never will be able to choose whether to do so or not.

Now retired and with both children settled, happy and living their own lives Ronnie and Beverley often chatted about how current affairs may or may not be signs of Gods final chapters, always looking for signs that the world was ready to accept God for who he really Is rather than some mythical Father Christmas, readily available to provide blessing when needed. How he longed for news that the world might have some concrete proof of God`s reality.

Ronnie, called out Beverley your Dinner is almost ready, you need to wash your hands and come in. A while later she found him slumped in one of their garden chairs, his head bent forward almost onto his chest. Prising the newspaper from his already stiffening fingers and with tears in her eyes she read the headline.

Amazing Find in Jerusalem. **Construction workers discover the coffin of ancient high priest Caiaphas**. Underneath a short paragraph explained how during construction works under the ancient temple a coffin had been found which experts had now proven to be that of the high priest Caiaphas who had been Instrumental in having Jesus crucified as a blasphemer, inside the coffin they had found his name in gold lettering woven into part of a robe or shawl.

WITHIN THE COFFIN THEY HAD ALSO FOUND THREE "BLOOD STAINED" NAILS

The Cup

How could a young boy born into Post War Britain even begin to understand that he had been selected to be part of a "Two Thousand Year Old" quest. But when his seemingly normal everyday life is hijacked and he is plunged headlong into a secretive operation to outwit the enemy he is forced to face the fact that perhaps he was born for this purpose.

Stumbling from disaster to disaster, he begins to realise that your enemy`s enemy is not necessarily your friend, and after one too many deaths, he pledges to do the right thing, whatever it takes.

The Women who shared his life, the Men who sought to guide his pathway, the Mysterious Siobahn, who he becomes entwined with, the British Secret Service and Mossad all contribute to maturing him at a young age as he seeks to make sense of what rapidly becomes an obsession.

Summer Balls and Garden Parties, Death at every turn, until finally exhausted by it all, and Running on Empty, he discovers the biggest secret of all

Copyright Ron Lamb 2021

Printed in Great Britain
by Amazon